Losing Hope:

Book One of the Sienna St. James Series

Losing Hope:

Book One of the Sienna St. James Series

Leslie J. Sherrod

www.urbanchristianonline.com

Urban Books, LLC
78 East Industry Court
Deer Park, NY 11729

Losing Hope: Book One of the Sienna St. James Series

ISBN 13: 978-1-60162-729-2
ISBN 10: 1-60162-729-7

First Printing September 2012
Printed in the United States of America

10 9 8 7 6 5 4 3 2 1

Distributed by Kensington Corp.
Submit Wholesale Orders to:
Kensington Publishing Corp.
C/O Penguin Group (USA) Inc.
Attention: Order Processing
405 Murray Hill Parkway
East Rutherford, NJ 07073-2316
Phone: 1-800-526-0275
Fax: 1-800-227-9604

Losing Hope:

Book One of the Sienna St. James Series

by

Leslie J. Sherrod

To challenges,
To courage,
To Christ, who makes us conquerors . . .

Acknowledgments

God is faithful, and His timing is perfect. And in His perfection and faithfulness, He continues to provide the people I've needed for support, assistance, and feedback. Thank you to my family: the Sherrods, the Datchers, the Greenes, the Coles, and every other clan that makes up my extensive family tree. Thanks to my church families, Mt. Pleasant Ministries, and my newly extended family members of the Upper Room Worship Center. Your prayers and support have been vital. Thanks to my friends, who continue to show their love and support through their prayers and words of encouragement: Angela, Mata, MaRita, Yolonda, Charese, Burnett, and Cheri. Stay encouraged! And, Carla, you get your own special shout-out for your help with this newest writing adventure. Thank you!

Thank you, Joylynn Jossel and Urban Christian, for continuing to allow me the opportunity to write publicly for Him. To the readers, book clubs, and reviewers who continue to support and encourage me, thank you! Special thanks to Deborah Smith and El-Shaddai Ministries and Evangelist Faye Dadzie and Victorious Life Ministries for your support backed up by action. God bless!

As a wife, mother, social worker, and writer, the most important things to me are my family, my writing, and my service for Him. *Losing Hope* is the first

Acknowledgments

book in a series that ties all these separate chapters of my life together. Hope you enjoy reading it as much as I did writing it. Be blessed!

Leslie J. Sherrod
lesliejsherrod@gmail.com

Hope deferred makes the heart sick,
But when the desire comes, it is a tree of life.

—Proverbs 13:12

Chapter 1

His ashes came with the morning mail.

I had just finished my second cup of mint green tea when the usual pile of bills and store circulars were dumped through the mail slot on my front door. I was not expecting the mail carrier to also knock. Thank goodness I had gone against my norm and dressed for work *before* eating breakfast. The sight of me in my neon orange head scarf and granny-length floral bathrobe would have been too much for anyone on a Tuesday morning. Guess that's why I am still single. Did I say single? That's not totally true.

It's complicated.

I looked at the box in the mail carrier's outstretched hands and sighed. *Then again,* I thought, *guess the title of single is now official.*

"Ms. . . Sienna St. James?"

I wanted to shake my head no, but I nodded, anyway.

"Sign here." The mail carrier pointed to a bright red X on the certified package, acting as if delivering boxes from the Crematório Rodrigues in Almada, Portugal, was part of his normal routine.

"Thanks," I mumbled, taking the large, plain cardboard box from him, then closing the door. It was heavier than I expected, as if a set of stoneware dishes from Walmart was waiting inside.

RiChard.

"Welcome home, baby." I bit my lip, waiting to feel the torrent of emotions I had been expecting to feel since last Wednesday, when I got the call.

Nothing. Numbness.

With the box of ashes still in my hands, I looked around my cramped rancher, searching for a place to put it. To put him.

God, help me.

The coffee table in the living room was piled high with library books and home-decorating magazines. The side tables had more of the same. No space. And there was no way I was putting that box on my kitchen table. Roman and I had to eat there. Oh, and before anybody asks, my bedroom was *way* out of the question. Too many memories. No, actually just too creepy.

I studied the box, running my fingers down the lines of heavy brown packaging tape, the box itself a weighty reminder that my life had not turned out the way I'd imagined it would when I was eighteen. And in love. Hard to believe that was almost two decades ago. A nearby silver teapot caught enough of my distorted reflection to remove any doubt. Though I still had my grandmother's heart-shaped face, my father's almond-shaped eyes, and my mother's honey maple skin, a few strands of gray blended in with the copper highlights of my retro Halle Berry–styled hair. And a few extra pounds padded my once thin and trim frame.

My mother used to tell me that I needed to add a doughnut to my daily routine to catch up to the hip, butt, and boob fullness of the women in my clan. She hasn't told me that in years.

One of my fingernails caught on an edge of the box, and I recoiled at the badly chipped raspberry polish. My fingernails looked like a preschooler's beloved art project. Sheena Booth, the diva who was my office mate, would call in sick before showing up to work with her nails looking the way mine did at that moment.

Work! The digital clock over the microwave read 7:42. The way I-83 got jammed in the morning rush hour, I should have left twelve minutes ago if I was to have any chance of getting to work on time. Although I was her favorite, Ava didn't play. I looked again at the box in my hands and then up at the kitchen ledge where I kept all my bills and junk mail. *I have no choice,* I reassured myself as I dropped the unopened box on top of my water, cable, and phone bills. A colorful advertisement for somebody's family-owned gutter-cleaning business lay to the side.

I mean, what else was I supposed to do with it? Seemed appropriate in a way—my long-lost husband's remains mixed in with my bills. How much had that man cost me? How much more did he owe me?

Some losses and debts couldn't be measured in dollars and cents.

It wasn't until I was halfway down I-83 that I realized what was wrong with RiChard's temporary final resting place. Roman did not have basketball practice today. He might get home before me.

My fourteen-year-old son knew very little about his father. His last memory of him should not be an unopened cardboard box from a crematorium in Portugal sitting next to the gas and electric bill. I had not told Roman anything about the call I'd gotten last week or the delivery I knew was coming. I hadn't told Roman much of anything. Truth was, I didn't think *I* knew much of anything when it came to RiChard Alain St. James.

I had to get home before Roman did.

I thought that getting home before four thirty would be my most difficult mission of the day, but I should have known better. Anytime anything RiChard St. James showed up, everything in my life collapsed in one way or another. I knew this. Lived it, breathed it. Survived it.

And I still wasn't prepared for what was coming next.

Chapter 2

"It's an easy case. You know I must like you. With Trevor quitting, we all have to pick up his clients—including me. I'm only giving you one of his, and it's easy. I know you already have your hands full with Keisha King and the Benson family. Sienna, are you listening to me?"

Ava Diggs was a big woman in every sense of the word. Large, loose golden curls framed her round brown face. The 3XL-sized tunics she wore were usually in bright shades of yellow or orange or had animal prints. Wooden beads of all colors clanged on her wrists, from her ears, and around her massive neck. The only thing quiet about the woman was her voice and her friendly, attentive eyes, the two attributes that drew me to her tutelage during my long, drawn-out grad school days. The only thing bigger than her hair and clothes was her heart.

"Sienna, are you with me?" Ava gently pried again.

I was sitting across from her at her desk. Twenty-five minutes late, I had missed the beginning of the weekly Tuesday staff meeting, and Ava wanted to fill me in before lunch.

"I'm here, Ava." I returned her smile. I still felt numb inside. There were no words to describe how I felt, no guidebook to map out what I was supposed to do from here. "I just had a, well, twist in my morning."

"Roman talking about girls again?" She chuckled.

I wish. "No." I blew out a loud, long sigh. "If only it were that simple."

"Simple?" Ava's chuckle grew louder. "Honey, that time you caught Roman on the phone with a seventeen-year-old girl who had three kids, I thought I was going to have to call a paramedic in here."

I gave a weak smile. "No, Roman's love life has nothing to do with my current drama."

Ava raised an eyebrow and leaned toward me. Although her meticulously kept desk sat between us, it felt like she was sitting right next to me, holding my hand. "Sienna, what's going on?"

I could tell from the slight coo in her voice that she was in full-fledged counseling mode. Although I had some of the same social worker credentials as Ava, I still melted under her masterful therapeutic skills. Indeed, her genuine empathy and perfected techniques had earned her the nickname "the Great One" among respected social work circles, professors, and clinicians.

The first time I met her—she was a guest speaker for a family therapy class I took at school—I was amazed at her wisdom and passion about spiritual wholeness and well-being. I was further amazed that she gave me her business card when I approached her privately with a question about her lecture after the seminar ended. I was a nontraditional student when I attended the masters of social work program at the University of Maryland in downtown Baltimore. "Nontraditional" is simply a nice way of saying "old."

Okay, I was not that old when I went—a year shy of thirty—but sitting next to those "newly legal" youngsters who knew nothing about bad marriages, shaky child care, and just plain struggling to survive until the next student loan refund came through, made me feel intimidated at best, unwelcome at worst. I almost quit six times. Ava Diggs became my mentor—no, my friend—and I know that I am where I am today in large part because of that warm smile, those gentle eyes, and her compassion and encouragement.

Going to school part-time while trying to take care of myself and my son was rough. It took me six years to get my bachelor's, another four years to earn my master's. Ava entered my life in year eight. God in His great mercy knew I needed a cheerleader for the final laps. When I finished last May, I was given four tickets for graduation. Although she was asked to speak at another local college's closing exercises scheduled the same day, Ava Diggs was sitting right next to my parents and my son as I walked across the stage, her smile as bright as my mother's.

But although Ava Diggs was my dear friend and informal life coach, when she offered me a position with her agency, I immediately decided that my work hours under her would be just that—work hours. I did not want my personal life to cross the boundaries of our professional relationship.

"Ava, I appreciate your concern, but this one I need to handle myself, in my own way and in my own time." I did not even know what that way and time were, but I knew that my closure with RiChard, whatever that meant, would come.

Taking my hint, Ava nodded, settled back into her leather seat, and put her glasses back on. The gold wire frames slid to the tip of her nose as she pulled a chart from a tall stack on her desk. We were back to business.

"Dayonna Diamond." She flipped through the chart without looking up. "A true child of the system. Born to a crack-addicted mother, father unknown, in foster care right out of the hospital. Due to reasons outside

of her control, she went through eight foster homes
the first seven years of her life. Due to reasons *within*
her control, she went through another six foster homes
from ages seven to ten. After three group homes and a
quick stint at baby juvy for a minor legal infraction, she
spent time at a residential treatment center in Florida,
where they diagnosed her with ADHD, bipolar disorder, PTSD, intermittent explosive disorder, conduct
disorder, and every other diagnosis they could find in
the DSM-IV."

She pointed to the massive manual of mental health
diagnoses she kept on her desk before continuing. "She
got back last Wednesday. The city wants her in therapeutic foster care with wraparound services. Hence the
referral to us. I handpicked the Monroes to be her new
guardians." Finally, she looked up at me as she spoke.
"I need you to check in on them two, three times a week
to make sure her transition goes smoothly. For reasons
I cannot go into at the moment, I need you to understand that this placement *must* succeed." She plopped
the seven-inch-thick folder in front of me. It landed
with an echoless thud.

"I thought you said this was an easy case, Ava. You
know I'm already stressing over the ongoing saga of
Keisha King. "

Ava tore open a wrapped fork that came with the
chef salad she'd pulled from a small refrigerator under
her desk. "Horace and Elsie Monroe are great people.
They never had children of their own but have helped
raise a village." She looked up at me over the rims of
her glasses. "Plus, they're members of Second Zion."

"So are six thousand nine hundred ninety-eight other people," I wanted to shout back in response to Ava's
reference to the respected mega-church. *What does
that have to do with me taking this case?*

"The Monroes' strong faith and their belief in the potential of every child—no matter how damaged or delinquent—have earned them one of the best records of all our trained foster parents." Ava crunched loudly on a lettuce leaf as she talked. "They have never had an unsuccessful placement. Every single child that has entered their home either ends up reunified with their birth family or successfully adopted into a loving home. Every single child."

She's really expecting this to work out. Not with Dayonna's history. I'd had only an MSW behind my name for just over a year, but all my previous work experience and internships had centered around child welfare and the agencies, departments, and foster homes that toiled in this heartbreaking field. I had worked with enough Dayonna Diamonds to know how this story would end, and the fact that Ava had hinted at the need for this case to succeed did not comfort me.

But I had no time for self-comfort. My cell phone was ringing.

"What do you mean, you have a half day of school?" I yelled into the receiver. I had excused myself from Ava's office and was headed to my own. Dayonna's file weighed heavily in my hands. "Who's idea was this?"

"Ma, calm down. It wasn't my idea, for real. It was listed on that calendar that came home the first day of school. Teacher development day, or something like that." My son's voice was in that stage when boyhood teetered on the edge of manhood. Every now and then a loud squeak broke through.

"It's okay, Roman. This half day just caught me off guard. You know I don't like not having a plan or activity to engage you after school." That was only half true. Roman was a good kid, not perfect, and I still feared for his safety from the Jezebels of the world, but my biggest concern at the moment was that he not get home before I did. I did not want him to see his father's ashes without preparation or explanation.

"Maa," he squeaked, "I'm fourteen. You don't have to plan every moment of my day. I'm in high school now. I'm almost a grown man." His voice cracked again.

"Grown man," I mumbled into the phone. "You've been in high school for all of what? Three weeks? Where are you now?" I held my breath.

"I'm still on the eight."

"Good." I sighed in relief. His magnet high school was in northern Baltimore County, and we lived on the west side. He still had to catch one more bus, which would take him across town, before he reached our neighborhood. "Hey, why don't you go down to the Police Athletic League center and play a smokin' game of . . . a pickup game with Officer Sanderson?" I regretted my words immediately, and not only because of my sorry attempt at sounding cool. I did *not* need Leon Sanderson thinking I was after him in any way, shape, or form. Sending Roman to the PAL center and having him ask for him would be just enough fodder for the old-school player to think I was actually considering his sorry advances.

"Uh, Ma . . . I was wondering if I could go . . . to Security Mall . . . with Skee-Gee. He can meet me there, and Aunt Vet said she could pick us up. She's gettin' her hair done there and can drop me off home by five."

"Okay. That sounds good!"

"Huh? Oh, okay! Thanks, Ma!"

"And don't forget to—" The phone was dead. My baby boy had already hung up. *I must really be in a state to have agreed so quickly to his plan.* Even Roman had sounded surprised. I shook my head and sighed again. Don't get me wrong. I loved my little sister, Yvette, and her five children, but I was never happy about Roman hanging around my nephew Skee-Gee too long without my supervision. But with a seven-inch-thick chart sitting on my desk, I did not have time to worry. I'd tried my best to raise Roman right. At some point I had to trust that he was making good decisions, right?

I spent about half an hour skimming through Dayonna Diamond's life. Ava had given an accurate summary. The notes I read were consistent with what she'd told me. They were also consistent with my rather pessimistic expectations. *Oh, well. Time to get started.* Ava had informed me that the Monroes were expecting me before the workday was out and Dayonna's home tutoring session would be starting soon.

Due to her recent return from out-of-state treatment, she had not been enrolled in a school yet. A home teacher would be coming a few times a week for now to assess her and determine the best educational placement for her. It was still the beginning of the school year, so the assessments were a priority to keep her from falling further behind her future classmates. The tutor was due to come soon, according to the notes. I resisted the urge to call back Roman and headed to my car.

I still felt numb to the world around me. With my feelings on mute, I figured nothing else in the day could get under my skin.

I should have known better.

Chapter 3

My mother was a fifth grade teacher when I was young. A vocal, not easily moved woman, Isabel Davis had spent hours in the evening, sometimes working until well into the night, preparing her next day's lessons, making sure that even the slowest child in her class would be able to grasp the objectives required by the Baltimore City Public Schools system. She had kept an ongoing supply of hats, coats, and gloves for students who came from homes where warmth and protection from the elements were a luxury. She would flip through my grandmother's old leather-bound Bible, searching for just the right scripture of encouragement to write down on index cards and mail to former students she'd heard had turned to the streets for continuing education.

I admired my mother. Wanted to be like her. Wanted the scent of hot tea and lemons she wore like a perfume to surround me and somehow change me into the essence of who she was.

But even I knew that was an impossible dream. Maybe that was why I fell so hard for RiChard.

I pulled up in front of the Monroes' home at about a quarter to two. They lived in an end-of-group row house in the Belair-Edison neighborhood of East Baltimore, an area still dominated by proud home owners and a strong community association. Their block was neat and tidy, with flower beds and sprinklers dotting little trimmed lawns. The Monroes had several yellow cushioned chairs and multicolored potted plants on their covered front porch. A large wreath of real daisies hung on the door. The blue- and yellow-checkered doormat read WELCOME DEAR FRIEND, and two wind chimes of angels and crosses tinkered in the breeze.

Dayonna Diamond was going to tear this place apart. I was sure of it.

Before I could knock, the door swung open.

"Hello! You must be the girl from the agency. Come on in." A coffee-colored, wiry, petite woman grinned up at me. Her thinning hair was pulled back in a neat bun, and her smile seemed to fill half of her face. "Horace, she's here!" The rich voice that boomed from her body betrayed her small frame.

I followed her into the bright and airy interior and smiled myself. The blue and yellow theme from the porch continued into the cramped living room. The space, though small and slightly cluttered with carefully placed knickknacks, reminded me of my great-aunt Josephine's home. I immediately felt welcomed. Mrs. Monroe's singsongy, though somewhat loud, voice added to the warmth.

"You have a lot of interesting pieces." I pointed to the scores of figurines and ceramics that dotted the room. As I stepped farther into the house, I realized that there was more bric-a-brac lining the walls and bookshelves than I had realized. A lot more. "Are you an artist?"

"No. I am not." Her voice cooled, and she frowned, making me wonder if I had offended her with my question. However, she quickly saved me from the slight awkwardness of the moment. "Come sit down," she said, directing me to a floral-print sofa. "I have some iced tea and my prizewinning coconut cake left over from my meeting with the pastor's aid committee. I'm the chairwoman." She beamed, exposing a small gap in her top front teeth.

"As you can see, my wife is too humble for her own good." A hearty chuckle filled the room. I had not seen Mr. Monroe emerge from the kitchen, but there he was, a tall, thin, honey-colored man with a wisp of a mustache and a few wavy strands of black trying to pass as hair on his bald head. Usually an unannounced entrance in a new home rattled me, but Horace Monroe's smile was as welcoming and engaging as Elsie's. I extended a hand to both of them, gently declining the offered food, ready to get to the business at hand. Ready to meet Dayonna.

I did not have to wait long. Before my behind could finish fighting through the pillows on the oversize, cushy sofa, a tall, slim teenage girl with quiet, fluid movements entered the room. I watched her and she watched me as she plopped down silently on a wing-back chair facing the sofa on which I sat. Wearing skinny jeans and a bright yellow fitted T-shirt that had small rhinestones on the collar, she propped up a foot on a plush ottoman and popped open a can of soda. A spiral notebook filled with purple paper rested in her narrow lap. Sandy-colored, shoulder-length relaxed hair was pulled back into a single smooth ponytail. A sparkling cubic zirconia butterfly clip rested strategically above a perfect part on the left side of her head.

She was the same age as my son, Roman, but she seemed lifetimes older.

"Hi. I'm Dayonna." Her surprisingly raspy alto voice broke through the incessant banter and chatter that had been swimming nonstop from the Monroes' mouths. I realized then that I had stopped paying at-

tention to the elder couple's conversation the moment
Dayonna had entered the room. Something in the
young girl's quiet, sad, and distant eyes unnerved me.
From the report I had heard and read that morning, I
honestly was expecting to meet a monster. In person,
this quiet, slim girl with the sad eyes looked barely able
to hurt a fly.

But I had been around long enough to know that
looks could be deceiving. I turned my attention away
from her and back to the Monroes, who were saying
something about an upcoming revival at their church.

"And Bishop Vernon Tracer of Sing a New Song Tabernacle will be the speaker. That's a gifted man, you
know," Mrs. Monroe gushed, beaming. I had no idea
who she was talking about, but I smiled and nodded
my head along with her.

"Sounds like you really have something to look forward to. That's exciting!" I said. "So . . . you've got a
beautiful home. I can tell you really take pride in keeping up with things here." Though I loved attending
a good service as much as anyone else who was into
Jesus, I usually avoided getting into discussions about
church and God with clients. Another lesson I learned
early on? Everybody is not coming from the same
place, and that can get complicated with the families I
serve. Fortunately, the Monroes did not seem to mind
the sudden shift in the conversation.

"We bought this house several years ago, and believe
me when I say it was a true fixer-upper," Mr. Monroe
replied, grinning.

"I wish I could say I helped fix it up, but all the credit
for the changes in here truly goes to Horace. Horace is
the best at fixing up old houses."

"Only because it's for you, my lady."

The elder couple gazed at each other in mutual admiration. A quick memory of RiChard standing on a hilltop in Zambia many years ago flashed through my mind . . . the look in his eyes, the heat in mine. I shook the image, the feeling, away. Quickly.

"You should see the work he's done all over this state, restoring homes and such," Elsie continued. "We got married late in life, well beyond the years we could have children of our own, but he's always made the houses we've lived in feel like family homes. Hence, we've always had a foster child within our gates. If we couldn't raise our own together, we sure enough can help another's poor baby."

Horace still beamed at his wife, but something had changed in his eyes. I tried to figure out what had just flashed in them, but I needed to stay focused on the reason for my visit.

"So Dayonna has been here a few days now. Tell me how things are going for each of you." I made certain to share eye contact with all three to ensure nobody felt excluded from my invitation to talk. In doing so, I did not miss the brief moments of silence that suddenly took over the room. The Monroes looked at each other again, though I could not read what emotion passed between them.

"Everything has been quite perfect, to be honest with you." The gap in Mrs. Monroe's upper teeth showed through her smile.

But her bottom lip was quivering.

"Yes, indeed." Mr. Monroe's voice sounded louder than necessary. "No problems here."

I looked over at Dayonna, who stared back at me with a blank look on her face. "Your thoughts on how things are going so far?" I inquired.

She said nothing, only continued to stare at me with that blank, unreadable look.

Teenagers were some of the most difficult people to navigate, even without a mental health diagnosis.

"Well . . . ?" I shuffled through some papers in my lap, trying to figure out what words would break the apparent agreed-upon code of silence suddenly permeating the living room. If Ava was there, she would know exactly what to say, what to do, where to go from here. Despite all my training, at times I still felt like a novice. "So . . . ," I said, beginning again, "everything is going well? No questions or concerns you—any of you—would like to bring up?"

"All is well." Mr. Monroe gave a plastic grin.

Mrs. Monroe nodded her head in agreement, a crazed smile on her face.

"Perhaps I can talk to each of you individually." I glanced over at Dayonna, whose lips were pursed, as if she was about to finally speak.

"That's a great idea, Ms. St. James," Mr. Monroe said, cutting through Dayonna's unspoken words, "but we are actually about to get ready for our Tuesday evening Bible study at church. Dayonna's tutor isn't coming today, so we wanted to take advantage of this time to go get some Word! How 'bout we plan on meeting with you one-on-one at your next visit?"

"Okay." I bit my bottom lip. I felt like whatever control I had over my role with this family was slowing shifting away from me. Everybody was smiling; nobody was talking. What was I supposed to do? I decided to just be bold and go for what I was after.

"You know, I will meet with you each one-to-one next time, but I am getting a sense that some things are not being said. Please know that I am here to help. If there are any concerns—"

"Everything really is fine." Dayonna's raspy voice cut through mine. Her face remained expressionless.

"Okay, well, how about we—"

"Ms. St. James, we appreciate you stopping by today, but as my husband said, we need to start getting ready for Bible study. Perhaps we can finish this visit another time?" Mrs. Monroe's smile did not waver.

There was nothing else for me to say or do. I gathered my things and casually headed for the door. "Okay. I'll come back on Thursday, same time, okay?"

"That's perfect." Mrs. Monroe clasped her hands together. "We'll have more time to talk then."

As I stepped out onto the porch, Dayonna was suddenly next to me, walking down the steps with me. She walked so close to me that my attaché was pinned between us.

"Wh—where are you going, little Miss Diamond?" Mr. Monroe called after us.

"Just walking Ms. St. James to her car," she shouted back. I stayed quiet, feeling like I needed to let things go wherever they were heading without my interruption. I could see Mrs. Monroe struggling to get out of her house slippers and put on her shoes. She wanted to come outside with us.

But I was already at my car.

"Is everything really okay, Dayonna?" I gave her my warmest smile. She was quiet as I opened the driver's side door and threw my attaché over to the passenger seat. She shrugged her shoulders and turned as if to leave but then was suddenly next to my ear.

"You gotta get me out of here." Dayonna's voice was a sharp whisper.

"Why? What's wrong?" I was pleased to finally be getting somewhere.

Dayonna frowned and looked me straight in my eyes. "They're going to kill me."

Chapter 4

My head swung all the way back. "Kill you? Why do you think the Monroes would want to kill you?"

"They killed my sister." Dayonna's words rushed out. "They killed her and ate her. Chopped her into pieces for cabbage stew."

I froze and looked in her eyes. A wild gaze stared back at me. I remembered seeing in her chart that she had at one time been prescribed Risperdal, an anti-psychotic, to calm her violent moods and soothe her psychotic symptoms. Had she seen a psychiatrist since her return to Baltimore? I made a mental note to find her one.

Immediately.

"I'm just joking. You know that." Her face broke into a smile. But her eyes still looked a little wild to me. I was becoming more uncomfortable. Some things you just don't joke about. And those eyes . . .

"Dayonna, Mr. and Mrs. Monroe seem like nice people. How are you feeling about being here?"

"Are you going to help me find her?"

"Find who?"

"My sister. She is gone. You have to help me find her."

I could feel my eyes blinking as I tried to think of what to say next. "Um, I did not know you had a sister. I know you have a brother." I had seen the name of one sibling, an older brother, somewhere in Dayonna's chart. I could not remember if a name was given, but I was certain I'd seen a birth date and a note that he had aged out of the system a few years ago. I had not paid much attention otherwise.

"I have a sister. And they chopped her and cooked her in cabbage stew. Are you going to help me find her or not?"

Before I could make sense of what she was saying, what she was asking, Mrs. Monroe had rounded the side of my car. In one quick movement, she put a thin arm around Dayonna's bony shoulders. I noticed the elder woman's shoes were on the wrong feet.

"All right, Ms. St. James." Mrs. Monroe's voice was extra chirpy. Or was that just my imagination? I'm not going to lie. I was feeling a little thrown off in that moment and not trusting my gut. "Thank you so much for checking on us," Mrs. Monroe continued. "We look forward to seeing you Thursday." She wrapped her thin arm so tightly around Dayonna, I thought she would cut off the child's circulation. "Come on, Miss Diamond." Mrs. Monroe smiled uneasily at her. "We have to get ready for church. Bye, now." She waved vigorously at me as she stepped back and away.

Dayonna smiled and turned to leave with her guardian, no hint of worry, fear, or agitation on her face. It was as if her words from moments earlier had not been uttered. "Bye, Ms. St. James." Dayonna grinned. "See you Thursday!" The two of them walked up the front steps together.

"Okay." I shook my head and started my car in earnest. I had to get out of there. Besides the fact that all of them seemed a little off their rockers, I saw on my car clock that it was now inching closer to three o'clock. I still had to go back to the office to do paperwork and then get home before Roman did at five.

RiChard.

Somewhere inside of me, pain wanted to swell up and take over. But I did not let it. Instead I reached for the play button of my car's audio system. The sudden movement of my hand knocked over my attaché.

"Darn it," I mumbled as I reached out to keep my big brown workbag from turning upside down on the floor. It was open and filled to the brim with papers, charts, and other work junk. I caught it just in time, but in doing so, a little torn piece of purple paper that had been sitting on top fluttered out. I did not recognize it at all, so when I stopped at a light, I picked it up and examined it.

I frowned at the four single words written in big, sloppy letters.

Her name is Hope.

"Hope Diamond? Hope Diamond. As in the big blue diamond on display at the Smithsonian?" My office mate, Sheena Booth, flicked some lint off her plum blazer with her long, perfectly manicured fingernails. "Seriously? That's the best name she could come up with? Creative. I give her that. I can't believe you are even giving this a second thought. You know our clients are crazy." Sheena adjusted the rhinestone-studded Bluetooth in her ear and turned back to her computer. Web sites for Facebook and Nordstrom filled her work screen. A half-written case note blinked underneath the open Web browsers. "Hope Diamond." She shook her head as she turned.

"That's assuming they have the same last name," I offered.

"That's assuming she actually exists." Sheena shrugged and then looked back at me. "You're not really buying into that mumbo jumbo are you? Didn't Ava tell you that Dayonna Diamond had some weight on her from all her medications? But when you saw her, she was as skinny as a stick? That should tell you something. That girl ain't taking her meds!"

"I know it sounds crazy, but sometimes you have to wonder where our clients get this stuff from. You know?" I had been at my desk for twenty minutes, trying to summarize my first visit with the Monroes in a coherent, professional-sounding note. *You never know when your documentation might be subpoenaed for court.* These words from Ava Diggs always stayed with me. "I mean, some things they say are *so* out there, you have to wonder where it comes from."

"Broken families. Messed-up childhoods. Crack in utero. Bad weed. Name it, Sienna, and our clients have lived it or said it, if only in their heads. There's a fine line between sense and insanity, and if someone's spent their whole life dealing with drama and trauma, it's not hard to see how the two can get blurred."

"Her name is Hope." I studied the scrap of purple paper one more time before sticking it back into Dayonna's chart. For good measure, I had rechecked her chart and confirmed that there was no mention of any other siblings except the older brother. Dayonna was just trying to get to me. I was sure of it. I shook my head, trying to dispel the unsettled feelings my new client had brought me. "Whatever. I need to get out of here. My son should be home in forty-five minutes, and I want to get there before he does. I don't know why this little fourteen-year-old is getting under my skin."

"He's fourteen. He's supposed to get under your skin."

"I was talking about Dayonna Diamond, but Roman is pulling a close second." There was no way I was going to share with Sheena my real reasons for wanting to get home before Roman. Nobody at Holding Hands Agency—not even Ava Diggs—knew the full story about my complicated past with RiChard Alain St. James.

"Look, if Dayonna is getting to you that much, talk about it with Ava tomorrow. She's gone for the day for meetings with the bigwigs at social services. I'm sure she'll be more than willing to help you get chopped-up sisters and cabbage stew out of your system. Oh, have mercy. Look at how fine this brother is." Sheena had turned to a copy of *Essence* magazine and did not look back up at me. Whatever audience I had with her was over.

Just as well. I had three minutes to log off and get back to my car, which was parked on the back lot. Rush hour was about to become full force on I-83 again, and I was on a mission. I had made it down the hall and was stepping onto the elevator when Sheena poked her head out of our office door.

"Wait, Sienna. Phone call. Your girl Dayonna just ran away."

Chapter 5

I met him the second week of my freshman year of college. Tall, slightly muscular, and a beautiful shade of golden brown, he had eyes the color of peridots—the pale green gem that was my mother's birthstone—and a smile that flashed brighter than any jewel I'd ever seen. In the summer, when the sun stayed on him, hints of olive underlined his perfect complexion, revealing his Mediterranean heritage. The biracial son of a history professor from Italy and a chef from the French Caribbean nation of Saint Martin, he was fluent in four languages—English, French, Italian, and Dutch—well read, and well traveled.

I was eighteen and fresh out of my mama's house, thinking that the rural acreage of my eastern Pennsylvanian college was exotic enough compared to my urban Baltimore upbringing. RiChard Alain St. James was a different type of foreign to me.

He was a visually and intellectually delicious man. And believe me, I tried my best to gobble him up.

The first time I saw him was at an impromptu student rally. He was standing on the steps of the student union, delivering a passionate call for student action on behalf of the Rwandan people. It was 1994, and the three-month genocide that the world community had largely ignored was starting to make real headlines. Too little too late.

But not for RiChard. He was a graduate student earning a master's degree in public policy and international relations, and his words were so potent and powerful, few could walk away. I watched football players cry. He told us that we had the ability and responsibility to be our brothers' and sisters' keepers, no matter what color or what country we all hailed from.

I loved him immediately and signed up for the public policy student organization over which he presided. I changed my major from theater arts to political science and nearly melted when I discovered he was the TA, the teacher's assistant, for my intro to political theory class.

The day he looked directly at me and smiled, I knew I wasn't going to make it to my sophomore year at that university.

We were going to go change the world together. . . .

"Ms. St. James, are you with me?" The police officer looked bored. A half-written missing person report dangled between his thick fingers, which were connected to thick arms that led up to a thick neck. Something about his facial features reminded me of a bulldog. The name Collins was written across a badge pinned to his uniform. The two of us were standing in the Monroes' too-yellow living room, but my mind was a decade and a half away.

"Oh, yes." I shook my head out of my daydream, out of my memories of RiChard, and tried to focus again on the situation at hand. Mr. Monroe sat stoically on the sofa, his fingers entwined in his lap. Mrs. Monroe alternated between wringing her hands and rearranging a shelf full of ceramic black angels. Every now and then a muted whimper escaped from her tightly pressed lips.

The display of nerves and angst in that room was getting to me in more ways than one. It was six thirty. I knew Roman was home. And I was not.

"We are so sorry." Mr. Monroe rumbled out another apology. "Like I said, we were driving to Bible study in my car, and when we got to Belair Road, Dayonna just jumped out of the backseat and ran off. We've never had a foster child run away from us. Ever. She did not give us any hint or clue that this was coming. I don't know what we did wrong." His voice trailed off, and I searched for something therapeutic to say, but Officer Collins was not interested in therapy.

"So, Ms. St. James, you were giving me the girl's date of birth?" He tapped on his pen impatiently.

"Oh, yes." I flipped through Dayonna's massive chart. "April twenty-third, nineteen ninety-seven." *That date.* That was why I had gotten sidetracked. *April 23, 1997.* That was the date of the last time I saw RiChard face-to-face. I will never forget the last time my eyes beheld him, just as I can never forget the first.

April 23, 1997. The last time I saw RiChard was the same day Dayonna first opened her eyes. A shiver went down my back, but I had to stay focused. My son was home with his father's box of ashes. I had to focus. I had to think of what to tell Roman. I had to get through this missing person report for Dayonna.

"Okay." I cleared my throat. "She is five-seven, one hundred eighty-three pounds. No . . ." I looked back up. "She is not that heavy anymore. She lost weight."

"She's a hundred twenty-seven," Mr. Monroe chimed in, his fingers still entwined in his lap.

"All right, DOB four–twenty-three–ninety-seven, five-seven, either one hundred eighty-three or one hundred twenty-seven pounds . . ." Officer Collins let out a loud sigh as he scribbled. "You already told me what clothes she was wearing. It would be helpful if we had a picture of her. No luck with that, huh?"

"Sorry." I shook my head softly. "We don't routinely keep pictures of our clients in their charts, though I think given situations like this, we probably need to start doing so."

"You guys don't have a picture, do you?" Officer Collins was folding up the paperwork, ready to move on to the next disaster in somebody else's living room. I started to wonder anew what was going on in my own home at the moment, but something in the officer's gaze caught my attention. He was studying the Monroes, who were staring at each other. Mrs. Monroe was no longer wringing her hands. Was that terror in Mr. Monroe's eyes?

"Um, no . . . yes. I mean, I . . . we do have a picture." Mrs. Monroe stammered through her words as Mr. Monroe's eyes grew even wider. I watched his Adam's apple move up and down as he swallowed hard.

Officer Collins raised an eyebrow. "Well, are you going to get it?" he nearly barked at the elderly woman.

"What? Oh, yes, the picture! If you think it will . . . help." Mrs. Monroe looked nervously back at her husband before scurrying up the stairs.

Mr. Monroe and I stayed quiet in her absence, while Officer Collins uncapped his pen to write down an extra note.

When Mrs. Monroe came back down the steps, a faded Polaroid snapshot rested in her open palms. She extended it gingerly to the officer, who studied it before handing it to me.

"Is this her?" His eyebrow was raised again.

I took the picture from him and nearly gasped. I had in my own records that she was once nearly two hundred pounds, but seeing the extra weight *on* her was different from simply reading a number off of a chart. In the faded photo Dayonna looked about eleven or twelve years old. She was standing in the middle of what looked like a narrow street. A blue shingled house with an orange porch swing stood in the distance behind her.

Either it had been nearing nighttime or the picture taker had not used the flash correctly. Either way, it was obvious that Dayonna was not happy in the picture. She stood sideways and looked back over her shoulder, as if someone had called out to her. She was wearing a puffy light pink jacket, and dirty snow and slush surrounded her feet. A scowl was unmistakable on her plus-sized face, and her hair stood uncombed all over her head.

"Where did you get this picture from?" I looked over at the Monroes, who were standing so close to each other, I wondered if they would both topple over if forced to separate.

"Oh, that p—p—picture . . ." A nervous smile played on Mrs. Monroe's lips.

"Dayonna had it," Mr. Monroe said with finality. "My wife found it in her things when she helped her unpack. It was the only picture Dayonna had in her belongings."

"That's right." Mrs. Monroe still looked nervous. "I hope it wasn't w—wrong for me to go through her things," she stammered. "I tried to ask her about it, b—but she did not want to talk." She looked from me to her husband, then back to the officer.

"Okay." Officer Collins took the photo from me. "If you think of anything else that could help, here's my number." He gave a card to the Monroes and looked back at me. "In the meantime, we'll keep you updated on our search. To be honest with you, since she's just coming back to the area from an out-of state-facility, she's probably out reconnecting with old friends. It might be a good idea for you to go through that whole

chart to see what other past placements she's had in
Baltimore. You might just find her yourself. We'll be in
touch." I did not miss the quick shared glance between
the Monroes as the officer bounded out the door and
back into his cruiser.

"I guess that is all we can do right now." Mr. Monroe
was holding the door open for me. I was a little slow
in realizing that they were expecting me to leave right
behind the officer.

For the second time today, I was being rushed out of
the Monroes' home, but before I could protest, my cell
phone began ringing.

Roman.

"Okay, good night." I played along with the Monroes'
hurried good-byes. "I will talk to you tomorrow—unless something else comes up tonight. Don't worry.
We'll find her."

"Yes, we will." Mr. Monroe nodded.

I turned away and nearly ran down the steps. My
phone was on its fifth ring. I did not want Roman to
leave a message. I needed to talk to him directly. I
squeezed a tear out of my eye, inhaled, and pressed
TALK.

"Hello, Roman?" I plopped down into the front seat
of my car. My eyes were closed.

"Mom!" His voice was two octaves higher than normal. "I can't believe this!"

"Let me explain, Roman." I imagined him standing
over the package with RiChard's remains, a look of
devastation on his young face.

Roman always looked through the mail as soon as
he got home. After a girl in his class last year sent him
a graphic love letter, which I quickly discarded, he
checked the mail daily to see if he had any other admir-
ers. The only person I had known my son to admire
was his father.

Though he was only an infant on April 23, 1997—the last time both of us saw RiChard face-to-face—Roman idolized his father. I had been careful not to talk badly about the man in his absence from our lives, and RiChard had kept up his end of the bargain by calling both of us from time to time and sending exotic presents and packages to Roman throughout the years. Though now his father rarely came up in his questions and conversations, every once in a while Roman would still ask me to tell him again about my and RiChard's adventures through remote villages and busy townships in Africa, Asia, Europe, and South America. The man was a legend in Roman's eyes, a larger-than-life legend whose worldwide humanitarian efforts outweighed his personal failings. To Roman, RiChard had never, would never, could never do wrong. His role of absentee father was an acceptable casualty in his warlike quest for social justice.

"I can explain this, Roman," I said, wondering if and how I ever could. My eyes were still closed, and I remembered suddenly a sunset I watched from a fishing canoe on a lake in Argentina. I knew from experience that there were some things that existed outside of the realm of explanation.

"Mom! I can't believe it. You were telling me the truth!"

"Listen, I . . . What? Of course I told you the truth. I'm not going to lie to you, Roman. Wait, what are we talking about?"

There was a man sweeping his front sidewalk across the street from me. The setting sun shone just enough light to reveal his cinnamon-colored, oval face and narrow eyes staring at me as he swept. Still sitting in my car next to the Monroes' house, I knew I must have looked a sight. I had never been good at maintaining my facial expressions, and the whirling cyclone of emotions I was experiencing in those few moments was doing a number to my face. I was sure of it. The man with the broom kept staring over at me with a quizzical look on his face. I felt like I was a living sitcom and both of us were waiting for the punch line.

"The ring! The lion's head ring! You weren't joking about it!" Roman's excitement was causing his words to run over each other.

"Roman, slow down. What are you talking about?" Of course I knew *what* he was talking about. Flashbacks from KwaZulu-Natal and the village elder who gave RiChard the prized possession flashed through my mind. The golden ring had a large lion's head on it with eyes made out of rubies and sapphires and a mane edged with diamonds. RiChard had worn the heavy jewel on a chain around his neck until he lost it while helping tsunami victims in Indonesia back in 2004. At least that was what he told me during one of our final telephone conversations. I knew *what* Roman was talking about, but nothing he had just said made sense. "Start over, please. Roman, I don't know what you are saying."

"The box that came in the mail! I'm surprised you didn't open it."

I could hear him crunching and smacking his way through something and remembered again that he'd just spent the afternoon with my nephew Skee-Gee. Who knows where they'd been, what they'd seen, what he'd eaten, but I'd have to debrief him about that later. He was talking about the box, and it sounded like he'd opened it!

"You opened that box?" I could feel my stomach open up and pull me down inside of it. The taste of bile filled my mouth.

"Of course! Mommy, you know that whenever it's a package from overseas, it comes from Daddy somehow!"

I don't know what bothered me more: the way he said the word *Daddy,* as if it rhymed with Jesus, or the way he was talking to me like I was two years old. But I did not have time to dwell on either irritation, because Roman was still talking.

"Anyway, Ma, I opened the box, and there was this big ole pot inside that looked like the kind Grandma has in her china cabinet or somewhere like that. That thing was heavy, but I opened it up, and all it had inside was bubble wrap and the lion's head ring right in the middle of it. I'm not going to say I thought you were lying about the ring, but I was just a little kid when you first told me about that story. I thought you were just trying to make me feel better 'cause I missed Dad."

I felt weak. And sick. "So you opened the box, and the only thing inside was . . . bubble wrap and . . . the ring? Nothing . . . nothing else?" My voice sounded the way I felt. Where were the ashes?

"Yeah, Ma. Were you expecting something else to be in there?"

I wanted to scream, cry, hyperventilate, or something along those lines, but I noticed then that in addition to the sweeper across the street, Mr. Monroe was watching me from his living room window.

And from an upstairs window, behind frilly lace curtains, I was being watched by none other than Dayonna Diamond herself.

Chapter 6

"I promise you I'm not crazy." Those were the exact same words I told my mother in November 1994. I was home for Thanksgiving break, and all the clothes, books, containers, and goods that my parents had helped me lug into my dorm room that past September were now sitting in their living room. I had moved out of my dormitory. I had stopped attending classes. I was dropping out of college.

RiChard was by my side.

"Mr. Davis . . . Can I call you Alvin? I love your daughter. I love the passion she has for the human race. I love the beauty she brings to this world with her genuine smile. She is a blooming flower in a land-scape of thorns." This was what RiChard was saying to my father, a truck driver for a local bakery. My father grumbled something and pushed another forkful of steaming hot mashed potatoes into his mouth. My younger sister, Yvette, sixteen at the time and pregnant with her first child, snickered in her seat at the table, glad, I guess, for once that she was not the object of my parents' wrath.

"Sienna has a full scholarship, and our family values education greatly. She is not leaving school." These words were my mom's, the woman who worked her way from fifth grade teacher to elementary school prin-cipal. She had her principal voice on then, talking to RiChard as if she were chiding a fourth grader caught talking during a spelling test, and not a grown man announcing to my family his intention to marry me and take me on his trip to a mountain village in China to help teach the locals English.

"Perhaps we in this country define education too narrowly," RiChard countered. He was afraid of no one, eager to share his thoughts with presidents and ambassadors, not backing down from dignitaries or chiefs. I admired his bravery. I *needed* his bravery for what I was about to do. "What greater classroom exists than the open-ended experiences allowed us in foreign terrains?" he continued.

My mother rolled her eyes and slammed her fork down on her good china. "Look, my husband and I have worked too hard to watch Sienna throw away her chance at success. It is all fine and good if you want to go globe-trotting to save the whales and rain forests, but once whale season is over and the rain forests are cut down and you have moved on to your next refugee camp, I need to know that Sienna can get a job and take care of herself. Sienna, you have lost your mind if you think you are going to throw away a full tuition, room, and board scholarship to follow this lunatic around the world."

"I promise you I'm not crazy." I found myself repeating those same words to Mr. and Mrs. Monroe as we stood in their living room once again. "I am one hundred percent certain that I just saw Dayonna looking out of your upstairs window." The bright yellow colors of the living room were starting to get to me. Even more unsettling were Horace's and Elsie's smiles. The painted lips on the porcelain dolls scattered throughout the room had more warmth and life on them than the pale, plastered grins on both the elders' faces.

"Ms. St. James," Mr. Monroe began again, "we appreciate your concern, but believe you me, if Dayonna was in this house, we would know it and you would know it. Like I told that friendly policeman, she jumped out of our car and ran off down Belair Road."

"It was an awful sight," Mrs. Monroe chimed in. "We were in the middle of traffic when she took off."

I eyed the two of them, trying—once again—to figure out what to say, but I'll be honest, as disturbed and confused as I felt over Dayonna's alleged disappearance, my heart and attention were not there.

I needed to see for myself that RiChard's ashes were *not* in that box lying on top of my bills at home. I wanted to take that heavy, gaudy ring from Roman and try to make sense of its sudden appearance after years of loss. And if RiChard was not in that box, where was he? *And why?* Once again that man was leaving me broken, lost, and confused. Anger, not sorrow, brimmed just under the surface of my collected demeanor.

"Look, Ms. St. James . . ." Mr. Monroe was talking again. I wondered if he had been talking the entire time. How much in life had I missed? From how many conversations had RiChard distracted me? "If it would make you feel better," Mr. Monroe was saying, "you can go check upstairs yourself and see that Dayonna is not in our home."

"Yes, please do." Mrs. Monroe nodded. "It would make me feel better knowing that you felt better. We are honest and decent people and have no reason to make up stories about Dayonna or anything else."

"That's right. We sure don't," Mr. Monroe affirmed emphatically.

Both Monroes glanced at each other.

"Okay." Out of routine, I held my bag close to me as I climbed the steps ahead of the older couple. Their row house had a layout familiar to any Baltimorean who'd lived in or visited the older brick homes that comprised many neighborhoods throughout the county and city. At the top of the stairs was a short hallway with two bedrooms in the middle and a bathroom and third bedroom at either end. A linen closet faced the stair landing. I walked toward the front bedroom that faced the street. The door was open, and the white lace curtains I had noted moments earlier danced softly in a breeze blowing through a cracked window.

"This is our room." Mrs. Monroe beamed with pride. The somewhat large master bedroom looked as frilly and flouncy as I expected it would. Dollies and ruffles and lace and ceramic knickknacks filled every corner, crack, and crevice. The room was decorated in shades of sea-foam green, white, and, yes, more yellow.

"I love the ocean, and my dear, sweet wife made our room look just like a cottage suite by the shoreline." Mr. Monroe was beaming now. The ocean was the last thing I would think about standing in the middle of that overdone room, but I was not there to critique their tastes in home decor. In silence, I scanned the room, opened the closet, peeked out the window, not really sure what else I was looking for, as Dayonna was obviously not in that room.

"You can check the other rooms if you'd like." Mrs. Monroe blinked and continued smiling as I followed them down the corridor. One by one, I began opening the other doors, taking in the peach-scented and peach-colored bathroom, the hallway linen closet, which smelled of cedar and gardenias, the navy blue guest bedroom, tripling as a home office and a craft room. Finally, I stepped into the bedroom that was currently serving as Dayonna's personal space.

Antique white furniture, including a small vanity, a chest of drawers, and a twin-sized ruffled canopy bed, was draped and wrapped in every shade of pink. The ribbon-framed mirrors, feather boa–decorated walls, shaggy carpet squares, even the ten or so arranged teddy bears on the crisply made bed were all shades of rose, fuchsia, coral, and magenta. Though somewhat faded and worn, everything in the room was perfectly clean, tucked in, and in place. With the detailed attention clearly given to the room, I figured it was safe to assume that the Monroes routinely took in only female foster children. No little boy or male adolescent would want to sleep in that pink festival of a bedroom. I made a mental note to review their fostering history back at the agency.

There was no sign of Dayonna.

Indeed, the only sign that she had ever even stepped foot in the room was a battered suitcase propped up against the closet. It was brown, plain, threadbare in sections, and out of place in the ostentatiously girly room.

"See, she's not here." Mr. Monroe looked clearly satisfied with his statement. He clasped his hands together under his belly and rocked back and forth on his feet.

"No, it does not look like she is up here," I conceded. "Do you have a basement?"

The two looked at each other, their expressions unreadable to me. "Well," Mrs. Monroe began slowly, "the only things down there are my crocheted dolls. I make 'em and sell 'em at the flea market when I have the chance. It . . ." Her eyes darted between mine and her husband's. "It's really a mess down there, but if you don't mind stepping over all my supplies, we can go take a peek."

I followed the two of them down the wooden steps that led to their unfinished basement and immediately wanted to go back the other way.

"This is interesting." The only words I could think to say. Crocheted dolls in all sizes crammed the dark, cool, expansive space. Skeins of yarn in every color of the rainbow were stacked in crates and boxes along the black tiled floor. Loose yarn zigzagged from the tops of the taller boxes, the walls, the ceilings, creating the feel that we had just entered the inside of a room-sized loom.

What got to me more than the maze of woven colors were the dolls themselves. I would say there were at least seventy-five, maybe a hundred, of those things. And none of them had faces. Creepy. No sign of Dayonna. *Time to go.* I hurried back up the steps. Both Monroes were right behind me.

As if reading my mind, Mrs. Monroe chimed, "I know it kind of startles people when they first see my dolls, you know, with no faces. But there is a reason I do not add eyes, noses, and the like."

The basement steps ended in their small kitchen. I stopped next to the refrigerator and turned around to give her my full attention. I hoped there was a sane reason for the featureless dolls.

"See, I make them because of the foster kids, all those countless children in the system who've been neglected or forgotten, abused or forsaken. I make those dolls to remember them. When people see those empty faces, they remember the reason why, after I tell them. And it puts those precious children with no families or homes into everyone's heart and consciousness. The money I make from selling them, I give as a donation to your agency, Holding Hands. Every cent. Been doing it for years."

No wonder Ava praised the Monroes so highly. They are helping to keep her agency afloat. "And you sell a lot of them?" I could not help but ask. How many people would want one of those dolls hanging around their house?

"You'd be surprised," she said and smiled, as if reading my thoughts. "When people know the story behind my dolls, they usually buy at least two or three of them. One man bought all the ones I had at my table when I was at the Patapsco flea market a few months ago. I do it for the children." Her smile turned sad; her compassion seemed genuine. "We can't keep all the foster kids in the system at our home, but we can help by bringing attention to the issue and raising money for support. It's my small way of making a difference under God's great sun." Her smile faded as she looked into the distance. "There is nothing worse than losing hope. . . ."

Mr. Monroe, who had been listening attentively to his wife's words, patted her shoulder and turned toward the living room. And then he froze, his eyes wide with disbelief. I quickly discovered the reason for his alarm.

Dayonna was sitting on the living room sofa.

"W—where did you come from?" The elder man's words were a whisper. Mrs. Monroe looked just as shocked as he did.

Dayonna gave a plastic, wide smile before turning back to the magazine through which she was thumbing. She said nothing, riffling through the latest edition of *People*.

"I'll let Officer Collins know she is back." I was ready to leave. Dayonna was back. I could tell from her body language that she was in no mood for talking. And I had no idea what, if anything, the Monroes knew about her disappearance or return. Or if she had ever even left. No one in that home was going to give me answers. I felt it in my gut. No need to waste my evening beating dead horses. I had other dead matters waiting for me at home that needed my attention.

"I'll call you tomorrow, and we'll talk," I said to nobody in particular as I walked myself to the door and headed to my car.

Not surprisingly, there was another note waiting for me. This one had been slipped through the small crack I had left in my car window. Had it only been twenty minutes since my world had turned upside down? *So you opened the box, and the only thing inside was . . . bubble wrap and . . . the ring? Nothing . . . nothing else? Yeah, Ma. Were you expecting something else to be in there?*

The note had landed on the passenger-side floor. I waited until I was at a traffic light several blocks away from the Monroes to pick it up. The message was again written in Dayonna's large and loopy scribble.

If you do not find my sister, I will keep running away until I find her. And if I find her, neither one of us is coming back, because they are going to kill us.

I crumpled up the note and threw it on the backseat. I was exhausted—mentally, emotionally, and physically.

Chapter 7

I finally pulled up to my home at 6:30 P.M., too tired to notice the police cruiser parked in front.

I guess I should have been paying more attention.

My only thought when I entered my living room was to find my son and make sense of the box before crashing on my bed. I truly was not prepared for the reality waiting for me instead.

"There she is, the finest woman on the planet. How are you today?" Even before I saw the flash of his gold tooth, I smelled the aftershave he'd obviously baptized himself in, and, oddly, I also caught a whiff of freshly baked chocolate chip cookies.

Officer Leon Sanderson.

"Wow. My day is now complete. I can go home now . . . to my empty, lonely home." The forty-something Police Athletic League officer was leaning against my excuse for a kitchen island. The tiny butcher-block cart on braked wheels looked ready to collapse under the weight of his solid frame. I wondered if he had even noticed that he was positioning himself for a hard fall.

"Hi, Leon. I see my son let you in." I did not even attempt to hide my disdain as I dropped my workbag onto my sofa and glared at Roman, who quickly began fishing through our refrigerator.

"Officer Sanderson baked cookies." Roman sounded defensive, attempting to explain why this man was in our home. Crumbs surrounded my son's mouth and spilled down his T-shirt. I wondered again if he really was fourteen.

Grown man, I thought, remembering his words from earlier that day, and shook my head.

"They're good, Ma," Roman said, slurping down a tall glass of milk at the same time.

"That's right." Officer Sanderson straightened up and produced a paper plate stacked high with chocolate chip cookies. "And these aren't those shortcut, prepackaged kind. I made these from scratch, my grandmother's recipe. Only you, Ms. St. James, are worthy of Alberta Sanderson's chocolate dream cookies. Some sweet chocolate for some hot chocolate." He extended the plate toward me as I passed by the kitchen on the way to my room.

"I don't have time for this. Roman, that's enough cookies. Please see Officer Sanderson to the door so his house won't be lonely." I had nothing against the officer, and to be honest, he wasn't a bad-looking man, but his pitiful pickup lines made everything about him seem like an outdated plastic camera—disposable. With all his corny jokes and over-the-top attempts to be romantic, it was hard to take him and his gold tooth seriously. Besides, although I'd never explained it to him, I was not exactly "available." Well, this morning, that possibility had been there, but now, with the ashes possibly nonexistent, I was once again in limbo regarding my marital status.

Too much to explain to an old-time player.

"Aw, Sienna, you play a hard game, but one day you'll realize you've met your match. No need to walk me to the door, young soldier. Your mother thinks she won this round, but she hasn't tasted my cookies yet." He winked at Roman, and out the door he went.

"Seriously, son." I shook my head at my first and only born. "You struggle when I tell you to take out the trash, but you have no problems letting it in."

Roman grinned. "Don't worry, Ma. I know the deal. I guess I saw no harm in eating cookies while we wait for Dad to come back home."

I turned away quickly before he could see my face.

There was so much I had not told my son. I hoped when he *was* a grown man, he did not hate me.

"It's all good." I blinked back tears, wondering if I believed my own words. I was standing next to my bedroom door, trying to remember what it was I wanted to do, where to begin, how I'd gotten there.

"It's right here," Roman said, interrupting my confusion. His right hand was cupped open. I already knew what he held. Feeling weak and nauseated, I stumbled my way to the long leather bench at the foot of my bed. Roman followed me into my room and quietly sat down next to me. He cupped the jeweled lion's head ring in his hand as if he were holding a butterfly, gently and firmly all at once.

"I'm going to get a chain and wear it around my neck like you said Daddy used to."

I watched him trace the rubies, sapphires, and diamonds with his left pinkie finger. "Not yet, Roman. Don't wear it yet." I did not trust my voice, did not know what else I would say with it.

"Yeah, you're right. You told me Daddy was going to give this to me for my eighteenth birthday. I can wait. Daddy would want me to wait. But then again, since he sent it now, maybe he thinks I'm ready. I'll ask him the next time he calls." The smile on Roman's face stabbed my heart.

"Roman, there is a lot . . . I think I need to explain. . . ." I sighed. What was I supposed to explain to him when I did not know the questions or answers about RiChard myself?

"Ma, you're crying."

Was I really? I lifted a finger to my face and discovered that a single tear had indeed washed down my cheek.

"I'm okay. I guess I am just a little surprised . . . to see this ring. Roman, I do not know where your father is. I do not know . . . if he is even okay." That was the best I could get out. And it was the truth.

"Oh, Ma, of course he's okay. He wouldn't have sent the ring if he wasn't. I gotta go tell Skee-Gee about this one." And with that, Roman was gone, leaving me alone to wonder for the umpteenth time in my life if I was a wife or a widow. Where were the ashes? Were there any ashes?

I was sick and tired of the constant limbo in which RiChard kept my life, my heart, my soul.

"Not today." I tried to shake off the constant sorrow that seemingly outlined the edges of my sanity and headed back into the kitchen. I kept a notepad on a shelf above my stove. I had scribbled on it the phone number of the stranger in Portugal who'd contacted me last Wednesday.

I guess I'd known even then that our conversation was not over.

Chapter 8

The cookies were actually good. And still a little warm. The chocolate morsels melted on my tongue as I waited for someone to pick up on the other end. Everything felt bizarre about eating cookies while calling an international phone number for a crematorium in Portugal. . . .

The woman who called me last week had told me that her name was Beatriz and that she knew very little English. Indeed, it had sounded like she was reading the few words she said. I could still hear the two sentences that made up most of the conversation. The words played like a scratched vinyl record in my head. *Hi. I am Beatriz in Portugal, and I am sorry to say that your husband's ashes are coming to you.*

I did not know her. I did not know what had happened. I did not even know RiChard was in Portugal. I was stunned at the call, which came at 2:51 A.M. Stunned and half asleep, I managed to get out one question. "What is your phone number?"

A man had immediately gotten on the line. He'd offered no name, no greeting, no explanation, just rote numbers in broken English. The call disconnected after he gave the last digit.

I'd debated about calling back to get more details since last Wednesday, but I thought getting more details would make the call seem real, and not just a fuzzy middle-of-the-night bad dream. Now the box was here, but no ashes. I needed answers.

The phone continued to ring.

I hung up and dialed again. Still no answer.

"Lord, I can't take it!" I slammed the phone down on the counter.

"Ma, what's wrong?"

How long had Roman been standing there? I made myself breathe and threw a half smile on my face.

"Nothing you need to worry about. I . . ." I searched for something to say. Dayonna Diamond reentered my mind. A perfect distraction. "You know what? I'm going to go get ready for church. And you can come with me."

"I was about to do my homework. Besides, I don't remember Pastor McKinney saying there was a service tonight."

"Boy, I know full well you were not about to do homework. Are you that against going to church?" Both of us chuckled, but I quickly put my "Don't mess with Mama" face back on. "Go get ready. We're not going to our church tonight. We're going to Bible study at Second Zion Tabernacle."

"Second Zion? Why didn't you say so in the first place?"

I watched a mischievous grin ease onto my son's round face. He had his daddy's nose. It wrinkled ever so slightly when he smiled. I shook the thought, the memories, the pain, the loss, the sorrow—the questions—and focused on the present moment with my son.

"Let me guess. Some girl from school goes there, huh?"

"Ma, everyone goes to Second Zion." His voice cracked as he struggled to contain the widening grin on his face. "I ain't worried about no girl from school."

"Mmm-hmm . . ."

The girl business aside, he was right. Seemed like everyone in town went to Second Zion. I was banking on that fact. I did not want the Monroes or Dayonna to notice me in the pews, and a worshipping crowd of half the city was just what I needed to remain unnoticed.

Chapter 9

We walked into the large royal blue foyer of Second Zion Tabernacle around quarter to eight. I had been in the massive facility once or twice before, but I still stood in awe of the majestic edifice. The narthex alone was grand. Floor-to-ceiling-length satin curtains lined the walls and windows of the foyer like stage curtains, complete with velvet tiebacks and posh tassels. The windows were works of art—commissioned stained-glass creations crafted by a local artisan in shades of blue, green, and gold. The entire ceiling, which soared high above our heads, was another commissioned art piece. More than just a painting of the blue sky, the ceiling artwork looked like the entrance to heaven itself. Billowing clouds, soft rays of sunlight, and chubby cherubim with faces in every color of humanity looked down on us with ethereal delight.

Bishop Vincent LaRue, the charismatic visionary behind Second Zion's tenfold growth over the past five years, had dreamed of a multicultural worship center. At the moment, however, mainly shades of brown filled his royal blue cushioned pews.

Roman and I flocked into the main sanctuary, which was already filled with a couple thousand congregants. Most churches seemed to have a difficult time getting people out to midweek Bible study, but the bishop ran his Tuesday night study more like a Sunday morning worship service, with the choir, band, and praise team in place. Only after an intense and inspiring musical praise prelude did the Tuesday night Bible study attendees pour into the massive classrooms adjoining the sanctuary. We'd gotten there just as the crowd was beginning to break into classes.

There were classes targeted to everyone from every walk of life: children, teen girls, teen boys, singles, marrieds, seniors. There were even specialized courses for mothers of preschoolers, single dads, pregnant teens, recovering addicts, and more. Biblically based workshops taught by licensed professionals were also offered, covering such diverse areas as household financial management, health and diet, grief, and small business start-up. I learned all of this by stopping at the circular information desk to the left of the foyer, where three women and one man answered questions and passed out brochures listing class names and locations.

"Sorry, Roman, but the teen boys meet in a classroom far away from the teen girls. Opposite sides of the building. Guess you're not going to run into that girl from school."

"I told you I wasn't worried about no girl." Despite his words, I didn't miss the disappointment filling his face. I shook my head and patted his back as he filed into a classroom lined with bold, bright posters.

He'd come here thinking he'd catch a glimpse of his crush, and I'd come here actually believing that I would somehow see the Monroes and Dayonna.

Like mother, like son. Delusional dreamers were we. Like father, too.

RiChard.

The backs of my eyelids burned anew as I fought to keep the questions from regaining control of my mind.

"Lord, what am I doing here?" I mumbled as I walked aimlessly along with the crowd. Even if I did perchance come upon the Monroes and/or Dayonna, what was I expecting to see? What did I want to overhear them say? What would *I* say if they ran into me? All I knew was that something was not adding up right with any of them. I felt it. I wanted to know more.

With no other plan or purpose, I sat down in a back seat in the closest classroom. STRESS MANAGEMENT WORKSHOP was written on a small dry-erase board pegged to the classroom door. The room was filled with about forty or fifty people, from business executive types taking notes on computer tablets and smartphones to old church mothers clutching square black purses and metal canes. A woman in her mid- to late thirties stood at the front of the room, her eyes closed as she walked the class through a deep-breathing exercise.

I recognized her immediately from the photo that graced the front of all Second Zion's bulletins. She was Marcie LaRue, the great bishop's young and beautiful wife. I guess a person in her position would have to know a little something about how to handle stress.

"As you inhale," she was saying, "meditate on these verses from Isaiah twenty-six. 'You will keep him in perfect peace, Whose mind is stayed on You, Because he trusts in You. Trust in the Lord forever, for in Yah, the Lord, is everlasting strength.'"

I watched as the young and the old alike, all with eyes closed, took quiet, deep breaths around me. I knew blood pressures were being regulated, anxiety was slowly being put in check, tension was getting released. I closed my eyes to join in the communal relaxation exercise.

"I want you to picture yourself in the arms of Jesus. Set your mind right there. Imagine His divine arms holding you, shielding you, hugging you, embracing you." The woman's voice was calm, steady. It was a comforting image. I let myself go there.

"Feel your muscles relax," she continued, "starting with your hands, then your arms, your shoulders, your neck. Keep feeling your muscles melt away in your face, your legs, your toes. Deep breath in . . . out. You can relax in the arms of Jesus. He is holding you up. His peace is eternal and strong. His peace nobody and nothing can take away from you. Find that last knot of tension inside of you, and feel it melt away in the presence of God. Inhale a deep breath of His grace. Exhale a deep breath of praise. Jehovah Himself will sustain you."

I was there. I could feel it. Relaxation. Peace. Divine tranquility. And then . . . *bump!* A large burgundy shoulder bag jabbed me in the arm as its owner passed me.

A man in an olive-colored suit bent down to whisper in my ear. "I am so sorry, sister." Something about his scent reminded me of the ocean, a lazy day, and a tropical breeze.

"It's okay," I said and smiled as I looked up. I had to catch my breath when I saw the raw handsomeness standing over me. At least six feet tall, he was the color of gingerbread, with a smile just as spicy. He had a fresh haircut and a slight after-five shadow, and the only imperfection on his face was a small scar over his left cheekbone. And even that looked intriguing.

"I'm glad you're okay, sister," he whispered, barely looking at me before readjusting his shoulder bag. I struggled to exhale, to figure out what I was supposed to say next, but he was already gone. Like a straw house slammed by a hurricane, something in me collapsed in his wake.

Pain, grief, guilt, sorrow . . . confusion.

I tried for several minutes to refocus on the teacher, her words, the scriptures. . . .

No use. *I'm sorry, Lord. I guess my mind has not stayed on you, 'cause I'm having no peace right about now.* Not wanting to be a distraction to anyone, I quietly slipped out of the room.

The Bible study sessions still had about another half hour to go. I meandered through the hallways, nodding or speaking to other stragglers, until I found an overstuffed armchair in a quiet corner. I collapsed into it, ready to block out the rest of the world and wait for Roman while wallowing in my silent pain.

And that was when I saw them.

Chapter 10

They were facing the doorway of another classroom. Mr. Monroe held Mrs. Monroe's hand as they both talked with sober faces to someone just out of my view. Dayonna was to the left of them, leaning against the wall outside of the room, looking away, her arms crossed. The seriousness on the Monroes' faces, the slight irritation on Dayonna's made me want to get up to hear what was being said.

Some classes were ending early, so there were just enough people in the hallways to make me feel like I could move a little closer to them without being noticed. Keeping my head slightly down, I joined a large group of women emerging from the singles' Bible study who were heading in the general direction of the Monroes. Again, I asked myself what I was looking for, what I was expecting to hear. Like with the rest of my life, I did not have the answers to my own questions.

The group of chattering, laughing, and profiling single women moved slowly through the corridor. I stayed in the center of the perfume-heavy crowd, feeling my heart beating faster as we approached the Monroes. There was no sign on the classroom door they were facing. The lights were dim. The room looked empty.

But they were definitely talking to someone. I was close enough to hear their muffled voices. Dayonna sighed loudly and looked up at the ceiling, her arms still crossed.

The group of women was starting to move faster, I realized. I upped my steps to keep up and keep my cover, but I quickly realized I was in danger of being noticed. They were heading directly toward the Monroes.

The Monroes noticed them coming, as well. I saw the two elders exchanging glances as the women neared. The ladies' steps were getting quicker, the sway of their hips more exaggerated.

I watched as the Monroes, hands still locked together, suddenly turned away from the classroom where they had been engaged in conversation with an unseen stranger. Mrs. Monroe reached out to Dayonna with her free hand, and the young girl joined their hurried departure.

The single ladies were now at the doorway, nearly clambering over each other to speak to the sole occupant remaining in the room.

A familiar face.

For a moment, I completely forgot what I was doing and who I had been trying to see.

"Hi, Brother Scott." The voices of the women rang out in a uniform singsong chorus. The object of their syrupy hello was the man in the olive suit with the burgundy shoulder bag, the man who'd bumped me out of my Jesus-hugging-me relaxation groove.

Brother Scott, Brother Scott, Brother Scott. I wanted to kick myself over how fine that man was. Seeing him full on only made him look better. It was like seeing a picture of an apple pie on a menu and then having the real piping hot thing placed in front of you.

Talk about a needed distraction.

One of the ladies patted his lapel with her hand. "Those were some mighty fine songs you led this evening."

Oh? How had I missed it? Brother Scott was the music director of Second Zion Tabernacle. I suddenly made the connection.

Another woman quickly chimed in, nearly batting the other woman's hand off the singer's jacket. "You really know how to usher us into the presence of God."

I felt embarrassed for them, until I realized I was still standing right in the middle of the pack.

Brother Scott, for his part, remained silent, only nodding with a slight smile at the flirtatious greetings. As he looked over the women, slowly easing away from their outstretched claws, I saw humility and gentleness in his brown eyes. I did not know a thing about this man, but I already respected him.

A familiar feeling began tickling my spine.

The student rally. The first time I saw RiChard. The instant need I had for the man I would marry. For the man who had disappeared so many times out of my life, even his ashes were elusive.

Nausea took over my stomach, and the taste of bile filled my mouth and stung my nostrils. I had to get away. Without thinking of how to make a more gracious exit, I pushed through the growing crowd of worshipping women. It was not until I reached the edge of the giggling sea that I remembered that he'd just been talking to the Monroes.

Second Zion Tabernacle was a church of thousands, and yet there was intimacy between the elder couple and the church praise leader. Something about their postures, their gestures.

The seriousness on the Monroes' faces.

Perhaps, depending on the nature of his relationship with the Monroes, he would be a good resource to find out what was the deal with them.

That was the story I told myself, anyway.

"There you are, Ma. I've been looking all over for you." My son pulled on my elbow. "We gotta come back here sometime."

"Is that right?" I couldn't help but raise my eyebrow at him. "So you enjoyed the all-boys Bible study class?"

"Yeah, it was cool. But the coed snack time afterward was even better."

"I'm sure it was, Roman." I smiled and shook my head.

As my son played away with the cell phone I'd sworn I would never buy him, I wondered how I could get in touch with Brother Scott to talk to him about the Monroes.

This was all becoming a very nice distraction from my reality, indeed.

Chapter 11

His name was Kisu, and he had been the eldest son of a village chief. His skin was dark as night, and his spirit bright as day. With a warrior's heart and a philosopher's soul, he was a close friend of RiChard. I met him once, the one time I ventured into the rich, heavenly land that had once made up the Zulu Empire. In this corner of the world, the earth, the water, and the skies spoke beauty in a language not captured by words. I saw things in nature there that to this day leave me speechless, breathless. RiChard was there on a mission trip—his own mission trip—determined to help the political cause of the Inkatha Freedom Party. It was the late nineties in South Africa, the end of apartheid, and the Zulu people were making their voices heard loud and clear. RiChard wanted to join in the shout.

The lion's head ring had originally been Kisu's.

Two o'clock in the morning and a flood of memories had made my sleep barren. Tired of tossing and turning in the bed, I reached for my bedroom telephone. I had the number memorized. I'd already tried it several times after coming home from church—before brushing my teeth, after wrapping my hair, while watching the numbers on my lighted digital alarm clock go from double digits to the single ones of the wee morning hours.

I dialed the international phone number again.

Still no answer.

The phone just rang and rang and rang, and I was so sick of not knowing what else to do. Where was RiChard?

I was about to enter the number into the handset again when a loud ring startled me. My cell phone.

Breathless, I clicked it on. "RiChard?"

"Ms. St. James?" a raspy voice nearly whispered through the phone.

I did not recognize the woman on the other end. Or at least I did not want to. Had I really just asked for him? Was I really hoping that he was still alive? What would it mean if he was?

"Ms. St. James?" the voice asked again.

"Yes? This is me. Who's this? Do you know where he is?" My heart was pounding so hard, I felt like a mob of wild horses would break out of my chest.

There was a long pause, then "It's me, Dayonna."

I sat straight up in my bed, quickly pushing down the disappointment that wanted to swallow me, quickly pulling up my social work hat.

I knew I didn't give that girl my cell phone number. Shoot, after my dealings with my other problem case, Keisha King and the Benson family, I didn't give any of my clients my cell phone number. The number listed on my business cards actually led to a computerized message system that sent a text transcription to my cell of any voice mail messages. Ava was old school and did not necessarily like my technology-based phone call screening system, but it worked for me.

Until now.

"Dayonna? Is everything okay?"

"Yes," the raspy voice replied. I pulled the phone away from my ear and looked down at the receiver, as if all of a sudden I would see the person on the other end of the line. The phone number had been blocked.

"Dayonna? Are you sure?" What I really wanted to ask was, "Are you sure this is you?" I'd heard only a few words from the girl's mouth, and I knew she had a somewhat raspy voice, but this caller's vocals were all out husky. Grown womanish–sounding. Maybe she was just half asleep. I knew I was. Maybe that was the problem.

"Dayonna?" I quizzed again.

"It's me!" the voice growled.

"What's going on?" I could not stop blinking, trying to stretch my heavy eyelids enough to focus again on my clock. Two seventeen.

"Don't look for Hope."

"Wha? How did you get my number?"

The line went dead.

Chapter 12

"So . . . let me get this straight. You've had this case less than twenty-four hours and already you want out? This isn't like you, Sienna. What's really going on?" Ava's gold wire frames were perched on the tip of her nose, giving her more the appearance of a studious teacher or librarian than that of the director of a therapeutic foster care agency. There was a frown tugging down the corners of her wine-colored lips, but I knew she was not disappointed with me. Just concerned.

"It's not just the case, Ava," I answered honestly. "The past twenty-four hours have been a little crazy, and . . . and Dayonna and her issues—which normally I could handle—are a bit much right now."

Her piercing gaze seemed to look right through me, as if she could see the outlines of my crying soul. I was exhausted, having never fallen asleep the night before. Seconds passed before she spoke again.

"Something going on with Roman?"

I closed my eyes and shook my head no, silently praising God that as far as I knew, nothing out of the ordinary was happening with him.

There was only so much drama a woman could take. This week was not Roman's turn.

"Ava, I appreciate your concern. I do. But like I told you yesterday, this is something I have to handle myself."

"I can't let you off the case, Sienna." Ava stuck both of her hands under her glasses, rubbed her eyes, and then used her fingers to push her large, loose golden curls off her caramel-colored face. "If I give you another case, there will be something crazy with that one, as well, and you will not have moved any farther than where you're sitting right now. I gave you Dayonna because I know you can handle her. This is a good opportunity for you to learn how to balance your personal crises and your self-care with the demanding needs of our clients. You're just starting your social work career. There will be a million Dayonna files waiting on your desk and a million more issues waiting for you at home."

She was not fussing. She was simply stating the truth.

"Dayonna called me at home last night."

"Then set boundaries with her immediately." Ava picked up a stack of folders and straightened them, no longer looking at me.

"What about this Hope Diamond business?" I couldn't let it go.

She looked back up at me over the rims of her glasses. Her frown deepened as she sat in silence.

"Ava, I'm not trying to back out of this case," I explained. "I'm just trying to make sense of it."

"I've been through her chart myself, Sienna. I've gotten the whole story directly from several of her workers over at social services. There's been at least five of them. I can assure you, Sienna, there is no missing sister. There is no sister at all. Just an older brother who left the system years ago. Dayonna has serious issues, mental chains and emotional scars. I would look into getting her a psychiatrist as soon as possible so that this placement will work."

"The Monroes are certainly acting like there are no problems."

"At the moment, yes. But if their *caseworker*"—she looked at me pointedly—"keeps trying to snoop around and convince everyone that there *is* something wrong, things will fall apart quickly. I can't believe that you followed them to church, Sienna. Are you *trying* to sabotage this placement?"

The accusation from my mentor hurt. I could not help but return with my own finger pointing.

"Of course not, but I think it's pretty obvious why you want this placement to work so badly. Mrs. Monroe is giving you all the profits from the dolls she sells."

I tried to sound mean, but we both ended up laughing.

"Honey, you think I'm willing to put you through all of this to keep getting ten dollars from Elsie Monroe's crazy-looking dolls?" Ava laughed so hard, she began clapping. "Now, don't get me wrong. I am open to any and all donations, but that is not why I have you working this case." Her smile slowly faded away. She stood and walked to the huge corner window, which was the single luxurious feature of her entire office.

Holding Hands Agency was housed on the fourteenth floor of an older building on the outskirts of downtown Baltimore. The panoramic view encompassed newly constructed high-end condos near Federal Hill on one end and dismal, neglected avenues of abandoned buildings and row homes on the other.

A city gone full circle.

I knew Ava's office choice had been intentional.

"I'll be honest with you," she suddenly blurted out, still facing the window. "There *is* money involved. But not from the Monroes. When I started this agency twenty years ago, times were different. People's hearts and priorities were in a different place. Now, in this day and age of cutbacks and setbacks, I'm struggling, Sienna, to keep this place afloat. I don't want to lay anyone off or turn any child away. Holding Hands has been recognized so many times as a successful therapeutic foster care program of final chances and last resorts. Dayonna's success with the Monroes will only solidify our chances of funding. I've gotten a guarantee on that."

She turned around to face me. Her lips were quivering. "Sienna, I need you to make sure this placement works. I don't care what oddities you hear or see, don't rock the boat if the water ain't troubled."

"I don't think I can do this." There. It was out. I'd been working with troubled children for years in many settings, but Dayonna seemed troubled on a whole different level. That child seemed too off and creepy for me to be messing with right now. "You know I have worked with challenging cases before, but if you are depending on me to help this foster family to keep the agency afloat, I don't think I'm the right person for the job."

"And that is why you must do it. If you were so confident you could change everybody and everything, I would have never asked you to work for me."

I tried to absorb her words, but one thing didn't make sense. "With all due respect, Ava, since this case is so important, and so much hinges upon it, why aren't you handling it yourself?"

Ava sat back down and finished signing off on some paperwork before looking back up at me.

"Honey," she said with great gusto, "I'm tired. If Dayonna doesn't make it, I'm retiring. I've had about enough of this."

We looked at each other a few moments, then burst into laughter. We were still laughing when I realized that I'd missed a call. My cell phone had been on silent mode, and the short voice mail message had been transcribed and sent as a text message.

Chapter 13

Three simple words filled my cell phone screen.

Get here now.

The call was from the Monroes' home, my complicated voice mail system revealed. I looked up at Ava, whose pen was frozen in midair.

"Is everything okay, Sienna?"

I already knew where Ava stood on the case, and I did not want to keep "rocking the boat," as she had put it. I threw a smile on my face, betraying the fingers of dread crawling up my back.

"It's all good, Ava. I'm going to go now." I smiled.

She nodded, and I hightailed it out of there, checking the voice mail message as I headed down the elevator.

The caller had whispered into the phone. I could not make out the voice.

When I pulled up to the Monroes' home fifteen minutes later, the first thing I noticed was the front porch was no longer blue and yellow. All the cushioned wicker furniture, the planters, and even the doormat and floral wreath were now in shades of lavender and teal.

Odd.

I knocked on the door, and Mrs. Monroe opened it with a startle.

"Oh, Ms. St. James."

I could not tell if it was a question, an exclamation, or just a statement of the obvious.

"Yes, it's me."

"Okay . . . Did you need something? I did not know you were coming today. " She stood in the doorway, smiling while blocking my view of the living room behind her.

Somebody was yelling inside. I could not make out the words, but the voice certainly sounded like Dayonna's.

"Is everything okay?" I moved my head around to try to see past her, but she continued to block my view.

"Uh . . . yes. Uh, Dayonna is just having a bad moment, but Horace is helping her calm down."

"I think I really need to come in." I realized I was shuffling from foot to foot, itching for a view. I didn't want to knock the elder lady down, but, seriously, this was all really starting to get on my nerves.

"We didn't know you were coming." She kept smiling and blinking, as if nobody was screaming in her house.

"Someone called from here and asked me to come."

"Oh?" The smile left, and she looked genuinely surprised. "I don't know why—"

"Mrs. Monroe, I'm coming in. If Dayonna is having a crisis, it is my job to help handle it." I stepped up to the doorway, and all she could do was move to let me in.

The living room was demolished.

Broken ceramic figures filled the floor. The sofa cushions were upturned; the pillows scattered. The floral centerpiece lay in shreds. A mirror that hung over an armchair had a long crack down the middle of it.

The screaming was coming from upstairs. I headed to the steps but had to quickly back up and duck for cover as dirty clothes and trash suddenly came flying down.

"Don't kill me! Don't kill me! Don't kill me!" Dayonna's voice sounded five octaves higher as she repeated those words nonstop from the landing above. I looked back at Mrs. Monroe and saw tears streaming down her face.

"I'm sorry." The petite-sized woman's lip quivered, and then her words gushed out like sloshing water. "I guess it's good that you are here. I did not want to call you, because it's so embarrassing. We normally can handle all the children that come through here, but Dayonna is . . . is . . . different. She keeps saying that we're going to kill her and cut her up for cabbage stew. Have you ever heard of such a thing? Horace is trying to calm her down. I'm so sorry. We really can handle her. Don't take her from us. We can handle her. Please don't take her from us. She needs our help more than anyone." Mrs. Monroe was shaking and wringing her hands.

Dayonna was still screaming.

I looked from Mrs. Monroe back to the staircase, where more clothes and trash were tumbling down. "Wait here, Mrs. Monroe."

I turned toward the steps, not sure what I was going to do, but knowing I had to do something. Clothes were flying everywhere, and I saw Dayonna at the top of the steps, trying to empty a hamper. A wastebasket lay sideways at her feet, its contents already scattered all over the staircase.

"Dayonna!" I yelled as I stepped carefully up the cluttered staircase. She appeared to be completely unaware of my presence, her mouth and screams seemingly stuck on a repeat button with the volume turned up, her eyes a vacant, hollow stare. Horace Monroe stood to the side of her, frozen in an awkward stance, as if about to grab her, but not sure how. He, too, seemed completely oblivious to my presence on the steps.

"Don't kill me! Don't kill me! Don't kill me!" Dayonna's screams continued to pierce my ears, and the laundry continued to fall. She was about to toss the entire wicker basket down when I reached her side.

"Dayonna," I said firmly and grabbed the girl in a tight restraint, something I had been taught to do during one of my social work internships at a special needs school. Though she still seemed oblivious to my presence, her body flailed in resistance to my hold on her. Her yelled words became lost in gurgling screams as she began fighting to bite my arms and bang her head into my chest. The cries coming from her thin frame did not sound human.

I held on to her, locking my arms and legs around her the way I had been taught, the way I had done only once before, when a child at the school where I interned had a meltdown that threatened the safety of his classmates. As I held on to her, rocking her slowly, Mr. Monroe snapped back to life. In silence he helped me move her away from the dangerously narrow staircase landing to the relative safety of the empty upper hallway. Slowly and steadily, her gurgled screams turned into heavy whimpers, her wild flailing became more subdued, and her eyes began to close. After minutes that felt like hours, I felt her body become like deadweight in my arms. Her breathing, though still heavy and forced, slowed down into a calm rhythm.

She was asleep.

For a second I could hear the workshop leader the night before guiding us into the visualization of being in the arms of Jesus. I remembered again the short moment of peace I'd felt before fine Brother Scott bumped me out of my serene space. I almost let my own eyes close. *Is that what I needed? Jesus to restrain me in the midst of my silent screaming?*

But I was not Jesus. And Dayonna was not me.

"She's all right now?"

I was not sure when Mrs. Monroe had joined her husband's side, but there she was, her hand shaking, covering her open mouth.

"For the moment she's okay." I loosened my grip on the young girl's body. Her head and thin limbs collapsed onto me. "What happened?" I looked back up at both Monroes. They looked at each other, and then Horace answered.

"Elsie tried to give her one of her crocheted dolls."

Chapter 14

Clothes, trash, broken ceramics, and porcelain shards were everywhere. For the average person, this would have been an overwhelming mess. For the Monroes, whose home had their own version of a neat, cozy cottage feel, I knew this was disastrous.

And yet it was obvious that they still wanted her there.

After helping me lay a still sleeping Dayonna in her bed, Mr. Monroe helped clear a safe path down the steps and through the living room. We sat at the untouched dining room table to talk. The catastrophe of moments earlier had been contained to the living room and staircase.

"I guess Dayonna was the one who called you." Mr. Monroe sighed and rubbed a hand over the wrinkles that lined his balding forehead. "My wife had just offered her one of her dolls, explaining that she gave one to all the foster children that come in our home. Then . . . well, then, Dayonna just went berserk. But we can handle it. We really can take care of her," he asserted.

"She keeps saying that we're trying to kill her," Elsie blurted out. "And that cabbage stew business! Have you ever heard such a thing?" The older woman nearly wept. For the first time I could recall since I'd met her, her voice sounded as frail and small as her frame. "Why is she saying all this? Are my dolls that disturbing?" She rested her head on Mr. Monroe's arm. He reached out his other arm and patted his wife's thin shoulders.

"No, sweetheart. Dayonna just needs some extra love and attention."

And medication, as far as I was concerned.

"Listen," I said, smiling at the love-filled couple, wondering if I would have a mate like that with whom to share my senior years. "I understand that you really want this placement to work, and I will do my best to support you. That is why I'm here. I need you to understand that."

The pair grabbed hands, looking less like a seasoned older couple and more like two youngsters getting chided. I continued with my lecture.

"In the future, if Dayonna is having a meltdown, you need to let me know as soon as possible. Please don't wait until after your living room is pulverized. I believe that you are really dedicated to taking care of her, but that does not mean that you have to face challenges alone." I remembered the new decor of their front porch. "What happened outside?"

"Last night." Mr. Monroe's voice was barely above a whisper. "After church. Elsie cooked us a late dinner. Baked chicken, potatoes, and . . . and cabbage."

"Say no more." I sighed loudly.

"We keep a second set of porch furniture in the shed. That's what's out there now. She stabbed the other set through and through with a butter knife." Mrs. Monroe shook her head. "It was bad. Our neighbor across the street, Everett, threatened to call the police with all the screaming and running around she was doing. But just as quick as it started, it ended, and she went up to her bedroom and went to sleep, like nothing had ever happened."

I remembered the cinnamon-colored man sweeping across the street yesterday and made a mental note to check in with him at some point for his observations.

"We should have called." Mr. Monroe glanced at his wife and cleared his throat. "But we've had such great success with all our foster children, and we could tell Ava Diggs had high hopes for us with this one. We did not want to look like we're failing."

A loud noise, like a ceramic plate shattering against a wall, sounded on the floor above us. I forgot what we were talking about as a single scream pierced our ears.

"Sisssterrrr!"

"That's the other thing . . ." Mrs. Monroe let go of her husband's hand and looked at me nervously. "Do you know anything about a doll baby named Hope?"

Chapter 15

The intake worker at Rolling Meadows Mental Health Center gave me a weak smile as she held out a clipboard filled with forms. IDA MCKERNAN was typed on her plastic name badge. I could tell from the way she kept checking the clock on the wall of the small admissions office that she was close to her lunch break or maybe even the end of her shift.

"You, or whoever, need to fill out all of these. I also need her medical assistance card."

"Sienna," Mrs. Monroe began again, "you really don't have to stay here for this. I've done this before with other foster children. I know the routine. I know you have other foster families to check on, and you've spent so much time with us already. Horace and I can handle it from here."

I gave her a warm smile. "I know I do not have to stay, but I promised that I would be here for support." Shoot, I'd been there to follow the ambulance and to witness the grand fiasco in the emergency room. The least I could do was hang around long enough to see which room Dayonna was going to be given.

I'd called 911 when the second round of throwing and screaming began at the Monroes. The doctors in the ER immediately agreed that the teen who came via ambo, on a restraining board, needed inpatient hospitalization. They'd had to drug her just to keep her from hurting herself or someone else in her out-of-control state.

"Um . . ." Ida, the intake worker, was still holding out the clipboard. "I'm not trying to rush you, but I do need someone to fill this out." She looked back up at the clock.

"I can do it." Mrs. Monroe took the forms and a seat. "Really, Sienna, you do not have to stay."

"Okay." She was right. I did have other clients to check on. "Just keep me updated. Please don't hesitate to call me anytime, day or night." I handed her my business card, knowing that I'd already given one to the family before. Then I remembered something else.

"Mrs. Monroe . . ." I stopped before I went out the door. The elder lady was pulling out a plastic sandwich bag filled with Dayonna's insurance cards and other legal documentation, a bag I knew she'd gotten from Dayonna's social services worker when they first took the girl into their home. "To your knowledge, does Dayonna have my cell phone number?"

"I don't think so." Mrs. Monroe had begun filling out the first form that would be added to the thick chart, which, I'd noted already, had Dayonna's name on it. "But if you've called our house from your phone, your number is probably on our caller ID." Her pen stopped moving, but she did not look up at me. "Why do you ask?"

"Oh, it's nothing, I guess. Just, well, the important thing is that Dayonna is here and will get stabilized to come back to your place."

"Yes, she is in good hands." Ida, the intake worker, tapped loudly on another clipboard. "You can always call if you think of any more questions."

My questions were not for Ida. I started to tell her that, but she didn't have time and I didn't have time, so I decided to move on. I turned back toward the doorway and almost ran into Mr. Monroe, who was entering the admissions office after having parked their car.

"You're still here?" He looked at me and then at his wife. Was that concern or irritation on his face? I could not tell.

"She's leaving now, Horace."

He gave a nod, seemingly satisfied with his wife's words and my quick wave good-bye.

Why was everyone rushing me out? I was only trying to do my job. I was halfway down the corridor, headed for the main exit, when a nurse poked her head out of a doorway across from the admissions office.

"Excuse me, ma'am?"

"Me?" I pointed to myself.

"Yes. Aren't you the social services worker that came in with the new girl?"

"Oh, I don't work for the Department of Social Services. I work for the therapeutic foster care agency that DSS contracted with to care for her."

"Close enough. Can you come here to witness while we do her intake exam?"

She disappeared back into the room before I could answer. I had no choice but to take on the duty, remembering from past experiences that the mental health facility usually stripped new patients of most of their clothing upon admission to ensure that they did not have any weapons, drug paraphernalia, or any other dangerous or prohibited items before being escorted to the locked units.

The first thing I noticed when I entered the room was that it was freezing cold. Why they would have the temperature so low when they knew patients had to undress in here was beyond my understanding. The second thing I noticed was that Dayonna was awake, alert, calm, and unrestrained.

"Hi, Ms. St. James," she chirped in that raspy voice of hers. "I like your shoes." She grinned at me like we were crossing paths in the supermarket and not standing in the intake exam room of a psychiatric facility.

"Hi, Dayonna. How are you today?" I kept up the charade as she began disrobing.

"I'm good." She smiled as she followed the nurse's directions to extend, then lift her arms. "On my next birthday I'll be fifteen. I can't wait until I get my learner's permit." She giggled, and both the nurse and I exchanged glances, the same sly smiles on our faces. I knew the nurse had the same thought as I did. Wasn't any way this girl would be driving anybody's car anytime soon, if ever.

"Does your son have a car?" Dayonna giggled.

My smile froze. "My son?"

"Yeah. Why didn't you tell me you had a son when we first met? What's his name?"

"How did you know I had a son?" I kept the smile on my face only because I was not sure what other expression to make. First, she knew my cell phone number—though I still wasn't convinced that the extra husky voice at two in the morning was really hers—and now she knew I had a son? Was I in the twilight zone?

"I heard the Monroes say so. They saw you at church last night. What's his name? Can I meet him?"

I was speechless. I'd spent nearly the whole day with them, and not once had the Monroes mentioned that they'd seen me at their church.

"Okay, little miss lady." The nurse handed Dayonna a hospital gown. "You'll have to wear this until someone brings you some clothes that match our unit rules. No buttons, zippers, or belts." The nurse's attention turned toward me. "Thanks for your help," she said and smiled.

Dayonna slipped the thin gown over her head and began following the nurse toward a door that led to another hallway.

"Dayonna, do you play with dolls?" I had to ask, fig-uring this was the safest place to broach the topic.

The young teen suddenly stood still, like her feet had become roots lodged into the linoleum floor. Her head turned ever so slowly to meet mine. Her eyes had taken on that familiar wild look. "I will tell you, just like I told them," she said in a gruff whisper. "Hope is not a doll baby. Hope is my sister. They killed her and they know it and I will be dead next." A low moan—almost a growl—began rising from somewhere deep in her chest.

"I'm sorry. You're going to have to go now." The nurse spoke quickly to me in a calm but firm voice as she reached to press a button on the wall.

As I headed back down the corridor to the facility's main entrance, I could hear the nurse's page over the hospital intercom system.

"All available hands. Room two."

Within seconds the empty hallway burst with activ-ity as doors were flung open and workers in a rainbow assortment of scrubs flurried toward the room I'd just left. When I reached the revolving doors that would take me to the visitor parking lot, I took one last look at the chaos I had created behind me. It was during the last few steps I took in the circular doors that a lone figure caught my eye.

While everyone was running the opposite way, Mr. Monroe stood still, facing in my direction, staring at me.

A sneer filled his face.

Chapter 16

Should I even try to make sense of it, the Monroes and Dayonna? Of course I could not. I wasn't even sure that I wanted to, nor did I have the time. After leaving the hospital, I squeezed in two quick visits with a couple of my other clients. I was supposed to see each of them only twice a month. Though I'd technically met my quota for Dayonna for the month, it was pretty clear that I'd be seeing her at least on a weekly basis, at least until she was stable.

I was almost back at the office to finish my paperwork when my cell phone started ringing.

Of all people, of all days, my sister. I loved my baby sis dearly, but she was one of those people who carried drama with her like a pocketbook—if it was not on her shoulder, it was nearby.

I answered the phone, anyway.

"Hey, Yvette. What's going on, girl?" I put my headset on so I could drive and talk at the same time.

"I know you better come get your son!"

Yvette was not one to waste words. No 'Hello. How are you?' Just the usual immediate demand.

Except she had just said something about my son.

"What are you talking about? Roman came to your house after school?" Had I missed a call or a text from him? I did not recall Roman asking permission to go anywhere other than home, especially since I had not yet debriefed him about his afternoon with Skee-Gee, Yvette's eldest, yesterday.

"*After* school?" Yvette was just getting started. "Apparently, he did not even *go* to school today. And now he got *my* son bleeding."

"Yvette, what are you talking about? Roman went to school today!"

"Humph. I hate to break the news to you, sister, but your little prince ain't perfect. All I know is you better come round here right now and get him. Punching and kicking my son? Oh no. I'm not having this."

The line went dead.

I snatched my headset off and threw it onto the passenger seat.

"What is going on now?" I made a U-turn to head back toward I-83. Yvette lived in Park Heights, near the Pimlico racetrack—the lower end of Park Heights, to be exact. The part the tourists never see.

I pulled onto Yvette's street at about a quarter to four, suddenly aware that I had not eaten all day. The permeating scent of jerk chicken coming from a corner store a few blocks away did not help my cause. My stomach growled as I got out of my car and stepped over empty sandwich wrappers, soda bottles, and other free-floating trash that littered the sidewalks like flower petals down a bride's aisle.

My sister lived in the sole occupied house in a row of abandoned homes with her five children and one of their fathers. Tim, Thomas, T-Man? I forgot his name. He and I really did not get along. She lived here and like this not because she had to, but because she wanted to make a statement. She'd been saying since she was fifteen that she would never be the type of woman our mother wanted and groomed us both to be, and on that point she had succeeded. Yvette and I were polar opposites of the same shoelace—she was the chewed-up, raggedy end, and I the end that had been repaired with transparent tape.

For better or worse, we were tied together.

"It's about time you got here!" Yvette was standing on the porch. Two years my junior, she looked twice my age. I would never say that out loud. She'd had a rough go of it.

Mostly by her own choosing.

I bounded up to where she stood, careful not to trip on the crumbling cement steps. She stood with one hand on her wide hip. Her hair, some of which was hers, all of which was dyed bright blond, fell out of a hurried ponytail at the crown of her head.

"Where's Roman?" I demanded, not recognizing my own voice for the fear and anger that were mixed in it.

"The heck if I know," Yvette snarled. "I fussed him out after what he did to Skee-Gee, and he stormed out of here 'bout fifteen minutes ago. When you can't take the heat, you gotta get out the kitchen." She swatted at a fly and crossed her arms.

I looked up and down the desolate street and saw no sign of my son. My heart started beating a little faster. Roman was not a child of the streets. *God, keep my baby safe till I find him!*

"What did he do to Skee-Gee?" I had to stay calm. My sister was riled up enough, and I needed more details before she really let loose.

"Sylvester Tyese Grantley the third, come here!" Yvette did not bother to turn her head or move as she yelled for her son. After a few seconds, my fifteen-year-old nephew plodded out the front door, the screen door slamming shut behind him. He had a black eye, a bloodied nose, and a half-inch scrape above one of his eyebrows.

Despite all that, he had his usual idiotic half grin on his face. "Hi, Aunt See." He leaned against a porch post as he greeted me with his personal nickname for me. I hated when he called me that, and he knew it.

"What happened? Where's Roman? He didn't go to school today? What's going on?" I had too many questions to stick to only one. Skee-Gee's smile only widened.

"Roman called me last night, talking 'bout he had to show me something. Talking 'bout some dumb ring his dad gave him from Africa. I told him it wasn't real, and so we were going to meet up today 'cause he was gonna show me it. That's all."

The ring! Why is Roman walking around with that?

"That's all?" I looked from him to Yvette.

"Tell her the rest, Sylvester." Yvette glared at me.

"Well, he came over here, and when he showed it to me, I asked him if I could hold it."

"Okay, I'm still waiting to find out what happened." My foot patted the ground.

"Well, he wouldn't let me hold it."

"So . . ."

"So I thought I would teach him a lesson about how you supposed to treat family and not put dumb jewelry before your own blood. It took all day, but he finally put it down to play with my DS when we came out here on the porch. When he went inside to the bathroom, I hid it under this brick right here." He pulled out a loose brick from the side of the tiny row home.

"Yvette, where is my son?" My patience was completely gone.

"Let Sylvester finish, please."

So now he's Sylvester and not Skee-Gee? I wanted to roll my eyes at both of them, but I held my tongue. I needed to know what happened.

"Well, when he came out the bathroom and didn't see the ring, he started hollering and screaming at me. I told him he needed to calm down and back up off of me. But he didn't listen. Instead, he came at me swinging." At this point, Skee-Gee stepped away from his post on the porch and began a live demonstration. "He put his arm out like this, see? Then I put my arm out like that, right? Then I made pretend I was going to punch him, and at first he stepped back. But then he got back in my face and banged me." Skee-Gee grinned and pointed at his bloodied nose as if he'd just won a trophy. "But I ain't no punk. I ain't gonna let nobody beat on me, especially no little cousin who gonna put a ring over his own family."

The ring came from family. I was at my boiling point with this, breathing hard but determined to stay calm until I got the information I needed to find my son. "So what did you do?"

"Wait a minute," Yvette cut in. "Did you just hear what your son did? Why—"

"Hold on. Let me finish, Ma." That smile was still on Skee-Gee's face. I wanted to smack it off. "Like I said," he continued, "I ain't gonna let nobody mess me over. I don't care who you are. So I took that little fake ring and threw it as far as I could. It went out over across the street." He pointed at the litter-filled vacant lot that completed the lovely view from Yvette's front porch.

"Just so happened that Bootman and his boys—you know they in a gang, right?—was standing over there. They picked up the ring, flashed a gun at us, and went on about their business. Fool Roman was about to run after them and say something, but I held him back. Ain't no need on getting killed over that stupid ring. Anyways, Bootman and his boys went that way." He pointed to the left. "And Roman took off this way." He pointed to the right, then sat down on the porch wall and poured half a bag of sunflower seeds into his mouth, seemingly satisfied with his tale of breaking my son's heart.

No words could even . . . I looked at Yvette and wanted to . . . Swirls of colors flashed. . . . Was I in a cartoon? Reality?

"Wait a minute, Sienna!" Yvette was yelling at my back as I marched to my car. "What are you going to do about your son beating on mine?"

My foot was already on the accelerator when I put the car in drive. Usually more cautious when on one-way, narrow streets, I zoomed within inches of cars parallel-parked on either side of me. But I could care less. My eyes were only on the sidewalks, the stoops, the bombed-out-looking vacant porch fronts that lined the street. My mission was to find my son.

Seven blocks down. Roman. Sitting alone on some-one's steps. His head was down; his shoulders slumped. His unused backpack thrown at his feet. I parked five cars away from him, the closest I could get. He did not hear me coming.

"Roman."

My fourteen-year-old son looked up at me. A single trail of snot hung from his nose. With no words, he stood to his feet, swinging his backpack up on his shoulder. We walked in silence to the car. He got in. I got in. A full eleven minutes ticked by before I started the motor.

We were almost home when I finally spoke, the only words I could say, the only words I knew he could handle at the moment.

"That ring survived a deadly battle, a tragic tsunami, and God knows what else. We'll get it back, Roman. We'll get it back." I looked over at him.

One corner of his bottom lip quivered, but the snot was gone.

Chapter 17

For the second day in a row, I came home weary, wounded, and tired. Only this time, instead of heading back out to church, I was sinking in my tub filled with baby blue bubbles.

I love the ocean, and anything that remotely reminds me of saltwater and sea breezes is usually enough to carry me away.

Usually.

Tonight, with Roman locked away in his room in silence, and my brain, heart, and head hurting, the ocean-scented bath bubbles reminded me only of the man who had bumped into me the night before.

Brother Scott. He had smelled like sweet escape.

Lying back on my bath pillow with my eyes closed, I thought of the bubbles that had zinged up in my stomach the moment I looked into his face.

RiChard.

Of course no one would ever compare to him. . . .

Somewhere, somehow, not surprisingly, my bath stopped being relaxing.

I pulled on my pajamas and tucked myself into my granny robe. Yeah, I looked like a little old woman with my floral-printed gingham ensemble, but who really cared?

Still seeking solace from the long day, I headed to the kitchen for something sweet. The only thing that was there was the plate of chocolate chip cookies Officer Leon Sanderson had brought over the night before. I warmed up a couple of them—okay, six of them—in the microwave and gulped down a cold glass of milk.

Perhaps Leon could help get the ring back. . . .

It was a fleeting thought, but the more I considered it, the more it made sense. According to Skee-Gee, a gang of boys had it. Leon Sanderson wore a uniform, so he had some kind of authority. Perhaps he had friends in that district who could pull some strings.

I knew as I thought it that nobody was going to risk rocking the boat with a group of young wannabe gangsters over a ring. But maybe it would be worth a try.

Rocking the boat.

Seemed like that was all I was doing lately.

My workbag lay sideways on the kitchen table. Folders, papers, and notes fell out of it, as I had never made it back to the office to type up and turn in everything.

For no reason other than wanting to find a distraction from myself, I pulled out Dayonna's file.

Rocking the boat.

Ava didn't seem to think there was cause to be suspicious about Dayonna's claims or the Monroes' evasiveness, but it just wasn't adding up right to me.

I'd been through Dayonna's chart before, but I started flipping through it once again. Pouring through the pages of her topsy-turvy life gave me a feeling of stability, like I was once again back in control of something.

I started at the beginning of her chart, my notepad next to me. The only thing I knew I was looking for was a sense of peace. Nothing about her case so far had allowed me that small indulgence. I began writing down every name, address, and phone number I could find.

She was born at Maryland General, weighing slightly over three pounds. There were so many drugs in her little newborn body that she spent over four months at Mt. Washington Pediatric Hospital. From there she entered her first foster home, a Sheila Lipscomb in Pikesville. She stayed in Ms. Lipscomb's home until just before her first birthday, when the elder lady apparently decided to go back home to Tennessee. For the next year or two, she bounced between four foster homes before being briefly reunited with her mother.

Crystal Rose.

I wrote down Dayonna's mother's name. Her address at the time was in Murphy Homes, high-rise projects that I knew were torn down back in 1999. No telling where Dayonna's mother was now. Then again, with her extensive drug history, which showed up in Dayonna's veins, no telling if the woman was still alive.

The reality of a life addicted.

I flipped through the rest of the pages quickly. More foster homes, some emergency shelters, and, as I already knew, visits to a couple of in-state and out-of-state residential treatment centers, facilities that offered more intensive twenty-four-hour care for children with severe emotional disturbances. There were several Department of Social Services caseworkers listed throughout her years. The current one was out on maternity leave, I noted. I jotted down all their names.

I worked my way up to Dayonna's entry into the Monroes' home. A week and a day ago. She'd just come back from a residential treatment center somewhere in Florida.

Hold up.

Something was not right. It didn't add up.

I flipped through the last few pages of the chart again, trying to figure out what I was missing.

She entered the facility in Florida three months before her thirteenth birthday. The pages before that date had her in an emergency shelter, with an AWOL date a full five months before she went to Scenic Brook Center in Florida. I checked and rechecked the pages, trying to make sure I had not missed anything. Obviously, a page or something was missing, I decided.

I noted the DSS caseworker she'd had around that time. Deirdre Evans. In the long list of DSS caseworkers I'd jotted down, I starred and circled Deirdre's name.

Five months was a long time to go unaccounted for in the system.

Chapter 18

"Sienna, you really need to talk to your sister. You know I don't like you two fighting."

I could tell my mother was at work. The voices, taunts, laughs, and cries of countless children nearly washed out her voice over the phone.

"Where are you? In a classroom or something? Left the quiet reserve of your office?"

"I'm checking on the before-care program held in the cafeteria, but don't try to change the topic, Sienna. The two of you need to sit down and talk."

It was first thing in the morning. I was on my way to visit a client I had been putting off for several days, and I did not have time to talk about Yvette and her ignorant son.

Not even to my mother.

I had let my mother's phone call roll to voice mail as I circled the inner loop, but had quickly called her back on her cell phone.

I had a little bit of sense left.

My mother was the principal of an elementary school in West Baltimore that had failing marks before she came on board. If I did not catch her now, I would probably not get through until the end of her school day.

And that was too much time for her to be focused on why I had not answered her initial call.

"Mom, Yvette and I aren't fighting. You know your youngest child and her children. Just some little bumps in the road we need to smooth out—and we will."

Even I knew I was understating how I felt at the moment, but where did I even begin trying to explain the continual void left in both my and Roman's life from RiChard's absence?

First the ashes. Now the ring.

The only thing I had left was my sanity, and even that seemed like it was slipping away on some level.

"Well, while you're calling it a small fight, Yvette is crying catastrophe. She said Roman beat up Sylvester over some jewelry. What is going on with him? That's not like my grandson."

"It was a ring from his father," is all I could say.

"Oh," is all she said.

That had made things quiet real quick. Since that Thanksgiving dinner when I announced I was dropping out of school to marry and travel the world, my mother had had very few conversations with me about RiChard. When I thought about it, I couldn't even remember the last time she even said his name. Neither she nor my dad—nor, really, anybody in my life—knew what had become of my marriage to the man who had changed some core part of me.

I knew my mother was waiting to hear the story, that she would be patient another ten or twenty years if necessary. All for the right to say, "I told you so."

I refused to give her that pleasure. I had my pride. Actually, not pride, I realized in that moment.

Hope.

I was bereft of all pride, dignity, and confidence when it came to the secret places in my heart. I'd loved one man, and he left me, he said, because he loved me so much that he could not let the world I lived in be a place in which evil could prevail. I guessed that was what he wanted me to tell his son. So that was what I'd spent the last fourteen years doing. Trying to convince a young boy that it was okay for his heart to bleed in the name of global peace and justice.

Justice.

What did that even mean?

The rooms in my heart had been swept clean and left bare, waiting for RiChard's return. No pretty pictures or fancy furniture to fill the space. All I had left was a little bit of hope that one day the rooms would be filled with something again. I wasn't even sure what that something was, but I knew that if I ever lost hope, I'd lose whatever else I had left going for me.

It made sense now why the past two days had left me so winded. My hope was leaving me, leaving me slowly like air in a balloon with a pinprick hole. Active deflation. Hope that my life and the rooms in it would be filled again. Would mean something beyond the nine-to-five grind. The daily monotony. The broken dreams. The shattered promises.

The love found and then lost.

I'd worked hard—exceedingly, painfully hard—to get to where I was.

And my life still felt so empty.

It had taken a while to realize this: I was losing my hope that I would one day feel full again.

Feel purposed. Like I had a reason to really be here. Like the world was truly different because I had been born. Like I had the power to change things—to heal, to help, to hold.

That was what RiChard had made me believe. About me, about himself. About everyone having that potential.

And then he left me.

He left me.

He. Left. Me.

Hope was leaving me. Hope that what he'd said, that what I'd chased, that what I'd believed had not been a lie.

There is nothing worse than losing hope. . . .

Mrs. Monroe had said that just yesterday, and the pronouncement felt familiar to me, as if the words that had been bouncing around randomly—endlessly—in my empty little spaces had just finally come together to make perfect sense.

"I'm going to find Hope." The mission formed even as I spoke it.

I did not know if Hope Diamond was a real person or just a broken fragment of Dayonna's scarred imagination, but finding Hope, whoever or whatever that was, now felt like a singular mission for me to fulfill.

Finding Hope gave me purpose.

"Sienna, are you even listening to me?" my mother flat out yelled into the phone. "I said I want you and Roman to come over for dinner on Sunday. I'm going to tell Yvette to come with Sylvester too. I can't have my family fighting each other, and we're going to reconcile all these differences over my chicken and dumplings."

All these differences.

My mother did not know the half of them. But she knew she had me hooked. Nobody in their right mind ever turned down Isabel Davis's chicken and dumplings, even if it meant ducking and dodging questions I knew I was not going to answer.

"Okay, Mom. I love you. I'll see you Sunday. I gotta go."

"Mmm—hmm." My mother's version of "Good-bye."

I disconnected the call and pressed my foot down on the accelerator. The traffic on 695 was starting to break.

Good.

I was on my way to finding Hope.

Chapter 19

I had a lot on my plate—calls to make, clients to see, Dayonna to check on—but I wanted to take a moment to absorb my newfound mission.

Or rather attempt to understand it.

My life felt like a whirlwind, and I needed some calm within the storm.

It had been years since I'd walked around Lake Montebello in Northeast Baltimore. A little over a mile around, the picturesque reservoir was a popular spot for bicyclists, joggers, walkers, and stragglers. On any given day, you could see everything from moms pushing strollers filled with toddlers sipping from juice boxes to dogs yapping and running alongside their owners, to bicyclists in spandex and bright helmets, looking like they were preparing for the Tour de France. If the weather was good, it was not unusual to catch a turtle basking on the large rocks that jutted out of the murky water along the stretch closest to Morgan State University.

Today I was not going to walk. I pulled my car into a shady area outside of the walking/biking lane. A few cars were scattered around me. Some of them were getting washed in the warm September sun. Others were providing a respite for solitary drivers flipping through newspapers and magazines. All of them were blasting music, mostly rap and light jazz.

I shut off the ignition and rolled down my windows just as a warm breeze stirred. Clean sunshine. That was what it felt like. That was what I needed. I sat there for about fifteen minutes, enjoying the clash of songs blasting from car stereos, the pounding of the pavement by nearby runners, the squeals of children, the casual chitchat of women and men walking in pairs. I took it all in with no thoughts or fears or concerns interrupting my quiet time. I could not remember the last time I had just let my mind go.

No, I did remember. Just the other night, during the relaxation exercise at Second Zion Tabernacle. I imagined again the arms of Jesus holding me, strengthening me for the next leg of my life's journey.

My life post RiChard.

Whatever that meant.

I took out my cell phone and keyed in the international phone number once again. It was more of a rote exercise, I knew, as I closed my eyes and laid my head back on the headrest, preparing to hear the other line ring incessantly.

"*Olá?*"

My head almost hit the ceiling of my car as I jerked forward in my seat.

"Hello? I mean, *olá.*" Stunned to actually get an answer, I scrambled for something to say. "Uh, uh, is this the . . . the Crematório Rodrigues?"

"*Desculpe-me?*"

"*Parlez-vous anglais,* I mean, English?" I wanted to kick myself for resorting to my ninth grade French. I knew the woman was speaking Portuguese, but I was so thrown off that I didn't know what language I was supposed to be speaking.

"*Desculpe-*me?" the woman said, sounding just as confused as I did.

Finally, I remembered something.

"Beatriz? You said your name was Beatriz."

Silence.

Then a loud click and the line went dead.

Beatriz, or whoever she was, had hung up on me.

"Oh no, you don't." I punched the numbers back in and waited. I felt too close to some real answers about RiChard's—or his ashes?—whereabouts. This woman knew something, and I needed her to tell me. The phone began ringing again, but this time, it did not stop. I hung up and dialed again. And again.

"I need answers!" I yelled, loud enough that an elderly lady power walking nearby with hot pink dumbbells in her hands looked my way. I realized my heart was pounding and sweat was forming on my forehead and just under my nose as I dialed the number a fifth time.

This time a man answered, his words unmistakable.

"No call here again!" The line went dead once more.

I dialed again, anyway, and kept doing so until I lost count. It was no use, I knew. Nobody was going to answer the phone. I threw my cell on the passenger seat, closed my eyes, and laid my head back.

But I was far from relaxed.

I reminded myself that I was on a new mission. *To find hope. To find Hope,* I told myself.

And to find closure.

I wasn't going to find what I needed from that woman or that man, so I was going to have to come up with another plan.

I grabbed my cell phone again and went online. After I had Googled and searched through several Web sites, a smile gradually eased onto my face. A new class in Portuguese had just started at one of the local community colleges. Only one session had been held so far. Within the next five minutes, I had registered for session number two, scheduled for Friday night.

Tomorrow.

I was not so interested in learning how to speak Portuguese. I wanted only to talk with someone who already could.

I left Lake Montebello with a smug sense of satisfaction. I had the makings of a plan in place. It might not work. It could backfire or make me fall flat on my face. It did not matter. It gave me a little hope.

For the moment, that was enough.

Chapter 20

I breezed through two client visits and walked into my office just before noon. Sheena spun around in her chair and looked at me.

"Girl, where have you been? Seems like I haven't seen you half this week." The twentysomething-year-old looked like she had just stepped out of a hair and nail salon. Everything about her—even the way her costume jewelry matched the exact shades of blue of her blouse and high heels—looked like a lesson in detail.

I smiled, then started to answer her, but there was no point. She'd already turned back to her workstation and her Facebook page, which was up on her screen.

"Seriously, Sheena, do you ever get any work done?" I shook my head at her, and she rolled her eyes at me.

"For your information, Ms. St. James," Sheena stated with mock attitude, "I'm all caught up. I doubt that you can say the same since you always seem to be trying to dig up more work than what's already in front of you."

I had to smile again, knowing there was some truth to what she'd said. Sometimes I made things harder than they needed to be. With that in mind, I sat down at my desk, trying to decide what would be the easiest way to determine if a girl named Hope Diamond really existed. I began to brainstorm ideas and started a "to-do" list. The obvious was to explore the matter in greater depth with Dayonna, but who was to say when she'd be in a state to talk about it coherently? I pulled out the list of her DSS workers. Perhaps one of them could shed some light. I had circled and starred Deirdre Evans's name. I really wanted to talk to her to get an explanation for Dayonna's five-month absence in her chart.

Then there was the brother. Dayonna's chart indicated that she had a brother who aged out of the system several years back, and Ava had mentioned this to me. I flipped through the thick pages and found his name. Dayquon Hardison, DOB November 13th, 1987. That would make him about two months shy of twenty-four. All things being equal, he would have aged out of the foster care system when he was twenty-one, nearly three years ago, unless he'd aged out as a teenager.

"Sheena, you used to work for a program that transitions older foster children to adulthood, right?"

"An independent living program. Yes." She did not look my way as she played around with her smartphone.

"If I wanted to find out what happened to someone after they aged out of an independent living program, how would I go about it?"

"Does this have anything to do with your current workload?" She gave me a sideways glance. When I responded only with a half grin and a twitch of my eyebrows, she shook her head. "Just get in touch with the last program the person was in, and see if anyone kept in touch with him or her."

"What if I don't know what program they were in?"

"Call DSS. Find out who their last worker was. Talk to them. But, Sienna, if this is not directly related to one of your current cases, you're going to have a tough time getting anywhere."

"That's probably true. Do you have any good contacts at the department? I haven't really kept in touch with any of my old classmates who went on to work at DSS, so I'm not sure where to begin." I pulled up the Web site for DSS and began searching to no avail for an index or directory of its workers.

Sheena studied me intently, tapping a long bright blue fingernail on her desk. "So this *isn't* related to one of your current cases?"

"It is . . . just indirectly so."

"Girl, you are never going to get anything done." She shook her head again but then began scribbling something down on a sticky note. "Here." She handed it to me. "I used to date a guy who was a supervisor there, Roland Jenkins. Be careful, though. He knows everybody and everything." She looked me straight in the eyes. "That means he can work for you or against you."

"Thanks, Sheena. And I'll keep your warning in mind." I turned back to my desk, wondering what harm a complete stranger could do me.

Thinking about complete strangers somehow made me think again about Brother Scott, the music director at Second Zion. I remembered wondering if he could be a resource for better understanding the Monroes.

I was willing to chase all leads, and the Monroes seemed like they knew more than they were letting on. Perhaps Dayonna had told them something in her initial days or hours in their home that had spooked them. They'd already proven that they would be willing to hide something from me if it in any way, shape, or form made them look less than spectacular or unable to handle her bizarre ways. Maybe if Brother Scott had a good relationship with them, he'd be able to help them trust me more. He certainly seemed like a man of integrity and good intent, I decided. Those women from the singles ministry were swarming around him like bees on honey, and he remained focused on being a light for the Lord.

I wanted to trust him.

I needed to trust somebody, I realized.

Of course, in the likely event that I could not earn his confidence, I would at least get another good look at his face.

Don't judge me for trying. I had to chuckle at my own self, knowing full well that my desire to find Hope at all costs was not the only reason I wanted a chance to converse with the man.

I liked the feeling that came over me when I looked into his face, when I smelled the scent of him and his burgundy leather bag.

I was too old to be having a schoolgirl crush, and Lord knows I was not really trying to go anywhere with it. I really just enjoyed having an innocent distraction from RiChard and the pain that resurged with every memory of him.

I pulled up the church's Web site and clicked on the "Contact Us" link. There was a long list of ministries, followed by the names and e-mails of the contact person for each. Some of the entries had photos of the ministry heads. I scrolled through the list, respecting the diversity of ages and backgrounds of those who were at the helm of Second Zion. From the food pantry ministry to the small business association to the garden club to the afterschool program, men and women stared back at me from their leadership photos, some in Sunday best attire, others in T-shirts and jeans.

I smiled when I saw Mrs. Monroe's photo next to the pastor's aid committee, her gap-toothed smile unmistakable under her flowery and feathery bright yellow hat. That woman loved her some yellow. I shook my head.

And then my head kept shaking for different reasons. I'd reached the music ministry link and the photo that accompanied it. "Brother Tremont Scott," it read underneath the studio quality close-up photograph of him. His eyes, the perfect combination of hazel and gray, pierced me from the snapshot with grace and solemnity. His smile looked no-nonsense but somehow still warm.

"Who is *that?*"

Sheena scooted her chair over next to mine so fast, I thought her weave would fall out from whiplash. "All right, Sienna, I gave you the seven digits to a man *I* know, so it's time for you to return the favor." She chuckled. "That is a fine-looking somebody right there. Do *you* really know him?"

I tried not to take offense at the way she'd said "you," as if there was no reasonable explanation for a woman like me knowing a fine man like that.

I guess I really did have esteem issues, which even marrying RiChard had not cured.

"Not exactly," I said, attempting an answer to her question. "I mean, I bumped into him at Second Zion Tabernacle the other night. He's the music director over there. I enjoyed the weeknight service, and I was looking to see what other ministries they had." I spoke cautiously, ready to change the topic, but knowing that if I did so too quickly, I'd be raising Sheena's suspicions and inviting more questions from her.

I did not want her asking questions I did not have answers to.

"Sure you were." She looked at me sideways again, a sly grin filling her face. I remembered looking at Roman the same way just before we went to the midweek service.

"Is that his e-mail address next to the picture?" She chuckled again. "I can think of a few praise reports I could send him. Girl, I'm ready to praise the Lord just for seeing that picture. You're gonna have me going back to church to get my shout on. Glory!"

We both let out a loud laugh as she scooted back to her desk.

"I'm sure he gets a lot of e-mails," she murmured as she turned to update her Facebook status on her computer screen.

She had a point, I realized, as I clicked on the link to his church-based e-mail address. I imagined him deleting half the frivolity that came through his mailbox. I cringed at the thought of what some desperate women might send him.

I needed my e-mail to stand out.

I was contacting him for professional reasons from my professional e-mail, so there was no reason to feel like I was doing something wrong or crafty, I figured. I wrote in the subject line "Your Assistance Requested."

To keep from gaining Sheena's attention again, I typed up the e-mail with speed and certainty.

Dear Brother Scott.
I am a social worker with Holding Hands Agency. I am hoping to talk with you about some congregants at your church who are currently serving as foster parents. I noted that you were engrossed in deep conversation with them earlier this week, and I was hoping to have your ear as I seek to find new ways of assuring them of my complete support of their challenging task. I recognize that my request to talk with you may seem a little bizarre, but my gut tells me that you may be just the re-

*source I need to continue building a positive rela-
tionship with this fragile foster family.*

I read through my words and immediately felt silly.
Sending this e-mail made absolutely no sense, I finally
admitted to myself. Was I that desperate for answers
and closure in so many areas of my life that I would
even consider contacting a man who did not know me,
and would believe he would just agree to help me get
through to the Monroes? I did not even know what
kind of relationship he had with them. I was going on
only the close body language the trio had exhibited
when I saw them talking alone in that darkened, empty
room two nights before.

*Thank you, Lord, for allowing me to catch the error
of my ways before it was too late!* I let out a loud sigh,
feeling both foolish and relieved that I had not pressed
SEND and made what probably would have been one of
the hugest, most ridiculous mistakes of my adult life.
What had I really planned to say if he had responded?

I clutched my computer mouse, directing the on-
screen arrow to DELETE. Just as I clicked on the mouse,
Sheena whisked back to my side, startling me and
throwing my attention and movements off in seconds
that happened too fast.

"So you *are* e-mailing that fine Brother Scott!" Sheena grinned.

"Oh, no!" I gasped aloud. In my startle, the arrow had
moved to SEND at the moment I clicked on the mouse.

"Your message has been sent," stared at me in big,
bold black letters.

Chapter 21

"Let me know how that works out." Sheena winked, completely oblivious to my sudden horror.

"Excuse me," I managed to whisper, trying to roll away from my desk. My head felt like it was too weak to stay on top of my neck, and my stomach felt like it had just dropped to my knees.

The only thing that kept me from passing out was another photo that caught my eye. "Wait, Sheena. Scroll back up."

My office mate had completely taken over my workstation and was going through the rest of Second Zion's ministry listings. Right after "Praise and Worship," "Prayer Team," "Revolution Youth Movement," and "Senior Saints" was a familiar face.

"No, right there. Stop," I directed Sheena and moved closer to read the small print underneath the photo that had caught my eye.

"Um . . ." My office mate raised an eyebrow at me. "Don't you think he's a little old for you?" She looked back and forth from me to the computer screen.

"Don't be silly, Sheena. This is not a dating Web site. It's a church. And that's not my wannabe future husband. That's one of the foster parents of Dayonna Diamond."

Horace Monroe.

The caption under the balding elderly man read "Substance Abuse Ministry Leader."

I felt my stomach sinking even lower. Both Mr. and Mrs. Monroe had leadership positions at the church. It would make sense for them to have a close relationship with Brother Scott as he was a leader also. Their shared intimacy might have no personal dimension to it . . . more business. Well, church business, anyway. How would I even begin to explain my e-mail to any of them?

Or to Ava?

All of this was bound to get back to her. I guess I should have just heeded her directive and quit "rocking the boat" before I got too far ahead of myself.

"I'm going to lunch," I mumbled to Sheena, though my stomach craved food about as much as a fish craves air.

"I'd go with you, but I'm meeting up with an old friend today. Let me know if you get in touch with Roland."

"Roland?"

"Yes, Roland. Remember, my contact at DSS?"

"Oh, yeah." I nodded as I reached for my purse and car keys. I had no idea where I was going. I stared at the sticky note with Roland's name and number printed on it, which was sitting on the side of my desk. I wanted to tear it up and leave finding Hope alone. All it had gotten me so far was potential embarrassment and trying to figure out how I was going to explain this to a bunch of folk, my boss probably being one of them. "Thanks, Sheena." I smiled for her satisfaction. I did not want her to ask me any more questions.

"No problem, big sis." She turned back to her Facebook page.

I envied the seeming simplicity of her life and loathed my knack for complicating mine.

"Still didn't see you get any work done," she teased as I walked out of the door.

She was right, I realized. I had spent all that time in the office and had not written a single case note.

Just a silly—and maybe even dangerous—e-mail.

The scary part about rocking the boat was not knowing whether the churning waves would eventually take me under.

Chapter 22

He wanted to complete the revolution. That was what he'd told the suspicious villagers through an interpreter. The interpreter was Kisu, the educated and brawny son of the old and respected chief. RiChard had met Kisu during a summer semester he'd spent at a university in London. The two had remained close friends ever since.

It was my fifth trip abroad with RiChard and my first and only to the breathtakingly beautiful land of KwaZulu-Natal, a southeastern province in South Africa. Apartheid had ended the year before, but violent skirmishes were not unheard of as the diverse nation tried to figure out precisely how to divvy up this thing called freedom. The people of the Zulu nation were no exception as shaky truces and unsteady political partnerships formed.

RiChard had wanted to be in the middle of it all, calling and singing for social justice beside village elders and chiefs, as if he had lived his whole life alongside them, waiting for this monumental moment in history. He'd planted himself in the rural communities in the rolling mountains, wanting to start there and work his way to the more urban townships.

He'd wanted me there to witness the mighty shaking and trembling of a newly free generation seeking to make new imprints, try out new wings. It was history in the making, he said, and we could help make sure it was made right. So I came, overcoming my fear of flying on yet another tiny, ancient aircraft while holding my breath, too scared to pray. I came, exposing my stomach once again to tastes and textures I'd never known existed. I came, dazzled by the colorful, intricate beadwork of the Zulu women; amazed by the colorful, intricate beauty crafted by the Creator Himself in the vast virgin landscape.

It was around this same time of year, I remembered. Just after the famous sardine run of the summer—when schools of the small fish rushed up the rich coastline, followed by more seabirds, dolphins, and sharks than one could imagine; and right before the yearly Reed Dance Ceremony of early fall, when the young women of the Zulu nation would parade by the thousands before the Zulu royal family.

I was both awestruck and anxious, entranced and terrified at being there with RiChard. My contradictory feelings had become the constant, the one sure thing of my life.

I could not talk to RiChard about the fears I had about fighting for social justice so far from home—and so close to violence. I could not talk to him about what "social justice" even meant, or how to even fight for it. I could not talk to him about not having a true address or missing my mother or wondering if I really should have given up my full ride at school to get a "life experience education," as he called it.

He already had a college degree. And he could use his fieldwork in foreign lands as fodder for his thesis—or even a doctoral dissertation.

Above all, I wondered if we even had a true marriage.

Yes, he told me he loved me, but I often felt like he loved the idea of me. Me, a partner, a shoulder, a witness, an extra hand to help with the dirty work of cleaning up the world's messes.

I wondered even then if he ever just saw *me*. Sienna.

That trip to KwaZulu-Natal was the last trip I made overseas.

After the incident that led to the village chief giving RiChard Kisu's lion's head ring, I knew I would never travel with him again.

I'd reached my breaking point.

"Roman St. James is in Mrs. Gillespie's class. . . . Yes, I'll hold."

Thinking about RiChard and that ring had reminded me that Roman had never made it to school yesterday. Calling myself being clever, I was on hold with his school's secretary, waiting for her to check the attendance log for the day.

If that boy had skipped school again, I was going to take away everything he owned that had a plug, a charger, a push button, or sound.

"Okay, Mrs. St. James?" The ancient secretary cleared her throat as she got back on the line. "I do not see Roman marked present for the day."

That boy!

"Thank you," I murmured into my cell phone, feeling an emotion that I could not name.

I was pacing the lunchroom of Holding Hands, the only one in there at twelve thirty—a true testament to the hard work and dedication of all of Ava's staff.

Seemed like I was the only one not getting anything done today.

"Call Roman." I used the voice-activated calling feature on my cell, unable to get both my mind and my fingers working together in unison to key in his number myself. Roman immediately answered.

"Ma, I know why you are calling, and I know why you are upset," he said quickly into my ear before I even had a chance to say hello, "but I'm getting Dad's ring back today. This fight is bigger than school."

And then he hung up.

I had not gotten a word in.

Of course I dialed back, again and again, leaving all kinds of messages on his voice mail. Of course he did not answer.

For the second time today, I was left with a phone ringing nonstop in my ear, with answers just out of my reach.

"Sienna, you okay?" A woman named Tynice entered the lunchroom and pulled a bag out of the fridge. She studied me with half interest. I realized my hands were shaking.

"Yes, I'm okay. Just dealing with my son," I managed to breathe out.

"Good luck with that one." Tynice shrugged her shoulders and looked away from me. She grabbed a plastic fork out of a drawer and headed back out of the room.

I knew that Tynice had two sons, both incarcerated. One for selling drugs and the other for aggravated assault.

"Lord, I have to do something." I did not know where to begin. I did not know where Roman was or what he was about to do. *Or what someone could do to him.*

Foolishness.

He had that same streak, that same look in his eyes at times as his father.

With my heart pounding, I did the only thing that came to mind. I called Leon Sanderson at our neighborhood's Police Athletic League center.

He was a cop. He cared about Roman.

He was the only person I thought could help.

Chapter 23

"I have a good friend who works in this district. I'm sure he'd be familiar with that gang of boys Roman's looking for." Leon studied the scene outside his car window, straining his neck to scour the streets around us. "We'll get it all sorted out."

"Thank you for helping." My gratitude was genuine.

The two of us were in Leon's late-model Altima, riding through the neighborhoods that made up Park Heights. When I'd called the PAL center, I found out Leon was off. However, the message I left must have gotten to him immediately, because he called me back not fifteen minutes later. Before I'd even finished telling him that Roman might be in trouble, he told me he was on his way to me. That was about an hour ago.

"Don't worry, Sienna." He glanced over at me before focusing back on the streets and sidewalks around us. "We're going to find your son, and I'll talk some sense into him myself. I don't like this missing school business and hunting down trouble. That's not the Roman I know. But don't worry. He'll be okay."

His words were meant to comfort me, but his expression only increased my anxiety level. Leon was usually pretty laid-back, spitting out corny jokes and cheesy one-liners. At the moment, however, his face held no humor; no smile sat on his pursed lips. The worry lines etched around his eyes mirrored mine.

A sound like a whimper escaped from my mouth, but Leon did not seem to notice. I followed his gaze to a group of young men standing near the door of an abandoned corner store.

"No, that isn't him over there," he murmured, seemingly talking more to himself than to me. "That boy in the red has the same book bag as Roman, but that's not him."

It was a small detail that Leon noted, but it spoke volumes to me. It was the third such detail he'd pointed out in passing during our drive through Park Heights. He seemed to have noticed little things about Roman that I thought only I'd been aware of. Not in a creepy way, but more like someone who took an interest in getting to know his mentees one-to-one. Roman was at the Police Athletic League center at least two or three times a week. Leon, I'd just learned, was there every day, on eleven-hour shifts during the summer months.

"How long have you been working for PAL?" I had to ask something that took my attention off of my worry for a moment. The intensity of my fear for Roman's safety was getting to me.

"Oh, I've been working at PAL centers for the past eight years." He slowed down again, studying another group of young men. This group had congregated on a porch about six blocks away from Yvette's house. "I used to be in homicide." He fell silent.

He continued talking after speeding up again, satisfied that my son wasn't among the congregants on the porch. "But after seeing so many young black men dead and cold, I decided I wanted to try to catch them while they were still alive and warm. And record free, if you know what I mean." He glanced over at me. "Working at the center is a great thing. I can try to make a difference before it's too late. I'm like a social worker, but with a badge."

We both gave a slight chuckle at his observation. In the quick moment of his smile, I noticed something was missing. The sparkle.

"What happened to your gold tooth?" I could not contain my curiosity or hide my disdain for his golden canine, even in that moment.

"Oh, that thing." He shook his head. "It's just a cap. I put it on only when I'm at the center."

"What? To get some kind of street cred or something?" Sarcasm seemed to come too easily to me.

"Not really . . ." He was no longer smiling. "It just helps me to remember my brother while I'm working with the youth. No matter how tough the wannabe gangster, no matter how many fights break out in the game room, I can look in the mirror and remember why I have to be where I am and do what I do." There was a solemnity to his tone as he looked straight ahead, no longer scouring the streets, like he had been seconds earlier.

I said nothing in response to his comment. I could tell neither one of us wanted to dig up the real story behind his gold cap and his work at the PAL center.

"Speaking of gold," Leon said, breaking our shared silence, "tell me about this ring you said Roman went after. It is something special to him, I'm assuming."

"It was from his father. My husband."

"Husband? You have a husband?" The man recoiled so forcefully, one would think I'd just said I had the Ebola virus. I almost waited for him to kick me out of his fine leather car interior to keep the husband germ from spreading.

"I . . . It's . . . a long story. I haven't seen him . . . Roman and I haven't seen him," I said, quickly correcting myself, "since Roman was almost two months old."

Seven weeks and one day old, to be exact. I remembered holding my infant son in my lap for our five-and-half-hour red-eye flight to the West Coast. April 23, 1997. The last time either one of us saw RiChard. I closed my eyes to shut out the memories that came with that date. Dayonna Diamond's birth date, I remembered.

Roman told people that he'd never been on a plane before. I never bothered to correct him, because he didn't know about his trip to San Diego with me. There was so much I hadn't told my son, so much I needed him to believe. That his father wanted to be a part of his life was a lie I'd made myself believe so that both Roman and I could survive without him.

"Sounds like you need to work out some things," Leon quietly commented before sliding back into our mutual silence.

If only he knew . . .

We were circling back around on a narrow street when I reached out my hand and touched Leon's arm. "Wait. Stop. Back up."

Leon had just driven past him. I'd almost missed him myself. It wasn't that I did not recognize my son. Of course I knew my only begotten.

I did not recognize his gait.

A few inches away from six feet tall and a few pounds away from being overweight, he usually carried himself like a slumping, big teddy bear, head down, shoulders hunched, as if to somehow hide in plain sight.

Now rage and grief had combined to make him a soldier marching vigilantly to his own demise.

My son was not a natural-born fighter. There was no way he could take on a gang of vicious thieves. Especially ones that were armed.

I hurt for him. In his foolishness, in his pain, I hurt for him.

The car pulled to a stop right beside him. He was so focused, he did not even notice Leon's beeping.

I rolled down the window.

"Roman!" All I could get out.

He looked at me, frowned, and kept moving forward with his death march.

Leon got out of the car and opened the back passenger's side door. "Get in."

Leon did not yell or scream, but there was a threat in his words, nonetheless. Roman heard it too. Without missing a beat, he turned back toward us and plopped down into the backseat.

Nobody spoke for the entire ride back to my office. Leon pulled up to my little Aveo in the parking lot but motioned for Roman to stay where he was.

"Ms. St. James, I know you want to talk to your son, but if it's okay with you, I want to have a few words with him first. Continue on with your day, and I can bring him home to you this evening."

I looked at my fourteen-year-old, seething in the backseat of the officer's personal car. Roman almost looked rabid, like he would leap and bite at the slightest wrong move.

"You can take him, and I'll deal with him later." I nodded.

I watched as the car roared off, my son still steaming in the backseat.

Chapter 24

"Sienna, Sienna, Sienna . . ." Ava was sitting in my desk chair. She backed up and sighed as I entered my office.

Sheena was gone, so I sat down in her seat, facing my supervisor.

"I've been trying to call you for the past two hours." Ava looked at me, a slight frown pulling down one side of her lips. "I even tried your home phone. Sheena did not know where you went. She said you just took off for lunch, and nobody's seen you since."

"I'm sorry, Ava. I saw your calls, but I was in the middle of dealing with a . . . crisis with Roman."

She raised both eyebrows. "Is he okay?"

"He will be."

"Are you okay?" She pressed her lips together.

When I said nothing, she turned back to my workstation, rubbing her eyes with both of her hands.

"Girl, you know you about gave me a heart attack. I worry about you. I know I push you, but I do worry about you. When you didn't answer my calls and nobody knew where you were, I thought something bad had happened. It's not like you to not answer your phone."

She looked back at me. I still said nothing.

"I wish you would just tell me what's going on."

"I'm sorry, Ava. I'm not trying to worry you or fall behind in my work or even avoid work. Life has been kind of complicated for me this week, for many reasons that I do not want to get into. I'm just trying to . . . not lose hope.

Hope.

I thought again of my mission and knew that I needed to stay focused and keep from being swallowed up in the quicksand of emotions threatening to overtake me.

This time Ava was the quiet one.

Finally, she spoke. "You asked to be taken off of Dayonna Diamond's case yesterday, saying she was only adding to whatever stress has been affecting you this week. I still think you need to hold on to her case to survive the lesson of balancing life and work. However, I think you might benefit from a day off from *every-thing*. It's what? Thursday? Go home, Sienna. Relax this evening. Do whatever you need to do in your personal life tomorrow and over the weekend. Come back on Monday. I'll cover your cases until then. Agreed?"

"Okay," I sighed, not sure if I felt relieved—or more stressed—at the prospect of having more time to dwell on the matters concerning me.

She looked at me sternly, but I knew it was more for show. I could see deep concern in her eyes as she accepted that I was not going to spill my heart to her. She saw that I wanted to maintain a business mode, and she was willing to play along.

"All right, Sienna." She patted my shoulder as she left my office.

"Thanks, Ava."

As I began shutting down my computer and closing up my files, I could not shake the feeling that something was not right. It was not until I had left the building and started up my car that I realized what was wrong.

In my haste to find Roman earlier that day, I'd left everything open on my computer screen. My e-mail account that said my message to Brother Scott had been sent; the Web site for Second Zion, with Horace Monroe's photo showing. Even the contact information for the Department of Social Services had been up on my screen.

However, when I'd shut down my computer just now, the only Web site up was one that offered maps and driving directions.

I had not opened up that Web site. I had not closed the others. And I knew from past experience that Sheena would not get on my computer unless I was in the office, alongside her. She did not want anyone going through her virtual world, and she'd made it clear that she would never do that to anyone else.

Ava had been sitting at my desk when I came in. What had she seen on my screen? I thought again of the map and driving directions that had been open on my computer.

And what destination was she looking for? I wished I had noted the address. *Oh, well.*

I was too antsy to go back home. And too hungry also. My stomach was letting me know. I headed out to a little lunch spot I went to on occasion, with the goal of getting both my nourishment and my research needs met.

Located on the outskirts of Baltimore's Hampden neighborhood, Charlie's Grill was easily passed by those not familiar with the area. On the corner of a street dominated by old warehouses and seedy-looking parking lots, the greasy spoon catered mainly to the working-class locals, mostly older white men, who came to grab a hearty meal of subs and chips and to play a round of keno over beer and loud conversation.

During lunch hours, the family-owned café became a dining spot for people of all colors and from all walks of life who'd discovered the freshly made sandwiches and Italian and Greek delicacies. This café embodied the unique charm of Baltimore as some envisioned it, a place where everyone was named "hon" and battered and deep-fried western fries and half-and-half—lemonade mixed with iced tea—were on the menu next to gyros, chicken cheesesteaks, and lasagna.

I settled in a deep booth with a triple-decker turkey club sandwich on toasted wheat bread and plotted my plan of action.

Ava wanted me to take some time off to pull myself together, reassemble my focus, and work toward resolving whatever issues were pushing me off track. For me, I knew my mission to find Hope was the answer to my problems. More than just another distraction, it gave me a sense of purpose, and a feeling that closure was indeed possible.

I needed that more than anything right now.

I pulled out the sticky note that Sheena had given me hours earlier and keyed the phone number into my cell phone.

"This is Roland," a deep voice inflected with attitude boomed into my eardrum.

"Yes, hello. Mr. Jenkins?"

"Yes, this is me, as I've already stated." Irritation joined the attitude that suffused the bass voice. How had Sheena put up with this man in a dating relationship? I had heard only two sentences from him and was already turned off.

Way off.

"Um, yes, I was calling to see if I could get some information from you about a young man who was formerly in foster care but aged out of the system a few years ago."

"And *you* are?"

"Oh, I'm sorry. My name is Sienna St. James. I am a social worker at Holding Hands Agency. Sheena Booth is my office mate, and she suggested I talk to you. I'm trying to find the whereabouts of the older brother of one of my clients. I need to know how to go about finding out which independent living program he may have been a part of before he aged out."

"Sheena sent you to me? Hmm." There was a long pause. "So you are trying to get information about your client's older brother. Not your client?"

"That's right, Dayquon Hardison is his name. My client is named Dayonna Diamond."

The conversation was briefly interrupted by someone on the other end handing Mr. Jenkins some files or something.

He came back to the phone. "Look, Ms. Sienna St. James," he said, enunciating each syllable of my name with exaggeration. "All I can tell you is that unless you have a signed release allowing me to give you information about Dayquon Hardison, I am not at liberty to disclose any information to you. I am sure that Dayonna Diamond's DSS worker has already apprised you of this fact."

"Dayonna's DSS worker? I believe she is out on maternity leave."

"Did you consult with the worker's supervisor to see who is covering the case?"

I wanted to kick myself for once again making a simple task complicated. Why hadn't I started there? "To be honest with you, I'm not sure who to contact. I just inherited this case this week." I tried to laugh off my failure of not starting with the obvious. Roland Jenkins was not amused.

"Ms. St. James, before you waste another moment of my time, please familiarize yourself with basic policies and procedures about what information we can give out and to whom. And, also, please inform Sheena Booth that if she desires to regain my attention, she needs to approach me herself. Incompetency is not attractive."

For the third time that day, the phone line went dead in my ear.

Chapter 25

I looked down at my half-eaten turkey club sandwich. Now, instead of hunger rumbling through my stomach, all I felt was nausea.

That man, Roland, was ridiculously rude. I wanted to call him back to tell him a little about himself, but fought the urge. A verse from Psalms crossed my mind. *Great peace have those who love Your law, And nothing causes them to stumble.*

If I was going to find Hope, I needed also to hold on to my peace.

I thought again of the verse from Isaiah that the bishop's wife had shared at the relaxation workshop: *You will keep him in perfect peace, Whose mind is stayed on You, Because he trusts in You. Trust in the Lord forever, for in Yah, the Lord, is everlasting strength.*

I considered how having hope was tied to having a sense of peace, which in turn was tied, according to the scripture, to trusting the Lord. It almost seemed too simple, but I was all about keeping it simple now. I'd complicated matters enough.

On this mission, I was going to have to trust the Lord with all the details, even when those details involved annoying people who stood in the way of the answers for which I was searching.

Searching!

Why hadn't I thought of it before? I'd been searching for so many other things online, why not look for a person? For all the technology I'd invested in for my cell phone, I did not have the best Internet access, but I did have my workbag, I remembered.

With renewed enthusiasm, and excited that the small grill offered a Wi-Fi connection, I reached for my company-issued laptop and Googled "Dayquon Hardison." I searched Facebook, Twitter, and every other social media network Web site I could think of.

Nothing came back.

What kind of twenty-three-year-old male did not have any online social imprint anywhere? I was back to square one, but then another thought occurred to me.

The Maryland Judiciary Case Search. The public online database that offered basic info about cases seen in district and circuit courts. If Dayquon had any traffic, civil, or criminal court case records as an adult, then they should show up in the free search engine provided by the Maryland court system.

I went to the case search Web site and entered his name and birth date. One record came back. It was for a traffic violation back in 2010.

An address was given: 1526 Lizbrooke Lane, #4G, in Greenbelt, Maryland.

I jotted it down, feeling like I finally had something or someone to turn to in my Hope quest. Greenbelt was in Prince George's County, about an hour away. Maybe I could try to drive out there over the weekend. The day had been long enough already.

I looked at the "to-do" list I'd created earlier and put a check mark next to Dayonna's brother's name.

"Are you finished with that, hon?" A woman in a dirty apron stopped at my table and pointed to what was left of my sandwich. She was smiling, but an eyebrow was raised. I looked down at my plate and saw why she looked so concerned.

My sandwich looked like it had been mauled by an angry dog.

Had I been that distracted and disturbed while attempting to eat my lunch?

"Yes, I'm done." I gave a curt nod and began gathering my things together. I had to find somewhere else to go. I was no longer hungry but still did not feel satisfied, still did not feel ready to retreat home.

I was halfway up 83 when I realized where I was going.

It was time to pay a visit to Dayonna.

I had no idea what time Leon was going to bring my son home, and I had no idea what I was expecting to get out of a visit to the hospital where Dayonna was housed.

I wasn't even sure that I would get to see her.

In reality, it was not her that I was hoping to see. It was her chart.

Chapter 26

One of the first lessons RiChard taught me is that every culture has its own currency that has nothing to do with money. Behind the dollars and cents that help determine power and wealth are the decision makers and the chosen ones who get to figure out where the bottom line should be. If you can figure out the language of those who have the money, then the money becomes as good as yours.

In the helping professions, it seems like the currency of power is paperwork.

Go to any office, clinic, hospital, or building where the healing arts are administered and behind the scenes and on every desktop is paper, paper, and more paper. Whether detailing policies and procedures, or outlining rituals and routines, a person's or a company's paperwork will tell you what or who is really calling the shots when all else is said and done.

I recalled seeing a thick chart with Dayonna's name on it at the hospital.

She had a history there, and I wanted a chance to see it.

I was especially curious to see if there was ever any talk about missing sisters and cabbage stew before her entry into the Monroes' home.

I had no concrete plan when I parked my car and entered the facility.

"Can I help you, ma'am?" A cheery-looking young woman with sun-bleached blond hair sat behind the receptionist's desk, which had been unmanned the last time I was there.

"Yes, I'm here to check on Dayonna Diamond. She was just admitted yesterday. I'm not sure what unit she is in."

The woman frowned as she clicked through files on her computer and glanced over at a wall clock hanging behind my head. After she noted the time, her smile returned. I remembered that these types of facilities usually had preset and limited visiting hours at various times of the day. I guess I'd made the cut.

"And what is your name?" The woman kept typing, her eyes glued to her computer screen.

"I'm Sienna St. James, her worker from Holding Hands Therapeutic Foster Care Agency."

"You're her DSS worker?" A slight frown pulled at the corners of her lips as she continued typing.

What on earth needs to be typed for so long? I wondered.

Again, paperwork.

"No, I'm not from the Department of Social Services. I work for an agency that DSS contracted with to help with the provision of her services."

The receptionist continued typing for a few seconds more before looking up at me, her fingers finally quiet.

"I'm sorry, Ms. St. James, but you're not on the list to see her." Her perky smile was really starting to annoy me.

"I'm not on the list?" *What is this? A nightclub? A private event?* "I'm sorry, but there must be some mistake. I'm her current worker. I'm with the agency that oversees her placement."

"I understand." Her head bobbed up and down as she continued smiling. "But all visitors must be preapproved before seeing patients, and unfortunately, your name is not on the list."

"Um, okay." I could feel my eyes blinking nonstop. "I understand that is your policy, but as her treatment foster care worker, I should be able to check on her condition."

"I'm sorry, but I am going to have to ask you to leave." The perkiness was leaving.

"Perhaps I can speak with one of the administrators here?"

"You don't understand, Ms. St. James." The woman was now blinking as much as I was. "It's not just that you are not on the list of preapproved visitors. Your name is down on a list of people who *cannot* have any contact with her during her stay here."

"What? That does not make any sense. Is that standard protocol? To have a list of who can't come?"

"Well, it's not the standard procedure, but when a request has been made, we have to honor it."

"Can you tell me who requested that I not be allowed to see Dayonna?"

"I would not have access to that information, but it's usually a parent or guardian or even the medical staff, if they have reason to believe that a particular visitor would not serve the best interest of the patient. Okay?"

No, it was not okay. I glared at the young woman, who simply went back to typing. Remembering the scowl on Mr. Monroe's face when I'd left here in a hurry last time, I took out my cell phone to call the Monroes. However, as the phone began ringing, I realized that my call would be futile. A visitors' sign-in sheet lay on the counter near where I stood. Both Mr. and Mrs. Monroe's names were on the sheet, with an "in" time noted and no "out." I was not going to get an answer or an explanation from them.

But that was not what really caught my attention on the sign-in sheet. It was the signature underneath the Monroes'.

Deirdre Evans.

Why did that name sound so familiar? I wondered as I turned to leave, knowing that I would not get any further with my mission at the hospital. Paperwork. The beginning and end of progress, it seemed.

Just as I stepped out the door, I remembered why that name sounded familiar. I turned around and went back to the receptionist's desk.

"Excuse me. Is there a DSS worker here to see Dayonna?" I asked.

"Yes, there is." Perky girl did not even look up at me as she continued typing.

"That doesn't make sense," I said aloud, though I was really talking to myself. Deirdre Evans was the name of the DSS worker who was in charge of Dayonna's case during the unaccounted for five-month period before she entered the residential treatment center in Florida, her last placement before the Monroes.

"She was on the list, so I had no reason not to let her visit Dayonna."

All I could do was shake my head and leave there more confused than when I'd come. Why would Deirdre Evans visit Dayonna? And why was I not allowed to see her?

I headed back to my car, wishing that I had Dayonna's chart with me to get the name of the current DSS worker's supervisor assigned to her case. I had no way of accessing her chart, so I did what I thought was the next best thing.

"Hi, Sheena," I sang into my headset, happy that my office mate had picked up her desk phone on the first ring. "Would you mind doing me a favor?"

"Sienna!" She nearly yelled in my ear. "I can't believe you are asking me to do another thing for you today! I have no idea what you told Roland Jenkins, but please don't ask me for anything else. I have work to do, and I don't have time for foolishness, his or yours!"

I beat her to hanging up, determined that I would not hear another dial tone in my ears today.

What in the world was going on?

Beatriz, Roman, Leon, Roland, Ava, Dayonna, the Monroes, Deirdre Evans, and now Sheena. In one day, more questions had arisen about both loved ones and strangers in my life than I felt like dealing with.

I decided to finally take Ava's advice. I went home.

Chapter 27

My bedroom was my personal sanctuary.

I'm not going to lie. The rest of my house was a semi-cluttered mess, but the room where I slept every night was a dream of peaceful perfection. I had decorated it in shades of lavender and pale green, and I always felt like I was lying down in a lush meadow filled with wildflowers. Every time I entered my room, I had the same exhilarating rush I'd felt once when I ran barefoot through tall grass beside RiChard, skipping stones across a brook like I was in a fairy tale, eating a picnic lunch with him on a red-checkered blanket like I was in a romance movie.

Yes, I'd lived that scene once.

I smiled at the memory, refusing to let any other thoughts creep in to remind me of how horribly my week was going.

But I could not stop my phone from ringing. It was Leon.

"Good. You're home," he said. "I'll have Roman home to you in about ten minutes."

As I hung up the phone, I realized that despite the clash of emotions my son had invoked in me earlier that day, I had not worried about him since he got into Leon's car. I had no idea where they had been or what had been said, but my heart told me that they had made it to the right destination.

Believe me, Roman was still in for the grounding of his life for cutting school and endangering his life and nearly giving me a heart attack. However, I was not afraid for him anymore. For once, and only this once, I knew it was good that Leon had been around.

When I heard Roman's key jingle in the front door, I suddenly became aware that I was wearing my granny robe and my bright orange head scarf.

"Hi, Mom," Roman mumbled as he rushed past me to get to his room.

"Roman?" I started to follow him, but Leon patted my elbow and shook his head.

"Don't worry. We had a nice long talk about a lot of things while shooting some hoops. You've got a good son. Just had a rough couple of days."

"Haven't we all?" I mumbled with a chuckle. I realized that Leon had not stepped beyond my front door. And if he was disturbed by the sight of me in my floral gingham robe and head scarf, he hid it well.

"Roman had dinner already. He insisted that we bring you back a plate, so here you go." Leon passed me a brown paper bag with a wrapped sectioned foam plate inside. "We went to this little soul food diner on the east side. Hope you like barbecued ribs, sweet potatoes, collard greens, and corn bread. Roman picked out your entrée. The peach cobbler was my idea." He smiled, and I noticed for the first time that he had a dimple. The gold tooth had been a glaring distraction from the finer qualities of his smile, I realized.

"Thank you, Leon." Again, my gratitude was sincere.

"There's nothing to thank me for. I just want to make sure that Roman continues on the straight path you've obviously been laying for him. You're doing a great job with him." He began backing down the porch steps.

"Thank you, Leon." I smiled at the man, who had a copper undertone to his flawless brown skin. Today was the first time I'd seen him without his uniform, and the button-down, short-sleeved blue linen shirt he wore showcased arms that obviously were intimately acquainted with weight machines. What I had thought were extra pounds on him was more hulk than bulk.

The things I noticed when I did not have that gold cap to distract me.

"No problem, Mrs. St. James."

Mrs. St. James? I could not remember the last time I had been called Mrs.

"Good night, Leon."

He was already down the porch steps and halfway to his car.

Like he was running away.

"Roman?" I entered my son's room. He was on his computer, looking up pictures of board games. "What are you doing?"

"Oh, I'm going to be helping Officer Sanderson with the elementary school kids after school a couple times a week. He told me I could help pick out some activities for them."

"Okay. So I'm assuming that since you're going after school, that means there is an *at* school component to your day."

Roman turned around to look at me. "Mom, I'm sorry, and it will never happen again. I know I'm grounded, but that's cool. I deserve it."

I rubbed my eyes and stared at him. "Who are you, and what have you done to my son?" We both laughed.

"Officer Sanderson is going to help me get back Dad's ring."

"Oh, that's good. Now the computer goes off."

He started to say something else but thought better of it. I started to say something else, but, really, what else was there for me to say?

You know, it had been a long, hard, twisted day. It was coming to a close with more questions, more confusion, more nonsense than I had ever imagined facing on a Thursday evening. There was more I could research, more calls I could make, more people I could hunt down, but I decided to let it all go. At least for the night.

As I stretched out in my wildflower bedroom, thinking about what tasks tomorrow held, a verse from the Bible I'd heard once preached in a sermon crossed my mind. *Therefore do not worry about tomorrow, for tomorrow will worry about its own things. Sufficient for the day is its own trouble.*

Lord, wasn't that the truth. . . .

I tried my best not to wonder what trouble tomorrow had waiting for me.

Chapter 28

We had been waiting all day for their return.

I'd stayed behind in the village that last day I was there, helping the rural women with their routine chores: fetching water, tending the vegetable garden RiChard had helped them plant. He and Kisu had traveled to another remote location in the scenic South African province to enlist more supporters for the cause.

He was organizing a protest.

The two had left just before dawn, when the first rays of sun spread like fingers across the unbroken sky. He'd held my face in his hands and kissed both my cheeks before planting a quick peck on my lips. Kisu had been steps away, looking off into the blooming horizon. A dark emotion colored his face, a foreboding shadow on what should have been a promising day.

Worry.

The worry on Kisu's face became like a contagious virus for me. I saw it on him, and it entered my conscience. Worry filled the air I breathed; my nostrils inhaled doubt, exhaled fear.

I knew before they left that the day would not end with the same beauty with which it began. I knew it, felt it, but still was unprepared for the sight that walked back toward us just as the sun was finishing its descent.

RiChard returned. Alone. With blood on his hands.

***

"You better be at this exact spot at three fifty," I said, threatening my son as he got out of my car. I was not taking any chances today. No more catching the bus for the time being. My son was going to have his own personal transportation service to and from school, whether or not he liked it. And I'd made up my own class attendance sheet for each of his teachers to sign when he showed up for class.

"Don't worry, Mom. I'll be here." He blew me a silly kiss, meant to lighten my mood and my lingering disappointment in him for cutting school the past two days. I shook my head and watched him enter the school doors.

"Lord, what am I going to do with that one?" I put the car back into drive, and Leon Sanderson wafted into my mind.

Only for a second.

I had big plans for the day. I was determined to find Hope and regain my peace of mind.

It was Friday morning. I had a Portuguese class waiting for me later that evening and a "to-do" list to keep me busy until then. Still disturbed that I had not been able to see Dayonna yesterday, I'd make it a point to try to talk to the Monroes today.

I might have been off of work, but that did not mean I was off my mission.

Visiting hours at the mental health facility where Dayonna was an inpatient did not begin for at least another two hours, so I knew they would not be there. I headed toward their Belair-Edison home for an early morning surprise visit.

"Ms. St. James." Elsie Monroe answered the door with a look of fake joy to see me. "I thought you were off today."

"You knew I was off?"

"Yes. Ava called us yesterday afternoon and said she'd be covering for you until Monday. She told us to call her if any problems arise. Is everything okay?"

Despite her best efforts not to do so, Mrs. Monroe looked over her shoulder and moved the door closer to her, trying not to look like she was attempting to block my view of her living room. Hadn't we already been through this scenario before?

"Yes, I am technically off, but I wanted to come by and talk with you. Is this a bad time?" I had to ask as Mrs. Monroe kept looking back over her shoulder. For all I knew, she and the mister had been enjoying their time alone while they had a kid-free home. It was early in the day, and I had not called to tell them I was coming, so the least I could do was be polite.

But I wanted answers, and I was not leaving until I got some. I wanted to know who had put my name down on the "do not visit Dayonna" list. And I also wanted to know why Mrs. Monroe kept looking over her shoulder.

I did not have to wait long to find out.

"Elsie, let her in." Mr. Monroe's voice boomed from behind the petite, wiry woman.

She stepped out of the way, and I walked into their living room, blinking to let my eyes adjust to the dimly lit room.

A man meticulously dressed in a tan suit and brown oxfords sat on the sofa, sipping a tall coffee. My heart skipped two full beats and the air in my lungs deflated as recognition settled in.

"I got your e-mail."

Brother Scott.

The four of us sat around the Monroes' dining room table, a mammoth rectangular piece of furniture, with the widest candle I'd ever seen filling in as a surpris-

ingly simple centerpiece. I had no notes, no files, nothing to work with except my questions and my concern
that I had crossed a line that I did not fully understand.

"You all serve in leadership positions at Second
Zion," I commented as Elsie rubbed her hands back
and forth. She and Mr. Monroe glanced at each other.
Tremont Scott stared only at me.

"Yes. I consider Brother and Sister Monroe to be my
spiritual mentors," he finally said, breaking the uncomfortable silence. There was a musical quality to his
voice. Soft, soothing. Without him even hitting a note,
an untrained ear could tell that he could sing.

"Brother Scott is being very generous," Mr. Monroe
chimed in. "My wife and I were both inspired by this
young man's dedication to using his talent as a vehicle
for worship. We're honored that he even talks this way
about us."

"Yes, he's a marvelously talented young man." Mrs.
Monroe beamed.

"Being the music director at Second Zion has been
my first real leadership position, and the Monroes have
pretty much taken me under their wings. They're like . . .
like parents to me, godparents."

His smile was so pretty, I nearly had to kick myself to
stay focused. How could any woman in her right mind
sit at a table with him and not get lost in his dazzling
facial features? I wondered if Mrs. Monroe ever took
a moment to gush at the "young man" beyond all the
syrupy banter going on between them.

"It's wonderful that you obviously have a warm relationship with each other." I nodded at the trio.

"Yeah," Tremont said, sobering. "That's why when I
got your e-mail, I immediately contacted the Monroes
to make sure that everything was okay. Sounds like
they have had a challenging past couple of days, but

otherwise things are under control." He flashed another smile, which I could tell was meant to calm my worries, but the only thing it did was raise my suspicions.

I'd never mentioned the Monroes by name in the e-mail.

How had he known I was talking about them with such certainty that he contacted them? Did he not share any other warm relationships with older couples at the church? It was a church of thousands. How had he known? I tried to think of a way to ask this question, but our conversation was apparently over. Tremont was rising to his feet.

"It was nice to meet you, Sienna." He extended a hand. I shook it and was quietly pleased at the warmth and strength and honesty that were in it. "Sorry, I have to go, but I have to get back to a project at church." He positioned a brown cap on top of his head, tipped it at the Monroes, and headed for the door. "Have a blessed day, everyone."

And then he was gone. And apparently so was the gushing. The Monroes looked at me with no humor in their eyes. Even their smiles were gone.

Mr. Monroe actually looked angry. "Ms. St. James, we appreciate your continuing concern about us, but I must tell you we were quite surprised that you contacted Brother Scott. Yes, he is like a son to us, but we also have certain boundaries that we keep, especially since all of us have leadership positions at the church. He's trustworthy enough not to spread our struggles with Dayonna around, but now we are not certain that you are. Who's to say who you'll talk to next?"

What was I supposed to say?

"I'm sorry. I really was not trying to upset you." *Yikes.* "I only wanted to gain your confidence so that you know I'm here to help with Dayonna."

So much for gaining confidence. I knew any hope of trust had been sufficiently shattered.

"We have a full day ahead of us, Ms. St. James." Mrs. Monroe's arms were crossed.

I took the hint and headed toward the door. The morning visit had been long enough without adding more damage-control duties to my growing plate of things to fix and/or uncover.

How would I explain all this to Ava?

"Again, I'm sorry for involving Brother Scott. Please know my heart was in the right place, even if my head was not." I let out a light chuckle, hoping to ease the tension.

I was the only one laughing.

"Um, well, enjoy your day. Are you planning to visit Dayonna?" I added.

"Of course." Mrs. Monroe still had her arms crossed as both of them walked me to the door. I was standing in the door frame when I remembered the main question I'd wanted answered during this visit.

"Were you the ones who requested that I not be allowed to see her?"

"What are you talking about?" Elsie Monroe raised an eyebrow. "Isn't it your job to check on her? Of course we wouldn't want to keep you from doing the tasks you are *supposed* to do."

"Of course not." I turned to walk away, not wanting to stir the pot even more.

But something was bothering me.

I hurried to my car, got in, and started the ignition, unable to shake the inkling of unease that was pricking my gut.

As I made a U-turn in the middle of the street and waved at their neighbor who was forever sweeping his front steps, I realized what was nagging me.

Mrs. Monroe had looked truly surprised to learn that someone had placed me on the "no-visit" list.

That same look of surprise was not shared by her husband.

Chapter 29

I'd been driving for only ten minutes when the call came.

"Sienna, my office now."

I made another U-turn and headed back toward downtown.

Even the security guard in the massive lobby of the building where Holding Hands was located seemed to sneer at me. Of course, I knew it was my imagination, but I felt like I kept making decisions that were either getting me nowhere or leading me into trouble.

Lead me not into temptation.

Not sure why that line from the Lord's Prayer crossed my mind just then. Maybe it was a hint from Jesus that I needed to be praying as I prepared to see my mentor, my boss, who, I could tell from her four brief words on the phone, was completely infuriated with me.

Ava Diggs was loyal, nurturing, and compassionate to a fault. But don't get on her bad side. She fought for which she believed, and if she believed that you were working against the good of her company or her clients, she would tell you so.

Just because I was her golden child did not make me exempt. If anything, it made me even more of a target, since I knew what she expected from me. Or in this case, flat out told me.

When the elevator door opened for me to go up to the fourteenth floor, Sheena stepped out. She was chatting away on her Bluetooth but still managed to shake her head at me.

"Girl," I heard her say, "my office mate is trying to get all of us in trouble. Me, the agency, DSS, and everyone else she can get a hold of."

Who knew that searching for Hope would create so much chaos?

I entered Ava's office, ready for my scolding, uncertain how I would even respond. She was busy filling out paperwork, her ink pen moving nonstop as I took a seat. Several moments passed as she checked and rechecked the forms in front of her.

Paperwork.

Finally, "Sienna, what are you doing?"

I said nothing, because I did not have an answer. Ava took off her glasses, and I noticed for the first time deep circles around her eyes.

"The Monroes called me. They expressed concerns about a breach of confidentiality?"

"I can explain."

"Please do."

"I contacted someone at their church—"

"The church where you went to spy on them . . ."

"Um, well, I sent an e-mail to someone I thought could help me earn their trust. I know you wanted me to leave well enough alone, but my gut tells me that all is not well. Something is up with Dayonna, and I feel like the Monroes know more about her than they are letting on. I think she may have told them something that might be important, and they are afraid of disclosing it because they want to continue proving themselves as worthy foster parents."

Ava rubbed her tired eyes. "What you are saying, what you are doing, is wrong on so many levels that I don't even know where to begin. In addition to breach-ing the confidentiality of one of our clients, you also continue to insist that something deeper is going on with this foster family, with no reasonable cause for concern."

"Ava, I realize now that I did not use good judgment, but I can assure you that my e-mail did not contain any names, not the Monroes or Dayonna's."

"Then how did the person you contacted know to contact the Monroes?"

"I have no idea. That's what I've been trying to figure out."

Ava got quiet at this, but her eyes never left mine. After several minutes she continued.

"I've never seen you get so troubled about a case, especially one that you've been working on for only three days. What is going on with this case that has touched off so many personal nerves and reactions for you?"

"I told you I've been having a challenging week. There are so many areas of my life that are not making sense. I guess I felt that if I could make sense out of Dayonna's life, there was hope for me to make sense out of my own."

Hope.

"I've changed my mind, Sienna. I'm taking you off the case. I still believe this is an excellent opportunity for you to grow, but I can't afford to let your personal growth come at a cost to our clients. You've crossed a line, Sienna, and whether it's due to bad judgment, stress overload, or a combination of both, I can't let you continue working with the Monroes and Dayonna, because I do not know what you will do next."

"I understand," I said, feeling ashamed that my mentor had to share this moment of my career with me. I felt bad and embarrassed at my professional mistake. Yet I did not feel relieved.

"Finish taking your time off, and I'll see you on Monday."

"Okay, Ava. I'm sorry." I stood up and headed toward her door, but just before I went out, Ava spoke again.

"By the way, who was the person you contacted at the Monroes' church?"

"The music director, Tremont Scott."

"Tremont?" Ava looked confused, which made me feel the same way.

"You know him?" I asked.

"Of course. He was one of mine. A foster child with our agency many, many years ago."

"Are you serious? You've served a lot of children over the decades, and you specifically remember him?"

"Oh, yes, I do. Tremont Leonardo Scott was a handful. I almost gave up on social work because of him. And now you're telling me he is the music director at Second Zion?"

I nodded my head, and she chuckled.

"Jesus really does know how to turn lives around." She shook her head as I turned to leave, trying to make sense out of this revelation. "Sienna," Ava called after me again. I turned to look at her, and all the humor had left her face. In fact, a frown tugged at the corners of her large lips. "I just remembered something else."

"What's that?"

"The Monroes were his foster parents."

I wanted to ask Ava if I could peek at his chart, but I knew that would only make things worse. She had already taken me off of Dayonna's case. There was no reasonable explanation for me to get her permission to access archived files. But questions still weighed on me as I headed for my car.

Why had neither the Monroes nor Tremont disclosed their full relationship to me? The revelation nagged at me, like a squeaky seesaw going up and down in my stomach. On one hand, it really was none of my business that he'd been a former foster child of the Monroes. That would explain why he was so close to them. It would also explain why he knew that I was talking about them in my e-mail.

But on the other hand, why not mention it? If there was nothing to hide about him or Dayonna, or anyone else, why keep anything hidden?

Dayonna officially was no longer my client, but I had no sense of closure.

I still felt like I needed to continue my mission to find Hope, and I had to believe that Tremont's past with the Monroes could somehow still help me understand their present with Dayonna.

He said he'd be at the church. It was my day off. I decided to go there. I wasn't pursuing the matter for Dayonna's sake, I told myself. My actions were for Hope.

I felt obligated to be Hope's advocate, whoever, whatever she was.

Chapter 30

I pulled up to the multi-acre complex of Second Zion Tabernacle, wondering what in the world I was trying to do. I admit, my actions and decisions over the past few days made little sense to me, but something was compelling me to move forward.

It bothered me that I could not quite put my finger on what that compulsion was.

I checked my phone and resisted the urge to call Roman's school again. He certainly had seemed more like his usual self this morning when I dropped him off. I planned to check and make sure that each of his teachers had signed my homemade check-in sheet the moment I picked him up after school.

I decided to leave my fears and thoughts about Roman alone for the moment.

Despite it being late morning on a Friday, the massive parking lot at Second Zion was about half full. It seemed like something was always going on at the church. I walked into the royal blue foyer for the second time that week, blinking in awe once again at the tapestry and the grand allure of the entryway. After giving the grand foyer its respectable due, I headed straight to the information desk. The circular wooden structure was manned this time by just two women, who were wearing identical navy blue blazers with plastic name badges identifying them as Sister Margaret Kelly and Mother Ernestine Jefferson.

Mother Jefferson flashed me a warm smile that made even my toes feel cozy as I approached the desk.

"Today is the day the Lord has made. Welcome to Second Zion. How can we help you, dear heart?"

It was easy to smile back at the elderly woman with the closely cropped, curly silver hair. She was what my mom would call a handsome lady, with flawless cocoa butter-colored skin and magazine-perfect makeup. She probably was over eighty years old, but I'd seen women twenty years her junior who looked older.

"Hello," I said, continuing to smile. "I was wondering if you could direct me to the music administration wing?"

"You're looking for Brother Scott too?" Her smile widened, and I immediately felt embarrassed.

"I . . . I, um . . ."

"They're in Grace Hall, at the end of this corridor. I think it is really wonderful what you are doing for the young people. Do you give private lessons as well?"

Before I could look even more confused or come up with an answer that would not make sense to her, Sister Kelly saved me.

"Ernestine, Deacon Roberts is waiting for you on line seven."

The elder lady nodded toward the hallway I should walk down as she took her call. All the common sense left in my head was telling me to get out now, to head back to my car and leave Brother Scott alone.

But again, a nameless compulsion kept my feet walking down the long corridor that led to Grace Hall. I opened the double doors to a scene I had not expected. I had imagined that the large room, painted baby blue and dripping with gold chandeliers, would be the perfect place to host a wedding reception, but at the moment it was hosting countless teens holding, blowing, plucking, or otherwise banging on all manner of instruments. They were sitting everywhere throughout the room, in groups of two or three or six or seven, playing songs off beat, off-key, and just plain "off"-ful!

Tremont Scott was in the middle of the room, waving around a baton with the seriousness of a conductor leading a philharmonic orchestra. I had to cover my ears at the chaos and understood immediately why the musical assemblage had convened in the extravagant room.

Grace Hall was soundproof.

"Okay," Tremont shouted over the broken notes. "Let's start again from the top." He tapped on a large black music stand, counting out the beats, and the chaos started up again. Somehow I managed to make out the beginning notes of "Just a Closer Walk with Thee." Just the beginning. After about twelve beats, the song collapsed into a tumble of shrieks, blasts, squeals, and cymbals.

"Okay," he shouted over the notes again. "We need to move on to the next song. Let everything that has breath praise the Lord. You guys are doing it! Keep praising Him." As he shuffled through some music sheets, I admired the perfection of him. Still donning his brown outfit from that morning, he'd taken off his suit jacket, revealing an oatmeal-colored T-shirt that fit his sculpted arms and chest nicely. His brown cap was still on but was sitting slightly to the side of his head. There was a carefree quality to his posture, and the smile on his face was easy and genuine.

"Yes, keep praising him, saints!" I could almost imagine my officemate Sheena saying. The thought made me smile, until I remembered that my conversation with her old flame, Roland at the DSS, had soured our relationship in some manner.

Something else to salvage on my "to-do" list.

Tremont was a couple of minutes into the next song when he noticed me standing near the double doors of the grand hall. I could tell that I had his attention because the carefree, easygoing smile and stance that had quietly captivated me suddenly disappeared. He finished conducting the song with a stiffened back and starched arms. When the song was over, he beckoned one of the teens to take over and headed directly toward me.

"Ms. St. James." He greeted me with a straight face.

"I'm sorry to intrude." *What is my purpose for coming here?* I asked myself again.

"Keon," he shouted to the teenage boy who held the baton, "go over this song two more times, and then do the Kirk Franklin song I introduced last week."

He led me across the room and opened the door to an empty restaurant-quality kitchen that stood adjacent to the lavish room.

"Let's go in here to talk." He motioned for me to step into the kitchen, and he followed. The soundproofing was amazing. The disjointed music faded into the distance.

"Church band?" I asked, uncertain where to go, being careful not to shatter the already thin ice I was creeping on.

"Not quite." Tremont picked up his cap and ran a hand through his hair. "We've formed a partnership with a couple of high schools who've had to let their music programs go. Every other Friday, the church pays for some buses to pick up these students, whose parents have consented, and I and a few other musically inclined church members have been trying to teach them how to play." He peeked out the door, and the brassy notes of a misdirected tuba player blared through. "At least we're trying to."

We both chuckled, but Tremont quickly sobered as he let the door close again.

"So, I know you did not come here to be serenaded by our music troupe. What's up?" His gray-hazel eyes searched mine with a slight squint.

"Well, first, I wanted to apologize about the whole situation with the Monroes. It was bad judgment on my part to send you that e-mail."

"No problem." The intensity in his eyes was unnerving.

"Secondly, I guess I was wondering why neither you nor the Monroes mentioned that you were a former foster child of theirs."

I watched as his eyes narrowed and his mouth hardened, so I quickly continued. "I'm not trying to get in your business. I just feel like too many people are hiding too many things. I would not otherwise care, but it's my job to ensure the well-being of the children I come across, and something just isn't feeling right. I can't put my finger on it, but secrecy only confirms to me that more is going on than meets the eye. The Monroes probably are not going to be saying much to me, but I guess I'm hoping that you will."

His mouth relaxed a little, but he bit his lip before speaking.

"I'm not quite connecting the dots that are making you uneasy. Yes, the Monroes were my foster parents, but I'm not sure what that has to do with your concerns regarding their current client."

The kitchen door swung open, and a youngster with a snare drum hanging around his neck tapped on it impatiently. "You coming back, Mr. Scott? Keon out there trippin' like he's really in charge."

"I'll be right out." Tremont flashed the teen a warm smile. When the door closed, he turned his attention back to me. "For whatever it's worth, Ms. St. James—"

"Please call me Sienna." I was probably only a year or two his senior, and the formality was making me feel old. And somehow ugly.

"Okay, Sienna," he continued, "I'll be perfectly honest with you. I did not bring up the fact that I was their former foster child, because they specifically asked me not to. Why? I don't know. Although I lived with them for two years of my life, there is still a lot about them I don't know. Or understand. Some people I just don't even question." He looked back at the kitchen door, almost as if he expected it to swing open yet again. "Look, I have nothing to hide, but I've always felt like the Monroes did."

"What do you mean?" My eyes widened at his confession.

"I don't know. I've probably said too much already. I'm not trying to get anyone in trouble." He looked back at the door.

"Who would be getting in trouble? And *why?*" My heart was beating faster, and it wasn't just because Tremont had stepped closer to me.

"My mother died from AIDS when I was fourteen years old. My father was in jail, and my grandmother did not want me. I was a wreck and a rebel before my mom died, and my grief, anger, and bitterness only made me ten times worse when she passed. I bounced around a couple of foster homes until I was sixteen. That's when the Monroes took me in. Their care and commitment toward me turned my life around, and by the time I was eighteen, I had pulled my life together enough to make it on my own. I owe a lot to them. I truly would not be the man I am today if it wasn't for them. That's why I don't question them. And I'm definitely not trying to say or do anything that will cause them trouble."

"So you think there's trouble to be found?"

"No, not exactly." He shook his head. "I'm just saying that feeling you have that something is not right, that they are hiding something, I've always had it too. But for the most part, I've left it alone."

"For the most part?"

"Yes. I said something once to my caseworker at the time. Actually, I think she was the director of the agency you work for."

"Ava Diggs?"

"Yes, that was her name."

Ava had told me that she had overseen Tremont's case. When she was short staffed or when her workers starting quitting to avoid particular clients, she was known to step in and handle things herself.

The door slammed open again. This time a disgruntled flute player, a girl of about sixteen or seventeen, stood there with her free hand on her hip, tapping her foot with impatience.

"I'll be out soon, Jasmine." He chuckled as she whipped around and marched back out of the kitchen. "I really need to go back to my students." He reached for the door handle. I followed him out, and he walked me back to the double doors of the spacious hall.

"Thanks for your time, Brother Scott. Just one last thing," I shouted over the musical mess as I stepped back out into the main corridor leading to the church's foyer. "What did Ava Diggs say to you when you went to her with your concerns regarding the Monroes?"

"She told me not to rock the boat."

Chapter 31

It troubled me, Ava's response. *Don't rock the boat.* She'd said the same thing to me when I first talked to her about Dayonna's claim that she had a missing sister. Ava Diggs was not one to give up easily on a matter. Indeed, a large part of her success had been due to her unwavering commitment to leaving no stone unturned in providing the best care for the foster children she encountered.

Why was she so willing to leave the Monroes alone when suspicions about their behavior were not new? Perhaps I was thinking too hard. I collapsed onto a plush sofa in the church's narthex and pulled a pen and a scrap of paper from my purse. I wanted to jot down the things that were troubling me about the Monroes.

First, they seemed to be doing their best to keep me from talking frankly with Dayonna. I wasn't buying that they had nothing to do with preventing me from visiting her at the facility—at least I wasn't buying that Mr. Monroe had no knowledge of this. Though Mrs. Monroe seemed genuine in her surprise that I had been put on an exclusionary list, Mr. Monroe had much the same look on his face as the day I left a screaming Dayonna in my wake.

Put like that, I realized it would make sense that he would not want me seeing her at the facility. Perhaps he thought I would just set her off. But why not tell his wife if he had been the one to make that request—or knew that someone else had?

As far as Elsie Monroe was concerned, I still found it odd that the elderly lady insisted that Hope was a mere baby doll. Why was she so convinced? What made her so certain, so adamant that any other option could not be discussed?

And then there was that photograph. I wrote down the word *photo* on my paper. I didn't believe I would have thought there was anything odd about the worn Polaroid that Elsie Monroe gave the police officer the evening Dayonna went "missing"; however, the way the Monroes continually looked at each other, it made me question the story behind it. I had to believe that Dayonna had said or done something that alarmed them when the photo surfaced in their home.

Lastly, I could not forget the whole running away episode itself. I knew I saw Dayonna in their window, but then again, even she acknowledged that she'd taken off. She'd managed to leave a note in my car, and the Monroes had looked just as surprised to see her sitting in their living room as I had.

I scratched the word *runaway* off my list but wrote it down again just because something still did not feel right.

I had learned years ago to trust my gut.

A flash of RiChard returning alone to the village in KwaZulu-Natal entered my mind. I shook my head to rid myself of the unspeakable memory.

"Are you okay, dear heart?"

I looked up into the smiling face of Mother Ernestine Jefferson, the information desk attendant who'd helped me earlier. Her navy blazer and a navy purse hung from her lower arm. I guessed her "shift" was over.

"I'm okay." I grinned. "Did you need to sit down? I'm about to leave." I realized that my purse, my paper, and my big behind were taking up most of the sofa situated near the main entrance of the church.

"Yes, it's probably a good idea for me to sit down while I wait for my ride." The older lady squeezed into the space next to me after I gathered my things."Are you a member here?" she quizzed.

"No, just visiting."

"What church do you usually attend?"

"New Eden Baptist Church."

"Oh, with Pastor Joseph McKinney?"

I nodded.

"I went to school with his wife, Lola. That was a *long* time ago."

We both chuckled.

"You don't look a day over fifty-five."

"Oh, I know you are being generous. I'll be eighty-seven in May." She flashed a full-toothed smile. "Yes, God has truly blessed me. That's all I can say. Now, how old are you, dear heart?"

"I'll be thirty-six in January."

"Married? Any children?"

"I've got a son. He's fourteen. And my husband . . ." My voice trailed off. I had never talked to anyone about RiChard, but something about her felt . . . safe. "My husband . . . ," I began again, with no luck. Mother Jefferson held up a gentle hand.

"Say no more, honey." She chuckled. "I had me one of them kind of husbands too."

"What kind is that?"

"The kind that can't be explained to nobody but Jesus."

I had my belongings together, and there was no reason for me to continue sitting there. But I did not want to leave. This woman was a complete stranger to me, but there was a knowing about her.

I had never talked to anyone about RiChard. All of a sudden I wanted to tell somebody everything.

"My husband is . . . was—" I began again, but Mother Jefferson patted my hand.

"Don't start that story now." She rubbed the back of my hand. "It's too big of a tale for this itty-bitty sofa. And you're not even sure where to begin." She reached for the pen and paper that were still in my hand. Under the word *runaway,* which I had written moments earlier, she wrote down an address.

"I'm home all day most days. Come over anytime. No need to call. I'll be there. When you figure out what it is that you need to tell somebody about your husband, just come over and we'll talk and pray." She pressed the paper into my palm and folded my fingers down on it.

A horn beeped outside the door, and I saw a white SUV parked by the curb.

"That's my ride, dear heart." She stood to her feet. "What is your name?"

"Sienna. Sienna St. James."

"Okay, Sienna. I'm going to be praying for you. And also for your fourteen-year-old son. Just come visit me when you're ready."

As Mother Jefferson walked out the door, a mild breeze blew in.

I felt it.

A soft wind of hope rustling back into my life.

I wanted to inhale, but finding breath was still difficult in the wake of so many unanswered questions.

Chapter 32

The day was halfway over, and I still had not made it to one of the main places I'd wanted to return to since yesterday. I was determined to find out who had requested that I not see Dayonna. The Monroes were a closed door, so I headed straight back to the hospital.

"For whom are you looking?"

What a loaded question. I had to shake my head at the chirpy receptionist, who once again pecked away at her computer keyboard.

"I need to see a manager," I said.

"Can I help you with something?" she asked, repeating what had been her first words when I approached her desk.

"Yes, you can send out a manager. I really need to talk to someone in administration."

"I am in administration, and I would love to assist you." She stopped talking for a moment and looked up at me. "Weren't you here yesterday?" She raised an eyebrow in disapproval.

"Yes, I was, and that is why I am back. I am a social worker with Holding Hands Agency, and I, I mean, *we,* have a client who is currently hospitalized here." I could not claim Dayonna as mine anymore. "Her name is Dayonna Diamond. I am not asking to see her. I already know that my name is on a list of people who are not authorized to see her. I just want to find out who asked that my name be put on that list."

"Usually restrictions are requested by—"

"I know. Parents or guardians or hospital staff." I was not trying to be rude, but I could feel my frustration level rising.

Somebody somewhere was going to give me answers. Today.

"You informed me of that policy yesterday." I softened my voice and threw a smile back on my face. This woman, as all receptionists were, was my gateway to the facility's powers that be. I did not need to burn a bridge. I needed her help. "I'm just wondering if I can find out who made that request so I can make sure I'm doing my job correctly. I promise I am not trying to cause problems for you or anyone else."

She liked my last sentence. I could tell because she resumed her happy keyboard pecking.

"Ms. Rose, I am glad to hear that you are not trying to cause any problems, because truthfully, I am prohibited from disclosing any information about a patient's care to someone who is not authorized to receive it. As a professional, I'm certain you can both understand and appreciate my responsibility for patient confidentiality."

"I'm sorry, but did you just call me Ms. Rose?" I struggled to remember why that name sounded vaguely familiar.

Perky girl scrunched up her face and began typing faster. "I'm sorry, but isn't your name Crystal Rose?"

"No, I am Sienna St. James."

"Oh, I see you. There were two people who tried to visit yesterday who were on the restricted list, and your name was just below my cursor." She squinted at her computer monitor.

Crystal Rose. I had heard or read that name recently. I was sure of it.

"Okay, thank you. May I please speak with a manager?"

This time my question elicited a loud sigh from the receptionist.

"Look, my supervisor—shoot, even the hospital president—is not going to be able to give you any further information about any patient in our care. I don't know what else to tell you."

We both stared at each other. Maybe glared is a better word. I guess I had the fiercer eye, because she finally relented.

"The best thing I can tell you to do is to contact your client's DSS worker. She may or may not have been here yesterday." The receptionist looked at the doorway behind her, which led to an administrative suite, and began typing again.

I could tell I had just been dismissed.

And helped.

I pulled out my workbag from the trunk of my car and sat down in the driver's seat, windows down. A soft, cool breeze filled the warm interior of my Chevy Aveo, and I was reminded of the gentle wind that had rushed over me as I watched Mother Jefferson leave Second Zion.

I was getting closer to Hope.

I felt it.

I sifted through the stacks of papers that filled my heavy workbag until I came to the notepad where I'd written tidbits from Dayonna's file days earlier.

Deirdre Evans. The DSS worker who had been assigned to Dayonna during the five months missing from her paperwork and also the DSS worker who'd visited Dayonna the day before.

I remembered seeing her name on the sign-in sheet, just under the Monroes'.

I dialed information and got the main phone number for Baltimore's Department of Social Services. I'd learned my lesson. No more calling people's contacts, ex-boyfriends, or former foster children. Any information I got a hold of now was going to come from my own research and efforts. I dialed the number and pressed through the computerized menu until I reached an operator. I requested the foster care division in my most professional, no-nonsense voice. I did not need any unwarranted questions anymore while on my mission. Finally, I reached an employee index that allowed me to spell out a worker's last name to get to his or her extension.

It took all of twenty minutes, but finally, finally, the extension for Deirdre Evans began to ring.

"Hi. You've reached Deirdre Evans. I am either away from my desk or on another call right now. Please leave a message and I will get back to you within twenty-four business hours. Thank you, and have a productive day."

When the beep came, I had my message prepared.

"Good day, Ms. Evans. My name is Sienna St. James, and I am with Holding Hands Agency. I wanted to talk to you about one of our clients who I know you visited yesterday at Rolling Meadows Mental Health Center. Please give me a call back at your earliest convenience. I have some questions that I believe you will be able to assist me with."

I rattled off my contact number, but as I hung up the phone, I realized that I'd just left my home number – and not my cell phone number — on Deirdre's voice mail. *Oh, well.* I was not going through that twenty-minute exercise to leave another message. I decided to simply check my home voice mail often to see if she returned my call. *Or better yet,* I thought, *why not just go home now and not even miss her call?*

It made sense to me. I was tired. I wanted a chance to turn my brain off and relax. Just thinking about the sanctuary of my bedroom loosened my tight shoulders. I shuffled the notepad and loose papers together in my lap to make one neat pile. Just as I started to put all the papers back into my workbag, a name jumped out at me.

Crystal Rose.

I'd written down her name just the other day. She was Dayonna's mother.

And, according to the receptionist, she had visited the hospital the day before in an attempt to see Dayonna. Like me, she had been denied visitation.

What was going on?

Chapter 33

His shoulders were not slumped; his back was not slouched. He walked toward the village with pride and confidence, though his hands were bloody.

His hands were bloody.

That was all I could see.

The other villagers wept and moaned when they learned of Kisu's death at the hands of men who did not appreciate his and RiChard's message. He'd been beaten and stabbed, and his prized lion's head ring stolen by his attackers, RiChard said. The two had, under RiChard's lead, gone to neighboring villages to try to round up support for a political protest.

I remember seeing Kisu's mother, shaking like a leaf trembling in the wind. There were no tears on her face, no sounds coming from her mouth. She just shook. Her husband, the aged and respected village chief, had the opposite response. He stood so still with his eyes closed, I recall thinking that if he had been lying down, one might believe he was dead.

Kisu's life had been ripped away violently, and his absence tore at the heart and soul of the village. He had been the first and sole university-trained son of his community. He had been their hope, their joy, their prize.

And he had been taken away from them because he'd joined along with RiChard. But that was okay, my husband reassured them. Kisu's death would outshine his life because he'd sacrificed himself in the name of social and political justice.

I remember standing there, feeling confused, angry even, that RiChard could continue standing there, rambling on and on about the fight, the cause, the righteousness of their battle, when all the villagers wanted to do was grieve.

But the blood on his hands.

That was what bothered me most.

After giving another speech on the sacrifices required for social justice, RiChard then announced that justice for Kisu's violent death had already been attained.

He had killed Kisu's attackers, he said. Ambushed them, fought them, killed them with his own bare hands. He detailed the bloody encounter without so much as blinking an eye or breaking into a sweat.

In all the time I had known RiChard, I'd always envisioned him as a man of peace, not as a murderer. But it wasn't murder, he assured us all; it was vengeance. He held up Kisu's ring as proof that he'd taken the lives of those who'd killed Kisu.

The village chief took the ring and studied the sunlight shining through the large blood-tinged jewels. I remember he mumbled something that no one could hear before kissing the ring and giving it back to RiChard as a reward for avenging Kisu's death. Both tears and cheers filled the village square as everyone crowded around RiChard to soak in his message and his method of fighting for whatever he said was right. No more questions were asked. As everyone clamored around him, I found myself being pushed farther back to the bare edges of the crowd.

The blood on RiChard's hands changed the way I looked at him, changed the way I looked at my life.

***

Sitting on my sofa, thinking about the lion's head ring, was not relaxing. That heavy, jewel-encrusted ring held memories of weeping and moaning; of murder and revenge; of my broken marriage; of my questions about life and meaning, justice and judgment; of my missing husband; of my devastated son.

I wanted some hot chocolate.

When I was younger, my mother would make homemade hot cocoa that was the perfect blend of bittersweet chocolate, creamy milk, and fluffy marshmallows. I thought about my mother and our upcoming Sunday dinner with Yvette and my nephew Skee-Gee.

Was there anything in my life that gave me peace?

A loud scratching noise at my door startled me. I jumped up from my sofa and grabbed a large cast-iron frying pan from my kitchen before peering out the peephole.

Officer Leon Sanderson.

"Leon?" I swung the door open and dropped the pan.

"Sienna?" He jumped back and looked at me with the same look of confusion I was giving him. "I wasn't expecting you to be home at this time of day. I was just leaving something here for Roman."

I looked down and noticed for the first time a large plastic bag sitting by my door. I looked back up at him, still confused.

"Every now and then a corporation on a PR kick gives us extra funds to help with programs and supplies at the center," he explained. "We're about to order a new shipment of games and activities for our elementary-school-aged kids, and I saw we had a little extra funds left over. I went out and bought some things for some of the older kids who I thought would benefit, as well. Roman was on my list."

I reached for the bag and opened it. Inside was a brand-new basketball and a chess set.

"Roman can have these," Leon continued, "but tell him he has to bring them along with him to the center at least once a week to share with the others there. Paying it forward. That's what I try to teach the young men and women I work with."

"Wow." I picked up the basketball and fingered the bumpy surface. "Thank you. I know Roman really will appreciate this, especially since he is grounded from doing anything that plugs in."

We both laughed, though I noticed Leon was slowly backing away as he chuckled.

"No sparkly tooth today?" I gestured to his pearly white grin.

Leon sobered, licked his lips, pulled at his trimmed goatee. "No, no more gold cap." He mused, "I wore it for a reason, and that was fine for that season, but at some point, you have to be able to move on from some things. Closure for me meant letting that cap go."

His words lingered in the air as he stood with one foot on the landing in front of my door and the other on the first step down.

"Does closure always mean having to let go of something?" It was an honest question from me, which he did not answer immediately.

"I don't know. What I do know is that sometimes when we are able to let go of something that symbolizes what we're unhealthily holding on to—or what is unhealthily holding on to us—freeing ourselves from those objects tells us and everyone around us that we have really moved on."

"You said your gold cap reminded you of your mission at the center. Something about your brother? Sounds honorable. Was that really something that you had to let go?"

He nodded his head, and a sad smile filled his lips. "I thought it represented my mission, that it reminded me of why I do what I do, but I realized yesterday, as we were searching for Roman, that it held another meaning to me, a darker motivation that has tried for years to be balanced out by good intentions, but it was there nonetheless."

"What was that?"

"Revenge."

He let the word settle in the space between us. I knew he had no idea of the emotional jolt I felt when he uttered that single word.

Leon broke our silence. "Don't try to understand it. It's a complicated story, my brother, that gold cap. Just know that I've finally learned my lesson from it. I've let it go, and no longer can my deeds meant to help others be colored in any way by wrong motivations. No need to try and save the world while your own soul is getting lost. That's why Jesus's sacrifice was so perfect. He was blameless. His motives were pure. Sorry to get all preachy on you. But that's where I've been the past twenty-four hours."

"Life-changing week for you too, huh?" I smiled. I was not quite sure what else to say. Hearing Leon talk about Jesus felt a little strange to me. Yeah, and a little preachy.

"It will be okay, Sienna." He shifted his feet on the steps. I felt uncomfortable too but could not quite put a finger on why.

"All right, Mrs. St. James. I'm off. Tell Roman to behave himself, or this old man will have to kick his butt in basketball again just to keep him in his place." He smiled and was gone.

Lord, have mercy. That was a lot to take in.

Roman was exactly where he said he would be when I reached his school. His check-in sheet was initialed by all his teachers. I took him to Denny's, where we had breakfast for dinner. I listened to him talk about all his friends at school, which teachers were getting on his nerves, which video game he was going to play first when he came off of punishment. I drank my hot cocoa. But all the while I was still trying to take it all in.

Chapter 34

My day was still not over.

After dropping Roman off at home for the evening, I headed toward 695. I had a class in Portuguese to begin.

The class was offered by one of the local community colleges but was held inside of a high school. The Web site listed it as a noncredit "life enrichment" course, along with other subjects like kickboxing, French cuisine, photography, and digital art. As I walked through the hallways, which were dimmed for the evening, I passed by numerous language classes: Spanish, French, Chinese, but mostly English for nonnative speakers. It was a few minutes after six, and I could hear teachers of all tongues as I walked down the hallway. The clashing of accents and foreign words made me feel like I was in a language buffet.

I stopped at the last room on the wing. INTRO TO PORTUGUESE: BASIC ELEMENTS was written on a sheet of notebook paper taped to the door. I entered the room and immediately wondered if I'd made a mistake.

"This is Intro to Portuguese, right?" I asked the young, coffee-colored, bald girl with bright blue foot-long feather earrings who sat at the front of the mainly empty classroom. A folded-over piece of paper on her desk read MS. TOMEEKA ANTOINETTE RYANS.

"Uh, that *is* what's written on the door." She rolled her eyes and giggled at the sole student in the room, a

Mediterranean guy who looked like he'd just stepped out of a Calvin Klein commercial, white tee, tight jeans and all.

"And you are . . . ?" I raised an eyebrow, confused.

"Your teacher, Ms. Ryans." She enunciated each syllable of her name, as if I could not understand English, then giggled at her other student again.

This little chick must be crazy or think that I am if she thinks I am going to be calling her Ms. anything. My son looked older than her. Yes, I'm exaggerating, but she could not have been a day over twenty-one.

"Are you going to sit down and join us? You're already late, and it is not fair to our students to continue with this interruption."

She actually said "students."

"You speak Portuguese?" I tried to sound civilized, but even I heard the bite in my tone.

"Obviously." Tomeeka rolled her eyes again.

I wanted to tell her that the only obvious thing about her was her stank attitude.

"Are you from a Portuguese-speaking nation?" I was trying to give the young girl the benefit of the doubt. There were plenty of places in Africa where Portuguese was spoken. However, she did not necessarily look like she was African, European, or South American. She looked and sounded like a good old-fashioned Baltimorean.

"For your information, I studied Portuguese for three years in college, and I spent a winter break in Brazil. Now, are you going to sit down, or do you need me to pull out my transcripts and photo album?"

We glared at each other a few moments more, but who was I kidding? I needed someone who could speak the language of the people who knew something about my husband, and Tomeeka currently was my one and only option.

"Sorry that I'm late." I slid into my seat.

"Very well. Let's take attendance. I had to cancel our first session last week, so now we can really get started."

Take attendance? Was this girl serious? I guess she was, because she unclipped a sheet of paper and began calling names.

"Martha Johnson?"

She scanned the room, and surprisingly, no one answered.

"Verdice Long?"

Again silence.

"Luca Alexander?"

The Calvin Klein model wannabe raised his hand.

"Fernando Alverez?"

Of course no answer. I could feel my temples heating up.

"Sarah Norman?" She looked up at me, and when I said nothing, she rescanned her list. "Those are all the names I have."

"I just registered yesterday. My name is Sienna St. James."

She looked displeased as she scribbled something down on her list.

"Do you need me to spell my name?"

She completely ignored my question. "Okay, I want you both to tell me why you have decided to begin learning 'the sweet language,' as Cervantes called it, of Portuguese."

Luca shrugged his shoulders. "I have a trip to Rio coming up, and I want to make the most of it."

"Ooh, Rio." The young girl's eyes glittered. "I'll have to tell you all the places you need to go. And you, Sienna? Why are you here?" she snapped as the glitter turned to stone.

I truthfully was beginning to wonder the same thing, but instead I answered, "Because I'm going to need your help finding my husband."

Tomeeka uncrossed her arms and leaned forward, a sudden look of curious mischief taking over her eyes. Her ears were itching for drama.

I could tell I'd just won her over.

Chapter 35

"Almada, Portugal. It is right here." With his index finger Luca pointed to a small yellow dot on the south-western edge of Europe. The small country of Portugal was between the Atlantic Ocean and Spain.

We were standing over a world map spread out over Tomeeka's desk. Tomeeka, who smelled like cocoa butter and feet up close, seemed overjoyed at Luca's discovery.

"This is so exciting and romantic." She giggled. "Trying to find your long-lost love."

Of course, I had not shared the entire story about RiChard. Ashes and murder and urns seemed too gruesome a tale to share with someone who couldn't seem to stop giggling. From her oversized attitude to her overwhelming giddiness, I was not sure what to make of this woman who was my best hope at the moment for getting answers about RiChard's whereabouts.

"Do you think he is having an affair with a European supermodel and wants to keep you from finding out?" She blinked innocently.

What is the girl talking about? I had to catch myself from wrongly answering her misdirected question by remembering the story I had just told them:

I had not seen my husband in many years after he left to complete a mission in another country, which I could not discuss. He might have run into problems in a city in Portugal. I knew this because he sent a cryptic

message through some residents there who were not
giving me any additional information, for reasons I was
not privy to. I was afraid that he might be in trouble,
and I was looking for assistance with breaking the
language barrier to see if I could get some clues to his
whereabouts.

Like I said, of course this wasn't the complete story. I
had not lied. Just left out some key elements. Such as it
had been nearly fourteen years since I'd last seen him.

And he might be dead.

"Do you think he's been kidnapped? Or is he into
something illegal?" Tomeeka seemed to derive great
joy from coming up with these scenarios.

"Do you watch a lot of movies, or is it just your nature
to think the absolute worst?" I said it jokingly, but I
meant it. Some people thrived on drama, and I thought
she had made it pretty easy to conclude that she was one
of those people. She laughed at my question.

"You should call one of those investigative news
shows. I bet they could get to the bottom of it and find
your husband."

"All right, um, I think I'm going to handle it from
here. Thanks for your help, but I probably need to go."
I'd had enough of the drastic speculation. This was not
helping anything. It was late. I was tired. I wanted to go
home. Once again, I wondered what I had expected to
get out of coming.

Another dead end.

"But did you still want me to try to call the phone
number you said you had?"

I thought about it. What did I have to lose?

"Use my cell phone," Luca said, joining in the conversation. "I just moved here, so my phone number will
not show up as a Maryland number *if* they have caller
ID. Less suspicion will be raised."

What was I doing?

"What will you say?" I eyed Tomeeka.

"Just give me the number. I won't say anything about your husband to tip them off. I'll just try to get some information about who they are or something like that. Maybe they're spies or drug dealers or international sex traffickers. I'm going to find out."

Yes, she'd been watching too many movies on cable. I shook my head and, against my better judgment, punched the numbers I knew by heart into Luca's cell phone and handed the phone to Tomeeka.

Someone must have answered immediately, because Tomeeka quickly grinned and offered a greeting into the handset. I felt my heart begin to race. Was I about to finally get some answers? She continued talking for a couple of seconds. I had no idea what she was saying, but I watched as her grin slowly disappeared and attitude began creeping across her face. My heart felt like it was about to pound right out of my chest wall when she finally looked over at me, her palm loosely covering the handset.

"European Portuguese is a little different from Brazilian Portuguese. I have no idea what she's saying. I might be wrong, but I think this lady works at a ceramic shop or somewhere like that. Sounds like she wants me to buy a clay pot." She looked bored, her dreams of high drama and romance dashed into pieces like a shattered vase.

"It is a crematorium."

Oddly, Tomeeka's face brightened at this new bit of dark information. Obviously, the possibility of death mixed in with deceit was intriguing to her. She began speaking into the phone again; this time her words were slower and deliberate.

"Estou procurando um homem ausente Afro Americano."

"Wait a minute," Instinctively, I tried to snatch the phone away from her. "What did you just say? Did you just say something about an African American?"

Tomeeka struggled against me, shouting something into the phone just as I grabbed it out of her hands.

It was no use. Nobody was on the other line. Beatriz, or whoever it was, obviously had hung up yet again. I handed the phone back to Luca, who checked it, a little peeved at the momentary mishandling of it by me and Tomeeka. I could only imagine what he was thinking. He'd actually come for a class, not a soap opera.

"See, you made them hang up." Tomeeka looked at me accusingly.

"What did you say?" I said, seething.

"I know you did not want me to say anything about your husband, but that is not how you go about getting information from the bad guys. You have to let them know that you are on to what they are doing."

"What did you say?" I did my best to stay calm, while feeling like my chances of finding out what was going on with RiChard were dwindling away.

"I told the woman who answered the phone that I was looking for a missing African American man."

I groaned and dropped my head into my hands. Instant headache.

"What? Isn't that what you are trying to do?" Tomeeka glared at me. You would think I'd known this girl for longer than forty-five minutes the way her nasty attitude freely turned off and on.

"First of all . . . I mean . . . really, it's too complicated to even begin to explain. I do not even know why I tried."

"What's so complicated? Your husband left you, and now you think he is in danger or in trouble in another country. What else needs to be said?"

Luca had sat back down, with one leg propped up on the chair in front of him. I wondered if he was going to ask for a refund for the class, or if he thought the entertainment value was worth the price he'd paid.

"It's more than that." I groaned again. "For starters, my husband is not African American."

Tomeeka gasped. "You're married to a white man?"

"No. I mean . . . See, he's biracial. His father was from Saint Martin. His mother was from Perugia, Italy. They met in Paris while his father was working as a chef at a restaurant and his mother was on vacation. Paris is where he grew up, but then he came to college here in the States, except for a semester he spent studying in England." Kisu flashed through my mind. I squeezed my eyes shut to try to stop the torrent of memories surrounding my last trip overseas with RiChard. "It gets even more complicated after that," is all I could say.

"A son of the world. Beautiful." Tomeeka had that dreamy look on her face again. "Girl, he's a mix of Caribbean and Italian? Your husband must look some kind of good," she teased.

I bit my lip, mad at myself for shredding up and throwing away every picture I'd had of RiChard sometime around Roman's fifth birthday.

RiChard was about as fine as they came. He looked as sweet as the chocolate Perugia, Italy, was known for, as smooth as its world-renowned jazz festival, as intoxicating as sweet rum from the islands, as refreshing as the Caribbean shorelines. Mix all those elements together and you had a man that left you breathless with one wink of his eye, with one kiss from his smiling and, yes, luscious lips.

With a decade-and-a-half absence accented by random phone calls, sporadic letters, and now an empty urn and a missing ring.

I'd told my son that the photos of his father had been in a jewelry box that had been stolen when my home was broken into years ago.

There was so much I had not told Roman.

I hoped that he would not be angry with me when he was a grown man and knew the full truth about his father and my relationship with him, or rather his relationship with us.

"His mother is from Perugia?" Luca said, piping up. I had not noticed that his leg had dropped off the chair in front of him and he had straightened up in his seat at my last words.

"Yes. Why do you ask?"

"I'm from Perugia," the dark-haired model wannabe explained.

Chapter 36

I stared at Luca, stunned, uncertain where to go with that new bit of information. But it did not matter.

My cell phone was vibrating, and I did not recognize the local number.

"Hello?" I answered, breathless, curious. Hopeful.

"Sienna." Leon Sanderson. "I have your son. I need you to meet me at the precinct near your house. Now." That is all he said before hanging up.

Tomeeka could see the fear and concern taking over my face. She grabbed my wrists with seemingly all the dramatic flair she could muster. "Don't worry, Sienna. We will find your husband. Right, Luca?"

"Sì," the Mediterranean cutie affirmed.

"Go handle your business. We can continue next week. Same time, same place," Tomeeka told me.

A million and one thoughts flooded my mind as I sped to the police precinct. What on earth was Roman doing there? *Oh, God.* The closest I had come to a prayer in I don't know how long. Though I was not that far away, the trip felt like the longest of my life. Terrible images surfaced in my mind, of Roman in handcuffs, of him bruised and bloodied. What had he done? What had someone done to him?

I pulled into the lot at a quarter of nine and immediately sighed in relief. Roman and Leon were standing outside, leaning against Leon's car. I parked in a space nearby and stormed over to them.

"What is going on?" I demanded, glaring at my son. He looked over at Leon.

"Don't look at me," the officer remarked. "Tell your mother what happened."

Roman looked away from both of us, his mouth a tight line of defiance, his hands in tight fists at his sides. When it became clear that he was not going to say anything, Leon did his best to fill me in.

"So I get a call from one of my old friends who works for the city police department. He tells me he's picked up a young boy in lower Park Heights that he's about to arrest, but the young boy asks for me. I get there, and this is who I find, sitting on the curb, in handcuffs, a five-ounce bag of marijuana sitting next to him. My friend, Officer Pettit, tells me it was in Roman's pants. I told him he was one of mine and that I'd deal with him. That's the *only* reason Roman is not at one of the intake centers for the Department of Juvenile Services as we speak."

I wasn't sure who was breathing harder, me or my son, but if fire could form in one's nostrils, I was certainly close to burning down that whole parking lot.

"What! Roman, have you lost your everlasting mind? What are you doing with drugs in your pocket? What were you even doing out?" I was a social worker by training, but in that moment I knew I was about to have to call child protective services on myself. I wanted to wring the boy by the neck. It took all I had to keep my distance from my son. I noticed that Leon was positioned perfectly between the two of us, and I knew it was purposeful on his part. "What? Are you selling drugs now? What is going on?"

Roman remained silently defiant, his eyes fixed on a traffic light swinging in the nighttime breeze. A storm was coming. Thunder rumbled in the distance.

"Roman, answer me." I did not even recognize my own voice. Something primal, primordial, was lodged in my throat, ready to surface in a scream. I felt like a mother grizzly, poised and ready to attack an unseen danger threatening her cub. When had the world become so evil as to try to claim my son?

"Roman?" The growl intensified.

Finally, he looked at me.

"You told me to go to school. I did. You said I was grounded. I haven't touched a single thing in my room. But I told you I was going to get Daddy's ring back." His eyes looked glazed over; I could not tell if it was tears or anger.

"What does that ring have to do with having weed in your pocket?" I demanded, trying to sort through the range of emotions that had taken over my mind and body at the thought of that ring again. I realized I was shaking.

"Skee-Gee said he would help me, but I had to help him first."

"Help him with what?"

"I ain't no snitch. Especially if we're talking about family." He looked back at the swinging traffic light, his face hardened. I knew that was all we were going to get out of him for the evening.

Leon knew it too. His next words were directed only to me. "Are you talking about Sylvester 'Skee-Gee' Grantley the third?"

"My favorite nephew." I rolled my eyes. "You have the pleasure of knowing him too?" I was not surprised.

Leon did not immediately answer, but when he did, his voice was barely above a whisper and his jaw quivered. "I knew his father, Sylvester Grantley the second." His eyes drifted off to the same streetlight that had Roman's devout attention.

"We're having dinner over at my mother's house this Sunday to talk to both my sister and her son. He and Roman had a bad fight earlier this week. Apparently, they've kissed and made up, but they've given us new things to discuss. With both of them." I glared at Roman, who still refused to look at me.

But Leon looked at me dead on.

"I know it's a family affair, but can I be a little rude and invite myself?"

His request did not strike me as rude at all. In fact, with all that had been going on with my son over the past couple days, it seemed like Leon *should* be there.

I scribbled my mother's address on some scrap paper and handed it to him. "Dinner usually starts at four, following services at New Eden."

Leon nodded, and I knew that our little parking lot meeting was over. It was time for me to take Roman home. It was time for the day to finally be over. As I herded my son to my car, I looked back over at Leon. He was still leaning against his car, his eyes drifting into space. A part of me wondered if it was a mistake to invite him to the dinner that would be happening the day after tomorrow.

I did not know Leon's history with Skee-Gee's family tree, but I noticed he was rubbing his uncapped tooth.

Chapter 37

I stared at my son's bedroom door, wondering if I could lock it from the outside, knowing that would do no good.

Roman had already proven that he was going to do whatever he was determined to do. Smiling and joking along in my face, scheming and *selling drugs* when I wasn't looking. Who was this person? I felt like I did not know him anymore. He was definitely his father's child. I swallowed to keep a sudden and unexpected wave of bitterness from washing over me.

"Good night, Roman," I whispered at the closed door, tracing a finger around the Baltimore Ravens poster he had taped onto it. I had no other words for him for that day.

Actually, I had no other words for anyone that day.

I was in the middle of dreaming about chocolate-covered wildflowers when a buzz from my cell phone woke me up. It was a text message.

Hi, Sienna. Sorry so late. This is Deirdre Evans from the DSS. Can you meet me at the entrance of Lexington Market tomorrow morning at nine? We can talk then.

Okay, I texted back and turned over in my bed. I was too sleepy to care or remember who Deirdre Evans from the DSS was or why we had to talk.

***

I found out I was pregnant with Roman on the Fourth of July. Independence Day. I remember because I had felt everything except independent. Lying in my parents' guest bed, staring at two pink lines on a stick while fireworks and firecrackers boomed and sizzled outside my window, I could not comprehend what having a child would mean for my life.

Would mean for my marriage.

I had returned to the United States from KwaZulu-Natal the week before.

Alone.

That was over fourteen years ago, and I still lay in a bed alone.

Somehow in the middle of these thoughts and memories, I awoke. A single ray of sunshine broke through a slit in my curtains, trying to trick me into thinking it would be a glorious day.

I knew better.

I'd gotten a text in the middle of the night, I recalled. Deirdre Evans.

The DSS worker who'd had Dayonna's case during the five months missing from her chart and the same one who'd visited her this week in the hospital.

That fact, I remembered, had been confirmed by the receptionist at that facility when I asked her who had put me down on the restricted visitors' list.

Could Deirdre Evans be the person who requested that I not see Dayonna? The question puzzled me, especially since I did not know this lady from jack, and as far as I knew, she was Dayonna's former DSS worker, not her current one. I nearly fell out of my bed reaching for my cell phone to reread her text.

"Roman!" I pounded on my son's door. It was already eight o'clock, and I was supposed to meet her at nine. "Get up! Get dressed! We're leaving in half an hour."

I waited a few moments, until I heard his big feet land with a dense thud on the floor. Satisfied that he was awake and moving, I headed back to my own room to get ready.

It was early Saturday morning, and I really did not have the best idea as to why I was meeting this woman. What I did know was that Roman was coming with me.

I'd already learned my lesson about leaving him alone while I chased Hope.

Lexington Market was one of the few landmarks in Baltimore City that I had not yet fully comprehended. A historic marketplace that had been around for over two centuries, it had vendors selling everything from fresh meat, produce, and candy to tax services, soap and body products, and, of course, crab cakes. But the other reality of Lexington Market was that it was a meeting place of sorts for those of every walk of life known to Baltimore. Against the eclectic backdrop of clashing sights and aromas, there was a clash of classes and cultures. One was just as likely to bump into a working professional standing in line at one of the delis as to be approached by a panhandler trying to sell food stamps in exchange for money. It was this unsettling vibe that made some tourists—and even some locals— leery of even coming near the market, but for those who did venture in, the food, the music, the ruckus were an experience all to themselves.

"Mom? Why are we here?" As big as he was, Roman was practically walking on top of me, like he did as a young child, when I held his hand to cross the street. His proximity to me was the only reason I knew he was nervous.

I followed his gaze to a woman who was probably in her thirties but looked sixty. She looked like she was doing an interpretive dance to a song no one outside of her head could hear, her arms and fingers moving in choppy rotations over and around her matted hair. A few seconds into her dance, she began to nod off, falling asleep as she stood there. Her body leaned forward to the point that I just knew she would topple over; but right before she did so, her head jerked back up and she was dancing again, this time moving her disjointed disco to the middle of Paca Street, much to the chagrin of drivers, who could do nothing but wait for her solo to finish.

"Mom?" Roman asked again.

"You want to sell drugs? I want you to see the long-term side effects your pharmaceuticals can have on people's lives. I guarantee you that for some of these folks, maybe even that poor woman, it started with one joint. That's somebody's daughter right there, maybe even someone's mother. You think this is what *her* mother pictured when she held her as a newborn baby?"

"Of course, my son had seen the tragedies of drug use played out in front of him before, but Lexington Market was an amphitheater of hard-core addiction. Whether you walked there, drove by, or caught the subway two blocks over, it was impossible to miss the multitude of broken lives trapped and dancing in desperation to the rhythm of the drug trade.

It was not a pretty sight.

I knew Roman had enough compassion in him not to want to contribute to anyone's demise.

At least that was what I hoped was somewhere in his genes.

We walked in silence as we went inside. Deirdre Evans was not due there for another ten minutes, and I wanted a breakfast sandwich and home fries. Roman, in a gesture I knew was meant to be a peace offering, paid for both of our meals. I started to ask him where he'd gotten the money, but I knew my son had better sense than to try to buy me off with blood money.

Blood.

The sight and smell of the chilled chicken and beef carcasses that were in glass enclosures nearby suddenly threatened my appetite as RiChard's bloody hands entered my memories.

"Let's go back outside." I pushed my son along, checking my watch. It was two minutes after nine.

"Are we waiting for something?" Roman asked after chomping down his sausage, egg, cheese, and grape jelly toasted sandwich a little while later.

I did not answer. Instead, I took some sips of my orange juice and checked my watch again.

It was eight minutes after nine.

"'Scuse me, ma'am." A finger tapped me on my shoulder.

"Yes?" I whirled around to face who I thought was Deirdre Evans, but immediately knew it was not.

"You got a quarter?" A birdlike man blinked at me. "I'm trying to get a bus pass to make it back across town."

I could not remember my usual spiel for these types of situations; I just knew I wanted him to move along so I could focus on finding Deirdre Evans.

"Here." I dropped three quarters in his hand. What he did with it was his business, not mine.

"Thanks." He nodded before fluttering away to another unsuspecting passerby.

"Mom, I'm finished. Can we leave now?" Roman's bottom lip curled over like he was eight years old. He thrust his hands in his jacket pockets and sighed loudly.

"Just wait. I would have left you home if I knew you could handle independence."

Independence.

The word chilled me.

I'd found out I was pregnant on Independence Day, and freedom had eluded me ever since. It wasn't Roman that kept me entrapped; indeed, he was the biggest blessing of my life.

It was the realization that my relationship with RiChard was over as the relationship with my then unborn child was just beginning. It was the realization that my definition of being free had never included being free from RiChard.

I'd never wanted independence from him, and yet I'd been fighting for fourteen years to gain it.

And now I'm standing here in front of Lexington Market, waiting for some woman I don't know to ask questions I can't remember in search of a Hope who may or may not exist.

"Let's go, Roman."

Enough was enough. It was nine twenty.

Maybe Deirdre Evans had come and gone. We had come back to the entrance a couple minutes after nine. Maybe we just missed her. I wondered how she expected to know who I was, anyway. I certainly did not know who to look for, and with me standing there with my son, perhaps she was thrown off too. I considered all these things as we walked one block up and one block over to our car.

"Uh-oh." Roman froze when we were about five feet away.

"What is it?" I asked, but he didn't need to answer. I saw it. The passenger window was broken. A large rock lay on Roman's seat.

And a note on mine.

My heart broke into a full-blown gallop as I reached for the single sheet of paper sitting in the shards.

Leave Hope alone before bigger things get broken.

"Is that your car, beautiful queen?" A man wearing a dashiki stepped out of a small nearby storefront. The scent of exotic body oils and incense wafted out with him.

"Yes. This is my car. Do you know what happened?"

"Not quite." His voice was calm and gentle. "I heard the glass breaking, and when I came out to investigate, I saw a woman running away."

"I was supposed to meet a woman at the market."

"You on *that stuff,* my sister?" The man lowered his face and gave me a stern look.

"No! I do not have a drug problem. Why would you ask that?" I knew from my line of work that drug addicts came in all colors, shapes, and sizes, but I hoped I did not come off like I had a monkey on my back.

"Ah, I'm not condemning you. It's just that woman, if she was the one you were looking for, she was high as a kite. I didn't get a good look at her, but the way she was running, I'm surprised she didn't get hit by a car. It's sad to be that far out of your mind." He shook his head and disappeared back into his store.

I pulled out my cell phone. There was no use in calling the police. What could they do? I pulled up my text messages and read Deirdre's words again.

What kind of woman was she?

I was about to call her back to ask her that very question when a realization hit me like a lightning bolt.

I hadn't left my cell phone number on Deirdre's voice mail. I'd left my home number by accident. Who had texted me?

I called the number from the text back twice. It was not in service.

Chapter 38

The lightning bolt left me sizzling hot. If whoever this was thought I would run off, quiet and scared, they did not know Sienna St. James, daughter of Alvin and Isabel Davis, mentee of Ava Diggs.

I came from people who did not back down without a fight. It was in both my nature and my nurture to swing back even if I was falling—and to do it with finesse. If I hadn't been on a mission to find Hope before, I was single-minded and single-purposed now.

Finding Hope had become personal.

Someone had had the nerve to threaten me and damage my property.

"Come on, Roman," I said, beckoning him to get in the backseat of the car. I had gotten all the broken shards I could see off of the passenger seat, but I didn't want him sitting there until I had a chance to give it a good vacuum.

I was not going to let my son get hurt on my road to finding Hope.

"Where are we going, Ma?" Roman looked perturbed. "And what is on that paper you're holding on to?"

"*You* are going to the PAL center, where I know you'll stay out of trouble under the watchful eye of Officer Sanderson. And I am going to take care of this note." I pressed down on the accelerator, going a little too fast for an outer downtown street, as the loud flap-ping of the plastic I'd used to cover the broken window alerted me.

"Someone you know broke the window?" Roman leaned forward in his seat.

"I don't know who did it."

"Then what was in the note?"

"I can't get into that right now." I pushed a little harder on the accelerator. I already knew where I was going after I dropped Roman off.

"Ma, do you think Daddy is dead?"

Good thing the light on Martin Luther King Boulevard was yellow, because I sure enough slammed on my brakes.

"What did you say, Roman?" I could feel my heart pounding in my chest. I closed my eyes and could feel them fluttering behind my eyelids.

I felt weak.

And nauseated.

"I was just wondering if you knew whether or not Daddy was dead."

The light turned green and I tried to go, but my foot felt like it had been superglued to the brake pedal.

"What makes you . . . Why do you ask that?"

"I don't know."

"Something made you ask that. Talk to me, Roman." I wished then that Roman was sitting in the passenger seat. I really wanted to see his face. "Why—" A loud car horn blared behind me. I still could not move.

"Ma, you need to go."

"Huh?"

"Ma, we need to move on from here. We can't stay stuck when we're supposed to be moving. People behind us are depending on you to go."

I heard him and knew that he was talking about the traffic light, but there was something deeper in his statement that rang out clear as a bell. *Or as loud as a horn.*

Cars, trucks, and maybe even a bicyclist, had joined in an angry chorus against me. Between the beeps, honks, and, yes, chimes, I knew I needed to do like Roman said and move forward. The time for wrapping my head around his words would have to come later.

And, more importantly, I needed to move forward so that I could answer my son honestly. At least I wanted to be able to answer him honestly; I was not sure that it was possible.

I waited until we were cruising at an acceptable speed to touch the raw spot again. I teetered gingerly around it so that neither of us would bleed.

"Hey, Roman . . ." I had to keep moving forward. "You've been thinking about your father, huh?"

"Yeah."

"Me too." I looked at him in the rearview mirror. "You're worried about him?"

"Yes. I mean, no. I'm sure that he's okay. It's just that you seem to be talking more to Officer Sanderson, and I, well, I don't think you should be, not while Dad's still around. You've never talked too much to any man before now, so I've been trying to figure out if, you know, if Dad's still alive."

I did not know whether to laugh, cry, scream, slap him, or slap myself to make sure I was hearing right. All this was over Leon Sanderson? Was the boy crazy?

"Roman, you know the only reason Officer Sanderson has been around is to help straighten out your behind. That's *all.*"

"But he likes you, Mom."

"Is that what he told you?"

"No, of course not. But I know how I feel when I see a woman I like, and he looks at you the same way."

"Okay. There are so many things wrong with what you just said that I'm not even going to touch it. But just so you know, you will never have to worry about me having any type of relationship with Officer Sanderson." Why was I even saying all of this to him? Seemed like the conversation should be going in the other direction, with me hounding him over some girl.

But the root of the matter, I knew, was RiChard. Always RiChard.

"So Dad *is* okay?"

Was the boy in my head?

"I don't get the connection."

"Well, the way I see it, you wouldn't be liking Officer Sanderson if Dad was still around. And you still don't like him, so Dad must be okay."

"Um, just so you know, Leon Sanderson is not the only man in the world. I hope he is not your measure of my love life." Why was I continuing this discussion with my fourteen-year-old son? I turned around to look at him. Our eyes met, and he quickly looked out the window. "What is it, Roman?" I asked, but I was not sure that I really wanted to know.

"That box. The one that Daddy's ring came in. I know it was from a crematorium. I looked up the address online, thinking I could find Dad."

I looked back at him again. This time he did not look away.

"Mom, can you please tell me where my father is?"

I was at a traffic light a couple blocks away from the PAL center. The light was green; I knew I could not stop here, no matter how much I wanted to.

"Roman," I said as I pulled to a stop in front of the building, "we'll talk. And I'll tell you everything I know about your dad."

I guess I was expecting him not to get out of the car, to put up a fight, to resist my attempts at delaying the inevitable.

But he did not do any of the above. He got out of the car and headed directly to the center door, even waving back at me before disappearing into the building.

Maybe telling him the truth about his father would be bearable.

For both of us.

Chapter 39

Bearable or not, I had a mission to accomplish.

With all the broken glass and broken hearts and broken spirits that seemed to be filling up my week—my life—finding Hope had become my road to keep from losing hope. Knowing that Roman would be safely occupied at the PAL center, I drove back home to get my old Mazda Protégé, which I held on to solely to give to Roman once he was old enough to get his license.

Then again, the way things were going, that might not happen until he is thirty.

My backup car roared to life, ready, it seemed, to show me that it had a lot of life left in it. I got back on the highway, heading toward my next destination.

Dayquon Hardison.

It was time to meet Dayonna's older brother.

Greenbelt, Maryland, was a suburban community near the college town of College Park, Maryland. The enormous flagship state institution defined the area around it, and the sprawling apartment complex that had been Dayquon's address—at least on November 15th, 2010, the one reference to him on the case search Web site—was no exception. I noticed FEAR THE TURTLE bumper stickers and University of Maryland flags all over the parking lot and the balconies of the rental complex as I pulled into a tight space.

Apartment 4G. I reread my notes and started the hike up to the fourth floor of the building in front of me. It was an older unit with plenty of wood panels and brown brick that blended into the mature trees surrounding it. Despite the dingy carpet and a stairwell that smelled of old pizza and stale beer, the building was quiet.

Then again it was still Saturday morning.

I checked my watch. Eleven thirty-seven. What time did people start getting up around here? I was debating on how loud to bang on the door to apartment 4G when I heard someone fumbling with the doorknob on the other side. Before I could get in a second thought, a tall, thin, lightly browned young man with shiny black hair was standing in front of me. He wore a gray tracksuit and had a bright red book bag slung over his shoulder. Both of us jumped back.

"Can I help you?" He spoke with a thick accent.

"Oh, I'm sorry. I think I have the wrong address."

"Wrong address? Who are you looking for?"

Before I could answer, another voice spoke from somewhere in the apartment.

"Preetish, who is at the door?" This voice had a thick accent as well.

"A lady who says she has the wrong address," Preetish called out. The second man joined him at the door; his black hair hung to his shoulders.

"Hi. Are you looking for the tutoring group?"

"No. I'm sorry. I have the wrong address."

"But that is the right apartment number you have in your hand." The second man pointed to the paper I held. "You are at the right place. I am Bisaj. Come in. You are early, but we will be starting soon."

"Really, I am at the wrong address. I was looking for someone else, but—"

"Oh, are you in Dayquon's study group?" the first one, Preetish, asked, rejoining the conversation.

"Dayquon? You know Dayquon Hardison?"

"Of course. He is one of our roommates." Bisaj looked confused. "But his group is meeting in one of the group study rooms in the basement of the Engineering and Physical Sciences Library. He started at eleven, so it will probably be over by the time you get there. You can stay here if you want. We're starting at noon."

I was already backing away from the door. "Thanks for your help!"

"But . . ."

I was not trying to be rude, but I was determined to find Dayquon, and as far as I was concerned, catching him at the end of whatever study session he was leading was perfect timing.

I had been on the massive university's campus only once before. One of my mother's former students landed on the basketball team and gave my mother tickets for his debut game. That was a few years ago, and the campus had grown even more since then. Thankfully, the engineering building was right near the main entrance. I found the library easily.

A group of students was emerging from the room as I entered. I took a chance.

"Is Dayquon still here?" I asked casually.

"I think he's still in there." A girl with orange and green yarn braided into her long blond hair pointed to another door.

I waited for the small crowd to disperse and then went into the room. A young man with shoulder-length dreadlocks pulled back into a ponytail was packing up a laptop and several thick textbooks. His back was to me as he shut down a projector and erased a small chalkboard.

"Dayquon Hardison?" I called out.

He turned around. The narrow, pointy nose and sad eyes were definitely similar to Dayonna's. Everything else about him was his own.

The legacy of having different fathers.

"We're done for the day." He barely looked at me as he spoke. "Here's the schedule for next week." He handed me a paper that listed times and dates for various math, engineering, and computer class study groups.

"You lead all these groups?" I was impressed.

"My roommates and I are all TAs for some of these classes. We rotate to help the undergraduate students when we can."

"You're a graduate student?"

"Yeah. I'm working on my master's in electrical engineering. What about you? I don't think I've seen you around. Are you new to campus?" He opened a can of cola and took a long swig before turning off the lights and heading to the door. I followed behind him.

"No, I'm not a student. My name is Sienna St. James, and I'm a social worker with Holding Hands Therapeutic Foster Care Agency in Baltimore. Do you have a second to talk?"

He stopped walking and looked directly at me, I realized, for the first time.

"Are you from that organization that keeps contacting me? If so, I've already said I do not want to be interviewed. There are plenty of other former fosters that you can talk to who've also taken advantage of the college tuition waiver program. I get that everyone wants to hear a good 'feel-good' story every now and then, but I'm tired of rehashing the details of my life. What may sound like a good story to you is nothing but painful memories to me. I've moved on."

He turned to leave, and I could not blame him. Although I was not from whatever group that wanted to explore his life story, I had the same aim.

And I understood a little something about not wanting to uproot pain-filled memories.

But I was on a mission.

I wanted to believe that finding Hope would bring healing of some nature to everyone involved.

"Dayquon, wait," I called after him. "I'm not from whatever organization you're talking about, but I do still want to talk to you. I am afraid your sister might be in danger."

He froze again, his back still to me. Slowly, he turned around.

"Which one?"

Chapter 40

"I haven't seen Dayonna in years. She's still in and out of hospitals, huh?"

"Yes, she's in one now."

Dayquon shook his head. "Poor thing. She had it the roughest out of all of us, I suppose."

We were sitting in the student union, in an area that looked like the food court of a mall. Dayquon was gulping down two slices of pizza, a cheeseburger, medium fries, and an extra-large chocolate shake, a meal that belied his solid athletic frame. I stuck to a bottle of water and a small taco. My frame had given up a long time ago, but I still tried to act right on occasion.

"So you do have more than one sister?"

"Yeah, I was the only boy. Seemed like my mother wanted another son, 'cause she kept trying, but she kept getting girls. Then again, the way she named them, I used to think she only wanted girls. She treasured them much more than she ever did me."

His face darkened, and I could tell from the ensuing silence that I could not afford to lose momentum in this conversation. He was a hurting somebody, and talking about his family was going to be difficult. Once the door closed, I knew it would go back to being tripwired and guarded.

"Hope Diamond."

"Excuse me?" Dayquon raised an eyebrow as he slurped down his shake.

"Hope Diamond. You were talking about the names your mom gave your sisters, and I was pointing out the uniqueness of Hope's."

"You mean Dayonna Diamond." He reached for one of his fries. "All my sisters have different last names, and she's the one named Diamond."

"Wait a minute. How many sisters do you have?" I resisted the urge to take out my notes. Something clearly was not adding up right here.

"Four."

"Four? How can that be? I've been through Dayonna's chart front to back a few times, and the only other sibling I've seen of hers is you." Even Ava had confirmed this fact.

"It doesn't surprise me that my other sisters weren't in Dayonna's chart. She and I were the only ones that made it into the foster care system. I don't think any social workers anywhere had dealings with my other sisters."

"So your other three sisters stayed with your mom?" I was pretty sure I'd read somewhere that his mother had her parental rights terminated. If she had other children, they probably weren't supposed to be with her.

"No. None of my sisters ever really lived with my mom for long. As far as I know, other family members took them in."

"Do you know who?"

"No. Whoever they were, they didn't take me."

"You don't remember any family outside your mom? Your father? Aunts? Cousins? Grandparents? Anyone?"

Dayquon set down his shake and blew out a long sigh. "No. The memories I have are of people in my house who were not relatives, if you know what I mean."

"No, I don't know what you mean."

"My mother. Her problems." He looked past me. "There were a lot of men, a lot of traffic in and out of our house. I don't remember them being family."

"So the only family you remember is your mom and your sisters?"

He closed his eyes and opened them again. "There was an aunt, I think. An aunt or a cousin. Or maybe she was just a neighbor. I don't remember. My mom called her Lisa. Or was it Sharon? I don't remember." He threw up his hands. "I was back and forth so many times between my mom's home and foster homes, I couldn't tell you who was who."

"Okay. So what about Hope? You said you all had different last names. What was Hope's?"

Dayquon shook his head. "Who is Hope?"

"One of your sisters, right?"

He shook his head again. "I don't have a sister named Hope."

"Are you sure?"

"Positive. It's impossible. That name doesn't even fit the pattern."

"Pattern? What are you talking about?"

"Our names. I'm Dayquon. You know Dayonna. And then there's Daynene, Dayvita, and Dayshonique. See, there couldn't be a Hope."

He had a point. Unless her name was Day-hope, or his mother had a change of mind during a later pregnancy, the odds that Dayonna had a sister named Hope seemed slim to none.

But there was rock on the floor of my Aveo and a crumpled note in my pocket that said otherwise.

I debated whether or not I should tell him about my mission to find Hope. Considering that I really did not know who or what I was looking for at this point, I decided to keep my mission to myself.

At least until I had more information.

"Listen, Dayquon, I know this has not been an easy conversation for you, and I appreciate your time. I'm also proud of your accomplishments, especially considering how many challenges you've had to face in your life. Thank you for talking with me. Before I leave, would you mind writing down the full names and birth dates of you and your sisters? Also, your phone number, if I have more questions?"

"No problem." Dayquon took the pen and paper I offered to him and began writing. After he handed both back to me, he extended his hand to shake mine.

"Nice meeting you, Ms. St. James. Honestly, I'm not sure exactly what you are doing, but I believe you are helping Dayonna somehow. I'm glad someone is. When you see her again, please tell her that her big brother still thinks about her every day."

I shook his hand, and he gave me a curt nod.

Some people live the lives of twenty and seem no less fazed.

We both stood to leave and turned in opposite directions. Just before we completely parted ways, I called back out to him.

"Dayquon, wait. I have one last question."

The young man turned back around, tucking a loose dreadlock back under his ponytail.

"Do you know where I could find your mother and other sisters?"

"I have no idea."

Chapter 41

Dayquon Hardison — November 13, 1987 (still 23)
Daynene Turquoise — December 5, 1989 (22)
Dayvita Topaz — November ? 1992 (19)
Dayshonique Sapphire — September 23, 1994 or 1995 (17 or 16)
Dayonna Diamond — April 23, 1997 (14)

Back in my car, I stared at Dayquon's neat hand-writing, trying to make some sense out of his sisters' names. He had not been lying when he said that his mother treasured her girls. Unless she had a penchant for dating men with exotic last names, Crystal Rose truly saw her daughters as her jewels.

Turquoise, Topaz, Sapphire, and Diamond. I scanned the unusual surnames once again.

So maybe there really was no Hope.

I remembered the large rock that still sat on the passenger floor of my other car, along with the remains of shattered glass. What was the explanation for that?

"My head hurts." I massaged my temples, wondering what my next move should be. "What am I even doing? What am I even looking for or hoping to find?"

Hope.

I'd forgotten that there was an old leather-bound Bible I kept on the back window shelf of this car. It had been my grandmother's and at her death had become mine. It was so worn and heavy that I'd never quite known what to do with it, so it became the symbol of my faith, riding along with me everywhere I went, until I had upgraded to my newer model.

Today, for the first time, I considered cracking it open. I was sure that there were bound to be verses and verses about hope.

Tears brimmed my eyes as I let out a heavy sigh. From the driver's seat, the Bible in my back window looked far away and heavy, just out of reach—much like most of my dreams and hopes always seemed to be.

Don't get me wrong. I'd been going to church all of my life. I knew Psalm 23 and the books of the Bible by heart, and I signed up to help with the annual youth conference at my church every fall. But for some reason, just looking at my Bible and trying to fit it into the complex context of everything that was going on in my life right now made my head spin and my heart heavy.

I knew there was hope in its pages, but my feet felt like they were stuck in muddy clay, making it hard, if not impossible, to move to where hope gurgled like a wellspring.

Hope.

I was too tired to even think about what it meant. Where it was. If Hope was even real. I just wanted my life not to feel so bland, so predictable.

So empty.

Meaning.

That was what I'd been hoping for, I guess. And Hope continued to evade me.

Minutes later, I was back on 95 for the hour-long trip back home. Before I stopped to pick up Roman, I ran into a small farmers' market on a side road in Howard County. I picked up peaches, grapes, and a freshly baked apple pie. Okay, and a pulled pork sandwich oozing with tangy homemade barbecue sauce.

It was nice to have some comfort food.

"Sienna, what a surprise to see you. How did you know I was here?"

"I saw that you made a purchase at a health food store near San Diego when I checked our bank account. I made some calls and found out you were here. I figured I'd surprise you and bring along your son, since you've never met him before."

Munching on the grapes from the farmers' market brought back unexpected memories. My trip with Roman across the United States to see his father. The surprise on RiChard's face. The confusion I knew was on mine.

He'd been back from South Africa for three weeks, I learned, and not once had he called to check on me or our newborn son.

Outside of him sending a postcard with suggested baby names when I first wrote that I was pregnant, I'd not heard from or seen RiChard since I left KwaZulu-Natal.

"Sienna, I've missed you." He'd kissed both my cheeks. I remembered nestling my head on his neck and feeling scratchy stubble on his face. "And my son, he is beautiful. Perfect."

It was my proudest moment, the way my husband looked at Roman for the first time, as if a priceless pearl had been created in my womb and I had just brought RiChard all that was good and wonderful in the world.

He loved his son. I never questioned that.

"His name is Roman," I'd told him, eager to show him my embrace of his ancestry. Although his mother was Italian, at the time I did not know Perugia from Sicily or Venice. When I thought of Italy, all I pictured was Rome.

RiChard frowned.

"Ancient Rome was a political monopoly that took over a quarter of the world, crushing the cultures and lifestyles of all it devoured." He must have seen my face drop, because he quickly added, "But it is a strong name that will serve as a constant reminder to our son to fight for what is right and just for those who are most vulnerable. He will grow to understand his place in the world because of his name."

He kissed my forehead, and I could smell black tea and hickory on his breath.

"So you've been here three weeks?" I looked at him, wondering how to even begin asking the questions my heart had not yet been able to form. I'd found him at a commune in Southern California. He'd been staying with a few dozen other people in a group of solar-powered adobe homes sprawled out over a large avocado orchard.

"Yes, this is where I've been, but it's not permanent. Think of this as a personal retreat for me. The last few months have been rough, traumatic, really. The work has been harder than I ever imagined. I didn't want to call you because I was in a bad place emotionally and spiritually, and I didn't want to give off anything that would unsettle you or, or . . . Roman." He looked down again at our child in my arms, letting Roman's little fingers curl around his thick thumb. Dark mud and dried blood had caked under his fingernails; and his skin, once smooth and healthy, was now blistered and sunburned.

I believed him when he said the past few months had been trying.

"It's good that you've come, Sienna. My retreat is almost over, and I was planning my next trip. I'm glad I got the honor of meeting my son before I left."

"You're leaving again?" I remembered wanting to ask him much more, but not finding the words. Or maybe the courage.

"Yes. I've learned about some things happening in South America. I want to go see how I can help."

"But what about Roman?" *And me!* I'd wanted to say.

"Ah, yes, I'll send you money when I have some."

Those were the last words he'd said to the two of us in person. There was no good-bye, no embrace. No kiss. Just a smile and a nod and a handful of grapes as he disappeared back into the greenery.

I was back on a plane, headed to Baltimore, three hours later.

He'd never even held his son.

I'd never told Roman that fact.

The grapes from the farmers' market were cold and crisp in my mouth. By the time I reached the PAL center to pick up Roman, I'd eaten nearly the entire bunch. I parked and stepped inside.

"They're down at the courts," called a young woman nestled in a metal chair and reading a book as I scanned the empty room. Wearing enough makeup to paint a wall, she looked out of place—and bored. I followed her pointing finger and headed toward a basketball court and a tennis court nearby.

"Ball, ball!" I heard Leon Sanderson call out. As I neared the double court, I almost laughed. It was a ragtag team of players if I'd ever seen one. Girls and boys of all shapes, ages, and sizes filled the blacktop, with just as many basketballs. Seemed like everyone on the court had one. I watched as a boy about six years old did his best to dribble a ball with both of his hands and then shoot. The ball went backward over his head and nearly landed on a teenage girl who'd been fiddling with her fingernails.

"Lamar!" she screamed in his face.

"Stacy, calm down. It was an accident." Leon smiled at the upset teen before giving solemn directions to the small boy. "Lamar, good try. Next time face the basket before you throw. Aim for the middle of the backboard."

Leon lightly patted both youngsters on their backs with all the seriousness of an NCAA Division I coach during March Madness. "All right, that's enough. Back inside, everyone." He mopped his head with a white towel and instantly transformed from basketball coach to traffic cop, directing the small mob of children and teens back to the PAL building. I searched for Roman and finally spotted him hanging out with a group of teens under some shady trees.

Mostly girls.

"Mrs. St. James," Leon called out to me just as I was about to march over and rescue my son from the she-devils. "Nice day out. Figured I'd let the kids enjoy what's probably one of the last warm days of September." He took a long swig from a water bottle as I joined him in herding the group of running children and bouncing balls back through the center doors.

I'll get to Roman in a minute, I decided.

Leon pulled up close to me, his dark brown eyes piercing mine. "Listen, Sienna, Roman told me you had some trouble this morning. Something about your car being broken into? He said you might know who did it."

"Oh, yeah, that. It's a long story."

I shook my head and looked back over at Roman, who was completely oblivious to me, surrounded by that pack of ravenous wolves. I swore one of those fast things was licking her lips. I looked back at Leon and then quickly looked away again.

Leon was wearing a yellow T-shirt and black running shorts. Though he was dripping with sweat, I could smell the body wash he must have used that morning. Something about seeing his exposed sculpted biceps and legs was bothering me. It didn't even feel right noticing these details. This was Leon Sanderson, for goodness' sake.

For his part, he seemed not even to notice it was taking all I had not to stare at his smooth mahogany skin.

"Is everything okay, Sienna?" His voice was a whisper as he worked to catch his breath.

Then again, maybe he noticed more than I realized.

"Huh? Oh, yes. Everything's fine." I wanted to smack myself for feeling, and acting, so ditzy.

"Put the balls back in that closet," he yelled out to a few hardheads and NBA dreamers who'd brought their dribbling game into the small room. Roman finally came in with his female fan club. I watched as all of them headed to a corner stacked with video consoles and games.

"Sorry about that, Sienna." Leon was talking to me again, still oblivious to my alarm over Roman's company. He and the other teenage boy with him were surrounded by about five or six girls.

And they looked way too grown up for my liking.

"Now, tell me about what happened to your car. What's going on?"

I was drawn back to Leon's eyes.

"It's work related. I have a client who claims to have a missing—or murdered—sister, depending on what state of mind you catch her in. Nobody seems to believe her, but ever since I started asking questions and digging for answers, strange things have been happening."

"This sounds serious, Sienna. Strange things like what?" He pulled on his chin with his thumb and index finger.

"Well, for one, her foster parents have been acting strangely, especially the foster father. Well, really both of them. They keep looking at each other like they've got something to hide, and they are not keeping me abreast of her behavior. I think my client may have possibly told them something important, but because they are determined to look like they can handle her and her issues, they are reluctant to tell me everything that is going on.

"Then someone pretending to be my client called me on my cell phone in the middle of the night, telling me not to look for this phantom sister. I don't believe it was my client, because the voice sounded like that of a grown woman. She's currently in the hospital, and I've been forbidden to visit her since I tried to question her more about her story. Then again, she went off so badly after I pressed the issue, I guess I could understand why I would be asked not to visit again." I pondered this for a moment but then threw up my hands. "And now my car."

"Yes, tell me about your car." Leon crossed his arms, his muscles bulging.

"There is a five-month gap in my client's chart," I said quickly to keep my mind from going off track. "I've been attempting to get in touch with the DSS worker who was responsible for her during that time period. Ironically, I found out she's been to see my client at the hospital, although, to my knowledge, she isn't assigned to her anymore. I'm assuming she's either close to her or trying to cover something up, since she's still involved in some fashion.

"Anyway, I left a message for her, accidentally leaving my home number. I got a text last night that supposedly was from her—on my cell phone, whose number I did not give her—asking me to meet her at Lexington Market this morning. Well, I got there and waited, and she was a no-show. Roman was with me, although he did not know what was going on. When we got back to our car, someone had thrown a rock through the window and had left this note on the seat."

I took out the crumpled piece of paper, unfolded it, and held it up for Leon to see. His mouth moved silently as he read and reread the single message.

Leave Hope alone before bigger things get broken.

"Hope is the missing sister's name?" Leon narrowed his eyes, as if in deep thought.

"That's what my client claims."

"Missing or murdered," he mumbled, scratching the back of his neck. "Either one of those scenarios would lead to strange behavior, secrets, and cover-ups." Leon looked squarely at me. "Or threats. Sienna, I really don't like the way this sounds, and I definitely don't like the idea of you possibly being in danger. Why don't you give me some names and more information, and I can look into this for you?"

"Thanks for offering, but for confidentiality reasons, I'm really not supposed to disclose any names or personal information. I've probably said too much already. Plus, I'm not sure that there's any danger to be found. Everyone else thinks that this girl is making up this story about having a sister, whether by intention or delusion, reasons unknown."

"Everyone else?" Leon quizzed.

"Yeah. My supervisor, her foster parents, shoot, even her own brother, who also spent years in the system, claim there is no sister named Hope."

"You met her brother?"

"This morning. I kind of tracked him down near Greenbelt."

"You tracked him down? You really are getting deep into this situation. If there is a girl named Hope that has been hidden all this time, someone is not going to like your attempts to expose her—or them. I'm not comfortable with the idea of you going at this alone. Is this really something you should be handling?"

He reached out a hand and rested it on top of my arm. I could have melted under the warmth that permeated my shirtsleeve. I looked away to keep from feeling like a fool under his intense gaze. That was when I noticed that the young woman who'd directed me to the basketball court when I first arrived at the center was staring intently at us. Her book was closed in her hand, and a slight frown pulled at the bottom of her too-bright-for-daytime lips. I looked down at Leon's hand on my arm, feeling silly for being so aware of the warmth of his touch. He must have picked up on my discomfort, because he immediately dropped his hand and took a half step back.

Darn.

"Leon, I appreciate your concern. To be honest with you, I don't know why I feel so compelled to keep pursuing it." Of course I knew a little of the reason why, but how would I even begin to explain my quest for reclaiming the hope that was missing in my own life?

"I admire you, Sienna, for your dedication. I just want to make sure that, like your son, you are safe from anyone who would mean you harm. Like Roman, I don't want you charging headfirst into a situation that could leave you hurt in any way."

At the mention of Roman's name, I looked back over at him.

He was looking at me and Leon.

He had the same look of displeasure on his face that I'd had on mine when I first saw him with the swarm of girls, who were still giggling and chattering around him. Leon still had not noticed.

"Again, thanks for your concern, Leon. If I ever do begin to feel unsafe, I'll let you know."

"Yes, please do." He fished inside his wallet and pulled out a card. "Listen, I understand about the whole confidentiality thing, but if there is anything that I can help with, or if at any moment you feel like you are in danger, get in touch with me right away. Don't even consider not doing so." He pressed the business card into my hand. It listed his business, cell, and work numbers. Twenty-four/seven access.

As he passed me his card, I could almost feel the fire breathing down my neck. Book girl, with the overdone makeup, actually had a snarl on her face. Her novel lay on the counter beside her. My son was frozen in the middle of the girl swarm, a solid rock in moving waters. The girls were beginning to notice his distraction, making all of them amp up their efforts. One girl, wearing tight blue jeans and a shirt that fit her like a latex glove, actually stretched her body along the length of the sofa that faced the video game console and propped one of her legs all the way up on top of the cushions.

That got Leon's attention.

"Young lady, please respect yourself and everyone else around you. Sit up and sit correctly," he demanded. "Ms. Patricia, can you please help our young sister with her sitting skills."

Book girl, or Patricia, as Leon had just called her, jumped into action with a smile too big for the situation, clearly pleased that he'd called on her for assistance.

"All right, Sienna. We'll talk again soon." He walked me over to where Roman stood, fuming.

"Are you still coming to Sunday dinner?" My question sounded innocent, but that was far from what I felt.

"That's right. I'll be there to help with the talk between Roman and his cousin Skee-Gee."

If looks could kill, I'd be dead twice. Neither Roman nor Patricia looked pleased with Leon's plans.

Or my smile.

As Leon walked away to break up a small squabble between two five-year-olds fighting over a crayon box, I was daydreaming about what outfit to wear on Sunday.

What was wrong with me? This was Leon Sanderson, for goodness' sake.

Chapter 42

Roman was quiet in his seat. That was fine with me. I really had nothing to say. All I wanted to do was go home, sit in the quiet of my bedroom, and try to figure out where my life had made a wrong turn, to the point of me going on a mad hunt for something or someone that might not even exist but had caused damage to my car. How did I even explain the rock through my window to my insurance company?

I could feel myself losing Hope.

"Mom . . ." Roman's voice was barely audible. "You said you were going to talk to me about Dad."

"Yes, we'll talk soon." My voice beat his in the weakness category.

We were ten minutes away from home when my cell phone began ringing.

"Sheena?" I answered without a hello. My office mate never called me unless it was lunchtime at work and she knew I was at Chipotle.

"Sienna, I don't know what you are up to, but you really need to stop before you get a bunch of people in trouble! This is getting out of control, and you need to rein it back in."

I could feel my face contort in irritation and confusion; old-fashioned attitude crept up my spine. I did not like her tone.

"Wait a minute, Sheena." I did my best to keep sounding Christian. "What are you talking about, and why are you raising your voice at me?" Like I said before, I come from a line of folk who aren't afraid of standing up when something isn't right.

Then why can I speak up in some areas of my life but not in others? The thought pierced me more sharply than Sheena's pointed tone. Why had I never challenged RiChard?

The thought was a monumental one for me, but I had to stay focused on my current conversation. Sheena had just said something about a bunch of people getting in trouble because of me. What was she talking about? I had just asked her, and she was hurriedly giving me a response.

"I'm sitting here at the hairdresser's, under the dryer, minding my own business, when my cell phone starts lighting up with texts. I mean one after another, and none of them make sense. The first one said"—she paused, as if scrolling through her phone—"it said, 'Tell her to leave it alone.' The next one said, 'She better stop if she knows what's best for her.' Then the next one was, 'Yeah, I got her number, but I'm telling you to make sure she listens.' And then there was one more. 'I got pictures, and they are not pretty.' Well, anyway, I'm sitting there, trying to figure out what these messages are about and how to respond to them, when my phone rings, and it's Roland Jenkins—"

"Roland Jenkins?" I interrupted, trying to place the familiar-sounding name.

"Yes, Roland Jenkins, my contact down at DSS, whose number I gave to you the other day." She sucked her teeth. "He calls me, screaming and shouting, telling me I better call you and tell you to stop harassing people, that you are messing with people's lives, jobs, and incomes."

"Sheena, I honestly have no idea what you are talking about. What people?"

"Oh, he rattled off a long list, but all I heard at the end of it was *me*. Sienna, I'm not going to lose my job because of something you've done."

"I assure you, I haven't done anything to jeopardize your livelihood—at least nothing that I know of. What list did he rattle off?"

"He said you were endangering him, you, Ava Diggs, and for some odd reason, he mentioned Second Zion Tabernacle and the citizens of Baltimore, and, like I said at the beginning, *me*. Well, he did not exactly say my name, but if something goes wrong with Holding Hands, that is going to directly affect me, and I'm not having it." I heard what she said, but I was stuck on one thing. *Second Zion Tabernacle?* I was about to ask her more questions, but my cell phone buzzed, indicating I had another call coming through. I did not recognize the number, but something told me I needed to answer it.

"Sheena, I want to talk to you some more, because I want to figure out what is going on myself. Hold on a moment, though. I have another call coming through, okay?"

She hung up without saying good-bye as I clicked over.

"Hello?"

"Hello . . . Ms. St. James?" It was a man's voice, and I sensed trepidation in it.

"Yes?"

"So this is really you?" the voice continued, and so did the fear.

"Yes? Who is this?"

I heard a loud sigh on the other end. "Ms. St. James, this is Tremont Scott. I got your phone number out of an e-mail I just received." He sighed again. "Can you please meet me at the church?"

"What's going on?" Now I was feeling nervous. *An e-mail? Who? What? Why?* The questions did not stop coming.

"I'd rather talk to you in person, if you don't mind." He paused for a moment, then said, "It's urgent."

I looked back at Roman, who was scowling at me from his seat.

Too many fires, too much drama for one day.

"Okay, I'm on my way." I let out my own sigh, wondering where all this was heading. And where it all had started. Was trying to find Hope that dangerous?

"Great. I'll meet you in the foyer."

He disconnected, and I did not even bother to call back Sheena.

Not yet.

I needed to know what hand of cards I'd just been dealt.

"Ma, why are we here?" Roman asked as I parked in an empty space in front of the humongous church. On a normal day I would have quickly put his tone and question back in check.

But this was turning out to be anything but a normal day. Week, really. For one, this was the most I'd been to church in one week, and that oddity was just for starters.

"I have a meeting. I'm sure there is something going on here that can occupy your time for a few moments." I scanned the full parking lot, figuring that among the many programs and activities occurring that Saturday afternoon, at least one had to be dedicated to the youth.

"You have a meeting?" he asked, following my gaze to the attractive music director, currently pacing in front of the main entrance of the church.

"Yes, Roman, but we'll find something for you to do."
His eyes narrowed as he looked back at me.

"No, Ma. I'm staying with you." He looked back at
Tremont as if he'd just spotted the enemy on a war
field.

"I'm not arguing with you."

"And I'm not leaving."

I left him sulking on the sofa near the front door, the
same cushy sofa I'd sat in the day before, next to that
sweet older woman. I forgot her name, but I still had
her address in my jacket pocket. I closed my eyes for a
nanosecond, remembering the comforting wisdom and
the calming presence she'd exuded. I recalled the quiet
breeze that had come over me as she walked out of the
edifice. *Hope.* I remembered thinking that I'd just felt
the gentle inkling of it.

That had been only a day ago, but the way I was feeling, the way things were going, it might as well have
been a lifetime.

"Thanks for coming so quickly," Tremont murmured,
clearly preoccupied as he led me down a long corridor.
"We're heading to my office in the music department,"
he explained, as if reading my mind.

I offered a weak smile, though inside I was terrified.
Tremont's gaze was intense, and not in a comforting
way.

"Okay, we're here." He unlocked a door and let me
enter the massive office suite first. It was a musician's
paradise. A baby grand piano sat in the center of the
room, surrounded by expensive-looking equipment
and other, smaller instruments.

"Sometimes we practice in here, and I like to record
our sessions to play them back and perfect them," he
offered in response to my awe at the elaborate setup.

He led me past the instruments and equipment to a smaller office in the back of the room. This space had the look of a more traditional office space, with a desk, a computer, and a couple of chairs.

One of those chairs alone looked more expensive than my entire living room set.

"This is your full-time job, right?" I could only imagine having an office like this to come to every day.

He nodded as he pointed to one of the seats for me to sit in. He took a seat behind his desk but then pivoted his flat-screen computer monitor so that it faced me.

"This is the e-mail I received less than an hour ago. Your name and cell phone number were attached." He clicked on a mouse, and a photograph appeared.

I gasped and quickly shut my eyes in shame.

Chapter 43

"Clearly this image has been digitally altered." Tremont looked furious.

I looked away and nodded my head in agreement, not wanting to view the graphic photo defiling his computer monitor, but wholeheartedly agreeing that the photo had been doctored. It was a picture of him standing next to an unmade bed, locked in a sensual embrace with the first lady of Second Zion Tabernacle, the strikingly beautiful young wife of the revered bishop.

Bishop Vincent LaRue had been widowed nearly a decade ago and four years later had taken a new wife not less than twenty years his junior. Only a few eyebrows rose at the age difference, however. Marcie LaRue had long been respected as a mighty woman of God, wise beyond her years, striking in her beauty. Her grandfather had been a respected elder in another denomination and had gone on to have a highly rated television show on cable. The bishop and the first lady's union appeared to be a perfect and heavenly match, and scandal had never marred it.

Until now.

Just Tuesdsy I'd sat in the session Marcie had led on stress management. Good thing she knew something about the topic, because she was going to need it now. I shook my head.

Though I agreed with Tremont that the photo had somehow been manipulated, I knew that if it was released, the gossip and the rumors that would follow could be enough to bring down the entire congregation.

In this day and age of mega-ministry meltdowns and controversies, even a dead lighter could start a forest fire.

"What can you tell me about this?" Tremont glared at me, as if I had created the image myself.

"I have no idea, Brother Scott."

"You've got to know something. Your name and phone number were attached as a separate document to this e-mail. Whoever sent it wanted me to call you."

"Who sent it?"

He scrolled back up the e-mail and pointed. A series of random numbers and letters made up the generic e-mail address.

"I already tried to reply," he explained, "and it bounced back. The e-mail address no longer is in service." He collapsed back into his chair.

"Sister St. James, I have worked and prayed very hard to get to this point in my life. I'll admit my past is not one that you would think would lead to success in God's Kingdom, but that's the beauty of grace and forgiveness. It would probably not be impossible for someone to unearth a photo of me like this from way back when, but to now involve the first lady in a blatant attempt to discredit this powerful house of God means that we're fighting against someone who can't stand the things and people of God. This isn't just a fight against flesh and blood. The enemy of our souls is busy, and the fight has just stepped up a notch."

"Brother Scott, I'm sorry that you're facing this. All I can tell you is that I've been getting clear messages that someone does not want me searching for a little girl named Hope."

"Hope. Who is she?" He said the name as a statement, not a question, and something about that small detail resonated with me.

"The sister of one of my clients." I decided to treat Hope as a fact too. Though I had no hard proof that Hope actually existed, the threatening note, the phone call, and now Tremont's e-mail were evidence enough to convince me that she was real to somebody.

"I'm assuming you're talking about Dayonna Diamond, the Monroes' new foster child. I remember meeting her after Tuesday night Bible study. The one you e-mailed me about earlier this week." Tremont studied the computer screen again, as if some detail would suddenly emerge to make a connection between it and Dayonna. I saw tears in his eyes.

"I'm sorry. I never meant for anything menacing to happen to anyone. I was only trying to find Hope, and I was not even sure she really existed." Seeing him look so vulnerable made me feel like crying too.

"What did Dayonna say about her?" He turned to me quickly.

"Ask the Monroes. I'm really not supposed to give out any details about my clients. Client confidentiality, you know. I have probably said too much already." I wanted to tell him everything but was careful not to give exact names or data. The way things were going, I needed to make sure I was in the clear when everything finally came out on the table.

"I understand." Tremont contemplated the matter. "One thing, though. Pay attention from now on to who you talk to about Hope. That way, if anything else happens, you'll be able to trace it back to someone."

"So you think I should keep pressing the issue?"

"If there is a child involved and someone is willing to go to these kinds of lengths to keep her hidden, then, yes, definitely. As scary as this is, at some point we've got to trust that God is bigger. Righteousness and holiness will win out for His name's sake. If someone does want to create a scandal, we've got to believe that justice will prevail."

Justice.

The word seemed to echo inside of me, as if there was an empty, cavernous space, devoid of feeling, thought, or reason. Devoid of hope.

How often had I sought to define that word *justice?* And to hear it grouped with such powerful words as *righteousness* and *holiness* left me wanting to take some time to digest it all.

But we did not have that kind of time.

"Do you think we need to go to the authorities?" I asked him, surprised at how weak my voice was.

"I was just thinking about that, and also whether or not I needed to alert the bishop."

My eyes widened at that thought, trying to imagine how I would explain to the larger-than-life pastor why his music director and his wife had been placed in a compromising situation, with my name and number attached.

"Look, Brother Scott, I don't want to make this a bigger situation than it needs to be. Let's wait until I can get more information before going to anyone else about it. I don't even know what's going on or who is trying to hide anything, and I want to be able to provide more than a hunch to the authorities . . . or the bishop."

Tremont seemed to weigh what I was saying, and then shrugged. "Okay. We'll go your route for now, but I'm going to be praying and fasting on this one, because this is one of those situations that will require true divine intervention. I have your number, and you have mine. Let's stay in touch."

He stood and so did I. As he walked me back to the foyer, a question came to mind.

"Brother Scott, do you know anything about Dayonna or her sister?"

"Why would you ask me that?" His eyes narrowed.

"Well, you weren't very forthcoming about the extent of your relationship with the Monroes, so I'm not making any assumptions about your knowledge about Dayonna. Maybe there is something the Monroes said to you when they told you about her that could help now."

He stared at me a few moments before answering. "I was not very 'forthcoming,' as you put it, about my relationship with the Monroes, because I did not think it was relevant. And to answer your question, no. I do not know anything about Dayonna Diamond, besides the fact that she is the Monroes' foster child, she's a handful, and she is currently in the hospital. That is all they've told me about her. That's it."

"Okay." I believed him. "But let me know if they share anything else with you."

"Will do."

We were back in the foyer.

"Good afternoon, dear hearts."

"Oh, hello, Mother Jefferson." Tremont threw on an instant smile and embraced the familiar information desk attendant. I had been so focused on my conversation with the music director that I had not realized we had stopped right next to the information desk and Ernestine Jefferson, the kind elderly lady who had helped me.

"I just talked to you yesterday, didn't I?" She winked at me. I could not help but smile back, though words escaped me.

"You know Mother Jefferson?" Tremont looked confused.

"We met yesterday as I waited for Marcie to come get me," she answered for both of us.

"Marcie?" I finally found my voice. "As in Marcie LaRue, the bishop's wife?"

"Yes, dear heart. She's my granddaughter," the handsome elderly woman replied with a smile.

I looked over at Tremont, suddenly understanding his confusion about my acquaintance with the first lady's grandmother. He was looking back at me.

With suspicion.

I had to get out of there.

"Okay, it was nice seeing everyone. I'm going to get my son and go." I turned to leave, trying not to run toward my son, who was still sulking on the nearby foyer sofa.

"You still have my address, Sister St. James?" Mother Jefferson called after me.

I quickly smiled and nodded, walking away even faster. Tremont narrowed his eyes, the furrow between his brows deepening.

"Just remember, my door is open whenever you are ready to talk."

Like that was going to happen. I remembered that Marcie LaRue's grandfather had been a respected elder with a highly rated TV show. And to think I wanted to talk to Mother Jefferson about my husband. There was no way she could come close to understanding my marriage to RiChard.

"Come on, Roman," I said, beckoning my son. I could not get out of there fast enough as Tremont stared me down.

It did not help that Roman was staring him down right back.

Chapter 44

Finally.

Home.

I collapsed onto the love seat in my living room just before 5:00 P.M. I turned off my cell phone, house phone, and computer.

I did not want to talk to or hear from anyone.

Roman was in the kitchen, gorging on a chicken box I'd bought him on the way home. With crispy chicken wings and western fries doused in hot sauce sitting in front of him, I knew I'd bought a few minutes of quiet, though uncomfortable, appeasement.

The minutes were short-lived.

"Mom." Roman stood in the doorway to the kitchen. "Can I ask you a question?"

No! I wanted to scream.

"Sure, son. Sit down." I moved the stack of magazines and other piles of junk that had been accumulating on my furniture to make room for him to sit next to me. He promptly did so.

"Mom." He bit his bottom lip before continuing. "How come Dad has never lived with us?"

It occurred to me just then that my son's voice, which had been squeaking and cracking like crazy over the past year, had a smoother quality to it—more bass, fewer breaks.

Roman was growing up.

I looked him straight in the face and decided to answer him as honestly as I could.

"Roman, your father was a complicated man. He knew how to be a diplomat, a civil rights leader, a mediator, and . . . and a fighter. He did not know how to be a husband and a father."

Roman nodded his head, slowly absorbing my words.

"So . . . you said he *was*. Not *is*. He's not alive, is he?"

"I don't know, Roman. I got a call last week from someone saying they were shipping his ashes to us, but they did not give any other information, and now they will not answer any of my calls. And you saw for yourself, your father's ashes were not in the package. I really do not know what that means."

Roman sat quiet for a long time. Then he said, "I never got a chance to know my father. And I've missed that."

"I miss him too, Roman. And yes, it makes me mad sometimes."

Roman took my hand and held it, a gesture that brought tears to my eyes.

"So what are we going to do about it?" he asked.

"Huh?"

He let go of my hand. "How are we going to find Dad, to know if he is okay, and then to find out when he is going to come home?"

I thought about my calls to Portugal; I thought about my calls, letters, even flights to various places over the years, to countries most people had never heard of, to villages that I wasn't even sure still existed. All the places in which I had tried to find RiChard, all the cracks and crevices he had used to keep himself hidden from the world.

From me.

From his son.

I was tired.

I had tried searching for Hope, and it had led no-where; and much like that quest, my search for RiCh-ard and what I meant to him had fizzled and died in so many ways, so many times. True, there was the occasional letter, gift, or trinket that came from him, enough to string along both me and Roman.

But at some point, I had to let it go.

Let him go.

"Mom?" Roman was still waiting for an answer, I realized. "How are we going to find Dad?"

"I don't know that we will, Roman. If Dad wants us to find him, he will let us know, and if all is not okay with him, we might just have to accept that we might never find out for sure."

Roman collapsed back onto the love seat, and we both sat quietly for a few moments.

"I can't accept that." His voice was still gentle, still quiet, but there was no mistaking the resolve in it. I turned to face him, ready to tell him that it was no use. My moment of bravery, however, was short lived. A knock pounded on my door.

She was a short, stout woman, with one thick spot of stubble to the left of her chin and large black moles that covered her face and neck like freckles. She held tightly to a metal cane and stared up at me from under bushy gray eyebrows. Terror filled her light gray eyes.

"Sienna St. James?" the brown-skinned woman whispered.

"Yes?"

She gave a quick look behind her before continuing.

"My name is Deirdre Evans. Can I come in?"

"You are Deirdre? From the DSS?"

"You know who I am?" Her eyes widened.

"I've been trying to contact you since yesterday."

The woman looked behind her again. "Who told you about me?"

"Nobody did. I just happened to see your name in a chart of one of my clients, and I had a question about her."

"Clients? What kind of work do you do?"

"I am a social worker for a therapeutic foster care agency."

"Really? Which one?"

"Holding Hands."

"You work for Holding Hands?" She eyed me suspiciously.

"Deirdre, please come in. Let's talk."

She gave one last look over her shoulder and then entered my living room.

"It's not usually this messy," I lied. *Lord, forgive me.*

"Oh, child, I'm not worried about your house. Actually, I'm admiring your collections. Looks like you've been all over the world." She nodded at the odds and ends that fought for attention in the midst of the books, papers, and magazines that filled my cramped living room and dining room. Handspun crafts made from cloth and carved from the elements peeked out everywhere, dropping reminders of Latin America, Africa, the Caribbean, Europe, and Asia to me and Roman on a daily basis. Some of the trinkets I had purchased myself in those first months I traveled with RiChard; most had been shipped by him as random packages over the years. They usually delighted Roman and depressed me.

"I guess I have been a lot of places." My eyes caught sight of the empty brown package from Portugal that had come to my door earlier that week. "And where I haven't been, my husband has, and he keeps finding ways to send a bit of his travels home to us. Do you travel much?" I was eager to change the subject and get to why this woman had entered my life.

I guess I was back to finding Hope. I groaned inside, wanting to be done with it and her.

"Oh, child, I'm not one to travel much." Deirdre Evans had no idea how terrible I was feeling as she continued. "Every now and then I go up to Atlantic City with a group from my senior building, but that's about it." Her words and her voice were casual, but nothing about her eyes or the way she was looking at me looked calm.

She still looked terrified.

"Ms. Evans," I asked quietly, "can you tell me why you are here?"

She narrowed her eyes at me. "I'm waiting for you to tell me. Didn't you say that you've been trying to contact me since yesterday?"

"Yes, but how did you get my address?"

"The man on the phone told me to come here right away."

"The man on the phone? What man are you talking about?"

Her eyes narrowed even more. "You know who I'm talking about."

"I really don't."

"Then why do you have them harassing me again?"

I crossed my arms, tired of the games and the confusion. "I really do not know what you are talking about. And what do you mean by 'again'?"

"I retired nearly two years ago, when it first started up, and I thought it was over. Until this morning." She looked at me sideways.

"When what started?" I could feel my nose and forehead wrinkling up in confusion. "Wait a minute. You're retired? But I left a message on your extension yesterday."

"My extension? That doesn't make sense." She cocked her head to the side. "Then again, when I was working, I had my extension forwarded to a pay-as-you-go cell phone because I was always out in the field. I lost that phone a long time ago. I guess it really could have just been stolen, and somebody held on to it all this time, although that really does not make sense."

"No, it doesn't. And neither does the fact that you visited my client—one of your old clients, in fact—at the hospital earlier this week."

"Visited a client at the hospital? I haven't been anywhere near a hospital since I had my knee replacement surgery five months ago."

"But I distinctly saw your name written down on the visitors' log when I went to see my client this week."

"Ms. St. James, now *I* have no idea what you are talking about." She started gazing over at my door with a look of unease.

It made me feel uneasy too.

"Dayonna Diamond." I let the name glide off my tongue, not even knowing it was going to come out when it did. Deirdre Evan's eyes grew wider.

"Her? So this is about her?" She pulled her purse close to her bosom and charged toward the door, her metal cane tapping along beside her. "I got to get out of here."

"Wait." I followed her, amazed that a woman with a recently replaced knee could move so fast. "Please, I need to get some answers."

"I knew I shouldn't have come," she was muttering to herself. "They probably followed me here. I retired to get out of this foolishness. Took my state pension and went back to minding my own business. Nobody believed me then, and I don't expect anyone to believe me now."

"Wait, please," I called after her as she marched down my steps. "I'll believe whatever you have to say. Please, tell me what happened. Why did you retire?"

She paused, her back still facing me. Slowly she turned around.

"I was a social worker for the state for over forty years. I've seen it all, heard it all. Nothing surprised me. Ever. Until I met that girl Dayonna. The things she said. The things she did. The things she said happened to her. Disturbing. She ran away from the last placement I put her in, and when she resurfaced five months later, her stories were even crazier and more bizarre. She started talking about a baby sister chopped into cabbage stew. I made the mistake of trying to make sense out of her senselessness, and that's when the phone calls and threats began."

Deirdre turned away, scoping the quiet street behind her.

"I'm going to tell you like they told me." She stared me dead in the eye. "Leave it alone. It's not worth the danger."

"But if a little girl is involved—"

Deirdre raised a hand to stop me. "I'm not even sure that Hope exists."

A chill passed through me. I realized in that moment that something inside of me *needed* Hope to exist.

"Do yourself a favor and stop your search now." Deirdre looked up at me from underneath her bushy gray eyebrows. "If you don't, believe me, they'll start calling you too, warning you to stop while you're ahead."

"They? Who *is* this 'they'?"

Deirdre looked around again. "When nobody at my job believed that I felt like I was in danger for trying to investigate Dayonna's twisted claims, I turned to my church for help."

Whatever had chilled in me before turned to solid ice.

"Let me guess. You attend Second Zion."

Her mouth dropped, and her eyes widened farther in fear. "How . . . how did you know?"

"Just a hunch." I thought about the e-mail that had been sent to Tremont Scott. Somebody in that congregation of six thousand knew something, I was convinced. "Who did you talk to?"

"I'm on the pastor's aid committee, and one of the members had me talk to her husband. I only did so because I knew that particular couple was well acquainted with the foster care system. Well, I talked to her husband, and he said he would help, but three days later he called me, afraid himself, and told me to leave it alone."

"What did he say?" I did not even have to ask who she was talking about. Elsie Monroe was chairwoman of the pastor's aid committee. What other couple could it be?

"I don't know who her husband talked to or exactly what he found out," Deirdre continued, "but he said that he wasn't going to press the issue any further and neither should I."

"Ms. Evans, who told you to come here today?"

"I told you. The man on the phone. The same man who kept harassing me and the same one I think started harassing that helpful couple at my church."

The man on the phone. I remembered she'd said that when she first showed up at my door.

"Who is he, this man who keeps harassing everyone?" I tried to imagine what type of person would frighten a dedicated social worker into retirement and a selfless elderly couple into silence.

"I never met him, but he calls himself 'Jewels.'"

Chapter 45

I watched as Deirdre Evans drove away in a battered blue station wagon. A white pickup truck suddenly zipped out of a parking space and followed close behind her. My heart began pounding and my eyes stayed glued to her car until I saw the pickup truck make a left at the next intersection.

"I am just as paranoid as her." I chuckled at myself as my heart began to settle down. Even still, I studied the street for a few moments more before going back into my home and shutting the door behind me.

Jewels. The name rang a bell to me. *Turquoise, Topaz, Sapphire, and Diamond*. The last names of Dayonna and her sisters, as told to me by their brother, Dayquon, echoed in my head.

There had to be a connection.

"Who was that, Mom?" Roman emerged from his bedroom, where he'd retreated during the whole of Deirdre's visit.

"It's a long story."

"Does it have anything to do with Dad?"

I could see a quick glimmer of hope in his eyes.

Hope.

"No. Nothing at all related to your father."

The glimmer fizzled away like a waning firework.

"Mom, I need to go online to study for a test I have Monday. Can I please use my computer?"

I didn't believe a word he said, but I was too exhausted to care.

"Go ahead. I have to run an errand. Do not leave this house. Don't even leave your room." I stared him down.

"I won't," he mumbled and disappeared back into his sloppy oasis, shutting the door behind him. The lock on his door clicked.

"Whatever," I sighed, grabbing my car keys. I did not have the energy to sort through Roman's mind. And I believed that by allowing him a temporary respite to use his computer, he would indeed stay put.

I was banking on that belief for the evening.

Today, right now, I was going to get some answers from the Monroes.

I pulled up to the Monroes' home just as dusk was settling over the city. The waning days of September in Baltimore meant daylight was beginning to slip away earlier, casting shadows and dim light on the Monroes' street. The first thing I noticed as I cut the engine was that all the windows looked securely shut and the shades were drawn. The next thing I noticed was the neighbor across the street blowing cut grass in his small front yard and staring at me. When I got out of my car, he cut off his blower and shouted over at me.

"They gone, ma'am."

"Excuse me?"

"I said they gone, ma'am. You lookin' for the Monroes, right?"

I waited for a car to pass by and then crossed over to him, hugging my arms. With the setting sun, a slight chill had filled the air, and I wished I'd had enough sense to wear a heavier jacket.

"Yeah, it's getting cold out here." The man looked to be in his late fifties, maybe early sixties, and had a well-fed stomach and maple brown skin. His head was almost square shaped, and a long mustache that was graying at the ends seemed to balance out his face.

"The name's Everett." He extended a hand. "Everett Worthy."

"I'm Sienna. Sienna St. James." I nodded as he shook my hand with a moist palm.

"Yeah, you one of them workers that be coming in and out of the Monroes' home, right? I seen you here seem like every day this week, huh? Them Monroes always got some agency checking in on them and those foster kids."

"Yes, the Monroes certainly are a generous and caring couple, opening up their home to children who need shelter."

"You got that right." Everett Worthy switched his quieted blower to his other hand. "My wife and I raised five children right under this roof." He pointed to the neatly trimmed row home that sat atop the small hill of his front yard. "Two boys and three girls. I barely had patience for them, so I know I couldn't take on another's young'un. 'Specially the kind like that girl they got living over there now. All that hollering and screaming and throwing. You shoulda heard her today. I was about to call the police, the way that chile was going off."

"Wait a minute. Today? You saw their foster child with them today?"

"Yeah. She'd been in that special hospital, but they brought her back home today. The way she was carrying on, I can't help but wonder if it was too soon to bring her home."

Dayonna was discharged?

"But none of them are home right now, huh?" I tried to look only half interested. I could tell this neighborhood watchman was itching for more details to share with the next person who came along. I didn't want him to get a whiff of the full story I was trying to piece together.

"Naw. They left a long while ago. The girl was with them, and they had a bunch of suitcases and bags with them."

I looked back at their house, trying to make sense out of what he was saying.

"Isn't that their car right there?" I pointed to the green LeSabre parked across the street.

"Yup. That is their car. They didn't go in that. That young man, the one they used to foster years ago who caused all them problems way back in the day, from what I understand—the one that was just here yesterday, when you came—he took them all off somewhere." Everett shook his head and pointed down the street toward Belair Road. "Had a nice car too. Black BMW. And he a church worker, from what I understand. That's why I don't trust them big churches. Taking all the money from the ones that need it and giving it to the ones that don't."

While Everett continued his rant against churches, I tried to absorb all that had been packed into his observations of the Monroes' apparent hasty departure. Their escort had to have been Tremont Scott, the music director at Second Zion. What kinds of problems had he caused them when they fostered him? I wondered. I started to ask Everett what he knew about him, but another question seemed more obvious.

"Do you know where they were going?" I asked, interrupting the older man's rant.

"Don't know for sure, but when I yelled out to them, Horace said something about spending some time out on the Eastern Shore. Bertha's people live out there." He turned his blower back on, ready to finish his yard work before the day was completely done.

"I'm sorry." I waved for him to stop. "Bertha? Who?"

"Horace's first wife." He looked at me like I should have known what he was talking about. "Horace still stayed close to her family when she left him a widower in his thirties, and Elsie, his new wife, had been Bertha's best friend. That's what I've heard, anyway." He shrugged.

This time he cut the blower back on, and I knew he had no more intentions of cutting it back off until he was finished with the yard.

It was all the same to me.

I felt like he'd just given me a glimpse of a gold mine of information. Now I just had to find the hidden trapdoor to access it all.

I could not put my finger on it, but in my heart I believed there might be Hope yet.

As I got back into my car, I knew exactly where I was going before the thought—or a plan—fully formed in my mind.

Chapter 46

My office building sat on a quiet and desolate street on the outskirts of downtown Baltimore. I never liked going into it after hours. On weekdays I was never one of the last ones to leave, especially in the fall and winter, when the days got shorter and sunlight disappeared. Coming to the building on a Saturday night was even creepier. Ernie the guard was not there, and the only way to get into the building was by entering a pass code into the front door. I'd never used it before, and as I punched in the numbers, I wondered if a camera was recording my entrance.

I did not care. I even looked up at the corners and the ceiling of the main lobby, imagining a hidden electronic globe capturing my mission of determination. I was not doing anything wrong. I just wanted information.

I was up on the fourteenth floor, standing outside the entrance to Holding Hands Agency, within mere minutes. Using my keys, I opened the front office door, walked through the narrow hallway, and then unlocked the secure room where charts for every single client and foster family we worked with were stored. Due to Ava's diligent efforts to ensure the agency operated at superior efficiency, I knew it would be a cinch to grab the Monroes' chart containing all the paperwork and history of their interactions with the agency. I stepped into the cramped room, which smelled of old paper and cardboard boxes. Despite Ava's commitment to proper storage and organization, she still kept things old school. There were no computer records. Just old-fashioned files, boxes, and binders.

I walked to the file cabinet where the files detailing our foster families' lives were kept. Quickly finding the folder labeled LMN, I fingered through the charts to find the Monroes.

"Lacy, McDonald, Miller, Nevins." I read and reread the alphabetized names on the chart labels. "Miller, Nevins . . . Where is Monroe?" I tapped my finger at the place where their chart should have been.

Charts were never out of place in the chart room at Holding Hands. If a chart was not where it belonged, it would be clearly signed out on the sign-out sheet Ava kept near the door of the secured room. I headed to the corkboard by the doorway, where the sign-out sheets hung, and flipped through them. There was no record of the Monroes' chart being taken out of the room.

"That's odd. Where could it be?" I wondered out loud, noticing the echo my voice made in the tight room.

I was about to leave the room when something out of place caught the corner of my eye. At the back of the room was an old desk that we sometimes used to peruse charts when there was no rush or need to check them out, like reviewing a chart to remember a court date, a birth date, an important name or address.

Usually the desk sat empty, except for the occasional coffee mug or stress ball that a coworker accidentally left behind. Tonight, however, there was something else on the small, shaky desk.

A chart.

And it was open.

Instinctively I knew it was what I had been looking for, and my gut feeling was proven correct as I neared it and saw the large black *M* on the side of the chart tab.

Monroe, Horace and Elsie.

The chart had been left open at a peculiar place, I noted, the part of the file that listed the hobbies, recreational activities, and interests of the foster family; and most of the activities listed for the Monroes had something to do with Second Zion Tabernacle. I skimmed the opened page.

Elsie Monroe: Chairwoman, Pastor's Aid Committee

Member, Senior Circle
Member, Home Visitors Ministry
Member, Grief Support Ministry
Other Interests: Gardening, Crafts/Crocheting

Horace Monroe:Member, Usher Board
Chairman: Alcohol and Substance Abuse Ministry
Other Interests: Home Restoration

I looked through the list one more time, chuckling at the interest in crocheting listed for Mrs. Monroe. I realized I had done my best to dispel those grotesque, faceless crocheted dolls of hers from my memory. I did not appreciate the reminder. I shook my head. I was glad, however, to be reminded that Horace Monroe was an expert home restorer by Elsie Monroe's reports. I remembered her saying that their current home had been a fixer-upper, which Horace had renovated.

"I wonder where they lived before?"

The question prompted me to flip to the demographic section of the Monroes' chart. To my surprise, several addresses existed. Before the Monroes moved to their present residence, they appeared to be hopping from one home to the next. The thought perplexed me until I looked again at the demos of the couple and was reminded that Mr. Monroe had been a career home renovator. With the housing market in the fluctuating state that it had been over the past decade or so, he had probably made out well buying broken-down homes and fixing them up to make them livable again.

I skimmed through the required home studies that had been completed on the residences, as they had served as foster parents at each. Though I was not sure what it was I was looking for, nothing unusual jumped out at me. For good measure, I jotted down each of the addresses, using a notepad and pen that had been left next to the chart, and then turned my attention back to the other sections of the tabbed folder.

"Foster history." I read aloud the next section. "They really are dedicated."

As I flipped through the pages, I had to admire the Monroes' commitment. The pages I glanced through confirmed that they had fostered over fifty-seven children for days, weeks, or years at a time over the past two decades.

I skimmed through the list of names, which had been abbreviated for confidentiality purposes, noting that a Tremont S. had been in their care from 1994 to 1996. That would have made the handsome music director around sixteen or seventeen years old at the time he lived with the Monroes, I estimated. I looked at the names following his: Kiana L., Breena J., Nadira P., Simone R., Therese K., La'Quayla M. . . .

"Wait a minute." I flipped through the rest of the list. "These are all girls' names."

I thought back to Dayonna's room at the Monroes' house. I remembered thinking even then that the elderly couple must have taken in only female foster children, as the overly girly decor of the room would have turned off the average boy. My suspicions were confirmed when I noted that Tremont had been the last male they'd welcomed into their home.

He really must have been a handful for them not to take on any more boys following their time with him. I shook my head and chuckled at the thought. *Unless there is another reason.*

I put the chart down and headed back to the shelves where client cases were stored.

"Tremont Scott, where are you?" Even as I asked the question aloud, I realized that I knew the answer.

Ava Diggs's biggest technological advancement for her company had been when she decided to archive old client files in a smaller format, as space had become an issue in the cramped chart room. I was still in graduate school when I helped her with the monumental task of organizing charts—many of which were over a couple inches thick—and getting them ready for a private company to put them into microfiche form.

Yes. Microfiche.

Despite everyone's best efforts to persuade Ava that the records would probably be better off in a digital format that could be read by any computer if need be, she was adamant that the old charts be treated much like documents in a library and converted into a format that she would not have to take a class to understand. At the time she did not know a flash drive from a floppy drive, so we all had to go with the flow. After a long, painstaking, and expensive process, all the files from 2000 and before were converted to microscopic images that could be seen only with the desktop reader she kept in a closet inside her personal office. The microfiche films were in that closet as well.

Both the closet and her office were locked with keys only she had.

I went back to the desk where the Monroes' chart still sat and picked up the pen and the notepad where I had written down their previous addresses. I wrote down Tremont's name and circled it, reminding myself that I wanted to learn more about his past. Even he had acknowledged that he had one.

Another thought entered and left my mind, and as I was searching to remember it, something else caught my attention.

Keys were jingling in the main door of the office suite.

"Oh, no." My heart began pounding as I ripped off the sheet of paper where I'd made my notes. I closed up the chart, leaving it where it was, and dashed out of the room. As quickly and as quietly as I could, I locked the door of the chart room and ran down the hallway to the office that Sheena and I shared. My hand was on the doorknob, ready to open the door, when I heard my name being called from down the hallway.

"Sienna, what are you doing here?" Ava looked at me with a raised eyebrow. She was wearing jeans and a hefty-sized sweatshirt, and a bag from a sub shop was clenched in her hands.

"Oh . . ." I let go of the doorknob. "I left something in here the other day that I need." I quickly tried to think of something that could be in my office to take with me so that I would not appear to be lying.

How far off the road had I fallen?

"Well, since you're here, can you help me carry this?" She held out her food bag, which I took, and then she reached back behind her in the hallway for a small box stacked with books and charts.

"I can carry that box if it would be easier," I offered, seeing the obvious strain on her face as she balanced the box between her arms.

"No, child," she grunted. "I got this."

As she pulled the box closer to her, I noticed that all the books and charts were set so that their titles and labels could not be seen. The fact that she nearly pushed her bosom over the small box seemed to validate my suspicions that she wanted the contents of her reading material to be known only to her.

"Can you unlock the door to the chart room?" she huffed.

My heart skipped a beat, but I reminded myself that I had no reason to be worried. How would she know I was ever in there today? I smiled and nodded, pulling out the same key I'd used earlier.

"I've got some charts to review and thought I'd get it done before the hustle and bustle of a new workweek begins," she said, answering my unasked question as she dropped the box on the floor of the chart room and began sliding it with her foot across the room.

"I was here earlier but had to run and get something to eat. You can set my food down right over on that desk." She pointed a finger but then immediately frowned.

The Monroes' chart was where I had left it—where I had found it—but it was closed.

I remembered at that moment that it had been open when I first found it.

Ava had been studying the Monroes, and now she was studying me, a hint of fear surfacing in her eyes.

"So, Sienna, I know this past week has been hard on you. Are things better now?" She was fishing for answers, for information, for something, but doing it in such a way as to avoid tipping me off about her intentions. I decided to do the same.

"Yeah, it has been kind of challenging this week, but I'm moving forward." I gave my best smile, hoping that she would just think that she'd closed the folder on her own. If I avoided acting awkward, then she'd have no reason not to believe that I was at the office for the purpose I'd stated.

I wanted more information before I talked to her about Dayonna, but she, apparently, was ready to bring up the issue herself.

"I'm researching Dayonna and the Monroes since I took you off the case. I'm going to handle this one myself." She nodded casually at the closed folder as I sat down her bagged sub. The scents of mozzarella cheese and a hearty Italian sauce wafted through the greasy brown bag.

"That makes sense," I replied. And it was true. There was no reason that her looking through the Monroes' chart would be odd, uncalled for, or suspicious.

Except that the chart had been opened to a page connecting the couple to Second Zion. And Tremont's name was in their history. And disturbing texts were being sent to all involved. And now the music director, the couple, and the client in question were all gone.

Of course, I could not tell her any of these facts without providing an explanation as to how I found out.

I'd rocked the boat so much, the whole thing was tipping over.

"Roman's okay?" She blinked, changing the conversation, I got the sense, for both of our benefits.

Except her question was a loaded one of its own.

"Hmmm." Is all I could get out.

"Why don't you take Monday off too?" she said a little too quickly, and she knew it. "I mean, if you think it would help with whatever is going on with Roman. I can tell he's got you worried about something." She let out a nervous chuckle.

Was she that eager to keep me away from Dayonna and the Monroes?

I was not used to having such a strained conversation with my mentor and friend.

"Um, I'm having dinner with him tomorrow at my mom's house, with my sister and . . . and a friend." The thought of Leon sitting at my mother's table warmed me for a brief second. "Hopefully, with all that backup help, I'll have him straightened out before the weekend is over."

"Oh, okay." She nodded and offered a broad smile. "Just let me know. About Monday."

She quieted and stood still.

"All right." I backed up toward the doorway, realizing that she was waiting for me to leave. "I will let you know."

As I traveled back down the elevator, I did not know what bothered me more: the questions I had about the Monroes or the new questions I had about Ava.

Why was she acting so strangely toward me? What was she trying to hide?

Roman was asleep in his bed when I returned home. I knew only because his door was open and a trail of potato chip crumbs led right to where he lay, bundled up in the mola quilt RiChard had sent us from Panama. Seeing him curled up in the warm, vibrant colors of the handmade patterned blanket, I remembered bundling him up in the quilts my mother handed down to me when he was first born.

I remembered watching him sleep back then, his miniature lips sucking an invisible breast as I stroked the tiny curls that framed his round face. I remembered the vast terrain of feelings I held on to during that first year of his life. Wonder at his perfection. Resolve to succeed as a single mother. Anger that his father was not there to share those precious moments of loving on his son.

Then again, had those feelings ever really left?

Roman stirred a little in his sleep, and it took all I had not to go over and pat down the curls that still framed his chubby face. Instead, I reached to turn off the desk light, which he'd left on. As I clicked it off, my elbow bumped his computer mouse and the screen jumped to life.

A map of Portugal filled the window, and snapshots of its people and culture filled frames of varying sizes all over the screen.

Roman had said he was not going to give up on finding his father. Dead or alive, I knew. But what could a fourteen-year-old boy do? I shook my head, grieving for the pain that I knew would be the only thing he'd find.

That was all I'd found over the years searching for RiChard. Pain. Hope for a different outcome had withered away and shriveled up in me, like an aged woman who'd lived a too harsh life. Like I'd told Roman earlier that day, I was done.

I took one last look at the map and then headed out of the darkened room, leaving the bright illustrations to blacken out on their own when the computer resumed hibernation.

But seeing the map had stirred up something in me.

A memory. A recent memory.

I'd just been staring at a map of Portugal the night before, along with that crazy teacher, Tomeeka Antoinette Ryans, and the model wannabe, Luca, in my ill attempt to reach somebody who could talk to someone at the crematorium in Portugal.

Luca had said he was from Perugia, Italy, the same city that was the birthplace of RiChard's mother.

Perhaps I still had one last hand to play. I just needed direction on how to play it.

And how to win.

Chapter 47

Sunday morning.

It was the first time I'd opened my eyes to a new week since my world fell off its course. First the ashes, then losing Hope, and now . . .

And now I didn't even know.

I decided to dedicate the entire day to church and to Roman. It had been a trying week for him, and for me because of him, and I guess I'd been holding on to the thought—the hope, Hope?—that everything concerning him would be perfected.

There was a Bible verse that went something like that, I remembered—God perfecting that which concerned me. I sat up in my bed, rubbed the sleep out of my eyes, and reached for my nightstand drawer.

"Where is my Bible?" I muttered, slightly irritated and embarrassed at myself that I could not remember where I'd put the precious Word of the Most High.

All over the place.

That was how my life felt.

That was what my house looked like, except my wildflower-themed bedroom.

That was what my nerves looked like. I was sure of it, imagining all the axons and dendrites running through my body looking like frayed wires, smoking at the ends.

I fished through my nightstand and found what I was looking for: a scuffed-up paperback Bible I'd brought home from my first trip with RiChard. It was to a little village in South America. I could not even remember the village's name, but I remembered the church service we attended at a mission run by a Protestant charity. I remembered rocking along to the music, laughing along with the children, even weeping along with the women as the elderly preacher from Scotland took us through an old-fashioned tent meeting service held Colombian style. I remembered being moved to tears at the beauty, the pureness, the simplicity of the gospel being celebrated in the outdoor camp.

And then RiChard, who'd sat unusually quiet during the whole thing, complained and criticized the simple service the entire walk back to our sleeping quarters.

"The white man always comes to destroy the culture and traditions of the world's most indigenous people. Why not let them be? Why not let them worship their own gods in their own way?"

I'd nodded my head, though an unease had filled my heart. While history had many stories of crusaders destroying entire lives and livelihoods in the name of righteousness, what I had witnessed at that simple camp meeting felt like something different.

Liberation.

Acceptance.

For all who believed.

I found it odd now, when I thought about it, that out of all the Bibles I'd been given, all the ones I'd bought over the years, the one from my first trip abroad with RiChard, the one that stood like the zero point between all that was positive and negative in our tumultuous bind, that was the one I kept in my nightstand.

Despite all my training, all my travels, and all my travails, I still wrestled with the meaning of social justice.

For I know the thoughts that I think toward you, says the Lord, thoughts of peace and not of evil, to give you a future and a hope.

That was not the verse I was looking for, but the words from Jeremiah 29:11 were the ones to which my Bible opened.

A future.

And a hope.

The verse jumped from the pages in a way it never had before.

A hope.

There is a Hope.

I needed it rekindled in my heart. Hope for my future. With or without RiChard.

God knew I needed it, and He let me find it that morning. In His Word.

I admit I hadn't sat down to read the Bible in a while. Okay, I could not even remember the last time I'd cracked open a page.

But as I read that verse that Sunday morning, I declare, I felt a small bit of something flicker inside of me.

Hope.

She wasn't lost. She was in me.

Now I just had to unveil her for the rest of the world to see.

Maybe that was the meaning of social justice. Giving people—all people—Hope.

Hope for a future.

"Amen." The only word I could get out. The most sincere prayer I think I ever prayed.

"It's about time you got here. And why is Roman wearing jeans?" My mother frowned her disapproval as she studied us up and down from behind her church fan.

MORGAN AND SON FUNERAL SERVICES.

I read the calligraphy on the back of her fan and noted the stern-looking black-and-white photo of, I guessed, Morgan and his son. I knew the picture of the two men in black suits standing next to a large flower arrangement was meant to offer an appropriate amount of somberness to such a weighty matter, but did they really have to look so solemn?

My mind was. All. Over. The. Place.

Roman and I had just joined in the eleven o'clock service at New Eden Baptist Church, the house of worship I'd been a member of, along with my family, since I was three years old. It was a small congregation of about three hundred people, and most of the congregants came from one of five families. My mother, Isabel Davis, had been one of the only stand-alones when she joined decades ago. My father attended the church twice a year: Easter sunrise service and New Year's Eve.

I'd been pretty active with my church family for most of my life, singing with the children's, then the teens', then the young adults' choirs; ushering; helping out with the monthly fried fish dinners for the building fund; and volunteering to chaperone the youth summer retreat camping trips—mostly because I did not trust those little girls around Roman out in the wild. I showed up every Sunday, paid my tithes biweekly, and helped organize the annual vacation Bible school that outreached to the children in our Woodlawn neighborhood.

Basically, I'd done everything there was to do with and at my church. I'm not saying that I was bored with it. Pastor McKinney gave a rousing word from the pulpit most weeks, and a few people in the choir could really sing. It was just that . . . Well, I didn't know. I didn't feel settled with going there anymore. Not like I used to.

Then again, very few things in my life felt like they used to. This week had been living proof of that, as I had been searching for something or someone as evasive as the contentment and peace I realized had been missing from my days for as long as I could remember.

I was tired of where I was in my life.

Roman, for his part, tapped his fingers on my shoulder.

"Look, Ma." He pointed.

Officer Leon Sanderson was walking down the center aisle, trying to find a seat in the packed sanctuary. He spotted us and headed toward our pew. Roman reluctantly moved his knees to let Leon slide by and sit next to me. Between the sneer on Roman's face and the curiosity on my mother's, I knew Sunday dinner was bound to be interesting.

It had been years since anyone had seen a member of the male species besides my son intentionally sit next to me in church. Did I say years? Maybe the correct word was *never*.

"Hope you don't mind me coming here today, but since I was coming to Sunday dinner at your mom's house, thought I'd join you for church too. Would have felt a little strange to have Sunday dinner without Sunday service."

When Leon leaned in to talk to me, I picked up the scent of soap and spice, the smell of fresh, clean man. I was afraid to inhale too deeply as I was already lightheaded from the mixture of emotions twisting my stomach into knots.

"No problem. Good to see you," I whispered with too big of a smile. I knew it was too big because he immediately looked uncomfortable.

"I really just want to help with Roman. He's got so much going for him, and I feel like he's in a dangerous life position. Too close to the edge. I don't want to see another young man fall off under my watch."

"I'm glad you're here. And you'll be glad you are too when you taste my mother's chicken and dumplings."

He gave a polite smile and focused again on the service. My mother patted the back of my hand and then stood to join along with the choir's song, her soprano voice ringing out louder than anyone's.

People were singing and shouting and praising the Lord. I just wanted the day to end with my life and my son and my future and my hope back on track.

And, I realized, I also wanted Leon to feel comfortable around me again.

That realization scared me, and I was not quite sure why.

Chapter 48

"And this right here is an authentic Roy Campanella autographed baseball bat. You know who he was, right? The legendary catcher for the Brooklyn Dodgers. Started out in the Negro Leagues."

"This is fascinating. You have quite a collection here." Comfort was the last thing showing on Leon's face.

My father was giving Leon a tour of his extensive sports memorabilia collection, housed in the basement of my parents' Randallstown split-level home. Usually on Sunday afternoons Alvin Davis budged from his recliner only when my mother finished putting all the serving platters filled with piping hot delicacies on their dining room table. Today, however, he had immediately sprung into action when Leon showed up behind me at their front door.

He had followed me to their home. My mother, who usually lingered after church to talk to her friends and finish whatever plans were needed for whatever function she was working on, had rushed home before us and appeared to be fixing two more dishes to go along with her chicken and dumplings, cabbage, and hot buttered rolls feast.

"Smells r—really good in here," Leon stammered and smiled at my mother, who had suddenly appeared next to my father.

"Oh, I hope you'll like the brown-sugared carrots and the apple pie I whipped up to go along with the chicken and dumplings. They're my mother's recipes with my own special twists." She winked. She was wearing my grandmother's apron, something she wore only on Thanksgiving and Grandma Lucy's birthday.

Inviting Leon over had been a mistake.

I knew it the moment my father began telling Leon the story about how he'd gotten his job as a delivery truck driver for a local bakery.

"I drive a truck for old man Antonello's bakery down in Little Italy," my father had begun not even three minutes after Leon stepped into the den. "And he told me on my first day that he was going to fire me when I finished my shift 'cause he did not want no coloreds near his bread. He'd only hired me to prove to his wife that he wasn't racist." My father chuckled. "Been there thirty years now, and we play poker every third Thursday. I usually win."

The last time I'd heard the story was when I made the mistake of inviting my classmate Terrance Goodwin over for a Friday game night at my parents' home. I was sixteen at the time and desperate to secure a senior prom date.

You would have thought I had told my parents that I had found the love of my life back then, that Terrance was a millionaire, and he was about to move the entire family to a villa in the Virgin Islands, the way my parents gushed and drooled over him.

Even after Terrance failed to ask me to the prom, my mother had still insisted that we have his parents over for dinner.

They declined.

"This right here is a signed boxing glove from Evander Holyfield. If you look real close, you can make out teeth marks from Mike Tyson." It was the same corny joke I'd heard when my parents told me to come over for dinner, only for me to find out that Mom's best friend's nephew "happened" to be coming over to help her fix a cabinet.

Roman had been four years old at the time. RiChard's name was never mentioned. And the nephew turned out to be married.

I was too, I reminded my parents that night, and my father disappeared again into his recliner.

The only time my father had been quiet at dinner with a man sitting next to me was that Thanksgiving RiChard sat at our dining room table. My father had only grunted while gnawing on a roasted turkey drumstick and then had sat in silence in the den with the television off and the lights on dim.

That was worse than him talking.

Men and dinners at my parents' house never mixed. I wanted to kick myself for not remembering this basic fact.

But this is for Roman, I told myself. Leon asked to be a part of this. To help Roman.

I looked over at my son, who was staring at me like I had set fire to his Wii and poured acid on his iPod. I didn't think I'd ever seen Roman look so angry.

It was disturbing.

Yvette and Skee-Gee had not yet arrived.

"Leon, what are you doing for Thanksgiving?" My mother beamed as all of us headed back up the steps. I wanted to lie down on them.

"I, um, usually spend it with my grandmother." He was not even smiling anymore.

I was actually glad to hear a knock on the door.

"Oh, good. That should be Yvette and Sylvester," my mother squealed and grabbed her oven mitts. "Go get the door, See-See, and I'll get the food out of the oven."

I didn't know what disturbed me more, my mother calling me by my childhood nickname or Leon following me to the door. I almost expected him to run out and not look back the moment I swung it open.

Based on what happened next, I wished he had.

I knew it was a mistake for him to come, but I was not prepared for the magnitude of the error.

Chapter 49

"You."

The single pronouncement stung like a single slap; the accusation in her tone sizzled with pure disgust.

"Yvette, let's start this off right. We came to help our sons make peace." I did not even know why I'd bothered with my mother's proposed solution, other than to make sure I got a take-home plate of her dumplings. I was beginning to wonder if the savory poultry stew was worth all this drama.

Yes.

I just had to endure it.

And then take my foil-covered plastic plate home.

"What are you doing here?" My sister's venom still spewed. She had not moved from the doorway.

"Yvette, why are you . . ." It was only then that I realized she was not staring at me.

Leon.

"Ma, what's the holdup?" Skee-Gee asked from behind her. He looked ready to push her the rest of the way through the door.

But she still did not budge.

"Sylvester, we are not going into this house. Not while the man who is responsible for your father's death is standing in there."

"Who the—" Skee-Gee began, but Leon cut him off.

"Sylvester Tyese Grantley the third, you look just like the second. I've been wanting to meet you . . . you both

. . . for some time." Leon seemed completely oblivious to the hatred oozing out of Yvette's eyes. Tears were filling up in his own.

"What are you doing here?" Yvette asked again, this time her voice a hoarse whisper.

"Teaching your son and Sienna's son a lesson about forgiveness."

"You can keep your lessons and your lies to yourself. Come on, Sylvester." She turned back toward the porch.

"No," Leon demanded. "This needs to happen. For you. For me. For Sienna. For your sons."

"I ain't stayin' for this." Yvette grabbed Skee-Gee by the elbow and started down the walkway.

"I never lied. I was undercover." Leon's voice cracked. "I was just trying to figure out who killed my brother. Everything went wrong. And when he pointed the gun at me . . . Well, you know what happens when someone doesn't put down their weapon when surrounded by cops."

"Sly did not kill your brother," my sister huffed as she spun back around. I tried to remember the loose details surrounding the death of Skee-Gee's father years ago.

Yvette had never talked much about her first love. In that regard, we truly were sisters.

"Sly betrayed my brother Lewis." Leon's gaze was intense. "Set him up. Sly didn't pull the trigger, but he might as well have. Lewis was beaten up so badly before getting shot, my grandmother only recognized his gold tooth."

"Sly did not pull the trigger on your brother, but you pulled it on Sly." Yvette crossed her arms, her eyes narrow slits.

"No. I didn't." Leon's arms were raised as if in surrender. "Another officer's bullet was the one found in Sly's heart. I didn't do it, but I've spent most of the last decade and a half wishing I did. And that's just as wrong."

Yvette shook her head as tears streamed down her face. "Why are you here?" she demanded again.

"I came tonight to tell you, to tell Sly's son, that I have forgiven his father. Not because he deserved it—because he *did* set up my little brother—but I need to be free. Both Sly and Lewis have been dead going on fifteen years. At some point, I can't let the pain control my life anymore. Forgiveness. That's all. It's not that I will forget or even understand what happened, but I need to be free, and forgiving is the only way to that. Now, Roman and Sylvester, I know you're fighting over the missing ring, but I think it's deeper than that. That ring stands for something missing in both of your lives. Your fath—"

Roman was nearly airborne as he lunged and landed on Leon.

"Shut up! Don't talk about my father! He is not missing. He is coming back, and you need to leave my mother alone!"

My son was all fists and tears and yells as everyone except Yvette and Skee-Gee grabbed him to pull him off of Leon.

Within seconds, my father was holding Roman back by the arms, and Leon was wiping a stream of blood off his bottom lip.

"See?" Yvette sucked her teeth. "That's exactly how Roman beat on my son. Y'all always acting like everything Sienna do is perfect, and she can't even control her own child. And where is *her* husband? Ya'll can say what you want about me, but everyone knows where all my children's fathers are. Only death or jail could keep them from being here for me and my children."

Skee-Gee joined the verbal assault. "And why ain't you shooting up Roman? He just jumped you and banged the mess out of you, and all my father did was look you in the eye man-to-man and you unloaded your gun."

I wanted to say that according to Leon's story, Sylvester's father had a pointed and loaded gun in his hand at the time of his death; that Leon did not kill him; that Skee-Gee had not been born yet when it happened; that I was a good mother; that my son was hurting; that RiChard had told me he loved me . . . that he had blood on his hands; that I was tired of hurting, of crying in my room, of pretending, of going through the motions, of living life with no joy, no purpose, no hope of feeling like I could ever truly recover from the decision I'd made back in 1994 to chase a man around the world who was never running toward me.

Hope.

The whole week piled on top of me. The whole week, *the whole past seventeen years*. Everything piled on top of me, and then I realized I was crying.

Sobbing.

"I'm sorry, Sienna. I only wanted to help. I'm sorry." Leon's voice sounded distant, and I realized he was standing outside.

Leaving.

Yvette and Sylvester were already gone.

My father had disappeared into the basement with Roman.

All that was left was me, my mother, and her serving platters sitting cold on the dining room table.

"Let Roman stay the night here. Your father will calm him down. Go home, Sienna. Go home and get yourself together. Roman does not need to see you like this. He can stay here, and we'll make sure he gets to school tomorrow."

"Mom, RiChard—"

My mother abruptly raised her hand. "I don't want to hear about it. About *him*." She shook her head firmly and pressed her lips tightly together. "Go home, Sienna. Get yourself together. I don't want to hear anything else about . . . it."

I still don't remember walking to the door, but somehow I did. I know I did, because I was standing on my mother's front porch, staring back at her, when she finally uttered the words I'd been waiting to hear from her since the day I returned from my last trip with RiChard, the one to KwaZulu-Natal.

"Sienna, I told you so."

Chapter 50

For I know the thoughts that I think toward you, says the Lord, thoughts of peace and not of evil, to give you a future and a hope.

I had started my Sunday by reading and rereading those words in Jeremiah. The day had begun with promise, a sweet reprieve from what had been a difficult week. I had wanted to believe that the words were meant for me, to encourage my spirit, to sustain me.

Now, alone in my house, I sat on the sofa, reading the words again, wondering if the message in them was really meant for me. I couldn't even say that questions filled my mind. Just facts.

My son was hurting in places I had not realized.

Leon was hurting in ways that he had never disclosed before tonight.

My parents were probably hurting. Yvette was hurting. Even Skee-Gee in his own way was hurting.

All this hurt in the world and what was there to do about it?

RiChard had tried to do his part but had left only more pain in his wake.

Was it even possible to be a vessel of healing without there being hurt involved? I thought about Leon, and how he had wanted to use his story to help Roman. He'd meant well, but everything had collapsed and quickly.

"Where is this hope, Lord? And this future? Who is it for?" My lips were cracked and dry, telling me that my tears had left me dehydrated.

"Is there really hope for me? My life feels a mess."

I thought about Jesus, how he died to bring healing to the world. But hurt had still been involved. He *died*.

Leon's words from the other day came to mind. *No need to try and save the world while your own soul is getting lost. That's why Jesus's sacrifice was so perfect. He was blameless. His motives were pure.*

But didn't RiChard have a pure heart? Weren't Leon's motives right?

I thought about all the work I had done as a social worker so far, the people I'd tried to help, the children I'd tried to protect, the vulnerable I'd tried to shield. I'd always put in my best efforts, as did most of the other social workers I'd been privileged to work with and under.

And yet burnout still came.

Hurt still surfaced.

I was tired of thinking about it, of trying to figure it all out. I crashed back into the cushions of my sofa. With nothing better to fill my time or my head, I grabbed the remote and clicked on the television.

"Great. Just the thing to cheer me up. The evening news." I pulled the sweatshirt I was wearing down to my knees and reached for the last of the warmed-up chocolate chip cookies Leon had brought over the other night.

A few days ago I could not get the man out of my house. Now I could not get him out of my mind.

And now, judging by the way he seemed to back up automatically anytime I was near, he seemed intent on staying as far away as possible.

I let the chocolate morsels glide over my tongue, finding solace in the bittersweet flavor. I curled into the corner of my sofa, ready to camp out in my living room for the night with my cookies and my cable TV.

"And back to the breaking news we reported at the top of the hour." The newscaster looked intently into the camera. "A local mega-church has been rocked by scandal with the release of pictures suggesting an affair between the music director, Tremont Scott, and the pastor's young wife, Marcie LaRue."

I jumped to full attention, turning up the volume and moving closer to the flat screen as blurred images of the snapshots Tremont had been e-mailed yesterday filled the screen, followed by still shots of the mega-ministry building.

"Oh, no." My hands covered my mouth as I watched the remainder of the report in horror. The news anchor explained that the photos had been submitted anonymously. Though I was certain it was only a matter of time before it was proven that the pictures had been manipulated, I knew the damage had already been done.

I had known this was a possibility, but I had never imagined it would come to pass.

Was this my fault? For searching for Hope?

I had tried to leave it alone. I had tried to ignore the questions that had arisen. Someone had tried to warn me and those around me to stop pursuing Hope.

But now I felt like it was up to me to expose the truth, whatever it might be.

Someone meant to quiet me, but they'd only lit a fire. And the fact that the church had been targeted was significant. Perhaps it wasn't me they were worried about. Special care had been taken to discredit the ministry of Second Zion, and especially Tremont Scott.

Why and who? And where is Hope?

She had to exist. I was sure of it. Why else would any-one go to great lengths to hurt so many people?

I stood to my feet, paced the room, bit what was left of my pinkie nail. It was late, but I had to do some-thing. Fast. I thought I would come up with some mas-ter plan, but whoever the master planner was behind this was quicker than me.

The story had not aired more than five minutes ago, and my cell phone was already ringing.

"Sienna." It was Tremont Scott, and he sounded out of breath. "Who have you talked to? We need to figure this out."

"Wait," I responded. "First, tell me where you are."

There was an unmistakable pause. When Tremont spoke again, he was whispering. "I can't really get into it right now, but I think you were on to something when you began to suspect that the Monroes are hiding secrets."

"I know they are with you. You picked them up today and took them somewhere. Along with Dayonna."

There was another pause, this one lasting longer than the first.

"Okay, you're right. They are with me. But things are more complicated than I realized. I will fill you in on everything, but I really don't want to do so over the phone. I'm going to give you a call sometime tomorrow with an address where we can meet. Until things blow over with these photos, I'm going to be keeping a low profile. Bishop's orders. I'm sure you understand."

"I do." But there was so much I didn't.

"Good. I will call you sometime tomorrow. And the whole truth, at least what I know, will be put out there on the table for you and for whoever else needs to know."

We hung up, and I was too tired to figure out what had just happened in that phone call. What I did know was that I could not wait for someone to explain to me what was going on. Something Tremont had said jumped out at me. *Who had I talked to?*

Though I had not even whispered Hope's name or added anything else about Dayonna, there was somebody who knew that I had been trying to get more info.

Ava Diggs.

It was almost midnight, but I headed over, anyway. I had been close to Ava for years, and this would not be my first late-night visit to her home in Towson. There had been two other times. The first was when I thought I was going to have a mental breakdown trying to balance a full-time class load and a full-time job working for the state's food stamp program. The other time had to do with Roman and an issue he was having with his eighth grade teacher that was driving me crazy.

This time I just wanted answers. She had to know something. Or at the very least, she had to know there was something that needed to be found out about the Monroes. Earlier that day both she and I had been looking through their chart. I knew why I was.

Now I wanted to know why she was.

The breaking news story told me that someone did not want me after them and that I was getting close.

Towson, a liberal, affluent, college-oriented suburb known for its high-end mall and growing city center, was about fifteen minutes east of me, just off 695. Ava lived in a small enclave of homes that made up one of the oldest African American communities in the county, East Towson, a residential area that bordered downtown Towson. A tiny AME church and a community center known for its affordable summer youth camp sat near the ninety-year-old, renovated Cape Cod Ava called home. Brilliant chrysanthemums in shades of orange, yellow, and red graced the steps that led to the huge wraparound porch, which held a porch swing and several potted flowers.

I rang the doorbell and was surprised that of all people, Sheena Booth answered.

Chapter 51

"What are you doing here?" My head jerked back.

"I should be asking *you* the same thing," she retorted. "I told you, I'm not trying to lose my job because of something you did."

"I haven't done anything except try to find out the truth about a little girl named Hope."

Sheena narrowed her eyes. "Sienna, are you still trying to figure out that crazy Hope Diamond story you heard from your client?"

"Look, Sheena, can you please just tell me why you are here? And where is Ava?"

Sheena sighed and looked back over her shoulder. "Out here," she directed and stepped out onto the porch with me, closing the door behind her. "You know my old connection at DSS, Roland, the one you called earlier this week?"

I nodded, remembering the man with the attitude who, Sheena had warned me, knew everything and everybody.

"Well, he called me a couple of hours ago, saying that he'd heard that Ava might be in a boatload of trouble, and that I better jump ship while I can. That's all he told me, but you know me. I can't just sit on that type of info, so I called her, and she sounded so hysterical when she answered the phone, I drove right down here. She's been on the phone the whole time I've been here, though. I don't know who she's talking to, and I can't

hear a word of what she's saying. You think you can
find anything out?"

I'd been nodding, trying to follow along, still not sure
that I saw a connection between Dayonna's story and
Ava's agency. "Let me go talk to her."

"Okay. I'm going to go for now, but call me the moment you figure out what's going on." Sheena left as
I walked into the warm comfort of Ava Diggs's living
room

Well, usually it was warm comfort. In addition to being a phenomenal social servant, Ava also had a keen
decorator's eye. The hues and arrangements she'd created for her foyer and living room let you know that the
rest of the house was worth exploring. And I do mean
exploring. Ava had one of those kinds of houses that
you wanted to browse, recognizing that each piece of
artwork, each afghan throw, dish, or charm had been
carefully chosen and artfully placed. At the moment,
everything was as neat and perfect as usual.

But a quiet chill had filled the room. Aside from the
heat being off and the night being cool, the warm, inviting spirit that made Ava's home a sanctuary seemed to
be missing.

I found her sitting in the kitchen, staring at a weath-
ered white cupboard. When I sat down next to her at
the small table she kept near a window, she barely
moved her head. We sat there in silence for a few long
moments.

"That cupboard," she finally began, "I found it at a
yard sale years ago."

"It's nice."

"Oh, it wasn't always." She let out a slight chuckle.
"When I first saw it, it was an ugly shade of brown.
The doors and shelves were crooked. The hinges were
barely hanging on."

"I know you are good at restoring things. I remember the desk you fixed up for the office."

"That old thing was a mess too, but this cupboard was the most difficult project I undertook. The people who sold it to me let me have it for three dollars. They would have probably given it to me for free, that's how bad a shape it was in. But I took it and worked on it for about five weekends. I sanded it down, painted it, put on new hardware, and now it's one of my favorite possessions."

"It's beautiful, Ava."

"That's what Holding Hands has been like for me. The work I do. My entire career. I started working on it with nothing, with clients and foster children who were broken, scuffed, neglected, and abused. And I put hours of labor into it, *into them*." She looked straight at me. "And I have watched many families and lives become whole and beautiful because I was willing to see their beauty and worth before anyone else did and invest in what was needed to make them shine. That's what I've done, Sienna."

"Yes."

"But now I've invested in the wrong thing, I think. I knew it was too good to be true." She looked away.

There were two charts sitting on the table in front of her. Silver utensils sat on either side of the short stack of paperwork and a green vinyl place mat sat underneath, altogether making the charts look like plates for serving. I thought it fitting. Ava lived, breathed, and was sustained by the work she did. Her job was her calling. Without her work, she would not be a fulfilled woman.

That was when I knew everything would somehow turn out all right.

But just as Jesus's sacrifice caused unbearable pain on some level, there would be hurt or suffering involved somewhere, somehow in the current circumstances.

I felt it but did not know where the ax would finally fall.

"Tell me what you know, Ava."

She turned to face me again. "You were right. About the Monroes. Something does not add up about them. I've been searching their charts all day. Reading through each line, trying to figure out what I missed. I don't usually miss anything, Sienna."

"I know."

"They are definitely hiding something."

"You mean like a child?" My heart skipped a beat. *Hope.*

"No. I don't mean like that. I guess a better way to say it is that they're covering up something. You know, Sienna, I really do not know what is going on." She tapped on the charts absentmindedly. I noticed for the first time that in addition to the Monroes', Tremont's chart was in the pile.

"You did not change his chart over to microfiche." I nodded.

"No, that boy was such a mess, I kept his file in the bottom of my drawer. I used to check it from time to time when I had an especially difficult case to remind myself of how not to handle things. I got a lot of on-the-job training from trying to deal with him. I'm glad God got a hold of his life, because truly divine intervention was his only hope."

"What kind of problems did he create?"

"Oh, honey, he was into drugs back in the day. Selling them, not using them. Drugs, and everything else that comes with that world."

"What was his relationship like with the Monroes?"

"That's what I'm trying to figure out now."

"You know they're all gone now. Dayonna too."

She frowned. "Can't say that I'm surprised. I feel like I missed something with them. I should have known something was up when I got the first installment."

"Installment?" I raised an eyebrow.

Ava let out a huge sigh. "Remember when I first told you that I wanted you to work on Dayonna's case? And I said that I needed it to work?"

"Oh, yes." I chuckled. "I remember. You seemed pretty intent on stressing that the arrangement between the Monroes and Dayonna needed to work, even when I told you I didn't think it could, given the girl's extensive placement history."

"You asked me then why it was so important that the placement work. I downplayed your question, but there was a reason. A true, legitimate reason. A noble one, a just one, I might add."

I watched my mentor blink back tears as she continued.

"Like I told you, times are different now than when I first founded Holding Hands almost thirty years ago. Back then it was more acceptable to help the most vulnerable. People and corporations were always willing to give out donations that assisted those in need. With the recent economic downturn and the shift toward viewing the poor as somehow evil or lazy and solely responsible for their own fates, funds for social programs for people who need it the most have dried up. Budgets have been slashed. Policies have been changed. So many nonprofits and community agencies have had to close their doors.

"Holding Hands has not been exempt from the times, Sienna. If you knew how close to the edge our budget runs each month, you'd be amazed that nobody's pay check has bounced. It's only been the grace of God that has kept us afloat. God's grace and the generosity of his people."

She slid an envelope toward me. It was addressed to her, and the return label had the logo and address of Second Zion Tabernacle.

"Open it, Sienna."

I lifted up the flap and pulled out the contents, a single piece of paper. A check. In the amount of five thousand dollars. It was made out to Holding Hands Agency. The payer was listed as Second Chance Ministry.

"What is this?"

"I've been getting grant money every month from this particular ministry. Mostly a thousand or two, if that much. For years. However, when I found out from DSS that Dayonna's case was coming to us a couple of weeks ago, the grant suddenly increased. I even received a letter from Second Chance stating that if we could keep Dayonna successfully with the Monroes, the monthly grant would increase to ten thousand dollars. Ten thousand dollars is a lot of money, Sienna, and with a guaranteed grant coming in every month in that amount, it would go a long way in helping to keep things afloat."

I guess it made sense, but there were still too many questions unanswered. I did not even know where to begin, but I remembered Sheena had come over in a panic, afraid that her job was coming to an end.

"Tremont and Second Zion are the leading news story tonight. What does this mean for you?"

"That's what I've been trying to figure out. There was a letter in my mailbox when I came home from the office today. Ever since you started saying that something did not seem right about the Monroes, I could no longer ignore that I've had the same feeling, as well. I started trying to figure out what the connection was between Second Zion and Dayonna and the grant I get from Second Chance every month. That's why I was studying their chart earlier today."

"So is Second Chance not related to Second Zion? The check came in an envelope with the church's letterhead." My brain hurt trying to piece this all together.

"Second Chance is a ministry of Second Zion. It's the official name of the alcohol and substance abuse ministry that—"

"Horace Monroe is the chairperson of." We said it together. I remembered that the chart had been open to that page when I found it in the chart room back at the office earlier that day. I could only imagine how Ava must have felt when she realized that Mr. Monroe was somehow paying her to keep Dayonna in his house.

"Do you think the church knows that the ministry Horace oversees has been giving out money to you every month?"

"No, I don't think so. I spoke to someone in the administrative office today and asked if they gave out grants through the substance abuse ministry, and the secretary to whom I spoke had no idea what I was talking about."

"So this is Horace's doing. Where's he getting all this money from?" I wondered aloud.

"I have no idea. Sienna, this was in my mailbox when I got home from the office this evening." She passed me a sheet of paper. It was purple and lined, but the handwriting on it was different from the one that was on the notes Dayonna had left in my car earlier in the week.

Someone who'd had access to Dayonna's things had written this note and left it.

Watch the eleven o'clock news. Leave Hope Diamond alone, or Holding Hands will be shut down before the week is over.

"Sienna, I cannot pretend to even know what this means, but I need you to find out. I can't handle it anymore. You are on field duty tomorrow. Find out what is going on. I can't handle it anymore."

Chapter 52

Tremont was supposed to call me. I was supposed to call Sheena. I wanted to call Leon. Roman called me instead.

"It's four o'clock in the morning."

Not the way I normally greeted my son on the phone, especially considering the way the weekend had gone, but I was half asleep and didn't know where I was or who I was when I answered my cell phone.

"Mom, I'm sorry."

"Oh, Roman . . ." My voice was hoarse as I struggled to sit up in my bed. "You don't have to apologize. You know that you can call me anytime, day or night, for any reason."

"No, Mom, that's not why I'm apologizing. I mean, I'm sorry for waking you, but I really just wanted to say that I'm sorry about last evening. And for how I've been for the past few days."

I did not want to say the wrong thing in my sleepy state, so I focused on just listening to him and trying to wake up.

"I'm sorry, Mom," he repeated again. "I feel real bad about how I've been acting. And . . . and how I jumped on Officer Leon like that. It was wrong. He's only been trying to help me. I just . . . don't understand why . . . my father isn't here for me . . . or for you."

I blinked back tears. "I'm sorry too, Roman."

"We're going to be okay, Mom."

I had to smile. "Yes, we will. And listen, not that it is any of your business, but I have no desire to be in any relationships until I figure out what happened to your father. I'm a married woman until I know otherwise."

"Well, it looks like Officer Sanderson feels the same way. I don't know why I got so upset with him when it's obvious he doesn't want to be anywhere near you."

The truth of Roman's words stung. I kept the smile on my face only to keep fresh tears from falling.

Who would have thought I'd have the hots for ole Leon? *Ew.* I felt like I was sixteen again.

"And another thing, Mom," Roman continued. "I thought you said you were done trying to figure out what happened to Dad."

"Yeah, I know I said that, but there is one more thing I can do, I think." I added Tomeeka Antoinette Ryans to my mental checklist of people to call tomorrow. Perhaps she could help me get in touch with Luca before next Friday's scheduled class.

I wanted answers.

Now.

By any means necessary.

It was going to be a busy Monday. I needed to finish getting my sleep to get started.

"Good, Mom," Roman was saying. "I'm glad you're going to keep looking. I think I'm done with Dad for now. But I'm glad you're not losing hope."

I pondered his last words before realizing I was taking too long to respond.

"No. I'm not."

Chapter 53

By 6:30 A.M. I was dressed and ready for the day. I considered it a working day, since Ava had specifically told me to find out what I could about the Monroes and Dayonna. I had my work cut out for me and I was dressed the part, wearing a plain black pantsuit with a blue silk top and, of course, comfortable flat shoes. I'd eaten a simple breakfast of a banana and strawberry yogurt topped with granola. And, most importantly, I'd written down a list, a plan of action for the day.

I knew exactly where I was going and with whom I planned to talk.

My life had changed course last Tuesday, when the package from Portugal came in the mail and Dayonna's chart came into my hands. It was day six of the saga, and I was determined that I would not enter the next seven days with the same confusion that had defined the past week.

Today, I was going after it all.

Answers.

Conclusions.

I was moving on. I had hope, and it was moving me forward.

I pulled out my GPS the moment I got into my car. I rarely used it, and truthfully, I knew where most of the streets I needed were located. However, I wanted to be a good steward of my time today and figured that a satellite looking over me would not hurt.

Even more importantly, God looking over me would help.

"Jesus, please guide my steps today. Let me get all the information I need at this point in my life, and bring a peaceful resolution to everything that is concerning me." The quick prayer jogged my memory about a verse I'd wanted to look up yesterday morning. I let out a sigh and reached for my grandmother's Bible, still sitting on its perch in the backseat window. The moment my fingers touched the ancient pages, I remembered where to find the verse. My grandmother had taught it to me when I was a child, visiting her home on Payson Street.

Psalm 138:8.

I read it aloud to encourage myself. "The LORD will perfect that which concerns me." I was about to shut the Bible back up when the verse above caught my attention. *Though I walk in the midst of trouble, You will revive me; You will stretch out your hand against the wrath of my enemies, and Your right hand will save me.* Something about that verse gave me comfort and fear all at the same time. How often had I not picked up my Bible for that very reason? Reading some passages that were meant to encourage often had the opposite effect on me, reminding me that there was trouble to be had. Pain in the purpose. Sacrifice before redemption. Hurt before healing.

"But the LORD will perfect that which concerns me," I reminded myself again, starting the engine and entering the first destination from my notes into the GPS unit.

It was still early in the day. Very early. I was hoping that the early hour would guarantee that someone would be home to answer the door.

***

I pulled up to the colossal row home on Druid Hill Avenue just before seven. Blocks away from the neighborhood YMCA, it was a narrow residence that billowed three stories above the street, much like the row homes that surrounded it. The intricate architectural details in the brick and arches told a story of a grand past dating back to the early twentieth century. I checked and rechecked the address, knowing that I was at the right place, but feeling like something was wrong.

The row house, like my sister's in Park Heights, sat in the midst of abandoned and vacant properties. Unlike my sister's abode, however, this home shined like a new penny. Obviously recently rehabbed, the marble steps gleamed in the new day's sun. The windows were vinyl replacement ones; the paint job, though somewhat aged, stood in stark contrast to the chipped and rotten horrors of the homes next door, most of which had boarded-up windows and doors painted over with graffiti and concert posters.

The doorway of this home led to a short hallway, I quickly discovered. Three unlabeled mailboxes were nailed to the wall, telling me that the three-story row home had been converted into a multifamily unit. A door was to the left of the mailboxes, and a staircase ascended to a dark unknown at the end of the narrow alcove.

I was studying the mailboxes when the door next to me swung open. A woman the color of worn khaki opened the door and bounded out into the hallway in a firestorm. She had a protruding forehead and tiny eyes that squinted upward. An MTA monthly bus pass was in one of her hands, and a set of keys dangled from the other.

"Come on! The bus will be here any second. You need to come now so you won't be any later than you already are!" the woman screamed into the darkened apartment.

"Go ahead! I'm coming. If I miss the bus, I'll just catch the next one. Shoot!" a young girl yelled back. I could smell pancakes and bacon, and I briefly wondered if my breakfast had been enough to sustain me for all the stops I planned to make that day. I smiled, trying to figure out what it was I wanted to say to the woman, who looked like she was about to bound down the marble steps to the sidewalk.

"Something sure smells good in there." I tried.

The woman, I realized, had not noticed me standing there next to the mailboxes. She jumped, almost screamed, really, and it was probably good that she had only a bus pass and keys in her hand. Anything else and I probably would have been knocked down, the way she nearly swung at me.

"Who are you? Are you the new girl moving in upstairs?" She looked more than a little agitated at my presence.

"No, I, um . . ." I struggled with what to say. "Hi. I'm Sienna St. James. I'm a social worker with—"

"Oh, you're a social worker?" The woman immediately cut me off, backing away from me. "What you from? Child Protective Services? You must be looking for that lady that lives on the third floor. That's the one. We don't have no problems down on this level." She stuck her head back into the apartment doorway. "Girl, come on! I'm about to leave you."

"No, I'm not from CPS. I . . ."

It was no use. The woman obviously did not want to have anything to do with me. She hurried out the doorway to the street outside. I could see a bus stop a few yards from their front steps.

"Okay," I sighed, trying to push down the frustration that was already threatening to take over my morning. Although I was not sure exactly what I was going to find at the first of the Monroes' previous addresses, I had expected that something would stand out. On Saturday I'd copied down all their prior residences listed in the chart, the same chart Ava had been reading through. I'd decided to go in chronological order, and this house on Druid Hill Avenue had been the first one listed in the Monroes' file. I wondered if the house had even been fully renovated when they lived there, if it had been one single house or the multiple-occupancy dwelling that it obviously was now.

"Horace is the best at fixing up old houses," Elsie Monroe had bragged, beaming, during our first meeting. My guess was that the row house I was standing in had at one time probably looked just like the ones next to it: broken down, beaten down, and abandoned. I imagined that the renovations I saw were probably Horace's handiwork.

These were all speculations, I knew, but I had to come up with some kind of working theory to make this trip worthwhile.

I let out a sigh and headed for the exit, uncertain what else I was going to discover in this first trip of the day. *A waste of time!* I tried to convince myself otherwise. The woman I'd talked to, who was now standing at the bus stop, eyed me suspiciously and pulled her purse closer to her. I couldn't blame her. Although I'd identified myself, I was not displaying my badge, something I customarily did when I was out in the field. This woman did not know me from jack, and I, too, would be a little nervous about a stranger hanging around my front door.

I wanted to talk to her some more to attempt to explain the purpose of my visit, to find out if she had ever even heard of the Monroes. But I knew that was a hopeless task. Aside from the fact that this woman would probably not give me the time of day, I heard the loud diesel roar of an MTA bus churning down the street. The woman heard it too, pulling her purse tighter to her side, sneering at me, and letting out one final yell to the open doorway behind me.

"Dayshonique Emaleah Sapphire, get your butt out here! The bus is coming."

I felt my jaw drop and my insides freeze as a girl of about sixteen or seventeen suddenly brushed past me, dashing down the steps, a zebra-print book bag bouncing off her behind.

"I'm coming, lady!" she shouted back, her voice raspy, with more attitude than the three words could even contain.

They were on the bus before I could even make sense of what had just happened, but in the quick second that the girl looked back at me, any doubts I had were completely erased.

Add about ten pounds, two years, and a bad case of acne, and that girl, Dayshonique Emaleah Sapphire, as the woman had called her, was the spitting image of her younger sister, Dayonna Diamond.

The bus roared away, leaving me coughing in a plume of black smoke.

I got back in my car immediately, punching in the address for my next destination. I wanted to get there before whoever was there left for school or work. My heart was pounding, not out of fear, but out of a knowing and a growing excitement. I took out the paper that Dayquon had given me on Saturday.

Dayquon Hardison — November 13, 1987 (still 23)
Daynene Turquoise — December 5, 1989 (22)
Dayvita Topaz — November ? 1992 (19)
Dayshonique Sapphire — September 23, 1994 or 1995 (17 or 16)
Dayonna Diamond — April 23, 1997 (14)

I took out an ink pen and put a check mark next to Dayquon's, Dayonna's, and Dayshonique's names. The GPS was telling me to turn right, so I obeyed and found myself heading for South Baltimore.

Highlandtown was one of those neighborhoods in Baltimore City that was in rapid transition. Long a community with residents of Polish and Greek ancestry, in recent years the area had become home to immigrants of a different culture and ethnicity. Countless families from South and Central America had begun forming their own community ties here. Now the barbershops, businesses, and carryouts that lined this part of Eastern Avenue reflected the change in cultural identity, with many signs and marquees written in Spanish. I drove a little ways down Eastern Avenue before turning onto a side street, where people of all shades and dialects were beginning their Monday morning routine. In this melting pot of countries and cultures, there were some African American families and households that dotted the neighborhood of tiny row homes. I saw one such family crowding into a cab right in front of the address to which I was heading.

A pretty young woman with a weave that extended down her back was half pushing, half tugging an entourage of small children into the cab. Two girls with neat pigtails hanging down their backs, fastened with brightly colored barrettes, waited inside. A little boy of about two or three kept acting like he was going to get inside the cab. He would take one step inside of it and then run back to the sidewalk, giggling the entire time.

The young mother did not share his amusement.

"Come on, Day-Day!" She chased after him, exasperation coloring her face. "We've got to go *now!*"

I had pulled my car to the curb behind the cab. I knew from my last stop that I probably had only seconds to make a connection. I hopped out of the car just as little Day-Day came rushing by. His mother, wearing high heels and leggings that tried in vain to contain her flabby legs, struggled to chase after him. I caught the mischievous youngster just as he passed.

"Thank you!" The woman gave a curt smile, barely looking at me as she grabbed him out of my arms.

"No problem," I said, trying to follow her as she rushed to the cab, trying to see if I could get in any other words. My hustle was of no use; the cab sped off with the four occupants inside, leaving me alone in front of the house. I decided to knock on the door to see if anyone was home.

There was no answer, but confirmation of my suspicions still came. An envelope, what looked like a utility bill, was sticking out of the mailbox next to the front door.

It was addressed to Daynene Turquoise.

The oldest of the jewel-named sisters.

I pulled out my list and crossed out her name.

Chapter 54

I had not had a conversation with a single person, but I felt like I was finally getting somewhere. Only 8:15 A.M., and I had already found two of Dayonna's sisters.

Sisters who, according to their brother, Dayquon, had never been part of the foster care system.

I still had two more addresses to go. Despite my success, I had a feeling that the rest of the day's journey would not be as simple. If finding Hope was just a matter of knocking on the right former door of the Monroes, I probably would have come across her already.

Which brought me to the obvious question.

What was the relationship between the Monroes and Dayonna?

Before I went knocking on anybody else's door, I wanted to get more clues to solve that puzzle.

I was heading back to church.

Mondays were usually a quiet day for Second Zion Tabernacle, or so I'd heard. Following days of classes, rehearsals, studies, and services, Monday was the church's weekend.

Not so today.

I'd already forgotten about the breaking scandal that had taken over Baltimore's airwaves.

The music director and the bishop's wife.

I realized as I pulled into the lot that I had been expecting the story to die quickly once somebody figured out the picture was doctored.

Or so the photo had looked to me.

From the number of television vans and the swarm of journalists set up on the asphalt surrounding the huge building, I could tell that this news story was not going to die a quick death.

I parked my car to the side of the lot and searched for a quiet entrance. There was a side door near a gathering of evergreen trees. With a speedy prayer that the door would be unlocked, and an even speedier trot to reach it unnoticed, I made my move and headed straight for it.

"Are you a member of this church?" A man in a dark suit who seemed to have jumped out of the bushes stuck a padded microphone under my mouth.

"No, I am not." I raised my hand to cover my face and kept up my march toward the door.

Praise the Lord! The knob easily turned. But the news reporter was not done.

"What are your thoughts about this twisted turn of events here at Second Zion? Do you think it's true? Are you surprised at the alleged affair?" He beckoned for a cameraman to zoom in on me.

My first instinct was to turn away, but then a thought occurred to me. Whoever sent those pictures had done so, apparently, because I had been asking around about Hope. He or she wanted me to be quiet, and this was my chance to show that I was going to be anything but that.

My parents had raised a fighter, and I was married to a man who was willing to sacrifice it all for justice.

Even if I had not always followed through, it was in my nature to be bold.

I turned to face the camera full on. The news reporter smiled and motioned for the cameraman to keep taping. He just knew he was going to get a riveting statement.

"Truth always outshines lies, and no matter how dark the lies get, I will not be the one to lose or let go of Hope. I am on a mission to find Hope and to find answers, even if I have to get hurt in the process. I've been hurt enough, and I'm determined to find purpose in my pain."

The news reporter frowned and motioned for the cameraman to turn away from me. He took over the shot with a plastered smile. "There you have it, folks. Community members are acknowledging that this scandal hurts their faith, and they will not let it go until they find some answers."

"No." I grabbed the microphone. "My faith is not broken. Indeed it's been strengthened as I wait to see how the Lord will shine and show Himself strong in this darkness. A Diamond's light can't grow dim and can be hidden only for so long." I pushed the microphone away, leaving the news reporter looking both confused and irritated.

As for me, I marched through the side door, letting my own words be absorbed into my heart, soul, and spirit.

I had come a long way from the one-time college dropout who'd mistaken another person's dream for her own. I had come a long way from just last week, no longer satisfied with the monotony of my life and the seemingly unending, unsatisfying quest to rediscover myself, my own dreams, my own values.

My own plan of action.

In addition to coming a long way, I realized immediately, I had just come the *wrong* way.

As the door shut fast behind me and my eyes blinked to adjust to the dim light, I realized I was standing face-to-face with none other than the great and respected Bishop Vincent LaRue and his beautiful, smeared-upon young wife.

Chapter 55

"My dear sister, who let you in?"

This was the man who preached fiery sermons on Saturday nights and Sunday mornings, who led a flock of thousands, who commanded the respect of city, even state, leaders.

And yet his voice in person, two feet away from me, had the quality of doves and quiet rainstorms—gentleness.

That was what it felt like, anyhow, as I stood there dumbfounded, uncertain what to say to this much-revered man of God, who had, it seemed, at least half the city of Baltimore under his sway.

"The door was unlocked," I finally managed to say, looking up into his deep brown eyes. I saw the fire in them, the boldness, the pureness of them, and I knew that this was a man who spent time with the Master.

There would be no playing games or sidestepping in here. I swallowed, wondering why I suddenly felt so exposed.

"Well, God must have a reason for you to be here. There are no coincidences in God's Kingdom." He smiled. "That door is always locked, but for some reason, somehow, you got in. Come in. Join the circle. We were just about to have prayer."

I looked around, realizing that the "we" was the bishop's true inner circle. Aside from his wife, Marcie, I recognized a few of the five or so faces as men and

women who served on his ministerial staff, the director of the church's deacon board, and the leader of the
church's youth movement. A smile from the corner of
the room caught my eye, and I smiled back.

Mother Ernestine Jefferson.

Marcie LaRue's grandmother, the wife of the late,
great elder.

The woman who'd said she'd had a husband like
mine. *The kind that can't be explained to nobody but
Jesus.*

My smile grew even wider as I considered the impos-
sibility of the comparison. There was no way that she,
the wife of a gospel great, could ever relate to my tale
of missing love, broken promises, differing priorities,
and, well, murdering mayhem.

I shut my eyes hard to block out the image of RiChard's bloody hands. I had to stay focused on my task
today.

Even still, my eyelashes were wet.

"Come join us." Marcie LaRue, the cool, calm, collected epitome of stress management, held out her
hand, making me realize I was holding up the prayer
session thinking about RiChard.

How many more times was I going to let that man—
dead or alive—hold me up from my own life? I swallowed the bitterness down and grabbed hold of the first
lady's damp palm.

I guess I had been expecting moans and groans,
shaking and quaking, and long, drawn-out petitions of
desperation and tears.

That was what I would be doing if my reputation and
ministry were on the line.

Instead the prayer was simple; the plea succinct.

"Father," the bishop began, "we know that no weapon formed against us shall prosper.

The enemy of our souls thought he could bind us with false reports, but we know that Your report will prevail. We ask you, Lord, that Your perfect plan will be revealed and that we will simply be obedient to Your moving. Thank You for this time of testing so that we may draw closer to You. Bless the ones behind this so that they will be moved to repentance and also draw close to You. We trust You. Our hope is in You. And now we praise You, for You have already perfected this situation. In Jesus's name, let's praise Him together, for we will not be moved."

And then a chorus of praise rang out from those standing in the circle. Not a flashy show of shallow shouts, but a quiet air of awe and reverence.

Standing there, holding hands with people who truly did not appear shaken, I felt something settle inside my own spirit. A calming, a peace.

It began when I found my way to worship. It continued as Mother Jefferson, sitting outside the circle, in a padded chair, quietly began quoting the entire sixty-second Psalm.

Truly my soul silently waits for God; From Him comes my salvation. He only is my rock and my salvation; He is my defense; I shall not be greatly moved. How long will you attack a man? You shall be slain, all of you, Like a leaning wall and a tottering fence. They only consult to cast him down from his high position; They delight in lies; They bless with their mouth, But they curse inwardly. My soul, wait silently for God alone, For my expectation is from Him. He only is my rock and my salvation; He is my defense; I shall not be moved. In God is my salvation and my glory; The rock of my strength, And my refuge, is in God. Trust in Him at all times, you people; Pour out your heart before Him; God is a refuge for us. Surely men of low degree are a vapor, Men of high degree are a lie; If they are weighed on the scales, They are alto- gether lighter than vapor. Do not trust in oppression, Nor vainly hope in robbery; If riches increase, Do not set your heart on them. God has spoken once, Twice I have heard this: That power belongs to God. Also to You, O Lord, belongs mercy; For You render to each one according to his work.

Like a parched tongue finding spring water in the desert, something inside of me lapped up the sacred words. Like finding food for my empty stomach, I absorbed the message and found solace for my weary way.

Pain. Betrayal.

Power and justice.

Salvation and defense.

Waiting.

And hope.

All in those words.

"Thank you, Lord." I joined the quiet chorus of praise around me. Yes, I was supposed to be there. I had not realized how much my soul needed reassurance.

Inner relief was not the only reason I was there, how- ever. I quickly marveled even more at God's purpose and timing after the prayer and praise died down. The mood in the room had gone from reflection to busi- ness. While I had been welcomed to join along with the prayer, I knew I was not going to get an invitation to the planning session. Indeed, the only reason I had not been kicked out so far, I concluded, was that Mother Jefferson had been nodding her head at the bishop about me since I first stumbled into the room.

The right person at the right time.

And then the right information.

As I headed toward a door that would take me to the main corridor, I noticed a stack of colorful brochures listing all the church's ministries. I picked one up and read through it as I entered the administrative wing of the church, which was located right next door to the pastor's conference room.

"Can I help you, ma'am?" A middle-aged woman wearing square black eyeglasses smiled at me from behind a large round desk.

"Yes," I said confidently so as not to raise suspicion. "I was looking through your list of ministries, and I had a question about the Second Chance substance abuse program led by Brother Horace Monroe." I squinted down at the brochure, as if trying to make out the tiny print. "That ministry seems to be doing a lot of good work in the community. Do you know if they get grants or any other financial support from outside the church to run their sessions and activities?" I blinked innocently.

"Um, not to my knowledge." The woman shook her head. "For the most part, all our ministries get funded directly out of the church's budget. On occasion, and with the pastor's approval, some special events or programs receive help from outside businesses or community organizations."

"Would Second Chance ever have events that would fall into that category?"

"I guess it's possible," she said, nodding, "especially with the type of work they do. I could see an outside agency collaborating with them from time to time, particularly for community outreach events that a government or local agency could get involved in to offer additional supportive services. There are too many people on drugs in this city, and the mayor always supports the church in our efforts to get those numbers down, those lives healed."

I liked the woman for her obvious optimism, her professionalism—and for not asking why I wanted all this information. I decided to ensure that the question would not even arise.

"Thanks for sharing all this with me. I'm a social worker, so sometimes I come across people or businesses that are looking to partner with programs such as those initiated by Second Chance. What would need to be done for a potential donor to offer help to this particular ministry?"

She looked at me with a sympathetic eye. I wondered if a loved one of hers battled a substance abuse problem. With the high rates of drug use in the city, as she'd correctly noted, it was highly unlikely that her life had been untouched.

"Here, let me pull that file, and I can give you the leader's contact information. I'm sure that he would be able to fill you in on that process, as I do not know the specifics."

She reached for a file cabinet behind her and shuffled through several papers before nodding her head and pulling out a thin manila folder.

"Hmmm, that's odd." She wrinkled up her face.

"What's that?" I tried not to look too eager to see what it was that had her narrowing her eyes in confusion.

"This is the folder for Second Chance Ministry, but it looks like it was emptied. There's nothing in here." She held it up for me to see, but as she did so, a small paper fell out and landed next to her desk. She did not notice it, but I did.

"What is that?" I pointed to the rectangular scrap.

"Oh, this came out of there?" She picked it up and squinted down at the tiny print. "It's a business card. Not really sure what this has to do with Second Chance. Must have fallen into the folder by accident."

She held out the card for me to see, and it took all I had to keep from snatching it out of her hand.

"Can I hold on to that?" I did my best to sound calm, despite my heart's sudden race to the finish line. "I might be able to find a use for it."

"Sure." She passed the card to me. "I'm sorry I couldn't be of more help."

"Oh, you've been plenty." I could barely hold in my excitement at this new bit of revelatory information that had literally been placed into my hand.

I tucked the card into my purse and headed toward the learning and resource wing of the mega-church building. There was a computer lab somewhere over there, and I needed an Internet connection.

Chapter 56

HIDDEN JEWELS OF THE CITY
HOME REHAB CO.

I smiled at the name of the business printed across the card and the slogan underneath: *From desolation to renovation, we turn shambles into treasures!* A scripture reference was underneath the slogan. Isaiah 54:11–12. I grabbed a nearby Bible and looked it up. Parts of the verses jumped right out at me.

Behold, I will lay your stones with colorful gems, and lay your foundations with sapphires. I will make your pinnacles of rubies, and your gates of crystal, and all your walls of precious stones.

The names of the jewels could not be a mere coincidence. I smiled, turning to the computer in front of me. A sign on the door stated that a computer literacy class would be starting in ten minutes, so I needed to hurry.

An e-mail address was the only contact information listed on the card. I knew sending an e-mail would probably serve no purpose, so I pecked the name of the company into the keyboard to do a search and waited for the results to show.

Nothing.

No Web site link, no address, no telephone number for a company with that name showed up anywhere in my search results.

I tried spelling out the word *company*, including the words *Baltimore*, *Monroe*, and even *Diamond*, for good measure.

Still nothing.

I took out my notes, which I had been carrying with me for the past couple of days. Dayquon's list of his sisters' names was on top, as I had been checking off the ones I'd found so far that morning. I typed in all their last names as a single search and added the word *homes* to see if anything would come up.

Still no information about the business.

But what did come up caught my attention just as much.

Entering the names of the various gems and stones making up the sisters' last names brought up multiple links to Web sites listing birthstones.

"Could it be?" I pulled up a site with a list of modern birthstones and double-checked the list of names and birth dates Dayquon had given me.

Dayquon Hardison — November 13, 1987 (still 23)

Daynene Turquoise — December 5, 1989 (22)

Dayvita Topaz — November ? 1992 (19)

Dayshonique Sapphire — September 23, 1994 or 1995 (17 or 16)

Dayonna Diamond — April 23, 1997 (14)

Sure enough! Each sister's last name coincided with her birthstone month. I wanted to absorb that new bit of information so I could try to figure out the significance of it, but I had only five minutes left before the computer literacy class was to begin. Indeed, the first of the attendees, a woman who reminded me of one of my great-aunts, strolled in.

"You the teacher?" she grunted, rolling toward me with her wheeled walker.

"No. I'll be out of here in a second." I did not have time to get into any conversations. Thankfully, the older woman didn't seem interested. She found a computer in a row behind me and collapsed into her chair with a loud grunt.

Lord, you've got to give me some direction. I had only three minutes left, and more class attendees were trickling in.

Then an idea.

I went to a government Web site for the state of Maryland and found a search engine that looked up business trade names. Typing as fast as I could, I entered in the name of the home rehab business and waited for the results to appear.

One did.

Hidden Jewels of the City Home Rehab Co., P.O. Box 111955, Cambridge, MD 21613

Cambridge, Maryland? I tried to place the city's name and then remembered it was a small city in Dorchester County, on Maryland's Eastern Shore. There was a small museum there celebrating Harriet Tubman, the famous Underground Railroad conductor, who had been born in that area. Visiting the museum had been on my list of things to do before Roman got too grown for me.

But at the moment the fact that the business address was on the Eastern Shore spoke volumes to me. I vaguely remembered the Monroes' neighbor, Everett Worthy, saying that Horace Monroe had family there, or something like that. A P.O. Box was not a physical address, I knew. I also knew that some people kept P.O. Boxes as a way of keeping their street addresses hidden.

What are you hiding, Monroes? Or rather, who *are you hiding?* I'd found all but one of Dayonna's known sisters in the Monroes' former residences, rehabbed and renewed. I felt like I was close to some answers, but there were many other questions out there.

"Welcome, everybody." A woman wearing a black business suit and a simple long ponytail came to the front of the room, a clipboard and laptop in hand. "I am Sister King, and we'll be starting our computer literacy class in a moment."

Four or five other people had taken seats in the minutes I'd been researching Cambridge. A thousand questions more or not, I knew it was time for me to head to my next destination.

There were two more previous addresses from the Monroes' file.

Chapter 57

When I pulled up to the aged Cape Cod on Ivanhoe Road in the Govans area of Baltimore City, I wondered if I'd finally reached a dead end. The house looked only partially renovated, as if a rehab job had been started but never completed. Most of the windows were boarded shut, and tall grass and weeds made the front yard look more like a jungle than a lawn.

Obviously, since it had been listed as one of the residences where the Monroes formerly housed foster children, it had to have once been minimally livable.

It was anything but that now.

I parked my car and headed up the crumbling cement steps and walked across the large front porch, where some of the wooden planks that made up the floorboards were rotting. One of the glass panes that surrounded the front door was broken. I stuck my hand through the jagged opening and reached for the inside doorknob.

Turned out that one gesture was more than what was needed. The door was already unlocked. I opened it and stepped in cautiously and immediately saw why the home had been abandoned.

Some of the walls were black with soot, and the hardwood floors had burned into a gray ash in the rear of the house.

There had been a fire.

I could not see it from the street, but the back of the house was clearly charred.

Though the house had most likely been condemned, it was clear that I had not been its only visitor since its fiery fate. Broken bottles, cigarette butts, and hypodermic needles littered the floor in the front rooms and the bare wooden stairs. I looked up the steps, wondering if I should take the trail of trash on them as a sign that the house was sturdy enough for me to continue my tour.

I did.

One by one I went up the dark steps, realizing that the lower floor had been well lit only because a couple of the windows had not been boarded up. The same was not true for upstairs. With the exception of a small skylight in what looked like a gutted-out bathroom just off the landing, all the windows were covered with wooden planks, making the interior of the vacant home feel more like nighttime than noon.

I looked back at the staircase. I remembered stepping over a discarded lighter in a pile of cigarette butts at the bottom of the steps. I headed back to it, and using a tissue I had in my pocket, I picked it up.

Flick, flick.

I tried a couple of times to light it, to no avail. The third time it worked, though I knew it did not have that much fuel left. I had to make my tour of the upstairs quick.

From the little flame in my palm, it looked like the house had three bedrooms on the second floor. The back room was charred as much as the rear of the house downstairs was. Perhaps the fire had started in the kitchen, I surmised, as I studied the blackened walls of what looked like a master suite. I turned around to check out the other two rooms, putting my faith in the continued trail of broken bottles and trash from previous visitors that the floor was sturdy enough to hold up under my feet.

The hallway was narrow and got darker as I moved away from the trickle of light leaking from the bathroom skylight. Using the single flame as a guide, I peered into the other two bedrooms. Nothing but more bottles, trash, and needles.

Why was I in this place? I shook my head at myself as I turned back around. Yes, I wanted answers, but what kind of information was I expecting to get from a rundown, partially burned-out vacant house?

I paused to think about what I knew at this point. Clearly, the Monroes had some kind of connection to Dayonna and her siblings, though I could not say for sure what that relationship was—or why it had been kept hidden. The couple was childless, I remembered Mrs. Monroe saying, so they weren't Dayonna's grandparents, I reasoned, trying to come up with a scenario that made sense. That did not rule them out as distant relatives of some nature—an aunt, a great-uncle, a second cousin, something like that. I wondered who Dayshonique's caregiver, the woman who I'd run into that morning, was. And what role did Tremont play in all this? He said he would call me sometime today, but I had yet to hear from him.

As I stood there, holding the lighter, trying to figure out what to do next, I heard a scratching noise.

Mice.

I did my best not to scream as I turned the lighter over to the wall where the critters were scurrying. Only it wasn't a wall where the scurrying was coming from. It was from under a door.

This house has four bedrooms? Or maybe it was just a closet.

I stepped over more trash and headed toward the closed door.

How many mice are in there? I stepped back, not certain that I wanted to enter a room full of rodents.

But I had come this far.

And had been in worse places.

Images of walking beside RiChard in villages where rats ran free like stray dogs flashed in my mind. I shut my eyes and pushed on the door to block out the sudden stab of pain that cut through my heart.

RiChard.

The day's adventures had been a perfect distraction from my unclosed past. I pushed my weight into the wooden door, as if opening this new door would somehow shut off all the old and broken passageways in my life that had led to nowhere.

The door was heavier than I expected, as if stuck or impeded. I threw my weight once more on it and it gave way—but the lighter fell from my hand.

Darkness swallowed me. I scrambled for the lighter and quickly flicked it back on. The scurrying became a stampede. And not of mice, I realized as large shadows bounded down the dirty hallway. *Rats.* I jumped back, stifling a scream, and then backed into the doorway I'd just opened. I turned around to see what the closed door had kept hidden, waving the flame in front of me.

A man stared back at me.

Chapter 58

I dropped the lighter again, and the room went back to black. In another desperate scramble, I bent over, running my fingers over the floor, terrified that I would connect only with broken glass or dirty needles or worse, waiting for the man I had just seen to grab me, choke me, or worse.

I thought about Roman.

Nobody would ever know what had happened to me. Who knows when my body would be found.

All these thoughts and it had been only seconds.

Frantic, I stumbled in the darkness, ready to kick, punch, head butt, whatever it took to get out of there, too terrified to even get out a scream. My fingers kept sweeping the floor, feeling nothing. I thought for a second that given the disarray of the rest of the house, it was odd that I had not felt even so much as one bottle cap on the floor of this newly opened space.

And aside from me stumbling through the darkness, there were no other noises. No rats, no footsteps.

The silence terrified me more than the darkness. Was he waiting for me in the corner, watching me trying to get away?

Finally, my pinkie fingertip touched the lighter. I flicked it back on just to see my way out of there, but I jumped back instead.

A full-sized poster of a rapper who'd been popular a year or so ago was taped to a tall chest of drawers right next to the bedroom door.

A poster of a man, and not a real one, had been the cause for all my terror, and the dresser had been the reason for my difficult entry into the room. I wanted to laugh at myself, but my heart had not calmed down enough to appreciate the humor. Indeed, as I pointed the lighter in every direction, I realized the poster and the chest of drawers were not the only things in the room.

It was furnished, fully furnished, the only room in the house that was.

This bedroom was at the front of the house. I walked over to the sole window and pulled off the wooden board that was hanging on by two loose nails. I'd never been so happy to see sunlight. The darkness that had been there milliseconds earlier dissipated into clean, fresh sunshine.

I took a better look around the room, amazed. In addition to the chest of drawers, there was a long dresser with a cracked oval mirror that hung overhead, a rocking chair that sat motionless in one corner, and a dirty queen-sized mattress lying in the center of the floor. A twin-sized pink comforter struggled to cover it. All the furniture, and even the dull brown area rug that lay underneath, was old, dilapidated, and falling apart. But clean. Despite the condition of the house, with its trash, needles, broken beer bottles, there was no trace of dust or trash anywhere in this room.

Except for one corner.

The remnants of a child's fast-food meal lay half eaten on a paper plate: a hardened cheeseburger on a moldy bun, dried-out and browned apple slices, spoiled chocolate milk. The rats had been feasting on this buffet, I realized, noting that even the pink unicorn toy that had come with the meal looked gnawed upon.

"Hope." I whispered the name instinctively, though I could not imagine that a child would have really been living in this house. And with whom? And why?

It did not make sense. Something still did not add up.

All of Dayonna's sisters I'd come across thus far lived in nice homes, rehabbed row houses or apartments that gleamed with new life in worn neighborhoods. The Monroes had somehow managed, for reasons still unknown, to ensure that the treasure trove of sisters had been housed appropriately. There was no reason to think that any one of them would be subjected to this rat-infested, fire-damaged place.

Unless the Monroes did not know about her . . . But why would they have run off? Unless they left against their will . . .

I was back to Tremont. What was his role in all of this?

I walked back to the window and peered down at the street below, as if just looking out into the sunshine would somehow offer light on the whole situation. *Lord, I need some more answers. None of this makes sense.*

Even as I prayed, I had to do a double take. From my perch above, I noticed the house directly across the street. Blue shingles covered it, and a large orange swing rocked gently in the fall breeze on the front porch.

"*Déjà vu?*" I blinked, trying to figure out why this scene felt so familiar. Where had I seen that blue house and orange porch swing before? Then it came to me.

When Dayonna had supposedly run away from the Monroes last Tuesday, Elsie Monroe had produced a picture for the police officer. Both she and her husband had looked uneasy about the whole thing.

The blue house and orange porch swing. They were in the background of that photo. I could see the picture clearly in my head now, Dayonna standing in the middle of the street. I remembered that she'd looked much heavier and extremely unhappy.

And surprised.

As if she had been caught off guard.

Maybe *she* was the last person in this house, I concluded. Maybe *she* was the child who slept and ate in that room. She did go missing, apparently, for several months. Five, to be exact, her former DSS caseworker Deirdre Evans had confirmed.

Once again, and to my disappointment, I realized my wish that there was a Hope to be found met bitter deflation.

Chapter 59

I was tired of the wild-goose chase. I had been all over Baltimore City and had talked to no one. I'd been to church, found out the name of a business, but no more than a P.O. Box address. The lines were not connecting, and I was tired of following the dots. If a picture was coming through, I wasn't getting it.

I picked up my cell phone to call Ava. I wanted to tell her that I was done with the whole disaster. I had too many issues in my personal life to be walking through burnt houses and trying to figure out when to make a trip to an unknown destination on the Eastern Shore to find the Monroes.

But I had one more address, I reminded myself, putting my phone back down. If this last residence did not offer any more clues to the Monroe-Tremont-Dayonna connection and/or validation about the missing Hope Diamond, then I would call it quits.

For real.

The last address I punched into my GPS system took me to a row home not far away. Still in Northeast Baltimore, the neighborhood of Chinquapin Park was less than a ten-minute drive from the vacant home in Govans. I pulled up to the row house, which sat across the street from a hilly green park, and smiled. I might actually get to talk to someone, finally.

An elderly woman wearing a wide black and orange housedress was sitting on the porch, reading a steamy romance. A little girl of about seventeen or eighteen months toddled nearby, a sippy cup and a play cell phone dangling from her hands. I walked up to the iron gate that closed off the porch, keeping the little one from tumbling down the stack of cement steps that led to the tidy-looking home.

The little girl noticed me first and offered me a five-tooth smile.

"Daymonica, come back here," the woman called out, her eyes still glued to her book. "Daymonica, what did I . . ." She finally looked up. "Oh, hello." She eyed me suspiciously, and I knew I had to win her over quickly.

"Hi, ma'am." I smiled. "I'm sorry to bother you, but I'm trying to locate the family members of Hope Diamond."

The woman wrinkled up her face and scratched the top of her head. She had mostly black, wavy hair pulled back into a curly ponytail. One large streak of gray passed down the center of her head.

"Who?"

"Do you know a Hope Diamond?"

The woman raised an eyebrow. "Are you one of Dayvita's friends?" Her suspicion was growing. She gently grabbed the little girl and pulled her close to her wide bosom, as if I was going to suddenly snatch her away.

"No, no." I shook my head, then thought to fish in my purse for my job badge. Ava had told me to get information, so I was there on official business, as far as I was concerned. "Again, I'm sorry to bother you. My name is Sienna St. James, and I am a social worker with Holding Hands Agency. I have a client who I think is related to you, and I am trying to get information about her family. Do you have a second to talk?"

The woman stared at my badge and looked me up and down. Finally, she said, "Let's go inside. Too many nosy ears out here."

Her kitchen was tiny and smelled like vanilla wafers and mildew. We were sitting around the small butcher block table because Daymonica, her seventeen-month-old granddaughter as I learned, needed her afternoon snack. The toddler sat in a high chair between us, happily munching on Cheerios and a chopped-up banana.

"This here is my heart." The woman, named Nellie Richmond, beamed at the little girl, whose face was covered with sticky crumbs.

I wanted to be careful not to disclose any more names or information than what was necessary. Fortunately for me, Nellie liked to talk.

"My son Ricky has a lot of children, mostly from women I ain't never met and probably never will. I wish he wasn't like that, 'cause all it means is that I don't get to know my own grandchildren, you know?"

A bag of doughnut holes sat in front of her. She tossed one into her mouth and offered me one. I declined. She continued.

"I have five or six grandchildren. I've met three of them besides Daymonica. I even started to raise one—Conya was her name—but the state got involved, and when it was all said and done, I lost her to her crazy mother. Conya was with me for the first three years of her life. Then, in one day, gone, and I haven't seen her since. That's why I decided the moment I got Daymonica that I was going to make sure to keep her completely out of the system. This grandbaby is all mine. Aren't you, sugar?" The elder lady made silly faces at the toddler, who flashed her five-tooth smile and squealed.

"Do Conya and Daymonica have the same mother?"

"Oh, no, child. All my son's children have different mamas. I don't know why he was like that, because that certainly was not the way I raised him."

Was.

The reference to him in the past tense did not escape me. Nellie popped another doughnut hole in her mouth and then clicked on the small television set in her kitchen. An *Oprah* rerun was on. Nellie paused to watch a few moments before turning her attention back to me. "Now, Daymonica's mother, she's the hottest mess of them all."

I decided to take a chance. "You're talking about Dayvita, right? Dayvita Topaz?" Hers was the last unchecked name on Dayquon's list.

"Yeah." Nellie looked at me sideways. "So you do know her? Where did you say you were from again?" The unease on the woman's face grew more distinct.

"I work for Holding Hands, a therapeutic foster care agency. You seem a little uncomfortable talking about Dayvita. Why is that?" I asked casually.

"Humph." Nellie crossed her arms and frowned. "Like I said, she's the worst of all of Ricky's children's mothers. She messes with them drugs. She's so addicted that she keeps getting in trouble for the things she does to support her habit, if you know what I mean. That's why I didn't even believe at first that Ricky was the father, all the men she was with. It didn't help none that she called me from the hospital five months after Ricky was buried, talking about could I come get my grandbaby. That's the one and only conversation I ever had with the girl about her own child. Not once has she even called to check in on Daymonica. Ricky never even told me she was pregnant, but the moment I looked into Daymonica's face, I knew I was going to raise her, no questions asked. She's in jail now, serving a five- or six-year sentence, from what I heard."

"Really?"

"Oh yes. I used to feel sorry for her, but not no more. That's the life she chose. That's the consequence she'll have to deal with."

"That's sad." I nodded along. "Do you know anything about Dayvita's family?"

"No, not really. I heard she has a bunch of sisters who for the most part turned out better than her. She takes after her mother, with the drugs and all."

"You've met Dayvita's mother?" I tried not to sound too curious about the woman who'd given birth to Dayonna and all her sisters. *Maybe even Hope.*

"Yeah, Crystal, Chrissy, something like that. She showed up at my door once, talking about she was going to file for custody of Daymonica. She was so high, I knew I had nothing to worry about, but just the same, I moved out my old house in Cherry Hill and came all the way up to this side of town so she couldn't find me again. Like I said, I don't want the system getting any hints about this here child. I take good care of her, and I don't want her exposed to the drama of either her mother or other grandmother."

"So Crystal wanted custody of Daymonica."

"Yeah, but I'm not too worried. From what I understand, she never had custody of her own children. Family stepped in to take in her daughters, and when that didn't work, the state took over. I don't want my grandbaby to go through any of that, so I moved just the same after that woman came banging on my door, screaming and crying that she wanted a child to raise. The way I see it, she had many chances and blew it. She is not getting my grandbaby." Nellie bent over and kissed the giggling Daymonica on the forehead.

A thought occurred to me. "You said you moved here after Dayvita's mother, Crystal, came knocking at your old place. How did you find this house?"

"A letter in the mail," Nellie answered promptly. "About two days after Crystal came to my old house, demanding I give her Daymonica, I get this letter in the mail from some company renting out rehabbed homes for dirt cheap. I tell you, it was like God heard my prayer and sent an answer right on time."

"What was the name of the company?" Of course I knew, but I needed Nellie to confirm it—and offer any other information without resurrecting her guard.

"I forget. Something about Jewels, Hiding Jewels. I don't remember."

"Did you meet anyone from the company?"

"I never met the owner, or nothing like that. I just dealt with the agent who showed me the house and had all the paperwork for me to sign."

Paperwork.

"You still have any of those forms?" It was a risky question. What would I say if she wanted to know why I wanted to see the paperwork? Fortunately, she seemed happy just to have an audience over the age of two. She reached for a drawer in a cabinet next to her.

"I mail a rent check to somewhere on the Eastern Shore." She shuffled through a stack of papers in the drawer. I could tell from her efforts it was going to take a while to find something useful in that stack.

"A P.O. Box?" I asked to hurry things along.

"Yeah, except once they sent me a letter and it had a real address. I remember because the envelope and the letterhead were different, like they had run out of their usual forms and had turned to personal stationery just that once. Oh, here it is." She miraculously fished out a single white envelope that was decorated with yellow floral blooms.

HIDDEN JEWELS OF THE CITY was handwritten across both the envelope and the top of the personal stationery—along with a street address. A lapse in the sender's judgment, but a break for me.

1119 WATERPOINTE ROAD, CAMBRIDGE, MD 21613.

I took the letter and copied down the address.

"The agent who showed you the house, do you remember anything about him?"

"Do I *ever* remember that agent." Nellie's face wrinkled up again, as if she had just smelled a spoiled boiled egg. "First off, it was a woman, not a man."

Mrs. Monroe, I assumed.

"Kind of petite, dark-skinned, real thin, slightly bald?" I used my hands to emphasize my description.

"Not at all. This woman was short but heavy, and not that pleasant to look at. She told me that she had retired from the state to take on a better position with this company. I remembered praying that I would age more gracefully than she had, and that was putting it nicely."

A retired state worker?

"Yeah, here's her name." Nellie pulled out another sheet of paper and pointed. "Deirdre Evans."

Dayonna's old DSS worker? Now I was thoroughly confused.

"She owns the company?" I was trying to keep up.

"No, she was just an agent. If I remember correctly, she hadn't even met the owner but took on the job because she was offered good money. Retirement in this day and age ain't no joke. You do what you got to do, you know?"

"And you haven't talked to anyone else in the company? Or even heard from Crystal since then?"

"Nope. I send my payment in the mail every fifth of the month and go on about my business."

Our conversation had to stop for a moment as Nellie took Daymonica out of her high chair and wiped mashed bananas off her cheeks, arms, and hands and out of her tightly curled hair. The toddler laughed again, and so did Nellie. As she cleaned her, a thousand other questions came to mind, but once I had her attention again, I could think of only one.

"Ms. Richmond, have you heard from or seen Deirdre Evans anymore?"

"Sure did. Yesterday, as a matter of fact." The elder woman brushed Cheerios crumbs off the little girl's shirt. "She came here asking the same question as you, but left right after I answered it."

Now I was the one with the wrinkled face. "What question was that?"

"Did I know a Hope Diamond? That's what she asked me. That's the only reason I let you in. I don't know about no Hope. What I do know is that I ain't giving up my grandbaby here for anybody or any reason." She planted a kiss on top of Daymonica's head. "That's all I know, and that's all I care about."

There was really nothing else for me to add, ask, or say. I thanked Nellie for her time, waved good-bye to Daymonica, and headed back to my car.

Just as I started to pull out of my parking space, Nellie's front door burst open and she came bustling down the steps, Daymonica in her arms.

"Wait a minute, Sienna! Wait!" A single paper flapped from her free hand.

I put my car back in park as she approached my window.

"I almost forgot," she huffed, out of breath. "Once I was a couple of weeks late for my rent, and someone called me. I was not home at the time, but they left a message. It was a man, if I remember correctly. Or maybe it was a woman. I don't remember. Anyway, I wrote the phone number that showed up on my caller ID down in case I ever needed it. I'm not really sure what's going on here, but I trust you, Sienna, so I'm giving you this number too. Find out what you can about whatever is going on. If you think there's even a chance that someone will try to take away my grand-baby, you let me know!"

She handed me the slip of paper with the handwrit-ten number on it.

"Thank you, Ms. Richmond."

"Stop by anytime, okay? It was nice talking to you. I don't hear from my kin too often, and I ain't one for talking much to the neighbors." The woman beamed. "Say bye-bye, Daymonica."

I could only grin as the toddler, Dayonna Diamond's little niece, scrunched her fingers together and blew me a slobbery kiss.

Chapter 60

Belvedere Square was a boutique shopping area not far from Nellie Richmond's house. Eclectic, inspiring shops and a fresh food market helped create a unique upscale atmosphere in this part of Northeast Baltimore City. I had not eaten all day, and the hunger pains were starting to interrupt and cloud my thinking. I needed a moment to regroup, refresh, and figure out what to do next.

I was sitting at an umbrella table outside, inhaling the steam from my generous bowl of vegetable curry, deciding on when to call the number that Nellie had just given me, when my cell phone rang.

Sheena Booth, my office mate.

"Girl, you just can't stop, can you?"

"Sheena, what are talking about?"

"The news, honey."

"Um, I still don't know what you are talking about, Sheena."

"I'm sitting here watching the four o'clock news, and there you are all up in front of the camera, standing next to Second Zion, talking about not losing hope. I have no idea what you were talking about, but someone out there must, because I instantly got a text message, and I'm assuming it's a message for you."

"Why do you say that?"

"It was your address, Sienna. Someone texted me your home address."

"What? What's that supposed to mean?"

"I don't know. Maybe whatever you said hit too close to home for the sender—and for you. I don't know."

I felt a chill inside as I considered the time. Roman. I had not checked on him all day, but he should be home from school. A stranger had our address, and my son should be home.

Just too much. Everything was too much.

"Okay." I swallowed, trying to keep from screaming. "Thanks for telling me, Sheena. I'll figure out what to do from here."

"Did you find out what was wrong with Ava last night? Are our jobs in jeopardy?"

"I don't know. I don't think so. I mean, I'm trying to find out what I can to make sure that she is okay, and that we'll be okay."

I need to get off this phone and check that my son and my home are okay.

"Well, although you are the one who seems to have stirred up all this trouble, you know I'll help with whatever I can to make sure Ava is okay."

I knew that she really wanted to say "to make sure my job is okay," but I appreciated the small gesture from Sheena. In a way, I felt like I was not totally alone in this.

"Thanks, Sheena. One thing. What number did the text come from?

There was a pause as she scrolled through her phone, and then she belted out the digits. My heart dropped as I read along with the number she was giving. It was the same phone number Nellie Richmond had just given me.

"Okay. Thanks, Sheena. I really need to go now."

I'd taken only two spoonfuls of my curry, but I left a few bills to cover the cost and a tip and hightailed it out of there.

I was in my car, heading home, my headset on and over my ear, ready to start making urgent phone calls within seconds.

"Call Roman," I directed my mobile phone for the fourth time. Again, the number rang and rang.

Where is my son?

After the raw feelings that came out last night at my mother's house, I had purposely given Roman some space today. I knew my parents would ensure he made it to school, and I had planned to have a face-to-face talk with him when I got home.

Now I wished I'd talked to him earlier. I had no idea what state of mind he was in.

"Call Leon," I shouted into my headset.

The number dialed in my ear, and once again, all I heard was a deluge of rings.

Where is everybody?

I was driving down Northern Parkway, headed to my home in Woodlawn, and the closer I got, the farther away I felt. I just wanted to get to my house and make sure all was okay.

"Information."

When the operator picked up, I requested the phone number for the Police Athletic League where Leon worked. My nerves were too worked up for me to try to remember the number on my own. The ringing began again, but this time someone answered.

A woman.

I remembered the young lady, Patricia, who had glared at me on Saturday, when I picked Roman up from there and confirmed that Leon would be meeting us for dinner.

"Hello." The sass in the voice of the woman who answered the phone let me know it was Patricia again.

"Is Officer Sanderson in?" My heart was beating faster, I realized, for many reasons.

She paused before answering. "No, he's not. Who's calling?"

"Do you know where he is?"

"I don't know where he went. He drove off a couple of hours ago with one of the teens who comes here sometimes."

"Was it Roman St. James? This is his mother." I held my breath.

"I don't know, miss. I just started here, and I don't know all the children's names. Give me your name and number, and if I hear from Leon, I'll pass along your message."

I did just that and disconnected, wanting to believe that Roman was with Leon. If he was, I knew he was in good hands.

I'm going to have to trust you on this one, Lord.

I was about to call the number Nellie gave me, the one from which the text to Sheena was sent, but I was close enough to my home that I decided to wait. First things first. I needed to make sure all was well on the home front.

"Roman!" I shouted as I stepped into my foyer.

No answer.

Only the scent of freshly baked chocolate chip cookies greeted me. My stomach growled ferociously in response as I followed the sweet aroma into the kitchen, where a paper plate piled high with the gooey cookies sat waiting, loosely covered in plastic wrap. A note sat atop it.

Again, I sincerely apologize about any confusion I may have caused your family yesterday. Roman and I are working out our differences. I will bring him home by nine.

– Leon

Taking one bite into one cookie made all the troubles, twists, and turns of the day feel minor. True escape. I thought about calling my mother, even my sister, for a family check-in, but I did not want to ruin the moment of perfection Leon had given me with the still-warm cookies. Roman must have helped him bake them, because I noticed my mixing bowls and a cookie sheet were clean and sitting in the dish drainer next to my sink.

I collapsed onto a stool next to the breakfast bar, enjoying the next bite, then the next. Perfection. Closing my eyes, I enjoyed the rest of the cookie and then reached for another.

That was when I saw the day's mail sitting on the counter.

That was when my moment of peace came to a screeching halt.

A letter from Portugal sat atop the junk mail and bills.

Chapter 61

My hands shook as I picked up the delicate envelope that was stamped and covered with international postage and postmarks. From what I could gather, it looked like it had been mailed the day after Beatriz called me to tell me that the package was on its way.

Almost two weeks ago.

There was no return address, and my name was written in block print.

My fingers continued to shake as I gingerly tore the envelope open. A sheet of paper was the single item inside. I took it out, smoothed down the creases, and felt my heart sink.

The entire letter was written in Portuguese.

I studied the foreign words, fingering the letters and commas, guessing at the message contained in the five paragraphs.

"RiChard, where are you?" My voice came out in a hoarse whisper.

I laid my head down on top of the letter, wanting to cry, knowing I had no time to do so. I'd have to deal with this letter later. A plan was already forming in my head. For now, I would finish the mission I'd started that day.

Finding Hope.

If I could find her, prove that she was real, and not just a figment of Dayonna's hurting imagination, then maybe I could begin coming to terms with the crippled hope in my own life.

I grabbed my cell phone and keyed in the number given to me by both Nellie and Sheena. Hidden Jewels of the City Home Rehab Co.

The phone rang three times before being picked up.

"Hello?"

I recognized the male voice immediately, though I was surprised at how surprised he sounded.

"Tremont?"

"Sienna?" He paused. "I was just about to call you. I've been finding out some troubling things over the past couple of days, and I wanted to talk to you about it. First, though, how did you get this number?"

"Tremont, or should I say Jewels, I think I should be the one asking the questions."

"Sienna, I really don't know what you're talking about. Who is Jewels?"

"Please, don't do this. I've found you, although I thought you were going to be Horace. Can you just tell me what is going on? And where is Hope Diamond?"

"Hope Diamond? So she *is* real?"

"Tremont, please! Let's be done with the lies and confusion. Just tell me what's going on."

"Sienna, that is what I am trying to do. I do not know all that's going on myself. Right now, I'm at this house—"

"On the Eastern Shore, right?" I interrupted.

"Y—yes. How did you know that?"

"I've been trying to find you and the Monroes—and Dayonna—all day."

"Okay, well, now you know where I am, and I really need to talk you. About Dayonna. About the Monroes. About everything I've been learning. Like I said, I've been trying to figure out what is going on with them myself, especially since that e-mail I showed you yesterday has made it to the media. I wanted to know who was behind it, and everything keeps pointing back to them. I've been doing my own investigating, and, like I said, I'm finding out some disturbing things."

"Tremont, I'm not an idiot. Just tell me—"

"I know you're not, Sienna. That's why I want to talk to you, and only you. You are the only person I know I can fully trust right now, because you have no agenda, no strings attached to any of this."

"What are you finding out, Tremont?" I rolled my eyes, growing sick and tired of the confusion that did not seem to end.

"I want to tell you, but I'd rather do so in person. And to be honest with you, I think you probably need to come here to find the answers you're looking for."

"To the Eastern Shore? You mean, like, now?"

"I know it's a two-hour drive from where you are, but I'm not leaving here until I find what I came here for, and my gut tells me that we are looking for the same thing."

"Hope?"

"I think you should come here, Sienna. I want to talk to you in person. It's too much to get into over the phone. This is heavy for me. I'm at this house in Cambridge now. The Monroes and Dayonna have stepped out. I was just kneeling here, praying for direction. The phone rang, I answered it, and it was you. You figured out this much. I think you need to see the whole story for yourself. I know it's getting late, but can you come?"

"Let me call you back, Tremont." I ended the call before he could say anything else, and now tears did flow.

It was all too much.

I remembered the first time Tremont bumped into me, just last Tuesday at church. I'd seen him four more times since, and what had struck me during each meeting was the sincerity in his eyes, the warmth in his hands. He'd just told me that I was the only person he was trusting right now. I wondered if I should give him the same courtesy.

I wanted to trust somebody in my quest to find Hope.

I think that was all I'd ever really wanted. Someone to trust with my hopes. RiChard had failed me. Disappointed me. Angered me.

I opened up the letter from Beatriz again, wishing I could make out what it said, turning to my last plan for answers to learn his whereabouts, his life and/or death status.

Tomeeka Antoinette Ryans.

The Portuguese teacher from the community college.

Roman had a scanner in his room. I held my breath and closed my eyes to the chaos of his sleeping quarters and, using his scanner, turned the letter into a graphic computer file. I found the syllabus that Tomeeka had passed out to me and Luca on Friday, remembering that her e-mail address was on it. The e-mail I sent her was short and simple.

A request to translate the attached file.

My energy was nearly depleted, but I knew I had a lot more ahead of me before I could say that the day was done.

I left a note on the dining room table thanking Leon for bringing my son home safely and instructing Roman to go to bed, that I would be home extra late.

It was already a little after five. The sun was showing hints of setting, my stomach was screaming for mercy in the form of food, but I had too much to do to stop now.

I was going to drive to the Eastern Shore to meet Tremont.

But before I did so, I had one more stop to make.

Chapter 62

What is right.

Those were the last three words in the last sentence I'd ever heard from RiChard's mouth.

Though the last time I saw him was when I'd made that cross-country trip when Roman was an infant, I'd had a few telephone conversations with RiChard over the years.

Six, to be exact.

He called on Roman's third birthday and then again on the day after Roman started kindergarten. He called one Christmas, when Roman was eight, and one Valentine's Day, when I was thirty. The next call came on a random Thursday in April when Roman was ten. The last call came on Roman's thirteenth birthday, when RiChard told Roman that he was now a man according to some global cultural traditions.

There had been letters and even more gifts and packages, but I—and Roman—lived for the times that the phone rang and RiChard's voice was on the other end.

When the last phone call came, Roman and I had just walked into the house following a dinner at my mother's to celebrate his transition into adolescence. I picked up the phone on what was probably its last ring.

"Hello, Sienna, my love. Is my son, the full-grown warrior, available?"

It was like hearing his voice for the first time. My heart stopped anew as I beckoned a wide-eyed Roman to the phone. The two talked for twenty minutes. I watched my son try to cram three years of school projects, sports victories, girl problems—what?—and some other odds and ends of his life into that conversation. When I took the phone back from him, I started with the same questions I had whenever I heard from RiChard over the years.

"Where are you?" "How are you?" "When will we see you again?" "How can we reach you?"

He always had the same answers.

He was on his way to a remote village with no phone service. He was tired but found strength in the righteousness of the cause. He had no idea when he'd be stateside, and the work was too dangerous for a woman and child—though he'd just pronounced Roman a man. He did not have a way for us to reach him, but he'd do his best to stay in contact.

He loved us, he missed us, and he'd call again as soon as he could.

That was how he was going to end the conversation, the way that had become the accepted standard between us. However, this time, I'd worked up my courage to ask a question that was not in our script.

"Why can't we all be more a part of each other's lives?"

It was not the true question that needed to be asked, but for me, it was a brave start.

I was not ready to handle the true answers.

RiChard played along.

"Sienna, I know I have been absent for a large part of your day-to-day life, but you must keep your eyes on the bigger picture. I need to do what is right."

What is right.

The words echoed back and forth in my head like a Ping-Pong ball, getting hit from all sides, whipped from all angles. I wanted RiChard to need *me,* to need me and his son in *his* day-to-day life.

But his needs were not my own.

I realized now as I was driving that the entire trajectory of my life would have been different if I had accepted that fact years ago.

For one, I would have moved. I'd stayed in the same house, afraid that if we moved, RiChard would not be able to find us when he was finally ready to come home.

I'd been hoping against hope that something in RiChard's equation would change, but I knew now that two plus two would always equal four. Any other outcome would mean different factors were involved.

I had never been willing to really examine the factors, to realize that while I was working on two plus two, RiChard was measuring triangles. It wasn't just about solving problems in different ways—we weren't even working with the same formula.

What is right.

Where do you even begin with that?

Mother Ernestine Jefferson lived in a senior condominium building on Clarks Lane in the Upper Park Heights neighborhood. This part of Park Heights, which was worlds away from my sister's end, was known for its large Orthodox Jewish community. Although it was not the Sabbath, I still saw small hordes of men in all black, wearing long beards and black hats, walking and milling about the neighborhood.

I pulled into a visitor parking space and smiled as the suited doorman, a light-skinned black man with a round face, a bald head, and pretty hazel eyes, whisked the lobby door open for me with a wink and a nod. Inside the lobby, an older black woman with curls as big as Ava's sat behind a glass wall. She slipped a sign-in sheet toward me through a small opening.

"Who are you here to see, ma'am?" she asked with a pleasant smile.

"Ernestine Jefferson in two-two-six, please."

"Is she expecting you?"

"Um, kind of?"

Mother Jefferson had told me I could come by anytime when she'd given me her address last week at church. She must have extended her offer to countless others, because the lobby attendant gave a short chuckle and called up to the apartment.

"Hey, Tina. Another one of yours is here." The attendant continued to chuckle. She hung up and nodded at me. "The elevator is down the hallway to your left, but she's right above us on the second floor, if you want to take the steps."

I followed her pointed finger and headed for the stairs. On the second-floor landing, the door to apartment 226 was already open. Before I even got to the door, Mother Ernestine Jefferson was standing in the doorway.

"I thought it would be you, Ms. Sienna St. James." She smiled. Although she was almost ninety years old, she had a youthfulness about her, which I didn't see in even some fifty-year-olds. Wearing a plum-colored velvet running suit and vibrant white sneakers, she looked like she could run circles around me.

"You remembered my name." I was genuinely surprised.

"Oh, dear heart, of course I remember your name. It's not too often I come across other women who have the same look on their faces as I did when I used to talk about my old Edmond."

I smiled, but inside I was shaking my head. This woman was married to a nationally, if not internationally, respected television preacher. What on earth did he have in common with RiChard, who probably would have had something negative to say about the elder's evangelistic ministry?

RiChard was not into Jesus. He called himself a man of many faiths, reading and studying the major religions of the world, even adopting the belief systems of whatever village or community he settled in.

I'd muted my faith to stand beside him. Maybe, I realized, I'd muted it so much that I'd forgotten where I put the volume button. When I'd needed it most, when I'd needed *hope* most, all I'd heard was silence.

No more.

"Come on in. Have a seat. I was just heating up leftovers from Sunday dinner. Meat loaf, green beans, and mashed potatoes with mushroom gravy. You want some?"

"Do I ever." I didn't even bother to hide my hunger. I don't think my body would have let me. Plus, I still had a long drive ahead of me. I had not planned on being here for a long stay, but I needed this pit stop.

Body, soul, and spirit.

"Good. Actually, instead of sitting down, can you help me get this food together?"

I did not mind the silence that ensued between us as we pulled out pots and pans from her refrigerator and set her dining room table with good china, real silverware, and etched glasses.

"I don't always get to have company for Monday night dinner, so I'm going all out for you, dear heart," she explained.

While we waited for the meat loaf to finish warming in the microwave, I could no longer hold in what was gnawing me.

"Mother Jefferson, you keep saying that you see in me the same thing you saw in yourself as it pertains to the relationship you had with your husband. How is that so? Your husband was a revered man of God, who served with integrity. You don't even know what I've been dealing with."

Mother Jefferson let out a slight chuckle as she spooned a mound of mashed potatoes onto my plate.

"Honey, I recognize that look in your eyes as if I was looking into a mirror."

"What look is that?"

"Loneliness."

She let the word sink in before sitting down in her seat and continuing.

"I know what it is like to watch the man you love and want to spend every second with share his days and nights with countless crowds. You admire what he does, but wish sometimes that he could just stop and spend his life with you."

"But that's just it. You admired your husband. You knew what he was doing, where he was, why he was doing it. And at the end of the day or the week or the month, he was back in your arms, and not in some unknown village across the globe, with blood on his hands for the sake of what he called justice."

Mother Jefferson put down the spoon and stared at me.

"You know, Sienna, you are right. I do not know the entirety of your life. I don't know your husband or where he is or what he's done. What I do know is that whatever mission he is or has been on in life, you were part of it. Your life intersected with his, but it did not end with him. You'll never be able to understand the weight of all he's done. You'll never be able to come to a final judgment of his actions—or inactions, as they may be. What you can do is make sure your hope is in the right place. Man will always fail you, but God is a rock. You must stay grounded for your own life's sake."

Hope.

I heard the word and shook my head.

"What is it?" She eyed me.

"Nothing. Just about sick of hearing that word hope."

"I'm not even going to ask the story behind that one, but since you say you're feeling so sick about it, consider this verse from Proverbs. 'Hope deferred makes the heart sick, but when the desire comes, it is a tree of life.' Don't get so caught up in your heartsickness that you miss the tree that's ripe with the fruit of your heart's desire standing right in front of you."

It was a lot to take in, and we both knew it. Silence became the third guest at the table as we finished the grand feast of leftovers. Though I was not sure that I'd been able to absorb all that was contained in the treasure of words she'd shared, I knew it was time to complete my mission for the day.

"I'm sorry about the awful rumors circulating around about your granddaughter." I could not look at her, wondering if she knew of my ties to the situation.

"Oh, we're not worried about that. No, it's not something we like or would have planned, but God is working out His purposes even in this. At some point, we just have to trust Him. When all looks like it is falling apart, inside and out, therein lays our hope." She winked. "God is perfecting *all* that concerns us."

"Amen." What else was there for me to say?

I helped Mother Jefferson with the dishes, and we laughed and carried on about random things, lighter things. No more discussion about husbands and heartbreaks, loneliness and hope.

I left there realizing that I needed everything that Mother Jefferson offered me that night: food, fellowship, and words to build my faith.

Simple moments were often the ones that had the most substance.

With a hope-filled heart and a satisfied stomach, I headed toward the Bay Bridge and Cambridge, Maryland.

It was already a little past six o'clock.

Chapter 63

I'd made many journeys in my life. I'd flown to countries I'd never heard of, met people with customs I did not quite understand. I'd traveled for recreation, for charity.

For love.

I'd had trips that took me out of my comfort zone and travels that redefined it. I'd lost some luggage and gained some friends.

Now, as I made my way past cornfields whispering gently in the cool evening breeze, I reflected on the many journeys I'd made—from villages in South Africa as RiChard's partner in revolution to home visits in Baltimore as a social worker. With my windows down to let the cold air numb my bones, my music off to listen only to the thoughts in my head, I knew that this trip to Cambridge—to find Hope—was symbolic of many trips I'd made before.

I was alone, seeking direction, not sure of the destination and the lessons to be had when I arrived. Like with the rest of my life, I was winging it, without a true plan, with just a general belief that I would end up at the right place somehow, doing the right thing for somebody.

I'd been a young woman when I thought my purpose was tied solely to RiChard and his ideals. When I stopped understanding him, I lost understanding of myself.

Yes, I had achieved much without him—my degree, my job, my home—but it had been done with the purpose of proving to RiChard that I was good enough for his ideals.

Now I knew my purpose could never be tied to a single person.

But Jesus.

With Him, my dreams, my desires, and my hopes were safe.

Eleven-nineteen Waterpointe Road turned out to be an old Victorian-style home on a dead-end street off of farmland that overlooked the Choptank River. With multiple porches and landscaped gardens, the property had to be worth close to a million dollars, by my untrained estimates. Though the house was probably about a hundred years old, spotlights placed strategically in the front yard showcased a dwelling that had been recently updated.

Even in the darkness, it was obvious that the house was the crown jewel of a home renovator's project list.

I parked in the circular driveway and walked up to the double front doors. Despite the spotlights that shone on the exterior of the massive Victorian mansion, I did not see any lights on inside. I tried to make sense of the interior darkness, wondering if I had come too late. Maybe I should have called Tremont to make sure he was still here. I pulled out my cell phone.

No signal.

I knocked on the door, not realizing it was already open. When it swung in with a loud creak, exposing a darkened foyer, I wanted to laugh at myself for the sudden fear that overtook me.

This is not a horror scene in a movie, I reminded myself, trying to calm my racing heart. *Nobody is going to come jumping out at me.* I thought about the man-that-turned-out-to-be-a-poster experience at the vacant home earlier that day and tried to keep a realistic perspective.

Just the same, I still did not feel comfortable.

"Hello? Tremont?" I stepped into the foyer, leaving the door open to have a little bit of light. "Anyone home?" As my eyes adjusted to the dimness, I noticed a floor lamp near the entrance. I pulled the chain and light flooded the room.

Despite the old-fashioned Victorian exterior, the interior of the home was a contemporary masterpiece done in shades of baby blue, cream, and sage.

Very calming.

Luxurious fabrics and finishes filled the foyer, living room, and dining room—the areas I could see from where I stood. Well-planned niches and tucked-away seating gave the feeling of escape. Though it was nighttime, I imagined that the large bay windows offered breathtaking views of the nearby river.

Honestly, the room was the antithesis of Elsie Monroe's ceramic and knickknack explosion decor. There was no way she'd had any say in the interior design of this home, I concluded, admiring the modern but inviting layout and furnishings.

"Hello?" I ventured deeper into the home, still leaving the front door open, as I did not want to feel like I had just made myself fully comfortable in another's home. "Tremont? Mr. or Mrs. Monroe?" I called out. "Dayonna?"

I flicked on another light and found myself standing in a beautiful and indulgent sunroom. This room was done in all cream with rich gold accents. A plush chaise lounge near the center of the room seemed to be calling my name, and it took all I had not to go over and collapse into the oversize pillows that sat on top of it.

That was when I realized I was exhausted.

"God, what am I doing here? All the issues going on in my life, with my son, and I am standing here in this empty house, two hours away from my home, searching for someone I am not sure exists."

I needed to go back home. I checked my cell phone again, this time with the thought of calling Roman.

Still no signal.

I flicked the lights off, but just as I did, something caught the corner of my eye and I turned them back on.

A magazine on the floor.

It was not so much the magazine but the address label on the back of it.

Crystal Rose.

Dayonna's mother.

I picked up the magazine, confirming that the address matched the house in which I stood. It did.

"Crystal Rose? What is she doing here?"

"I wondered the same thing, Sienna." The voice came from the darkened hallway.

Chapter 64

"Tremont?" I jumped to keep from screaming, his presence so unexpected. "Where did you come from?"

"I'm sorry, Sienna." He took a step back. "I did not mean to scare you. I was upstairs." He motioned to the back of the house. I noticed a dim light in what appeared to be the kitchen. A back staircase led to an upper floor from there.

"Are you here alone?"

"No."

I noticed tears in his eyes.

"What's going on, Tremont?"

"I think you should come upstairs and see."

"I'm not feeling . . . very comfortable right now." It was a brave thing for me to say, but I said it.

"I understand, but you've come this far, Sienna, so I know you are determined to find whatever it is you've been looking for. I've been on my own mission since I talked to you. I've definitely been getting answers, and, well, it's been painful, to say the least. Come upstairs. I need you to see what I've learned."

With nothing else to do, nowhere else to go, I followed him through the dimly lit hallway to the back staircase in the kitchen. When we made it to the upstairs landing, I realized we were not finished with our hike. I also saw where the light was coming from. A second set of steps spiraled upward where the first one ended, leading to what looked like a finished attic. A door with light peeking around the frame blocked my view of what lay ahead, but an unmistakable familiar sound came through nonetheless.

Whimpering.

Dayonna.

Even Tremont seemed to hesitate as we got closer to the door. The whimpers were getting louder. With a loud sigh, he opened it, and I realized the whimpers were really full-blown screams. The finished attic must have had some type of sound barrier or insulation built into it.

As I blinked my eyes to adjust to the brightly lit, windowless room, I saw that Dayonna was not alone. Horace Monroe stood in a corner, under the eaves, his large hands rubbing his forehead in angst. Elsie Monroe was seated on a metal twin bed, Dayonna draped across her lap. The elderly lady had a wet washcloth that she was using to dab Dayonna's forehead.

"We're sorry, Tremont," Mr. Monroe mumbled. "This isn't how we wanted you to find out."

They all must have thought I'd figured out everything, because nobody said anything else for a long time. At a complete loss for words and direction, I moved closer to where Mrs. Monroe and Dayonna sat on the bed. Tremont remained frozen in the doorway, his eyes wide, as if in shock.

I noticed as I approached that there were a couple of pictures stacked on the bed. Silence remained even as I reached for them. The first was a family photo, of a younger Horace Monroe in a black hat, with a charming smile, and a woman who was most definitely not Elsie Monroe.

And a girl of about seven or eight who had the familiar slanting eyes and thin nose that I'd come to recognize as a family trait for Dayonna and all her siblings.

"The woman in this picture—"

"Bertha." Elsie Monroe cut me off. "My best friend from childhood. And Horace's first wife."

I paused to make sense of that bit of information, along with the strained look on Mrs. Monroe's face and her blank stare off into space.

"And the girl?" I asked, gently prying, though I already knew the answer.

"Crystal Rose." Mrs. Monroe looked at me.

"Your daughter?" I looked over at Mr. Monroe. He nodded and gave me a weak smile.

"Yes. She didn't have our last name, because Bertha wanted to be different. She was a free spirit, an artist—a gifted artist. A lot of the knickknacks and ceramic figurines at our house are her handiwork. She wanted Crystal, her greatest creation, to be named after her birth month, June." His smile strengthened slightly, then waned.

"And rose is the birth month flower for June?"

He nodded again.

"It suited her," Mrs. Monroe chimed in, a blank look still plastered on her face. "At least in the beginning. Crystal was a free spirit too, but addiction, unfortunately, became her artistry."

"It was in her genes." Mr. Monroe almost sounded defensive. "I was an alcoholic when Crystal was young. It only got worse when Bertha died. But then Elsie stepped in and helped turn my life around."

Mrs. Monroe's face brightened as she focused in on her husband. "And now he helps lead the substance abuse ministry at Second Zion." She beamed.

"Crystal, she wanted to continue her mother's tradition and gave her daughters surnames based on their birth months," I said. "But she used birthstones instead. Topaz, Sapphire, Diamond. . . . I'm forgetting one."

Mr. Monroe's smile dropped as he and Mrs. Monroe exchanged glances. "Y—you know about the other girls?"

"And Crystal's son." I nodded firmly.

"Dayquon? You know where Dayquon is?" Tears glistened in the older man's eyes.

"I have his phone number. And address."

"Praise the Lord!" Mr. Monroe dropped into a worn armchair. "He went into foster care at an early age, and because of the breakdown in our relationship with Crystal, we weren't able to keep track of him—or get him back. After that experience, I promised myself that no other child she gave birth to would leave our family. Crystal was so high, she didn't even care that I saw to it that family members took in her offspring. Dayonna was the only other one who got away."

"So you started taking in only girls, hoping she would somehow show up."

Mr. and Mrs. Monroe exchanged glances again.

"And when she did, you weren't going to lose her, no matter how difficult her behavior."

"I have done everything in my power, with all my resources and all my might, to keep my grandchildren somewhere in my care. I was so afraid that I would lose them to the system, like we did Dayquon, if anyone outside of our family found out about them. Kinship care, even as grandparents, is not always so cut and dry once the foster care system gets involved. The authorities want to know every detail of your life, and we just wanted to live our lives, no questions asked. I wanted my—I mean, *our*—grandchildren to have as much of a normal life as possible despite Crystal's, well, shortcomings." He smiled over at Mrs. Monroe, who blinked rapidly but smiled back.

"God forgive me if any of my strategies weren't as honest or straightforward as they probably should have been," Mr. Monroe continued, "but I did not know what else to do or where to turn. I was determined to save everyone without stirring up too many questions from those outside our family."

"But we haven't been able to save Crystal." Mrs. Monroe looked away again. I noticed for the first time that Dayonna had stopped whimpering.

I looked back over at Tremont, who still looked stunned.

"Tremont, I know the path I took to come here, but how did you end up here today? You knew about all of this."

"I knew nothing." His voice came out in a whisper. "But I knew Crystal. When I was a foster child in the Monroes' home, she was always around. I was selling drugs back then, and Crystal, well, she was . . . beautiful . . . and feigning for her next high. That combination . . . well, you can put two and two together."

I watched as Mr. Monroe squinted, as if a searing pain had shot through his body.

"The picture that's floating around on the news, of me and the bishop's wife?" Tremont continued. "Like I told you, it was fake. What I didn't tell you was that the picture was based on a real one. It is me in that photo, but the woman in the original was Crystal. When the picture first showed up in the Monroes' mailbox years ago, when I was living with them, understandably, Mr. Monroe kicked me out."

"I was just doing what I thought was best for my daughter at the time." Mr. Monroe looked and sounded apologetic.

"Please . . ." Tremont held up a hand. "I've told you before and I'll tell you a million times, you kicking me out was the start of me getting my life together. When I had nobody left but Jesus to turn to, that's where I turned, and I'm better off for it."

Elsie nodded. "You got better, and Crystal seemed to get worse. We didn't see her too much after you were gone. Poor thing." She shook her head.

Tremont shook his head too. "Anyway, like I said, that picture was from years ago. When it showed up in my e-mail the other day, I knew it had to somehow be related to Crystal. I called the Monroes, demanding answers, but I'm still struggling to accept the answers they're giving me. How could you have kept this information from me?" Tremont sounded like he was still demanding answers as he stared at Mr. and Mrs. Monroe.

"What is he talking about?" I was trying desperately to make the connection.

Mrs. Monroe made it for me. "Dayonna is Tremont's daughter."

"And you came all the way here to tell him that?"

"Yes." Mr. Monroe stated flatly. "I renovated this house for Crystal, thinking that if she had her own private detox place, she'd finally get it together."

"But she hasn't," Mrs. Monroe noted. As if recognizing the shortness in her tone, she quickly added, "So we use this as our own private getaway. We thought that in addition to having a peaceful place to tell Tremont about his daughter, this would be a good place for him to hide out of the public spotlight until things calmed down in Baltimore. There's really nowhere he can go back home where he is not recognized. Plus, we figured Dayonna would benefit from having a personal retreat. It's been a challenging week for her, and when the hospital discharged her, we knew immediately that we were coming here." Mrs. Monroe looked down in her lap and patted the still quiet Dayonna with the wash-cloth.

I nodded along, trying to absorb all this new infor-mation. But some of the dots still were not connecting. "Okay, I get what you are saying, but what about the picture and the crazy texts and phone calls? Who is behind all that?"

"That's what we are trying to figure out, Sienna," Mr. Monroe said. Tremont and Mrs. Monroe firmly nod-ded.

Silence ensued as I tried, along with the others, to piece together the complicated puzzle.

"Deirdre Evans?" I threw out her name.

Mr. Monroe raised an eyebrow. "You know about Deirdre? Wow, you really have been digging." He leaned forward in his chair. "As I said, after we lost contact with Dayquon, I wanted to do all I could to keep my other grandchildren out of the system. I did not want their names to even come up. And why should they? They are being well cared for by family members who wanted to take them in. We knew Dayonna was in the system and caught wind of her whereabouts about a year and a half ago, when Deirdre Evans was her DSS worker. She was also the worker for a foster child we had in our home at the time, and she was not as consci-entious as you, Sienna. Dayonna was her toughest case, and she talked about her constantly, names, addresses, and all. Through her, we knew that Dayonna went missing for a while, and that she was subsequently placed into a residential treatment center.

"Deirdre was the type of person who knew a lot of people and asked a lot of questions. I could not take any chances of the system finding out about my grand-children, splitting them up and sending them who knows where," Horace explained. "When it seemed like she was getting too close to finding out about my other granddaughters, I found a way to offer her a better position, paying better money with fewer hours, and she took it. It was good for her and good for us, as we still had a way to keep tabs on Dayonna. Deirdre doesn't even know that I used her pull to get Dayonna hooked up with Holding Hands once she came back from the out-of-state center. She just knew not to keep asking too many questions."

"Hold on." I held out a hand. "Just to clarify, you are Jewels, right?"

Mr. Monroe ran a hand over his balding head and dropped his eyes. "I've overseen many home renovation projects and rentals throughout the Baltimore metropolitan area, and even out here on the Eastern Shore. My business has been very profitable for me, and it had to be. The money I've made has been bread and butter for my family members, especially the ones who've taken in my grand-girls. But again, I did not want anyone getting a whiff of any of them so that there would be no risk of losing them to the system, like what happened to Dayquon. I've managed to avoid too many inquiries about my business, especially since I donate most of what's left after caring for the girls to the church and other charitable causes without my name even attached."

"It's been a blessing to be able to help so many," Mrs. Monroe commented.

I wanted a moment to absorb all that was being said, but Mr. Monroe was not finished with his explanation.

"Deirdre Evans was not only a caseworker, but also a member of our church. When she began to ask too many questions, I managed to quiet her down by convincing her that somebody wanted us all to stay quiet. Jewels, naturally, was the first name that rolled off my tongue. But I never called her or texted her with threatening messages. I haven't been able to figure out who knew what was going on and what was being gained by scaring that poor woman. Anytime anyone asks questions about Crystal and all her children, strange calls and threats start happening. But what could I do? I didn't want any of this to become public knowledge."

"So you think Crystal could be behind all this?" I asked. Crystal certainly seemed like the likely candidate. I stared over at Tremont, who looked just as confused as I did.

"I've wondered that myself." Mrs. Monroe answered. "Crystal has not been happy that all her children have been taken from her, although she signed documentation giving family members guardian rights. Most of the time, she's too high to really care. But when she does care, her behavior can get extreme." Mrs. Monroe continued wiping down Dayonna's head as she spoke to me.

"But who took the picture?" I looked back over at Tremont, who had never left the doorway of the brightly lit attic.

Mrs. Monroe sighed and shook her head. "I don't know. I guess there are still too many unknowns."

"Yes. There are. For one, where is Hope?"

"Sienna," Mr. Monroe stated plainly, "I may not know the answers to all the questions you have, but I do know one thing. I do not have a grandchild named Hope."

"You lie!" Dayonna suddenly sat up. "I have a sister named Hope! They killed her and chopped her up for cabbage stew. Somebody help me find my sister! They are going to kill me and cook me too!"

It was even more disturbing the second time around. The accusations.

The confusion in her claims.

The screams.

Tremont broke from his frozen stance and rushed to Dayonna's side.

"Get off of me!" Dayonna screamed at the touch of Tremont's hand on her arm. "Get off!" She let out one last shriek before collapsing back into Mrs. Monroe's lap. I waited a few moments as she quieted down before asking one last question.

"Where can I find Crystal now?"

Mr. Monroe stared at me with sad eyes from the armchair under the attic eaves.

"I built this house for her, but only God knows where she is."

Chapter 65

Mr. Monroe was right. Only God knew Crystal's whereabouts and whether or not a girl named Hope existed. I left the house in Cambridge only half satisfied. On one hand, I felt like I could put to rest my unease about the Monroes and Tremont. True, the social worker in me knew that a lot of counseling and support would be needed in the coming hours, weeks, and days. Before leaving, I offered my continued support to them and respected their desire for personal space and privacy.

On the other hand, nobody could answer for certain who was behind the threatening texts, e-mails, and calls being aimed at me, Tremont, Second Zion, and even Ava, Sheena, and her connection at DSS.

Her connection at DSS. Roland Jenkins.

I tossed around ideas about his involvement but decided in the end he was just one of those people in the center of intricate connections. He wasn't a culprit, or even a co-conspirator, just a nosy, gossiping mouthpiece.

But someone in his path knew something, or it would not have trickled down to him.

"Who have you talked to?" Tremont had asked me that when the doctored photo first made the evening news, and his question had encouraged me to start connecting the conversation dots.

Only now I had talked to the entire city of Baltimore via the local news. Thinking of that reminded me that someone had texted Sheena my address.

I pressed the number one on my phone's speed dial. Roman. No answer.

I tried Officer Sanderson. No answer again.

"They must still be together," I decided.

I started to call my mother, but I was not ready to talk to her or any of my family members.

"I am alone." I thought about my dinner with Mother Ernestine Jefferson just a few hours ago, her wisdom, wit, and words of encouragement. "God, you're going to have to help me. Only you have the answers. Please guide my steps, and let me have peace." My spirit still felt unsettled as I thought about Hope's existence.

Halfway across the Bay Bridge, a thought occurred to me that I could not shake. I pressed my foot to the accelerator. The closer I got to Baltimore, the more the thought bore into every thought I had. By the time I could see the twinkling downtown skyline in the distance, my plan was in place.

Why hadn't I thought of this before?

I tried Leon's cell. This time he answered.

He spoke before I did. "Sienna, I know it's late, but I have both Roman and your nephew with me. It's been intense, but we're making progress."

"Oh, okay."

He heard the pause in my voice. "What's wrong? Is everything all right?"

"Yes. I, well, I don't want to take you away from Roman and Skee-Gee. I'll just—"

"We're at your parents' home. They can stay here. Where are you, Sienna?"

"I'm on my way to a house in Govans. I need to go somewhere, and I would feel more comfortable about it if I wasn't alone."

"What's the address?"

I gave him the street name and the number to the vacant home I had visited earlier, and he promised to meet me there in thirty minutes.

Because it was late and the traffic was light, I had made it back to Baltimore in just over an hour and a half. It was almost ten thirty.

I got to the house before him. Common sense told me I needed to wait for him. Urgency pulled me in instead.

I remembered that I kept a flashlight in my glove compartment and decided to use that as my weapon against the deep darkness of nighttime. Leon should be there any moment, I knew, as I entered the abandoned home's front door. I shone the light up the steps. The trail of trash and needles, and everything else, was still there.

"Hello?" I shouted.

Only silence greeted me.

"Lord, please let Leon get here soon," I prayed as I started up the dirty staircase. I followed the upstairs hallway to the furnished room.

The door was closed.

I was certain that when I'd left the home earlier, I had not shut the door behind me. Maybe I needed to go back outside and wait, like any woman in a darkened, vacant home, with half a brain, would do.

What is wrong with me?

I turned around to leave, but something caught my eye.

The doorknob was turning.

I had a single second to decide what to do: whether to turn and run back down the steps, or stand there and face whoever was coming out of the room.

Time was not in my favor.

I grabbed the flashlight into my fist, ready to strike if need be as the door swung open. Immediately, I aimed the light into the person's face, knowing that the direct bright beam would temporarily blind him or her in the darkness—and give me a chance to see who I was up against.

A woman.

Tall and lanky. Clothes disheveled. Hair matted. All skin and bones.

Strong odor.

She held her forearm up over her head, blocking her eyes from the beam of my flashlight.

"Crystal Rose?" My voice echoed in the narrow hall.

"Who . . . who is it?" Her voice was raspier than Dayonna's. She stumbled a little as she shook her head, still trying to adjust to the light.

She was high.

"Let's go outside to talk." I turned the flashlight off of her face, a friendly gesture meant to gain her trust.

"Who are you?" she asked, barely able to keep her head upright under the lull of narcotics.

"I'm Sienna. I work for Holding—"

Before I could get out another word, she lunged for me, grabbing both my shoulders and pinning me against the hallway wall. My flashlight fell and rolled away, casting long shadows on the soot-filled interior. Now I was the one struggling in the dark hallway.

"Where is she!" she screamed, her face close enough to mine that I could smell her sour breath. I pushed back, but I had underestimated the strength and determination of the woman in front of me. She spun me around and grabbed my neck in a headlock.

"Crystal, wait! I'm trying to help!" I grabbed her wrists as she slapped my face, her breathing frantic in my ear.

"Tell me where she is!" she screamed, her grip around my neck tightening. "Where is Dayonna? I haven't—"

"Dayonna?" I gasped.

"I haven't seen her since the month she turned twelve! Where is she?"

"Dayonna?" I repeated. "Don't you mean Hope?"

Crystal shrieked and let go of me.

"Hope?" she whispered. "So she is real? I didn't just imagine it all?"

With my neck free from her grip, I darted down the hallway and grabbed my flashlight. When I shone it back on her, she was doubled over, as if in pain. A low moan escaped from her mouth.

"You have a daughter named Hope Diamond."

"No. I don't know. Oh God, what have I done?" She was still bent over, her head shaking from side to side.

"She was born in April. Like Dayonna. Diamonds. Your April birthstone treasures."

"Noooo." Her moans were turning into sobs. Tears and snot dripped off her face as she began vomiting. "What did I do? I'm sorry! I'm sorry!"

"Why are you sorry? Did you hurt her?"

"No!" Her tears suddenly turned to hisses. "She lied! I wanted her. She should have been mine. She better not be dead. I was going to raise her! She was going to be *my* baby." She started walking toward me down the hallway. I realized then that I had broken one of the cardinal rules of social work home visits. Always keep a straight, unbroken path to the exit. Crystal was blocking my way to the staircase.

And a piece of broken glass was in her hand.

"I'm tired of the lies," she hissed. "I'm sick of the lies. Everyone keeps lying to me. Lies! Is Hope really dead?"

"She's not dead," I said calmly, thinking quickly. Crystal was still approaching me, the glass in one hand. A used needle in the other, I realized. "Hope is not dead."

The words reverberated through me.

A car motor rumbled outside. Leon! My heart leaped in hope as the motor neared the home. It sunk as the motor pulled slowly away. I realized that either it was another person's car or Leon was trying to make out addresses on the dark street.

I had to keep thinking on my feet.

"Crystal," I said firmly. "You called me, telling me not to look for Hope. You've been texting people and sending e-mails, and all this time you haven't even known where she is?" I was thoroughly confused, but I had to keep talking.

"I haven't called anyone. I just want my Hope back. I was supposed to raise her. Do you know where she is?"

"Yes." I said it with such certainty, I believed it myself.

I just knew I had to get out of that house without any broken glass or dirty needles blocking my way.

"Come with me. I can take you." I watched as she hesitated, and then turned toward the stairway. The motor outside cut off, and footsteps sounded on the front porch.

That was when I made my move.

Without a second to reconsider my plan, I screamed as loud as I could and ran toward the staircase. I threw the flashlight at Crystal, trusting myself to remember my way out in the dark. She screamed, and all I could hear was glass crunching under my shoes and rats scurrying in the darkness.

"Sienna!" Leon's voice sounded so far away. But close enough. I ran toward it, but apparently, so did Crystal. Both of us ran to the front door and tried to push our way out.

"Watch out, Leon. She's going to attack!"

He grabbed Crystal just as she was about to swipe him with the glass in her hand.

"I want my child! I was there! I was going to raise her! Where is my Hope?" she screamed and collapsed into him, sobbing. "You said you knew where she was and that you would take me to her!" She looked at me, desperation on her face and in her voice.

"Sienna, what is she talking about?" Leon's voice was calm in the middle of the confusion.

The moment felt surreal as I stared up to the heavens. A streetlight cast a haze on the sleeping neighborhood. The only other light came from an upstairs light inside the house across the street.

The house across the street.

The blue shingled home with the large orange porch swing.

The house that had been in the picture of Dayonna.

The picture the Monroes said they found of her, taken when she had more weight on her, taken with her caught off guard.

"I do know where she is." I turned to face Crystal and Leon. "I know where Hope is."

Chapter 66

"I knew you'd be back, but I didn't expect it to be this soon."

Nellie Richmond looked at the three of us through the wire mesh of her front screen door.

"Can we come in?" I asked the frowning older woman. It was a little after eleven thirty, nearing midnight. "I know it's late, but this is important." We'd just driven to her home in Chinquapin Park, Leon escorting Crystal in his car behind me.

Nellie hesitated but then finally unlatched her door. She walked away as we stepped inside. "Might as well get this over with."

She sat down on a love seat as Leon, Crystal, and I took the sofa. A late-night talk show was muted on a television on the other side of the living room.

"This is Leon. He's a police officer who's been helping me." I started with that statement to keep everyone's temper and actions in check. "And I know you already know Crystal Rose."

Nellie turned up her nose but nodded. "We've met once. When she came pounding on the front door of my home in Cherry Hill."

"Dayvita told me her baby was here, and I wanted to see her. Daymonica is *my* grandchild! You don't even know for sure that she was your son's," Crystal yelled.

"You're right! You and your daughter have turned so many tricks, who knows what man contributed his

DNA. But I'm the one who's been taking care of Daymonica since she was a newborn. I'm the one who's been up all night, feeding her, singing lullabies, nursing fevers, soothing colds! You've been too busy getting high to even raise your own children!" Nellie charged.

"You don't know anything about me!" Crystal screamed.

I was glad Leon was there, because I could tell these ladies were seconds away from a physical confrontation. I noticed that even he had moved closer to the edge of his seat.

"Ms. Richmond, I need to see Daymonica's birth certificate." I broke through the growing tension, determined to keep the conversation on track.

Nellie eyed all three of us with disgust and then, after a long pause, walked over to a coat closet near her front door. She stood on her tiptoes, shuffled through something, and walked back toward us, a faded piece of paper in her hand.

"Here." She flung it at me, then sat back down on the love seat, dropping her head into her hands.

I looked at Leon and Crystal, who both were reading the form over my shoulder.

Daymonica Hope Diamond, 04 April 2010, 4 lbs., 3 oz.

The mother was listed as Dayvita Topaz. The line for the father was blank.

Crystal jumped to her feet.

"Hope?" She shook her head. "That cannot be! That's impossible! I was there when she delivered! No! It can't be!"

"Dayvita's delivery?" I looked at Crystal and Nellie. Leon had been absolutely quiet. Though I was certain he had no idea what was going on, I could feel his support surrounding me.

I was glad he was there for backup.

"Dayvita delivered her in a crack house, then dropped her off in front of a hospital, with a note that had the information for the birth certificate and a message that I was to be the infant's guardian," Nellie explained. "She called me from a pay phone in front of the hospital and told me my new grandbaby was waiting to see me. I knew the moment I saw her little body lying in the NICU that Daymonica was *not* going to go into foster care, as far as I was concerned. The hospital staff welcomed me when I came to claim the newborn that had been left in front of the emergency room," she huffed.

"But Dayvita did not give birth to Daymonica Hope Diamond, did she?" I finally voiced the growing realization that had been gnawing at me ever since I had first seen that picture of a heavyset Dayonna, standing confused, unkempt, surprised in the middle of a narrow street, which I now knew was Ivanhoe Road.

"Hope Diamond is Dayonna's child." I looked directly at Crystal. "You must have run into her somehow and seen that she was pregnant. When nobody else knew about her pregnancy, you kept her with you for what? Five months? You thought that her baby would finally be the one you could raise, and nobody would know any different. But it did not work out that way."

I shut my eyes at the horrid thought.

Dayonna pregnant at, what? Eleven, twelve?

There was a story there, if what I was asserting was indeed true. Teenage boy? Foster father? Consensual relationship? Rape?

Dayonna's fourteen years had been so tragic, who knew what secrets were hiding behind those piercing eyes.

Tears streamed down Crystal's face.

"Yeah, you're right," she blurted, her high long gone. "I saw Dayonna one day, and I could tell she was pregnant. She was staying at an emergency shelter with a bunch of other kids when I seen her standing in the play yard. I could tell she did not even know she was pregnant. I got her to come with me, and I kept her drugged up enough that she didn't even know what was going on with her own body, or probably even where she was."

"In that house we just left, right?" I asked.

Crystal nodded slowly. "How do you know all this?"

"I saw a picture of Dayonna standing outside of that home on Ivanhoe Road. She had a lot of weight on her, and I erroneously assumed that it was a side effect of the medications she was on. Then I realized it was not that she was overweight in the photo. She was pregnant."

Crystal began trembling. "The night she had Hope was horrible. There was blood everywhere. Dayonna was in and out of it. I didn't even know what I was doing. I thought we was all going to die. I named the baby Hope 'cause we didn't. We all survived, and I thought I was finally going to have my hope fulfilled, my own baby to raise. But when I woke up the next morning, both Dayonna and Hope was gone. I never knew what happened. And I never realized that Daymonica wasn't Dayvita's. I rarely talk to that child of mine. When I found out she'd had a child named Daymonica, I never questioned it. I guess Dayvita's been so out of it herself, she hasn't been around to question it, either."

"Where did you get the birth certificate from, Ms. Richmond?" I asked, gently prying.

"The hospital used the information in Dayvita's note to fill out an application, and it came in the mail to me." The defeat on her face was heartbreaking.

"So all the hospital had was a note that was left with Daymonica when she was found outside of the emergency room." I was trying to make sense out of all these new details. "Did the hospital give you anything else?" I asked.

The elder woman hesitated before slowly getting back on her feet and walking over to the coat closet.

"Just what was in this bag. I kept it all."

She stood on her tiptoes, reached for the top shelf, and grabbed something. An old diaper bag was in her hand, and she sat it on the coffee table in front of me. I opened it, and the first thing I pulled out was a small sealed sandwich bag that contained what looked like a dried-out plant.

"What is this?" I held up the bag. Leon took the bag from me and squinted at it, turning it over and upside down.

"Cabbage leaves," Nellie answered.

That caught my attention.

"Cabbage leaves?"

"Like I said, I kept everything. Apparently, cold cabbage leaves are used by some new mothers to help ease the pain that can come when their breast milk comes in. They stick the leaves right in their bras for relief. The discharge nurse told me that Dayvita had left them near the baby to help calm her down. They had the scent of her mother on them."

"Her mother. Dayonna, she remembered the cabbage leaves." I closed my eyes, hearing in my head Dayonna's screams about Hope being chopped up for cabbage stew. Between the drugs Crystal had pumped into her body, the sloppy delivery, and the cabbage leaves for her engorged breasts, the entire experience had to have been traumatic enough to mess up her mind, among everything else she had suffered through in her short life. I thought again about the cabbage leaves.

I went on. "Someone was helping her. Someone else knew about her pregnancy but wanted to keep it hidden, just like you did, because Dayonna did not show back up in the system for about another month and a half after she gave birth. Somebody had her, and just like you, they wanted to keep her pregnancy hidden. Nobody was supposed to know."

Crystal's eyes were closed as she rocked slowly back and forth.

I reached back into the diaper bag. The contents that remained were typical newborn gear: a hospital-issued blanket, an impossibly small diaper, a glass bottle of formula.

"That was everything, huh?" I asked.

"Yes, that's it," Nellie confirmed, her hands wringing in her lap. "Oh, wait a minute. There was one more thing that had been left with her when the hospital staff found her outside. I keep it in Daymonica's room. She sleeps with it every night." Nellie heaved herself up and slowly plodded up the stairs. I looked over at Leon, who gave me a reassuring smile.

When Nellie came back downstairs, my eyes widened at what was in her hands.

A faceless crocheted doll.

"Elsie Monroe," Crystal hissed. "She never did like me. She never wanted me around. I should have known she was behind all of this. I guess Dayvita had nothing to do with this at all. It must have been Elsie who dropped Daymonica off at the hospital, who managed to hide Dayonna right after she had the baby. It was all Elsie. For years, she told me she would help me get Hope back if only I'd stay away from her and my father."

"Elsie knows about Hope?" I asked.

"I called my father the morning after Dayonna gave birth, when I saw that both her and the baby were missing. Elsie answered the phone. She told me then that she would help me find Hope, as long as I stayed away. For years that's what I done, only 'cause she seemed to be genuine. All this time, she's been the one keeping Hope away from me. She put her here with this lady and been lying to me the whole time."

"You talk to Elsie?"

"We meet every last Friday of the month at Lexington Market. I only do it because she always gives me money and what I thought was updates on Hope's whereabouts. I don't have to turn tricks anymore to get high, but now I know she was just buying me out with lies. All lies." Crystal's face hardened. "I'm sorry about your car window, but she told me that I had to stop you. She the one who told me about you. Sienna St. James, the woman who was trying to steal my Hope from me."

"Hope was never lost," I assured her. I assured myself. "She's been in good hands. We just had to find where she was so that we could keep moving on with our lives."

As if on cue, a loud giggle sounded from the floor above. Nellie pulled herself up again and bounded up the stairs. Seconds later, Daymonica, wearing a bright yellow sleeper and her five-tooth smile, was in Nellie's arms.

"Hello, Hope." I smiled.

The toddler looked at me and squealed.

Chapter 67

"So that's the whole story, huh?"

Ava Diggs was sitting next to me in my mother's living room. It was seven o'clock Tuesday morning, a full week after my quest to find Hope began.

"That's everything." I let out a sigh. It felt like the longest exhalation of my life.

"I missed a lot with this one." Ava shook her head.

"Well, it's easy to miss what's been purposely hidden."

"True. But even still, honey, I'm getting too old for all this foolishness. I'm really thinking it's near my time to retire and pass the baton on to someone who is willing to keep it going."

"I'm sure Sheena would take that baton and twirl it like a drum major at a homecoming halftime show."

"Sheena is not who I had in mind." She winked.

Before I could wrap my head around what she was saying, the mention of Sheena's name reminded me of a question that had not yet been answered.

"Ava, last night, when I came to your house, Sheena told me that you had been on the phone in deep conversation with someone. If you don't mind my asking, to whom were you talking?"

"Oh, that." Ava looked down and swallowed hard. "I had called one of my oldest and dearest friends to apologize. In my desperate attempt at getting answers, I tried to visit Dayonna at Rolling Meadows the other day. When I identified myself as a social worker, the staff there automatically assumed I was from DSS and signed me in with the last caseworker's name they had in Dayonna's extensive chart history there."

"Deirdre Evans." I recalled seeing her name on the sign-in sheet.

Ava nodded. "We worked together when we both first came out of school many, many years ago. I saw the receptionist put her name down, and I should have corrected her, but I didn't, because they were letting me back to see Dayonna. In the end, it did not matter. Dayonna was having an episode, and I was asked to leave before I even made it to the unit."

"I guess someone else must have seen Deirdre's name on the sign-in sheet and started harassing her again."

"I think that's exactly what happened, because she called me in a terrible fit last night. I apologized for not fixing the error immediately, as it somehow opened the door to her being harassed again."

"The Monroes. They must have seen her name and went back into action." I considered Mr. Monroe's determination to keep his grandchildren out of the system, by any means necessary, it seemed.

My mother yelled out from the kitchen, cutting our conversation short.

"Breakfast is ready! Roman and Sylvester! Stop playing around down there, and come get your pancakes!" The boys were down in the basement, sneaking in a video game before they both got dropped off at school. I had no idea what Leon had said or done with the two of them last night, but the two were acting like brothers again, for better or for worse. I smiled.

Leon, for his part, was in the kitchen, helping my mom with the impromptu breakfast.

"My grandmother Alberta Sanderson would make stuffed pancakes on Tuesday mornings," I overheard Leon say. "Every week was a different surprise filling . . . blueberries and pecans, cherries, or lemon crème. We never knew what would be waiting on our breakfast plates."

"Mmm-mmm, that's sounds good and yummy. I think I'll have to pull some pages from your grandmother's recipe book," my mother responded.

I knew even then, like it or not, Leon Sanderson was part of my family now. He fit comfortably in my mother's kitchen, in my son's social network, even in my father's basement club room, where he had his discussions and debates over sports memorabilia.

But it stopped after that.

There was no other space carved out in my life in which he fit perfectly.

He knew it.

And I did too.

As if on cue, Leon joined Ava and me on the sofa, piping hot plates extended in both of his hands.

"Ladies, a new day calls for a big breakfast. Your mom made the pancakes, and I fixed the omelets."

Both Ava and I smiled at the stacks of pancakes topped with strawberries, powdered sugar, and whipped cream and the perfectly made omelets stuffed with fresh spinach, chopped bacon, tomatoes, and mounds of gooey mozzarella cheese.

"Perfect." I grinned.

"Just like you were in handling this whole situation." He smiled back.

"Thanks again for helping last night. I'm surprised you didn't say anything the entire time," I told him.

"There was no need for me to say anything. You were standing on your own. You did it, Sienna. You did not need me or anyone else to validate you, what you were doing, or why you were doing it. I was support. You were the star. And you shined. You really shined. And an entire family is better off because of you." He winked.

I had already filled Ava in on what had happened after we discovered the betrayals, breakdowns, and lies that had been keeping the Monroe family bound for years. After we realized that Mrs. Monroe's bitterness at Mr. Monroe's unceasing commitment to his daughter, despite her drug use, was at the root and center of the confusion, we had a starting point for healing and direction. Through a tear-filled midnight conference call, we agreed to meet in the coming days to sort out the secrets and put the pain out on the table, in plain view, so that it could be digested—and eliminated.

Mrs. Monroe was sick of the moving, the fixing-up-ping, the fact that the best home renovation had been reserved for Crystal, despite her continued addiction. Hiding Hope had been Mrs. Monroe's last card in a hand to keep Crystal away. She'd used Mr. Monroe's complicated scheme to hold on to his grandchildren against him, even finding a way to have Deirdre Evans unwittingly involved in hiding Hope under everyone's noses.

Mrs. Monroe had cared for Dayonna in the days after she gave birth, hiding her in one of Horace Monroe's renovated, but unrented properties while her mind faded in and out of consciousness. The elder lady had seen the pregnant Dayonna and her mother at the abandoned residence one day when she drove past the property, and she began her planning.

Elsie Monroe had been the one who'd left baby Hope in front of the hospital, knowing that pretending Hope was Dayvita's drug-addicted newborn would not be difficult to pull off, especially since the newborn was truly drug addicted. When Dayonna mysteriously showed back up at the emergency shelter from which she'd been AWOL for five months, her subsequent mumblings and bizarre claims had been chalked up to an unstable mental state and she'd been sent to the residential treatment center in Florida. Mrs. Monroe had not counted on Mr. Monroe demanding that Dayonna become their new foster child upon her return—and what could she have said to Mr. Monroe about Hope?

Neither one of them had expected Dayonna's broken memories to find glue within their home.

The threats, the phone calls, the texts, the e-mails, even the photo, were all Elsie's doing, a last resort to keep the deal that kept Crystal away from their lives.

"I've spent my entire marriage under Bertha's shadow," Mrs. Monroe had wept into the phone. "Her artwork filled my home, when all I've gotten are horrified stares at my dolls. Her grandchildren consumed my husband when I could not even give him a child of my own. And Crystal—she seemed like she was in the middle of it all, strung out, dirty, and disrespectful. Hiding Hope to keep her away from us was the only control I had of anything, outside of being chairwoman of the pastor's aid committee. I am so sorry for all the hurt I have caused my family and my church home."

The Monroes were meeting with Bishop LaRue at that moment to disclose the complicated web of lies and secrets that had tangled not only them, but also the church and the surrounding community.

We would meet later in the week to plan for the family's future, to piece it all together. What was decided outright, however, was that Dayonna would remain with the Monroes under an official kinship arrangement, with additional support to address her problematic behaviors and shattered emotional and mental state; that the circumstances surrounding her tragic pregnancy would be investigated; that Crystal would try detox again; and that Daymonica Hope Diamond would remain with the only family she knew: Nellie Richmond. There were still questions to be asked, answers to be found, but finding Hope had been the first step in finding healing for this family.

And in finding healing for me.

Leon was right.

I had accomplished something by following my own instincts, my own values.

My own faith.

"Mom."

"Where did you come from that fast?" I stared up at my fourteen-year-old son, who was suddenly standing in front of me, munching down three slices of bacon.

"I've got something for you." He managed to get the words out between bites. In his hand was a brown lunch bag with toilet paper sticking out of it.

"Toilet paper?"

"Imagine that it is sparkling tissue paper in a pretty pink gift bag. All I had on short notice." He grinned as he held out the grease-stained, wrinkled lunch bag.

"Pathetic." I shook my head but took the bag, anyway. As I ran my hand through the mounds of cottony soft toilet paper, Roman could not contain his laughter.

"I don't get the joke." I shook my head again, until my fingers touched something hard and cold and heavy.

"Roman?" I nearly choked on my own tongue as I let my fingers bring up the single item.

The lion's head ring.

A new deluge of memories overtook me as Skee-Gee came up behind Roman.

"I got it back for y'all, Aunt See." He nodded his head.
"How—"

"You don't want to know." Skee-Gee's lips curled into a smile as he shook his head so hard, the baseball cap that covered his braids nearly fell off.

"Um, no, we don't." Leon was smiling, but there was a serious note to his tone. He looked over at me, questions, concern unspoken but all felt in his gaze.

There was a blurry line between right and wrong, justice and just cause when it came to anything RiChard.

That was his legacy, it seemed, and I'd have to find a way to live with that fact.

"You can keep it, Ma. I don't need it." Roman pressed the ring deep into my palm.

I didn't like what flashed in his eyes, but he turned away and slung his book bag over his shoulder before I could tell him that the ring was not what he needed to let go of.

I swallowed hard.

"We need to get everyone off to school." Leon's voice sounded far away. "Us adults got to get to work, and Sienna has to get—"

"Some sleep!" my mother and Ava said in unison.

I was still quiet, frozen, really, as one by one the people I loved—and who I knew loved me—began piling out the door. Commotion, ruckus, taunts, the usual upheaval of a weekday morning rush pushed its way out of the living room, all to the beat of my sister Yvette's impatient car honks.

Within seconds, the living room was as quiet as it had been noisy. I closed my eyes and fingered the large ring that still weighed down my palm. I was about to sink back into my mother's overstuffed leather sofa and pull the knitted throw she kept on it up to my shoulders when the front door swung back open.

Leon.

"Forgot my keys," he mumbled, grabbing a simple key chain from off a side table my mother kept near the bay window in the living room. A breeze sent the white curtains that covered the window into a slow billow. As he turned to exit again, I saw him look at the ring in my hand. He paused. "Sienna, get the answers you need for you, for Roman, first." He bit his lip, then stared me straight in the eyes. "I'm not going anywhere."

The door closed quietly behind him. I could hear his footsteps pound down the walkway. I listened as his car roared to life, drove off into the distance.

Answers.

I'd sent an e-mail to Tomeeka Antoinette Ryans, the Portuguese teacher, I suddenly remembered. The letter from Portugal I had scanned and attached to the e-mail. I jumped up from the sofa, but my feet became lead as I got closer to the ancient, dusty large black box of a computer my father kept in the basement, right between a boxing robe from some great boxing legend and an autographed basketball.

"Does this old machine even have an Internet connection?" My fingers shook as I booted it up and waited for the screen to turn from black to blue.

It did.

I could feel the rest of my body joining the trembles of my fingers as I pulled up my e-mail account.

One new message.

From Tremont Scott, the music director at Second Zion.

Thank you, it read. We are all going to heal. We've come this far by faith.

I exhaled, imagining his perfect voice breaking out into the chorus of that classic gospel melody, the congregation only strengthened by his testimony, encouraged by his sincerity.

Yes, we are, I typed back. I wiped away a tear and reached for the mouse to click off my e-mail account.

Check your junk folder.

I'd been listening to my gut—the still, small voice in me that had been directing my steps all week. Why should I stop now?

My fingers shook even more as I clicked on my junk folder. Even through the tears that blurred my vision, I saw it in the midst of spam e-mails.

Tomeeka had written me back.

I took a deep breath and opened the e-mail. Tomeeka had skipped all formalities. The entire body of the e-mail was the letter transcribed.

My name is Beatriz. I spoke to you yesterday by phone to tell you that a package with your husband's ashes is coming. My brother does not know that I am writing you, and he will be very upset if he finds out, because we promised not to tell, and we needed the money.

I am a pottery maker in Portugal. This is our family business, and we are not doing well. A few weeks ago a man came to view our wares. After quietly studying our best work, he paid us great money to craft an urn. He came back for it yesterday, and then after inspecting it, he put a small box inside of it and told us that he would pay us twice the amount he'd given us for the urn if we would only call you to tell you that your husband's ashes were coming and then mail the urn to you. My brother agreed, because we greatly needed the money, and to make the story more authentic, my brother used the address of a crematorium in a neighboring town for the delivery. When you asked for the phone number during my call to you, he meant to give you the one for that crematorium, to keep you from finding us, but he instead accidentally gave you our number. I took that mishap as a sign from God that it was meant for you to know the truth, especially with what happened last night.

Late last night the same man who asked us to mail the package was found unconscious in a hotel room near our town. The news media here put out a story to try and get more information about him, since he appeared to be traveling in this country alone and illegally. I do not know his name, but a link to the newspaper article can be found at this Web site. There is a picture on the Web site of the man.

I do not know what was in the small box that the man put inside the urn. If it is truly your husband, I am sorry for your loss. What I do know is that I cannot live a life of dishonesty, no matter how much money is offered, and I have not had peace about staying quiet regarding this.

Please do not try to contact me. I do not want my brother angered, as he does not usually get involved in such affairs. I am telling you all I know.

Tomeeka had highlighted and hyperlinked the phrase "a link to the newspaper article can be found at this Web site," letting me know that I could click on it to get right to the picture.

My heart rolled like thunder in me as I clicked on the mouse one last time, with my eyes closed.

I did not want to open my eyes until I knew that I was ready to see what I knew had to be a photo of my husband, RiChard Alain St. James. The words *found unconscious in a hotel room* spun around in my head like a topsy-turvy spinning top. I did not want to imagine RiChard crumpled up on the floor of a room in a foreign land. I could still see him as I did the first time, when he was shouting "Revolution!" from the steps of the student union on campus. He was the color of chocolate-laced vanilla, his hair a wind-blown mop of gleaming black curls, his smile easy, his eyes a beautiful shade of brilliant green.

I smiled and finally opened my eyes and nearly jumped out of my seat, as if I'd just seen a ghost.

In a way, I had.

A man with skin as dark as night and a spirit as bright as day filled the computer screen.

Not RiChard.

"What is he still doing alive?" I tried to make sense out of senselessness. I had seen the blood on RiChard's hands myself when he'd avenged his violent death fifteen years ago.

Or at least that was what RiChard had said at the time.

But there he was, though in an unconscious state in the picture, alive and in Portugal, at least a couple of weeks ago, and taking up the monitor's space.

Kisu.

I took the lion's head ring back out of Roman's homemade gift bag and laid it on the small desk. The jewels sparkled even in the dim light of the basement. Several minutes passed as I stared at it.

"RiChard, wherever you are, this side or the next, I wish you well. There are answers out there somewhere, but I'm tired of chasing after them. I know only what you have let me know."

I could try to seek out Kisu. I could even try to see if there was a way to connect with RiChard's international family. Luca, the young model from the Portuguese class, had ties to Perugia, RiChard's mother's hometown, I recalled.

I could try to seek and search out and push forward until all stones had been unturned. But the path to answers looked unending.

And I was tired.

My father kept a safe in the back of the basement, where the most valuable pieces of his sports collection were stored. I had a fleeting memory that the combination was either my or Yvette's birth date. I tried both, and the lock gave way. I pushed the large ring as far back into the safe as I could, plunging my hand deep into the plush red velvet interior.

My fingers lingered on the cold metal a few seconds before I did what I now knew I had the strength to do.

I let go.

For now.

Readers' Group Guide

1. The entire trajectory of Sienna's life changed when she decided to leave school and marry RiChard. What major decisions in your past have contributed to where you are today? Are you satisfied with your choices? Why or why not? If not, what changes can be made? Are you facing any life-defining decisions now? How do you handle major decisions?

2. What was RiChard's mission? What did he sacrifice to pursue it? What did he gain? Was his absence from his family's life justified?

3. Leon believes that it is possible to have good intentions but wrong motivations. What are your thoughts?

4. Sienna noted that she could stand up for herself in certain situations but shied away in others—particularly when it came to her relationship with RiChard. Why was this? Have you ever found yourself in a similar situation?

5. Is it okay for Sienna to pursue a relationship with Leon or any other man? Why or why not?

6. Throughout the novel, several characters teeter on the edge of right and wrong when handling situa-

tions of importance. What "gray areas" are ventured into by Ava, Mr. Monroe, RiChard, Roman, and other characters who handle their affairs in what may be perceived as questionable ways? What makes these areas "gray?" Do "gray areas" even exist? If so, how are they to be addressed?

7. Elsie Monroe allowed bitterness and resentment to control her emotions and actions. What are the fruits of bitterness, both for the one experiencing it and for others? What is the best way to keep a root of bitterness from growing? Consider Hebrews 12:15.

8. The fictional mega-church Second Zion Tabernacle offers a long list of ministries, both traditional and nontraditional, for its congregants and the surrounding community. What types of ministries or services, if any, should churches be providing, and for whom? Why or why not?

9. Ava Diggs served as a professional mentor for Sienna, while Mother Ernestine Jefferson served as a spiritual one. What are mentors? What purpose do they serve? What qualities should they have? Is having a mentor necessary?

10. In her social work career, Sienna noted the varying outcomes of the children in her care. Even when they come from the same family with the same traumatic background, some children grow up to find success while others land on more difficult pathways. Why do these differences in outcomes occur? What factors contribute to a wounded child's future success? How is success even defined when horrific circumstances have colored the outset of someone's life?

Author Bio

Leslie J. Sherrod is the author of *Like Sheep Gone Astray* (Grand Central Publishing, 2006) and *Secret Place* (Urban Christian/Kensington, 2011). She is also a contributor to the *A Cup of Comfort* (Adams Media) devotional series and the short story anthology *But, Yet, Still* (Plenary Publishing, 2012). A social worker providing therapy to children and families, Leslie resides in Baltimore, Maryland, with her husband and three children.

UC HIS GLORY BOOK CLUB!

www.uchisglorybookclub.net

UC His Glory Book Club is the Spirit-inspired brain-child of Joylynn Jossel, author and acquisitions editor of Urban Christian, and Kendra Norman-Bellamy, author for Urban Christian. This is an online book club that hosts authors of Urban Christian. We welcome as members all men and women who have a passion for reading Christian-based fiction.

UC His Glory Book Club pledges our commitment to provide support, positive feedback, encouragement, and a forum whereby members can openly discuss and review the literary works of Urban Christian authors.

There is no membership fee associated with UC His Glory Book Club; however, we do ask that you support the authors through purchasing, encouraging, providing book reviews, and of course, offering your prayers. We also ask that you respect our beliefs and follow the guidelines of the book club. We hope to receive your valuable input, opinions, and reviews that build up, rather than tear down, our authors.

What We Believe:

—We believe that Jesus is the Christ, Son of the Living God.

—We believe that the Bible is the true, living Word of God.

—We believe that all Urban Christian authors should use their God-given writing abilities to honor God and share the message of the written word God has given to each of them uniquely.

—We believe in supporting Urban Christian authors in their literary endeavors by reading, purchasing, and sharing their titles with our online community.

—We believe that everything we do in our literary arena should be done in a manner that will lead to God being glorified and honored.

—We look forward to the online fellowship with you.

Please visit us often at:
www.uchisglorybookclub.net.

Many Blessings to You!
Shelia E. Lipsey,
President, UC His Glory Book Club